RADIANT
STATE

By Peter Higgins

Wolfhound Century
Truth and Fear
Radiant State

RADIANT STATE

PETER HIGGINS

orbit

www.orbitbooks.net

Orbit
Hachette Book Group
1290 Avenue of the Americas
New York, NY 10104
www.orbitbooks.net

Printed in the United States of America

RRD-C

First U.S. edition: May 2015
First published in Great Britain in 2015 by Gollancz

10 9 8 7 6 5 4 3 2 1

Orbit is an imprint of Hachette Book Group.
The Orbit name and logo are trademarks of Little, Brown Book Group Limited.

The Hachette Speakers Bureau provides a wide range of authors for speaking events. To find out more, go to www.hachettespeakersbureau.com or call (866) 376-6591.

The publisher is not responsible for websites (or their content) that are not owned by the publisher.

Library of Congress Control Number: 2015931019
ISBN: 978-0-316-21966-2

Ice cliffs melt
under truth's solar burn.

OSIP MANDELSTAM (1891–1938)

Part I

Chapter One

We will leave our planet by a radiant new path.

We will lay out the stars in rows
and ride the moon like a horse.

Vladimir Kirillov (1889–1943)

On the canals of Mars we will build the palace of world freedom.

Mikhail Gerasimov (1889–1939)

1

She sees with eyes too wide, her ears are deafened with too much hearing, she feels with her skin. She is the first bold pioneer of a new generation: Engineer-Technician 2nd Class Mikkala Avril.

Age twenty-three? Age zero! Fresh-born raw today, in the zero day of the unencompassable zero season of the world, she descends the gangway of the small plane sent personally for her, the only passenger, under conditions of supreme urgency. *Priority Override*. (The plane is still in its shabby olive livery of war: no time is wasted on primping and beautifying in the New Vlast of Papa Rizhin.) Reaching the foot of the wobbling steel stair, she steps out onto the tarmac of the Chaiganur cosmodrome, Semei-Pavlodar Province, and into the heat of the epochal threshold hour.

To be part of it. To do her task.

The almost-bursting heart in her ribs is the heart of her generation, the heart of the New Vlast, a clever strong young heart pounding at the farthest limit of endurability, equal parts dizzying excitement and appalling terrible fear.

Today will be a day like no other.

It is not yet quite six years since the armies of the enemy surrounding Mirgorod were swept from the face of the planet in a cleansing, burning wind by Rizhin's new weapon, a barrage of atomic artillery shells. Not quite six years – the vertebrae of six long winters articulated by the connective tissue of five roaring summers – but for the New Vlast the time elapsed has delivered far more and felt far longer. General Osip Rizhin, President-Commander of the New Vlast and Hero of the Peace of a Thousand Years, has taken time by the scruff of the neck. He has stretched the weeks tight like wire and made each day work – *work!* – like days never worked before.

Some may express doubt that all this can been achieved so quickly, Rizhin said on First Peace Day, outlining his Five Year Plan, his Great Step into the Future. *But the doubters have not grasped the true nature of time. Time is not a dimension, it is a means of production. Time is too important to be trusted to calendars and clocks. Time is at our disposal and will march at our speed, if we are determined. It is a matter of the imposition of human will.*

Rizhin had seen the Goal and envisaged the completion of Task Number One. It would be delivered at the speed that he set.

And so it was. In two thousand hammer-blow days, each day a detonation like an atomic bomb, he made the whole planet beat with a crashing unstoppable rhythm perceptible from a hundred million miles away. The New Vlast was a pounding anvil the sun itself could feel: it shook the drum-taut solar photosphere, the 6,000-degree plasma skin.

But no day will ever beat more strongly or echo more enduringly down the corridors of the coming millennia than this one day, and Engineer-Technician Mikkala Avril will play her vital part.

She pauses on the airfield apron, savouring the moment, fixing it in memory. The furnace weight of the sun's heat beats on her face and shoulders and back. Hydrogen fusing into helium at a steady burn. She feels the remnants of the solar wind scouring her cheeks and screws her eyes against the bleach and glare. The air tastes of bitter herb and

4

dusty cinder, of hot steel and of the sticky dust-streaked asphalt that peels noisily away from the soles of her shoes at every step. Breathing is hard labour.

Chaiganur is a scrub of desert steppe, baked dry under the rainless shimmering sky, parched to the far horizon. Flatness is its only feature. The dome of the sky is of no colour, the sun swollen and smeared across it, and the steppe is a whitened consuming lake bed of silent fierce unwatchable brightness. Nothing rises more than a few inches above the crumbling orange-yellow earth and the low clumps of coarse grey grass, nothing except pylons and gantries and hangars and scattered blockhouses: only they cast hot blue shadows. Miles to the south lies the shore of an ancient sea, and when the hot breeze blows it brings to Chaiganur a new covering of salty corrosive grit: ochre dust, clogging nozzles and caking surfaces.

The workers at Chaiganur put scorpions in bottles and watch them fight.

Throughout the two-hour flight from the Kurchatovgrad Barracks, Mikkala Avril had studied the technical manual, memorising layouts and procedures she already knows by heart. The night-duty clerk woke her in the early hours of the morning, agog with news, his part in her drama. A telephone call had come: instructions to go instantly to Chaiganur, transport already waiting. Her principal, Leading Engineer-Technician Filipov, had been taken suddenly and seriously ill and she – she, Mikkala Avril, there was no mistake, there was no one else, none qualified – was required immediately to take Filipov's place. Not an exercise. The thing itself.

As she put on her uniform she spared a thought for Filipov. He and his family would not be heard from again. Their names would no longer be spoken. It was a pity. Filipov had trained her well. Her success this day would be his final and most lasting contribution.

The plane bringing her to Chaiganur flew low. She watched through the window as they crossed the testing grounds and saw scars: the wide grey splash-craters of five years' worth of atomic detonations, the fallen pieces of failed and exploded engineering, the twisted wreckage of spent platforms cannibalised from war-surplus bridges and pontoons. Half-buried chunks of stained concrete resembled the dry bones and broken tusks of dead giants.

Didn't mammoths once walk this land? She might have heard that somewhere. Hadn't someone – but *who*? – taken her once, a girl, to rock outcrops polished smooth by long-dead beasts (by the scraping of scurf and ticks from their rufous hairy sides). That might have happened to her, she wasn't sure. Whatever. Nothing thrives now in all that flatness of stony rubbish but scorpions and rats and foxes and the sparse nomadic tribes with their ripe-smelling beards and scrawny horses.

The plane that brought her leaves again immediately, engines dwindling into sun-bleached silence. She heads for the control block, picking her way across pipes and thick cables that snake along the ground. She might be only one small component in the machine, one switch in the circuit, but she will execute her task smoothly, and that will matter. That will make a binary difference; that will allow the perfection of the most profound accomplishment of humankind. She will make no mistake. She will do it right.

2

Exactly one hour after the arrival of Mikkala Avril, a convoy sweeps at speed past the security perimeter of the Chaiganur cosmodrome trailing a half-mile cloud of dust. Three-and-a-half-ton armoured sedans – chrome fenders, white-walled tyres – doing a steady sixty. Motorcycle outriders and chase cars. They are heading straight for Test Site 61.

The sun-baked sedans carry the entire membership of the Central Committee of the New Vlast Presidium, and in one of the cars – no one is sure which, the bullet-proof windows are tinted – rides the President-Commander himself, General Osip Rizhin. Papa Rizhin, the great dictator, first servant of the New Vlast, coming to witness this greatest of triumphs and certify its momentousness with his presence.

Two jolting trucks bring up the rear. A sweating corps of journalists is tucked in among their movie cameras and their tape recorders. The men in the open backs of the trucks crook their arms in permanent angular shirt-sleeved salute, cramming homburgs, pork-pies, fedoras down tight on their heads against the hot wind of their passage. None but Rizhin knows what they are coming to see.

The party might have flown in to the cosmodrome in comfort but Rizhin refused to allow it, citing the presence among them of ambassadors from the new buffer states. *We must never permit a foreigner to fly across the Vlast*, he said. *All foreigners are spies.* That was the reason he gave, but his purpose was showmanship. He didn't want his audience seeing the testing zones or getting any other clues. None among them, not even the most senior Presidium member, had any idea how far and how fast the project had progressed. And so they all rode for three days in a sweltering sealed train with perforated zinc shutters on the outside of the windows, and then in cars from the railhead, five hours across baking scrubland, to arrive red-faced and dishevelled at Test Site 61, where a cluster of temporary tin huts has been erected for the purpose of receiving them.

The temporary huts crouch in the shade of a two-hundred-foot tall, eighty-foot diameter, snub-nosed upright bullet of thick steel. The bullet is painted crimson with small fins near the base. The fins serve no functional purpose but Rizhin demands them for the look of the thing, to make it more like a rocket, which it is not.

The Vlast Universal Vessel *Proof of Concept* stands against its gantry, an ugly truncated stub, a blood-coloured thumb cocked at the sky, a splash of hot red glimmering in the glare of the sun.

3

Three time zones west of Chaiganur and eight hundred miles to the north, in the eastern outskirts of Mirgorod, a short train ride from the shore of Lake Dorogha, a woman in a shabby grey dress picks her way across a war-damaged wasteland.

Five years of reconstruction across the city have passed this place by, and the expanse of bomb craters and ruined buildings is much as she last saw it: tumbled brick-heaps, charred beams, twisted girders, tattered strips of wallpaper exposed to the sun. There are brambles now, nettles and fireweed and glossy grass clumps on slopes of mud, but otherwise nothing has changed. It is still recognisable.

The place she is looking for isn't hard to find. She chose it well back then. It is a warehouse of solid blue brick, a bullet-scarred construction of blind walled arches and small glassless windows: roofless, but so it had been back then. During the siege this place had been contested territory: again and again the tanks of the Archipelago passed through and were driven back, and each time the warehouse survived. An artillery shell had taken a gouge from one corner, but the walls had stood. She'd used the upper windows herself for a week. It made a good place to shoot from when she was waging her private war, alongside the defenders of Mirgorod but not of them.

She crosses the open ground to the warehouse carefully, taking her time, moving expertly from cover to cover, using the protection of shell holes and bits of broken wall. There are no shooters to worry about now, only wasps and rats, nettles and thorns. Almost certainly there is no one here to see her at all, no faces in the overlooking windows, but it's as well to take precautions. She mustn't be noticed. Mustn't be seen. The sound of the city is a distant hum. She is getting her dress dusty and mud-stained, but she has anticipated that. She carries a change of clothes in the canvas bag slung on her back. She is nearly forty years old, but she remembers how to do this. She was good at it then and she is good at it still.

Inside the warehouse the stairs to the cellars are as she remembers them. She has brought matches and a taper, but she doesn't need them. She finds her way through the darkness, familiar as yesterday, by feel. Nothing has changed. It is possible that no one has been here at all since she left it for the last time on the day the war's tide turned and the enemy withdrew.

She crouches at the far wall and runs clenched, ruined fingers along the low niche, touching brick dust and stone fragments and what feels like a couple of iron nails. For a moment she cannot find what she is looking for and her heart sinks. Then she touches it, further back than she remembered but still there. Her fingertips brush against an edge of dusty oilcloth.

Carefully she hooks the bundle out from the niche. It's narrow and four feet long, bound with three buckled straps cut from an Archipelago officer's backpack. The touch and heft of it – about twelve pounds weight in total, she estimates without thinking – brings memories. Erases the years between. She notices that her hands are trembling, and she pauses, takes a breath, centres herself and clears her mind. The trembling stops. She hasn't forgotten the trick of that, then. Good.

In the blackness of the warehouse cellar, working by feel, she brushes the grit and dust from the oilcloth bundle and wraps it in the towel she stole before dawn that morning from a communal washroom. (The towel is a child's, faded pink with a pattern of lemon-yellow tractors, the most innocuous and suspicion-disarming thing she could find. If she's stopped and searched on the way back, it might just work. Camouflage and misdirection. Though she doesn't expect to be searched: she'll be just one more thin drab widow lugging a heavy bag. Such women are almost invisible in Mirgorod.)

She stows the towel-wrapped bundle in the canvas bag, hooks the bag on her shoulder and climbs back up towards the narrow slant of dust-filled sunlight and the morning city.

4

In a temporary hut at Chaiganur Test Site 61 the ministers of the Central Committee of the Presidium and the other dignitaries assemble to hear a briefing from Programme Director Professor Yakov Khyrbysk. The room is unbearably hot. Dry steppe air drifts in through propped-open windows. Khyrbysk's team has mustered tinned peach juice and some rank perspiring slices of cheese.

President-Commander of the New Vlast General Osip Rizhin fidgets restlessly in the front row while Khyrbysk talks. He has heard before all that Khyrbysk has to say, so he is working through a pile of papers in his lap, scrawling comments across submissions with a fountain pen. *Time moves on, time must be used.* Big fat ticks and emphatic double side-linings. *Approved. Not approved. Yes, but faster! Why so long? Do it now!* Rizhin likes to draw wolves in the margins. *I am watching you.*

He listens with only half an ear as the Director runs through his spiel: how the experimental craft will drop atomic bombs behind itself at the rate of one a second and ride the shock waves upwards and out of the planetary gravity well. How the ship is not small, as space capsules are imagined to be, but built large and heavy to withstand the explosive forces and suppress acceleration to survivable levels.

'Vlast Universal Vessel *Proof of Concept* weighs four thousand tons,' he tells them, 'and carries a fifteen-hundred-ton payload. She was designed and built by the engineers of the Bagadahn Submarine Yard.'

He tells them how the explosions generate temperatures hotter than the surface of the sun, but of such brief duration they do not harm the pusher plate. How *Proof of Concept* is equipped with two thousand bombs of varying power, and the mechanism for selecting the required unit and delivering it to the ejector is based on machinery from an aquavit-bottling factory. That gets a chuckle from the back of the room.

The ministers of the Presidium play it cautiously. They keep their expressions carefully impassive, neutral and unimpressed, but inwardly they are making feverish calculations. *Who does well out of this, and who not? How should I react? Whose eye should I catch? What does this mean for me?*

Rizhin listens with bored derision to their sceptical questioning and Khyrbysk's patient answers. *So that thing outside is a bomb?* No, it is a vessel. It carries a crew of six. *How can explosions produce sustained momentum not destruction?* It is no different in principle to the operation of the internal combustion engine of the car that brought you here. *Is the craft not destroyed in the blast? Will the crew not be killed? I hear there is no air to breathe in space and it is very cold.*

Fucking doubters, thinks Rizhin. *Do they think I'd have wasted time on a thing that doesn't fucking work?*

But he listens more carefully as Khyrbysk explains how each bomb is like a fruit, the hard seed of atomic explosive packed in a soft enclosing pericarp of angel flesh. The angel flesh, instantly transformed to superheated plasma in the detonation, becomes the propellant that drives against the pusher plate.

'We call the bombs apricots,' says Khyrbysk, which gets another laugh and a flurry of scribbling.

Rizhin is deeply gratified by this exploitation of angel flesh. Since Chazia died at Novaya Zima and the cursed Pollandore was destroyed, he's heard no more from the living angel in the forest. No falling fits. No disgusting invasions of his skull. All the angel flesh across the Vlast has fallen permanently inert, and the bodies of the dead angels are nothing now but gross carcasses, splats on his windshield, and he is moving fast. Even the mudjhiks have died. Nothing more than slumped and ill-formed statuary, Rizhin had them ground to a fine powder and shipped off to Khyrbysk's secret factories. Yes, even the four that stood perpetual guard at the corners of the old Novozhd's catafalque.

'And now,' Khyrbysk is saying, 'we will retire to the cosmodrome and watch the launch from a safe distance.'

But there is a brief delay before they can leave. Rizhin must honour the cosmonauts. A string quartet has been rustled up from somewhere, and sits under the shade of a tarpaulin playing jaunty martial music: 'The Lemon Grove March'.

The cosmonauts, three men and three women, march up onto the makeshift podium and stand in a row, fine and tall and straight in full-dress naval uniform in the roaring blare of the sun. Brisk apple-shining faces. Scrubbed, clear-eyed, military confidence. Rizhin says a few words, and shutters click and movie cameras whirr as he presents each cosmonaut in turn with a promotion and a decoration. *Hero of the Vlast First Class* with triple ash leaves. The highest military honour there is. The cosmonauts shake Rizhin's hand firmly. Only one of them, he notices, looks uneasy and doesn't meet his eye.

'Nervous, my friend?' he says.

'No, my General. The sun is hot, that's all. I don't like formal occasions. They make me uncomfortable'

'Call me brother,' says Rizhin. 'Call me friend. You are not afraid, then?'

'Certainly not. This is our glory and our life's purpose.'

'Good fellow. Your names will be remembered. That is why the cameras and all these stuffed shirts have turned out for you.'

On the way back to their cars the dignitaries stare at the stubby red behemoth glowing in the sun: the Vlast Universal Vessel *Proof of Concept* with its magazine of two thousand apricots, rack upon rack of potent solar fruits.

Rizhin is walking fast, oblivious to the heat, eager to be on the move. Secretary for Agriculture Vladi Broch breaks into a waddling jog to catch up with him. Broch's face is wet with perspiration. Rizhin flinches with distaste.

'Triple ash leaves?' says Broch. 'If you give them that now, what will you do for them when they come back?'

'When they come back?' says Rizhin. 'No, my friend, there is no provision for coming back. That is not part of the plan.'

'Ah,' says Broch. ' Oh. I see. Of course. But ... so, how long will they last?'

Rizhin shrugs. 'Who knows?' He claps Broch on the shoulder. 'We'll find that out, won't we, Vladi Denisovich? That is the method of science. You should get friend Khyrbysk to explain it to you some time.'

5

In the control room at Chaiganur the tannoy broadcasts radio exchanges with the cosmonauts. From the edges of the room the whirring movie cameras follow every move with long probing lenses, hunting for the action, searching for the telling expression.

'T minus 2000, *Proof of Concept*. How are you doing?'

All is good, Launch. Very comfortable.

The cosmonaut's voice grates, over-amplified and crackling.

'I remind you that after the one-minute readiness is sounded, there will be six minutes before you actually begin to ascend.'

Understood, Launch. Thank you.

The cosmonauts have nothing to do. No function. No control over their vessel unless and until the launch controller flicks the transfer switches. Their windows are blind with heavy steel shutters, which they will take down once they reach orbit.

If they reach orbit.

The last of the ground crew is already three miles away, racing for the safety perimeter in trucks.

And so the cosmonauts wait, trussed on their benches, separated by the thickness of two heavy bulkheads and a storage cavity from a warehouse of atomic bombs. They are sealed for ever inside the nose of *Proof of Concept*, locked in by many heavy bolts that will never be withdrawn, and the ship beneath them is alive with rumble and vibration, the whine of pumps, the whisper of gas nozzles, the thunk and clank of unseen mechanisms whose operations the cosmonauts barely understand.

The technicians who actually control *Proof of Concept* are ten miles away inside a low concrete caisson, a half-buried blockhouse built with thick and shallow-sloping outer walls to deflect blast and heat up and over the top of the building. Not quite twenty in number, the technicians occupy a semicircle of steel desks facing inwards towards the launch controller at his lectern. They lean forward into the greenish screens of their cathode readout displays, flicking switches, twisting dials, turning the pages of their typescript manuals. They wear headphones and mutter into their desk microphones. Quiet purposeful conversations. For them this is no different from a hundred test firings: everything is the same except that nothing is the same.

Behind the controller a wide panoramic window of sloping glass gives a view across the flatness of the steppe. The assembled dignitaries and journalists sit in meek rows between the controller and this window on folding chairs, the sun on their backs, not wanting to cause a distraction. In something over thirty minutes they will turn to watch *Proof of Concept* climbing skyward to begin her journey. They have been issued with black-lensed spectacles for the purpose. For now they clutch them in their laps and observe the technicians, alert for any hint of anxiety in the muted voices. They watch for the flicker of red lamps on consoles, the blare of an alarm, a first indication of disaster. More than one of them wants to see failure today: a grievous humiliation for Director Khyrbysk and his protectors could mean great advantage for them. Others are cold-sweating terrified of the same outcome: if Khyrbysk's star wanes, theirs will tumble and crash all the way to a hard exile camp or a basement execution cell.

Guests and technicians alike smoke relentlessly.

President-Commander Osip Rizhin has not yet arrived in the control room. An empty chair waits for him between Khyrbysk and the chief engineer, whose name is never mentioned for he is a most secret and protected national resource.

*

'T minus eighteen hundred, *Proof of Concept.*'

Thank you, Launch.

'You are all well?'

There is an implication in the question. The captain of cosmonauts carries a pistol in case of … arising human problems. The psychology of each cosmonaut has been thoroughly and expertly examined, but the effects on emotional stability of massive acceleration, prolonged weightlessness and extreme separation from the planetary home are unknown. Every member of the crew is equipped with a personal poison capsule. The foresighted bureaucratic kindness of the Vlast.

We're all good, Launch. We could do with some music to pass the time.

'We'll look into that, *Proof of Concept.*'

The launch controller's gaze sweeps across the technicians at their workstations and settles on Engineer-Technician 2nd Class Mikkala Avril. He raises an eyebrow and she stands up.

Five minutes later, hurrying back down the passageway from the recreation room with an armful of gramophone records, hot with anxiety to return to her console, Mikkala Avril runs slap into men in dark suits armed with sub-machine guns. Rizhin's personal bodyguard, walking twenty-five steps ahead of the President-Commander himself. Papa Rizhin – Papa Rizhin! In person! – is bearing down on her.

Terrified, the young woman in whom beats the heart of the New Vlast presses herself flat against the wall and shows her empty hands, the stack of records tucked hastily under her left arm. She has been taught what to do in such an extremity. *Always look him in the eye, but not too much. Stay calm at all times, be respectful, answer all enquires with humour and firmness, above all conceal nothing.*

Mikkala Avril stands against the wall, back straight, eyes forward. The gramophone records are slipping slowly from the awkward sweaty grip of her elbow. Any moment now they will fall to the floor and there is nothing she can do about it. Desperately she squeezes them tighter between arm and ribs, but it only seems to make the situation worse.

Papa Rizhin glances at her as he passes and notices her confusion. Stops.

'Are you working on the launch?'

His voice is recognisable from his broadcasts but it is not the same. It is surprisingly expressive, with the tenor richness of a good singer.

Up close his cheeks are scattered with pockmarks like open pores, something which is not shown in portraits: the legacy of a childhood illness, perhaps.

'Yes, General,' she says.

'What is your task?'

'To monitor the telemetry of the in-atmosphere flight guidance systems, General. The vessel carries small rockets to correct random walk—'

'Yes,' says Rizhin, interrupting her. 'Good. You are young for this responsibility. And is all in order? Is there any concern?'

'No, General. None. All is in perfect order.'

Inevitably the sweat-slicked gramophone records choose this moment to fall slap in a heap at Rizhin's feet.

Mikkala Avril stares blankly at the wreckage: the titles of the musical pieces in curling script on the glossy sleeves; the monochrome photographs of mountains and lakeside trees. She feels her face turning purple.

Rizhin shows no reaction and does not look down.

'What is your name?' he says.

'Avril, General. Engineer-Technician 2nd Class.'

'That is good then. *Avril*. I will remember the name. The New Vlast needs young engineers; it is the noblest of professions. You are the brightest and the best.'

He glances at last at the fallen records and smiles with this eyes.

'Youth must not fear General Rizhin,' he says. 'He is its friend.'

When he's out of sight she crouches down to scrabble for the records. *Shit*, she mutters under her breath over and over again. *Shit. Shit. Shit.*

'T minus twelve hundred, *Proof of Concept*. We have some music for you.'

A syrupy dance tune begins to play over the tannoy: 'The Garment Workers of Sevralo'.

Yakov Khyrbysk groans inwardly and glares at the launch controller. *Must we?* He glances at his watch and wonders where Rizhin has got to. Wandered off, sniffing out buried corpses. It makes Khyrbysk uneasy, and he is edgy enough already.

On the other side of Rizhin's empty seat, the chief engineer is leaning forward, long dark-suited limbs gathered in tight about him. He steeples his long slender fingers. The fingernails are ruined: blackened sterile roots that will not grow again. The chief engineer (whose name on Rizhin's order is never spoken now, not even by himself) survived five years in prison camps before Khyrbysk found him and managed to fish him out. He hunches now like a bird on a steep-gabled rooftop, watching in silence. He has the pallid complexion of a man who lives his life underground and takes no exercise, but he is hot with energy. It stares from his eyes. Fierce, stark intelligence. Such energy would have burned through a weaker person long ago, but the chief engineer's constitution is a gift of nature. It is hard to tell how old he is, a young forty or a harrowed twenty-five. His hair is cut short at the back and the sides like a boy's.

The convoy of sedans waits outside, lined up, engines running, ready to race Rizhin and the dignitaries to safety in case of disaster. Khyrbysk wonders if someone has thought to issue the drivers with dark glasses. He is considering checking on this when Rizhin arrives and takes his seat. Kicks back, legs stretched out, reclining.

'Today we start the engine of history, Yakov,' says Rizhin. 'Today we blow open the door on our destiny.' He fishes for a paper packet of cheap cardboard cigarettes and lights one, drawing the rough smoke deep into his lungs. 'Those are good phrases. They have a smack to them. I'll use them in my speech.' He exhales twin streams through his nose. 'No problems, eh, Yakov? No fuck-up?'

'We've made test firings every week for the last three months.'

So many tests that the Chaiganur desert is scorched and glassed and pitted for hundreds of miles in every direction, the landscape pocked with scar-pits that show the corpse-grey rock beneath the orange earth. So many tests. Yellow plumes and dust streaks still linger in the upper atmosphere like nicotine stains.

The first test launches carried automatic radio transmitters. Later they sent up dogs and pigs and apes. One of the first monkeys to fly slipped free of its muzzle and screamed for three days until they had to cut the radio off. After that they equipped the beasts with remote-controlled execution collars. A bullet in the back of the neck. Nine grams of lead. Now there is a small menagerie of mummifying corpses orbiting overhead in thousand-ton steel tombs. The success rate was improving all the time, but nothing is certain. Khyrbysk knows that.

Nothing is certain except his own fate if *Proof of Concept* pops its clogs and goes *phutt!* in front of the entire Presidium and the assembled press corps of the Vlast. Nine grams of lead for dear old Yakov Khyrbysk then.

If he were a weaker man, he would think it unfair. He would think Rizhin ungrateful. Was it not Yakov Khyrbysk who sent the shipment of atomic shells to Mirgorod so Rizhin single-handed could break the siege? It was. And was it not Khyrbysk who expanded the town of Novaya Zima into a huge, sprawling secret city where penal labourers built the armoury of manoeuvrable atomic field-weapons that tipped the balance of the war? It was. But Khyrbysk is a canny operator: he has never made the mistake of reminding Rizhin of all that he owes him.

Six months after the victory at Mirgorod, when the war against the Archipelago was still in the balance, Rizhin had ousted the feeble government of Fohn and Khazar and made himself President-Commander of the New Vlast. After that, the first thing he did was fly north to Novaya Zima to see Yakov Khyrbysk.

'You must forget these bombs, Yakov,' Rizhin had said. 'I've got ten men who could run this show better than you. Talk to me about the other thing. Task Number One. Tell me about the ships that will carry us to the stars.'

Khyrbysk's stomach lurched. It was sheer brutal astonishment. *How did he* know?

'And bring me Farelov,' Rizhin added.

'Farelov?'

'Are you the *brain* here, Khyrbysk? Does all this come from *your* head? I do not think so.'

Khyrbysk had blustered. He cringed to think of it now.

'Well,' he said,' of course the theoretical foundations were laid by Sergei Farelov. Sergei is a brilliant mathematician and a visionary engineer, truly visionary, but he is not the sort of fellow to be the leader of an undertaking like this. I *made* Novaya Zima. I am the organiser, I am the efficient man. I am the will that drives it on.'

'Bring me Farelov,' said Rizhin. 'And Yakov ...'

Rizhin paused, and Khyrbysk, caught off guard, found himself looking unprepared into the gaze of a potentate. The neutral brown eyes of a man who knows for certain and unremarkable fact that he can do to you anything that he wants, anything at all – cause you any pain, destroy you and those around you in any way he chooses – and there is no protection for you, not anywhere, none at all. It was not a fully human gaze.

'Do not keep secrets from me, Yakov,' said Rizhin. 'Never try that again. I don't like it.'

Farelov arrived, tall and slender as a birch tree with wide nocturnal eyes.

'You are the great engineer, then,' said Rizhin, raking him with his gaze. 'You are a vital national resource. You belong to the Vlast. Your very existence is a state secret now. Your name will not be spoken again.'

Farelov returned his gaze without speaking. He nodded slowly.

'How long will it take?' said Rizhin. 'How long to build this thing so it works?'

'I will answer,' said Khyrbysk hastily. A promise not kept was a death warrant. He hesitated, mind racing. 'Fifteen years,' he said. 'At the outside, twenty.'

'Five,' said Rizhin. 'Make it five.'

'*Five!* No. Five is impossible.'

'Why impossible, Yakov?' said Rizhin. 'This, nothing else but this, is Task Number One. Tell me what you need and you shall have it. Without limit. The resources of the continent will be at your disposal. A hundred thousand workers. A million. Twenty million. You just tell me. Never hide your needs. How does a mother know her baby is hungry if the baby does not cry?'

Khyrbysk looked at Farelov.

'It can be done,' said the chief engineer quietly. 'In theory it can be done.'

'So,' said Khyrbysk. 'OK. Five years then.'

And in five years, though it was impossible, he had done it. He'd brought Task Number One this far, to this point of crisis: *Proof of Concept* baking quietly on her launch pad in the country of the hot panoptic undefeated sun.

6

In Mirgorod the new clocks are striking noon as the woman with the heavy canvas bag on her shoulder crosses towards her apartment building. The block where she lives is harsh and slabby: a cliff of blinding colourlessness under harsh blue sky in the middle of a blank square laid out with dimpled concrete sheets that are already cracked and slumped and prinked with grass tufts and dusty dandelions. Scraps of torn paper lift and turn in the warm breeze.

She climbs the wide shallow steps and pushes through the door into the dimness of the entrance hall. The sun never reaches in here and the lamps are off. There is no electricity supply during the day. No lift. She nods to the woman at the desk and crosses to the stairwell.

Her room is five flights up. The stairs smell of boiling potatoes and old rubber-backed carpet. On the landing of her floor an oversized picture of Papa Rizhin is taped to the wall. He is smiling.

She opens the door of her apartment into a blast of hot stale brilliance. The brassy early-afternoon sun is glaring in through a wide window. There is no one there. The women she shares with – young girls, sisters from Ostrakhovgrad – are out at work, but the room is heavy with their scent and full of things. The three beds, a table and chairs of orange wood, and shelf upon shelf of purposeless gewgaws and tat: make-up and toiletries, small china ornaments, magazines in faint typeface on thick brittle paper filled with advertisements and optimistic stories. The one big flimsy yellow cupboard stands open, overflowing with nylons and cheap summer clothes. Both girls are conducting affairs with high-ups in the Ministry of Supply. There is a can of raspberries tucked in the underwear drawer.

One of the sisters brought with her to Mirgorod a poster from the wall of the Ostrakhovgrad Public Library and tacked it inside the cupboard door: a photograph of strong women with the sun on their faces, shoulders back, heads up, the wind in their hair. DAUGHTERS OF THE VLAST, COME TO THE CITY! CITIZEN WOMEN! REBUILD OUR LAND! So many men were killed in the war, there was free accommodation on offer in Mirgorod to women of working age with no children.

The woman unwinds the pink towel with the lemon-yellow tractors and lays the long oilskin-covered bundle on her bed. Kneels on the floor to unbuckle the straps. Forcing clumsy hands to do what once went smooth as breathing.

She'd done a good job almost six years before. She'd left the rifle cleaned and wrapped in strips of cotton damp with lubricant, and it had kept well. No damp or grit had reached it. Awkwardly she strips it and cleans and oils each part. The touch and smell of the rifle is as familiar to her as her own body. The wood of the stock is still smooth and dark honey-brown. The magazine and firing mechanism, the telescopic sight rails, the pierced noise-suppressing muzzle and flash guard, all still blue-black steel, are a little scuffed and scratched – she remembers every mark – but there is no sign of corrosion. Only her own broken hands, finger bones snapped and carelessly re-fused, have to relearn their work. Figure it out all over again.

The Zhodarev STV-04 – gas-operated, a short-stroke spring-loaded piston above the barrel, a tilting bolt – weighs eight and a half pounds unloaded and is exactly forty-eight inches long, of which the barrel is twenty-four. Muzzle velocity is two thousand seven hundred feet per second. Effective range with a telescopic sight, one thousand yards. The Zhodarev is not a perfect weapon: it is complex to maintain, a little too heavy, the muzzle flash too bright even with a flash guard; it tends to lift, and the magazine can come loose and fall out. The woman had always wished she had a Vagant. But she knows the Zhodarev intimately. She fitted the muzzle brake herself to counteract the lifting. It is her weapon.

She reassembles the rifle, lays it aside and checks the rest of the kit. Wrapped in a separate bundle of oiled cotton is the olive-green 4-12 x 40 VP Akilina telescopic sight, rarer and more precious by far than the weapon itself, its graticule adjustable both vertically for range and horizontally for windage. And there are paper packages, still sealed, containing five-round stripper clips of 7.62 x 54mm Vonn & Belloc rimmed cartridges. One hundred and twenty rounds. One combat load. Not really enough for what she needs but it will have to do.

'T minus six hundred, *Proof of Concept.*'

Ten minutes to go.

Engineer-Technician 2nd Class Mikkala Avril settles herself at the familiar console and tries to calm the churning of her mind. She runs again through the routines. The launch controller is making his final tour of workstation checks before launch. Calling on each desk in turn for confirmation of go. Her turn soon. A matter of seconds. She scans the columns of figures again. All displays are showing within normal parameters. Dead on the line.

She has never actually done this task herself before, not at a real launch, not once, not even under supervision; except for practice exercises, she has always sat at Filipov's left hand and watched while her principal made the necessary settings and corrections. Even so, she's ready. She understands the procedures. It's not that complex. Ever since she joined the Task Number One programme, fresh from graduating top of her year (the first graduating year of the New University of Mathematical Engineering at Berm), she has spent every spare moment in the technical libraries at Kurchatovgrad and Chaiganur studying the classified reports.

It was Khyrbysk's policy to encourage technicians on the programme to learn as much and as widely as they could about the project as a whole and not limit themselves to their own area of work. His attitude to access to papers was liberal, and she took maximum advantage, beginning with the chief engineer's own seminal paper, *Feasibility of an Atomic Bomb-Propelled Space Vessel*, and working her way along the shelves: *A Survey of Shock Absorption Options*; *Trajectory Walk Caused By Occasional Bomb Misfire*; *The Capture of Radiation by Angelic Materials*; *Radiation Spill Around An Impervious Disc*; *Preliminary Sketch of Life Support For A Crewed Vessel*. There weren't many people at Chaiganur who knew more about the history, physics and engineering of Task Number One than Mikkala Avril.

She checks the central readout once more. The eight-inch-square display is connected to a von Altmann machine beneath the floor, which will, when called upon, analyse the telemetry from the vessel in flight and calculate any necessary corrective thrust from the banks of small rockets set in the midriff of *Proof of Contact*. It is her job to send the instructions for those corrections to the rockets themselves. It requires concentration, rapid reflexes, a steady hand. But all she has to do now is confirm readiness.

Launch is looking at her.

'Guidance Telemetry?' says Launch, relaxed and neutral.

And Mikkala Avril freezes.

Her screen has gone dark.

After half a second a short phrase blinks into life: *Fail code 393.*

Everything else, all the rows and columns of figures, have disappeared. She has no contact with the ship.

Fail code 393? It means nothing to her. Heart pumping, hands trembling, she riffles through the code handbook in mounting panic. *349 ... 382 ... 397 ... 402 ... What the hell is 393?*

There is no 393. Not in the book.

Launch asks again, impatient now.

'Guidance Telemetry, are we go?'

Think. Think.

Faces are turning towards Mikkala Avril. She feels the gaze of Director Khyrbysk on her back. The chief engineer is watching her. Papa Rizhin himself is watching her. She can *feel* it.

'Guidance Telemetry?' says the launch controller a third time. 'What's happening, Avril?'

'I've got a 393, Launch.'

'What is that?'

'I'm working on it, Launch.'

Ignore them. Focus only on the immediate need.

She has no idea what Fail code 393 means. It isn't in the book, which suggests it's a core manufacturer's code, not set up by Task Number One. It might be trivial, only a glitch in the machine. But it could equally be a fundamental system failure that would send *Proof of Concept* pitching and yawing, tumbling out of the sky to crash and burn.

It is either/or, and the only way to find out is to switch the machine off and start it up again. And that will take ten minutes.

'Last call, Avril,' says the launch controller. There is tension in his voice now. The beginning of fear.

She hesitates.

It is the epochal moment of the world, and it turns on her.

If she says go and the guidance systems misfire … No, she will not even think about the consequences of that … But if she calls an abort, Papa Rizhin's flagship launch will collapse in ignominy in front of the entire Presidium, the ambassadors, the assembled press of the Vlast. It will be days – possibly weeks – before they can try again. And if the abort turns out to be unnecessary, only a twenty-three-year-old inexperienced woman's cry of panic at an unfamiliar display code …

She hears her own voice speaking. It sounds too loud. Hoarse and unfamiliar.

'Guidance Telemetry is go, Launch. Go.'

'Thank you, Avril.'

Launch moves on to the next station.

With trembling hands, Mikkala Avril powers off her console, counts to ten, and switches it back on. The cathode tubes begin cycling through their ponderous loading routine.

'T minus three hundred, *Proof of Concept.*'

Thank you Launch.

Five minutes. The sugary music cuts out at last. There is a swell of voices and a scraping of chairs as the dignitaries turn to the window and put on their dark glasses.

'Can't see a bloody thing from here,' mutters Foreign Minister Sarsin. (The Vlast needs a foreign minister now. So the world turns.) 'It's below the fucking horizon.'

'You will see, Minister,' says Khyrbysk. 'You will certainly see.'

An argument breaks out as camera operators try to set up in front of the dignitaries.

'You don't have to do this. There's another team on the roof.'

'Something could go wrong up there. We should have back-up footage.'

Khyrbysk makes angry signs to the press liaison officer to close the disturbance down. He hadn't wanted the press there at all, or the ambassadors for that matter, but Rizhin insisted. Rizhin is a showman; he wants to astonish the world.

'The risk,' Khyrbysk had said to him on the telephone. 'What if it flops?'

'You make it *not* flop, Yakov. That's your job.'

Rizhin *needs* risk, Khyrbysk realises. He burns risk for fuel. Everything races hot and fast, the engine too powerful for the machine. Parts that burn out are replaced on the move, without stopping. The whole of the New Vlast is Rizhin's *Proof of Concept*, his bomb-powered vessel heading for unexplored territories and goals only Rizhin understands.

The cosmonauts feel the colossal engineering beneath them sliding into life, the coolant pumping round the shock-absorbing pillars, the bomb pickers rattling through the magazines in search of the first charge. *Proof of Concept* is a behemoth of industrial construction, but it is also very simple.

Mikkala Avril's screens come back up with ten seconds to go. Everything is fine: readouts dead on the line. She is so relieved she wants to cry, but she does not allow herself; she is stronger than that and holds it in. She is the heart of the youth of the New Vlast and she is good at her job and she will not fail.

Two seconds to go, she remembers to put her dark glasses on. She turns up the brightness on her screen, closes her eyes, presses a black cloth against her face and begins her own interior count. For the first ten bombs it will be too bright to see, and *Proof of Concept* will be on her own: then Mikkala must open her eyes and be not too dazzled to work.

Before the chief engineer discovered the properties of angel flesh propellant, what Mikkala was about to do would have been impossible: the bombs' electromagnetic pulses would have broken all contact between ship and ground. But now the ship's instruments will sing and chatter as she rises, and be heard.

The cosmonauts' cabin shivers with the clang of the first apricot locking into the expulsion chute.

Launch control is whited out in a flash of illumination that erases the sun.

Bomp – bomp – bomp. Bigger explosions each time. Brilliant blinding flashes. Slowly at first then faster and faster *Proof of Concept* rises, riding a crumb trail of detonations, climbing a tower of mushroom clouds.

The cosmonauts groan as each detonation slams their backs with a brute fist of acceleration. The whole ship judders and creaks and moans like a bathyscaphe under many thousand atmospheres of pressure.

For the observers in the launch control blockhouse at Chaiganur Test Site 61, the ship itself is lost, the explosion trail hard to watch. The repeated retinal burn forms blue-purple-green jumbling images. Brilliant drifting spectral bruises in the eye. President-Commander Rizhin stands at the window, the hot glare pulsing on his face, an atomic heartbeat.

I am the fist of history. I am the mile-high man.

A long time after the light the sound waves come.

Chapter Two

… in the deep country
Where an endless silence reigns.

Nikolai Nekrasov (1821–78)

1

In Papa Rizhin's world the clocks race forward to the pounding iron-foundry beat, the brakes are off and the New Vlast tears into the wind, riding the rolling wave of continental cataclysm-shock, flung into the future on the impulse-rip of centrifugal snap, taking a piston-blur express ride – six years now and counting and there's no slowing it yet. But pieces break off and get left behind. Because the past is sticky. Adhesive. Reluctant to let go. The continent is littered with broken shards. Arrested fragments of slower time. Unhealed unforgotten memories and the dead who do not die.

A house and a village and a lake.

On a day in the eleventh year of her dislocated life Yeva Cornelius comes gently awake in the first grey light of morning. There is some time yet to go before the rising of the cooler, circumspect, conciliatory sun. Yeva stays quite still on the couch, breathing slowly, watching the curtain stir. Lilac and vines crowd against the house. The room is leaf-scented, leaf-shaded, cool.

Her hair has been braided again in the night with loving gentleness: she feels the tightness of the intricate knotted plaits against her skull and smells the clean sweet fragrance the domovoi anoints her with while she sleeps. The prickle of tiny decorative twigs. Trinkets of seed and bird shell.

Take the domovoi's attention as a mark of favour, Eligiya Kamilova had said. *It's glad there are people again in the house. Leave a little salt and bread by the stove and it won't trouble us.*

The domovoi laid trails of crumbling earth across the floorboards, long sweeps and spirals along corridors from room to room. Eligiya Kamilova was right: it didn't want to hurt, not like those in the rye and oat fields – they were bad. Watchful and furtive, they came at you out of the white of noon and raised welts and sore rashes on your skin. Sly thorn scratches that stung and drew beads of blood. But the ones to be really afraid of were the ones that moved around outside in the night. Darkness magnifies. Darkness changes everything.

Daylight gathers and hardens in the room. Moment by moment the curtain is more visible, rising and collapsing. It's as if Yeva is moving it with her breath. Experimentally, she holds back the air in her lungs and eyes the curtain to see if it pauses too. Half-convinces herself that it does.

The atmosphere of a complicated dream is ebbing slowly away. Her mother was in the dream. Her mother was looking for her.

Her mother looks for her always, every day. She will have come back to the apartment and found it not there because of the bomb. But somebody will have told her the soldiers took them away, her and her sister, and put them on the train, and she will look for them. Only she won't know that Eligiya Kamilova took them off the train again, that Eligiya did something with her hands and broke the door of the train and took them into the night and the snow, and they ran away. Her mother won't know that.

Everywhere they go, Eligiya Kamilova leaves behind messages and notes so her mother can know they have been there and where they are going next. But her mother might not get the messages. She might not know who to ask. Eligiya posted letters to their old address but her mother can't go back to that house, not ever, because the soldiers sent everyone away. Some stranger will have read those letters. Or they'll be in a pile in a big post office room in Mirgorod. Or burned.

They walked south through the winter, Yeva and her sister Galina and Eligiya Kamilova, keeping off the roads and out of the villages, staying in the trees and the snow. The cold was like a dark glittering blade, but Eligiya was a hunter in the woods: she didn't talk much but she knew how to trap, how to make a warm place, how to build a fire in the night that didn't show light and a barricade of thorns against the wolves. Sometimes she slipped away to a village and came back with something they needed. Sometimes she found a hut or a farm where the people would let them sleep, maybe in a barn.

Yeva remembered every night. Every single night.

Her sister Galina was sick for a long time but she didn't die, and in the first days of spring the three of them came out of the trees, following a black stream flecked with brown foam, and found the house in the middle of a wide field of waist-high grass: a big square house of yellow weatherboards under a low grey roof, the glass in the many windows mostly broken. They waded over to it, leaving a trodden wake in the grass that buzzed and clattered with insects. Eligiya Kamilova went up under the porch and broke open the door, just like she had opened the door of the train. A wide staircase climbed up into shadow, and on the bare boards of the entrance hall was a pile of leaves and moss. Twigs laid out around it in patterns like the letters of a strange alphabet. Eligiya stepped round it carefully.

'Don't disturb it,' she said. 'Be careful not to touch that at all.'

There were pieces of furniture in some of the rooms. Mostly they'd had their upholstery ripped open, the stuffing pulled out and carried off for nests. There were chalky splashes of bird mess in the corners and streaks of it down the curtains. In the kitchen there were lamps, and oilcloth spread on the table.

'Are we going to stay here?' said Galina. 'For a while?'

'Perhaps,' said Eligiya Kamilova.

Yeva knew that Galina needed to rest, to stop moving for a long while, to be strong again.

Eligiya Kamilova hadn't give them any choice when she opened the door of the train and took them away into the trees and made them walk. It all happened too quickly to even think about until after it was done. But if they'd stayed on the train and gone where it was taking them, their mother would have known where they were and she could have come there to get them. Eligiya said the train was going to a bad place, a cruel terrible place, and no one ever came home from there, but she didn't even know what the terrible place was called, and Yeva wasn't scared of being in terrible places.

Every day she remembered the bomb. It always jumped her when she was thinking of something else. It wasn't like a memory. Memories change until you don't remember the actual thing any more; you remember the remembering. But of the time when the bomb fell nothing was forgotten and nothing was changed. When it jumped her it was like opening the same page of a book again and again, and the words were always all there, and always the same: Yeva's life hammered open like a bomb-broken building, the insides scattered and left exposed to ruinous elemental fire and rain.

Part of her stopped moving forward when the bomb came. Part of her got stuck in that piece of time for ever, always back there, always smelling the dust and burning, always looking down at Aunt Lyudmila squashed flat, always going down the stairs that used to be inside but were outside now, with nothing to hold on to. Part of her stayed back there, and only part of her was left to carry on. *Now* was a shadow remnant life of numbed and lesser feeling. Now was only aftermath. Aftermath.

That day when they first found the yellow house in the grass they didn't stay there but after looking it over they walked on down the stony dry track into the village. Long before they reached the village fields, Yeva could taste the tang of raw damp earth and animal dung in the air. Rooks chattered, squabbled and wheeled across the wide flatness of black soil just turned, thick and heavy and gleaming blue like metal. In the distance women were stooping and crouching at their work. They wore long red or green skirts, and their hair was wrapped in lengths of white cloth.

The village was a collection of ramshackle dwellings under heavy mounds of thatch, and beyond it was the lake and a line of tall pale trees on the shore, blue and dusty and far away. They walked in among skinny chickens and wary, resentful dogs, grey wood barns, grey corrugated-iron roofs. Scrawny cattle browsed in the dust behind a low fence of woven branches. A tractor leaned, abandoned, its axle propped on a rock.

'What's the name of this place?' said Eligiya Kamilova to the knot of men who gathered to meet them.

'Yamelei,' they said. 'This is Yamelei.'

Women from the nearest field came to join them, treading heavily over the upturned mud in rag-made shoes. Eligiya showed them the intricate brown patterns on her dark sinewed arms, and their eyes opened wider at that. A big old fellow with a ragged beard scoured the skyline behind them.

'There are no men with you?' he said.

'No.'

'A mother and daughters, then.'

'I am not their mother.'

'Grandmother?'

'No,' said Eligiya. 'Who lives in the big yellow house?'

'They left,' a woman said.

'How long ago?'

The woman pursed her lips. It was a question without an answer. Seasons rolled, and once in a while a new thing happened.

'And no one lives there now?' said Eligiya.

While Eligiya was talking to them Yeva watched the people of the village, their broad flattened faces, flattened noses, narrow dark curious eyes in crinkled skin. The men wore linen shirts and sleeveless jackets of animal hide, the pattern of the cows' backs on them yet, and shoes of woven bark that looked like slippers. They had knotted hands and swollen knuckles and their teeth were bad. They were looking at her, and she was looking at them, but the space between her and them was like thousands of miles and hundreds of years. She couldn't feel what they were thinking. They talked the same words but it was a different language.

Eligiya Kamilova told the people of Yamelei she would fix the tractor and make their boats stronger and steadier for the lake, and it was agreed that she and the two girls could stay at the yellow house for a while.

*

'Whose house is it?' said Galina as they walked back. 'It must be some-body's.'

'Small house,' said Eligiya Kamilova. 'Small aristocracy, long gone now.'

'Why doesn't someone from the village go and live there?'

'If someone did that,' said Eligiya, 'the others would have to resent them, and it would lead to trouble.'

They took water from the stream to drink and cook and wash in. Eligiya Kamilova trapped things in the woods. Pigeons and hares. Yeva didn't mind the plucking and the skinning and pulling the inside parts out. Galina wouldn't do it, but it gave Yeva no bad feelings at all.

There was a place behind the house closed in by a high wall of horizontal weathered planking between tall solid uprights. Inside the wall was a mass of ragged foliage, a general green flood: shoulder-high umbellifers and banks of trailing thorn. Week by week Eligiya and the girls cleared it away and found useful things still growing there: cabbage and onion and currant canes and lichenous old fruit trees. On a high shelf in a tool shed Eligiya found a rust-seized shotgun and a half-carton of shells. She fixed the gun up with tractor oil and it seemed like it would work, but she didn't want to try it out because the noise would reach the village and the men would come.

When summer came the walled yard was gravid with acrid ripeness. Lizards sunned themselves on the planking and wasps crawled on sun-warmed fruit. Eligiya Kamilova and the girls went into the garden and ate berries hurriedly, greedily, three at a time, bursting the sharp sweet purple taste with their tongues against the roofs of their mouths, staining their fingers with the blue-black juice.

Every day Eligiya Kamilova went down to Yamelei to work. Yeva was glad when she was gone and the sisters were on their own together without her. Then there were long afternoons of slow lazy time when few words were said or remembered, only the smells and colours and the day-flying moths in the house and the feeling of the long grass against their skin. Yeva would lie on her back by the overgrown stream and shut her eyes and look through closed lids at the bright oranges and soft, swirling, pulsing reds and browns. There were rhythms there, like the rhythms of her breathing. A plenitude of time. Galina got stronger, and in the evenings the sisters swam together in the big deep pond where the stream was dammed, until the air streamed with night-borne scents and the first stars rained tiny flakes of light that brushed their faces and settled on their arms. Then the night fears started to come out of the trees and across the grass, and Galina said it was time to get dressed and go into the house. Galina was getting better, but she still went silent sometimes and far away as if she was looking up at Yeva from under water.

In the evenings, before she went to sleep, Yeva would empty her pockets onto the shelves in the bookless emptied library and pick through the collection of the day. Feathers, empty dappled eggshells, twigs and leaves and moss, stones and fragments of knotty root. The best of them she put out by the stove for the domovoi.

Morning is fully come now. Yeva can see every thread in the thin curtain, and the dust smears on the broken windowpanes. Soon she will get up and put some wood in the stove and get water and wash her hair and brush the tight braids out. Then she will go down by herself into the woods by the lake. But for now she lies without moving and watches the curtain, and her sister is warm and heavy beside her under the blanket, eyes still closed fiercely in sleep. Galina will stay like that for another hour or so yet. Although there are rooms enough in the house to sleep in a different bed every night for a week, the sisters share the couch in the library. Eligiya Kamilova sleeps out on the veranda with the loaded gun.

2

*I*n the coolness under the trees down by the lake at Yamelei the dead artilleryman brushes aside his coverlet of damp memorious earth. Conscript Gunner K-1 Category Leonid Tarasenko. The grave mound is sweet and crumbly, layered with rotting leaves and matted fungal threads. Parts of his body are wrapped in warm, wet, skin-like, papery stuff.

The dead man's mushroom face feels the gentle touch of the conciliatory *morning sun in patterns of leaf shadow. The head turns from side to side, moving its dirt-stuffed mouth. Eyes large and dark as berries stare without blinking. As yet they see nothing.*

There is a faint perfume on the air.

Soldier Tarasenko, throat unzipped and bled out long slow years ago – a whizz of hot shell casing, a shiv wouldn't do it neater – rises slowly from the shallow accidental grave where he was planted like a seed.

Yeva Cornelius, night braids brushed out from her hair, leaves the house and her sister and Eligiya Kamilova still sleeping. The early fields are filled with air and light to overbrimming like a cup.

The path down to the lake passes between sea-green rye and scented hummocks of dried manure. In the bottom land the sorrel bloom is over, the crop coming on heavy and dark. Thick green heady vegetable blood. Yeva comes out onto the yellow grass of the lake margin. Old Benyamin Zoff is there already, on his hands and knees, crawling in his best grey suit along the edge of the water. He moves slowly, intently, with sacramental concentration, murmuring words that are quiet and musical but not a song. He will crawl like that all morning. There is a sunken city under the mirror-calm lake. An underwater world. In the village they keep water from the lake in their houses, in bottles and basins, and in the winter people go sliding face down on their bellies across the frozen surface, staring down, trying to see what is there.

The soul of the people is forever striving to behold the sunken city of Litvozh.

Eligiya Kamilova said that soon after they came to Yamelei. It was a quotation from a book. *They long not for something that will be but for the return of something that was. They have not forgotten and they never will.* The window frames of the village houses are carved with pictures of streets and towers under watery waves.

There are brown wooded islands in the lake and low hills on the horizon beyond the further shore. Yeva waves to Benyamin Zoff, who ignores her, and turns away from the water's edge to climb up into the woods. There is a dead man standing among the trees. She passes quite close to him, but he is not watching her, and Yeva pays him no regard. Yeva isn't bothered by the dead: they are preoccupied with their own thoughts and take no notice of her.

*

War, like storm and famine, has come around the shore of the lake and passed from time to time through Yamelei. The woods near the village are scarred by tank tracks, shallow shell holes and random trenches sinking under bramble, ivy and thorn. The trees are ripped and tattered by gunfire. Here, in these woods, colliding companies of the lost, rolling along on random surges of retreat and advance, attack and counter-attack, stumbled over one another, panicked and rattled bullets into each others' bodies. Field guns set up among the oats and rye in the upper ground rained desultory shellfire on unofficered and bootless conscripts crawling for shelter under thorn bush and bramble mound. One time a whole truckful of people from somewhere else was driven in under the trees, shot and shovelled into three-foot ditches.

In the woods around the lake the killed have not died right. Uneasily half-sentient, not rotting well, they can be disturbed, upset, awakened. Their uncommitted bodies rise through the earth. They will not sink. They float. From time to time they get up from their beds and wander a while under the trees and lie down somewhere else. When the villagers come across a shallow-buried corpse in the woods they cut its head off, sever the tendons in its legs and drive a wooden peg through the ribcage to pin it firmly down. But they will never find them all.

You put new plaster on the walls but the old stains still seep through. That's what they say in Yamelei.

Conscript Gunner K-1 Category Leonid Tarasenko, dead, stands with his forehead pressed against a tree trunk and traces the fissures in the bark with his hands. Pushes his fingers into the cracks and tries to pull pieces of the bark away, to see what is underneath. The pieces of bark won't come free. They slip through the tips of fingers that are sticky from the gash in his throat. His second, silent mouth.

The dead man has probed the inside of the tear in his throat to feel what is in there. He has found soft things and hard things. The hard things are sometimes slippery smooth, and there are some pieces in there that are sharp. There is a hole deeper inside that he can slip fingers into, but the hole is deeper than his fingers are long.

The interiors of things interest him. The inspection of the tree absorbs his attention. He touches the tree with his tongue. Feels roughness, tastes taste.

It occurs to him that the tree is not part of him.

Where is the end of me? the dead man wonders, looking up into the top of the tree. Where is my limit? I am up there. I go past those branches and those branches and up into the bright place up there that looks wet but has no smell of wet. I go past those trees over there, and those trees, and those trees behind me, and that is not the end of it and that is not the end of me. But though I am over there and up there, I am here and not there. It is strange. Fingers and tongue don't go up there to the top of the tree. They stop short.

The dead man apprehends that the tree doesn't stand on the earth but continues down into it. The tree reaches into the ground and fastens there, but it isn't the same with him. Unlike the tree, the dead man seems to be free to go to a different place.

That is interesting.

When he thinks about himself and what he knows and feels, the dead man finds pieces of knowing and pieces of feeling but the pieces are not connected. One of the pieces is angry and one of the pieces is sad because something important has been lost. One of the pieces feels sick, unfathomable horror and despair.

The pieces look at each other as if they have eyes, but they don't have eyes, not really. Eyes are on the outside, in the sticky-soft raggedy face thing, here, where you can touch with hands. When fingers touch eyes, eyes cannot see trees any more and fingers come away sticky. If you press eyes with fingers you see flakes of light, strange muted flakes of different light, but you only see the light and not the other things, not the trees you could see before. The light you make with fingers in the eyes, that light is inside the head.

Yet inside the dead man mostly there is darkness. He can touch the darkness in his throat with fingers, but the darkness is always there and doesn't come out. He cannot press that into light. That too is interesting. The dead have a lot to think about. But the piece in him that is sad and the piece in him that is angry want something. They are saying to go down the path.

What is path? says the piece of him that has all the questions. There isn't any piece with an answer to that, but the feet are walking now, and that seems to be good. That seems to be the answer to the path question.

He notices that if the feet stopped walking then all the other things – all that is not him but other stuff, trees and not trees – stop moving also, and wait, and watch the dead man watching them, waiting.

I am the centre then.
I see that.
That I understand.

Yeva Cornelius passes the dead man by. As she moves away, he catches the sense of her crossing a splash of sunlight between trees, and his heart is surprised by a deep dim anguish, a recognition of kinship.

Leonid Tarasenko does what the dead don't do. He starts to follow.

3

In Mirgorod the woman with the heavy canvas bag on her shoulder takes the tram all the way out to Cold Harbour Strand. She starts out along the spit and, when there is no one to see, leaves the path and disappears into the White Marsh. An hour and a half of hard walking brings her to the edge of a wide muddy expanse of marshland. She unpacks her bundle, spreads the oilskin out on the ground like a mat, sheltered from the breeze in the lee of a fallen tree trunk, and lays the Zhodarev on it. She crouches next to it to push the telescopic sight into the rails and set the graticule. Prises ten rounds from two stiff stripper clips into the toploader. Four hundred yards away across the mud another tree leans sideways in front of a mossy stone wall. She cuts a branch into three short lengths with a knife and binds them with twine to form a makeshift tripod barrel mount. Then she sets the graticule and settles herself into position, kneeling then lying alongside the fallen trunk. Remembers how it feels to be tucked away. Hidden from view. Safe.

She settles the stock of the rifle against her shoulder. Closes her left eye and fits her right eye against the back of the sight. Lets herself relax and sprawl on the ground. Becoming part of it. Settled. Rooted. She has to cock her wrist awkwardly to bring her clawed trigger finger to bear. It feels wrong but she will get used to it.

She fixes the tree in the cross wires. Centres on the place where a particular branch separates from the main bough. Squeezes the slack out of the trigger. The graticule is shivering and taking tiny random jumps. Her heart is busy in her chest. She breathes out, emptying her lungs – calm, calm – and pulls the trigger. The muzzle kicks and deafens her. A puff of dust rises from the wall five feet to the left of the target tree. Waterfowl lift from the mud and circle, puzzled.

Not good.

The woman resettles herself and takes another shot. Forcing her clawed finger to squeeze smoothly.

Two feet to the right of the target. Still not good. But better.

She has put ten rounds aside in a safe place ready for the task itself, which leaves her a hundred and ten to practise with. At ten shots a day that's eleven practice days. Eleven days in which to remember. Eleven days in which to learn again how to put an entire magazine into a spread she could cover with one hand. She used to be able to do that, six years ago.

Eleven days to get it back. That will be enough.

She has eight cartridges left for this morning's work. She adjusts the graticule again and prepares herself for another shot.

4

Galina Cornelius wakes to the empty house. Her sister Yeva is wandering in the woods by the lake and Eligiya Kamilova has gone down to the village to work. Galina is glad to be alone. She has a secret place to go.

She crosses the black stream by a wooden plank and pushes her way along the overgrown margin of the pond, following the rim of still, deep water. The grass, in shadow and still morning-damp, soaks the edge of her skirt. Thorns snag at her clothes and roots try to trip her, but she presses forward. Old statues watch her from the undergrowth with pebble-blank eyes: naked women holding amphorae to their breasts; burly, bearded naked men, long hair curling to their shoulders; a laughing boy riding a big fish. The dark green foliage has almost absorbed them, and some have already lost limbs and faces to winter frost and summer heat. There is a rowing boat beached among the reeds on the lake shore. The oars are still shipped in the bottom but the sky-blue paint on the hull is peeling away. Every time she sees it Galina pictures a mother and her girls, a lilac parasol, a shawl against the cool of the shade, in that boat on the water in the afternoons of summer. She tried to pull it onto the water once, but the wood was soft as cake and came away in pieces.

Galina pushes on towards her destination.

The little concrete building is still there, grey and weather-stained, half ivied-over under the shade of trees. Figurines look down at her from the corners: fat naked children smiling, crumbling, patched with moss. Galina pushes the door open. Inside, in the semi-darkness, there is a dark mouth in the ground, the start of a spiral stone staircase. The air in the stairwell smells cool and earth-scented with a taint of rust. She descends. At the bottom is a narrow tunnel with tiled walls that bow out and then lean in to meet low overhead. The tunnel leads away into gloom, heading out underwater across the floor of the lake, and at the far end is a dim green light. Galina feels her way in near-darkness towards her secret underwater room.

Who knows what kink of imagination caused the people who once lived in the house in the grass to build such a place, a hemispherical glazed dome of white steel ribwork, an upturned glass bowl twenty feet high on the bed of the lake? The water that presses against the glass walls is a deep moss colour at floor level, fading to the palest, faintest green at the top. The steel framework is streaked and patched with rust, and on the other side of the glass is the dim movement of water vegetation and shadowy water creatures. Obscure larvae and gastropods. Muffled fishes. Over the course of the years the lake has rained a gentle silt upon the outside of the chamber, staining the glass yellow and flecking it with patches of muck. The underwater room is filled with dim subaqueous forest light, but when Galina arches her neck to look up she can see light and the undersides of ripples lapping in the breeze, and sometimes the underneath of a waterfowl disturbing the circle of visible surface.

Down here in the underwater room the temperature is constant and cool. The room is furnished. Rugs, a sofa, an empty bookcase, a cupboard, a chair, a desk. A pot of earth stands in the centre of the circular floor, the remains of some long-dead, long-dried plant slumped across it. As Galina moves around, circling, touching, she surprises traces of cigar smoke. The smell of brandy and laudanum lingers in pockets of air.

She has told no one about this place and brought no one here, not Eligiya Kamilova, not even Yeva. It is her own place, where she can come and be herself and think about what she should do. Eligiya Kamilova is not their mother. She has never been a mother to anyone at all. She stays with them and takes care of things, but she would travel further and faster without them; she would go even as far as the endless forest in the east. Eligiya has been in that forest, has travelled there, and it stains the air around her. Part of her is in the forest always and has never come away.

Their mother is in Mirgorod.

I have been too ill to do anything but follow where Eligiya Kamilova went, but that time is coming to an end. I must take Yeva back to Mirgorod. I am the older one, and it is my job to do that. Soon I will be as well and strong as I will ever be, and then I must do that.

But I am not ready, not quite yet.

The rusalka presses its chalky face, expressionless and pale, against the silt-flecked glass and stares in at Galina, watching her intently. It moves its hands through the water slowly as if it were waving. But it is not waving. It is only watching. The first time it came Galina mistook it for the reflection of her own face.

The dead soldier Leonid Tarasenko follows Yeva out from under the trees into the emptiness of tall light. There is a tiny anguished hook of memory somewhere inside him, a diamond-hard strange survivor in the heart, a piece of disconnected understanding no larger than a single word, and the word is child.

The dead man follows child. Child fills his heart with happiness and tears and need. In all the world of the dead man there is only child and follow and no other purpose at all, and the existence of even this one irreducible shard of purpose is a mystery more mysterious than the endless ever-faithful burning of the sun.

But child (all unaware of the following) moves faster than the dead man can. The separation between them stretches and stretches.

The dead man would call out after her if he could, but there is not enough wonder and mystery in the world to provide him with concepts like voice and call. He has been given only child and follow, and it is not enough.

Child is gone.

He moves on, following the line she took. Child is gone, but of following there is no end and nothing else to take its place.

The line of his following brings him again to an edge of trees, different trees, but trees. Trees are familiar to him and the smell of earth is familiar beneath them, and that is a soothing ointment for his heart, but also not soothing at all; nothing takes away the happiness and the tears and the need for following child.

Because trees are familiar to him the dead Leonid Taresenko follows his following in under the trees.

Galina Cornelius stays a long while in the underwater room, but eventually it is time to return to the house because Yeva will soon be home from the woods. As Galina is crossing the plank over the black stream, the dead soldier steps out from a tree and comes towards her.

She sees his open earth-filled mouth, the woodlice in the folds of his face and neck.

She screams. It is blank terror.

All the way to the house she runs, heart pounding, fear-blind, and at the veranda she stops and turns. The dead thing is following her, loping unsteadily through the waist-high grass.

Galina screams again.

'Yeva! Yeva!'

The dead soldier is out of the high grass and coming up the path, coming towards her with fixed and needy dead black eyes, hand stretched out for companionship.

Eligiya Kamilova's gun is lying on the couch on the veranda.

It could blow up in your eyes. Eligiya had said. *Only use it if the other thing will be worse.* But she had shown them how.

Galina seizes the gun and swings the barrel up into the face of the dead soldier. His foot is already on the first veranda step when she pulls both triggers together and takes his head apart. The stock kicks back into her shoulder and knocks her down. She can't hear her own screams any more for the appalling ringing of the double gunshot in her own ears.

Eligiya Kamilova finds the two girls sitting side by side outside the house, on the couch on the veranda, staring at the corpse of twice-killed Conscript Gunner K-1 Category Leonid Tarasenko, a good and simple man but not a lucky one. When she heard the shot she was already on the track up to the house, work abandoned halfway done, weightless, spun out of orbit by the kick of the newspaper in her hand.

The girls look up at her in silence when she comes. Their faces are strained and pale, their eyes rimmed red and wide with shock. She knows that she should comfort them, but she doesn't know how, she hasn't got it in her; she searches but it isn't there, the right thing to do to take that shock and pain away. She stands stiffly on the veranda, bitterly, emptily aware of the newspaper rolled and clutched by her side. The ineradicable, undeniable truth of it burns in her hand. She hasn't anything to give them for comfort, not even news, not good news, only bad.

There's no good time to tell them what she knows. She is tempted to wait, but waiting will only make things worse, compounding fact with deceiving, and she has never told them less than truth. She cannot give them loving comfort but she can give them that and always does.

She holds the newspaper out to Galina.

'Look,' she says. 'Read it. Read the date.'

Eligiya was down in the village working on the boats when the musicians came out of the east, walking in with their rangy dog: the gusli player with the long straggled hair and thick coal beard resting on his chest, one leg lost in the war, swinging along on crutches, and the tall old man in the long coat, drum like a cartwheel slung on his back. The drummer carried a newspaper stuffed in his pocket that nobody in the village could read. Kamilova bought it from him for a couple of kopeks.

Galina stares at the newspaper blankly.

'What?' she says. 'What about it? What?'

'The date.'

Galina makes an effort to squint at the stained print.

'It's a couple of months old.' She hands it back to Kamilova and wipes her fingers in the lap of her dress already splattered with the soldier's drying mess. 'It's greasy. It smells bad.'

Galina's eyes aren't focused properly. They stray back to the half-rotten corpse on the veranda boards.

'Not the month,' says Kamilova. 'The year.' She holds the paper up again for the girl to see. Galina stares at it for a while. Furrows her brow in confusion.

'It's a mistake,' she says. 'A printing error.'

'No,' said Kamilova. 'I talked to the men who brought it into the village. I asked them questions. It isn't a mistake.'

'What?' said Yeva. 'What are you talking about.'

Kamilova sat down beside them on the end of the couch. She felt suddenly exhausted. Not able to manage. Not able to lead the way, not at the moment, not any more. The strength in her legs, the straightness in her back, was gone. Yeva squeezed up to make room.

'What is it?' she said.

'I'm sorry,' said Eligiya Kamilova. 'I'm so sorry.'

What?

'We've been walking in the trees,' said Kamilova, 'and we've been living here in the village by the lake, and it's been seven months, nearly eight – a long time but not quite eight months – that's all.' She takes the paper from where it lies in Galina's lap. 'Look at the date.'

Yeva reads the small print at the top of the page.

'But that's wrong.'

'No.'

'But it is wrong. It's five years wrong.'

'Five and a half. Five and half years gone.'

Kamilova has had longer than the girls to think it through.

The three of them roll the corpse of the twice-killed soldier onto a sheet, wrap it and drag it through the grass far away from the house. They dig a hole up near the woods. It takes all day and they are dumb with exhaustion and heat and stink, and the sun has gone and the fear is coming out of the woods. They go inside and light candles and put wood in the stove, and when the water is hot they wash in the kitchen in silence, the whole of their bodies from head to toe. It takes a long time to get the dirtiness off and they don't quite manage it even then.

Rank warm cheese and a stump of hard bread on the shelf. Oilcloth on the table. Candles burning. The house and the village and the lake. Some people cannot look at their memories, and some people cannot ever look away.

'Our mother thinks I'm sixteen,' says Yeva. 'Sixteen. Or dead. Either way she didn't find us. She never came.'

'I didn't know,' says Kamilova. 'There wasn't a way to know.'

'She couldn't have come,' says Galina. She looks at Eligiya Kamilova. 'But tomorrow we'll go home,'

'Home?' says Kamilova. 'What do you mean "home"?'

'You don't have to come with us, Eligiya. You've done enough; you've done more than you needed to for us. You can have your life back; you can go where you want; you can go into the forest again, or stay here and live for ever. '

Galina's words lacerate Eligiya like the blades of knives.

'I ...' she begins. The pain she feels is shame and guilt and love, inextricable trinity, hands held open to receive the price you had to pay. 'Everything will have changed,' she says. 'You have to think about that. She ... Your mother might not even—'

'You don't have to come, Eligiya.'

'I will come,' says Eligiya Kamilova. 'Of course I will come.'

Chapter Three

If you're afraid of wolves, stay out of the forest.

Josef Stalin (1878–1953)

1

The rain came in long pulses, hard, warm and grey, and the noise of it in the trees was loud like a river. The galloping of rain-horses. Rain-bison. Rain-elk. Maroussia Shaumian followed the trail through rain and trees, splashing through mud-thick rain-churned puddles, the bindings on her legs sodden and clagged to the knee, pushing herself, back straight and face held high, into the future. Her clothes smelled of wet wool and woodsmoke and the warmth of her own body. Rain numbed her face and trickled down her chin and neck. It tasted of earth and nettles. Rain slicked and beaded on the ferns: tall fern canopies trembling under the rain, unfurling ferns, red fern spore. A boar snuffled and crashed in the fern thickets. His hot breath. The smell of it in the rain. There were side paths leading in under the thorns; mud ways trodden clear that passed under low branches. The larger beasts were further off and elsewhere, under taller trees. Cave bear and wisent and the dagger-mouth smilodon.

The land rose and then fell away: not hills but a drifting swell that wasn't flatness. Coming down, the trail took her among broad shallow pools. Maroussia cut a staff and kept her head down and walked against the rain, churning knee-high through water, mud-heavy feet slipping and awkward. Most of the ground here was water. Roots and stumps and carcasses of fallen trees reached up through the rain-disturbed surface, paused in arrested motion, waiting, balanced between worlds, and everything distant was lost in the rain.

Maroussia crouched to dip her hands in the water, letting the rain beat on her back. Rolling up her sleeves she reached right down to the bottom and ran her fingers through the grass there. It looked like hair and moved to her touch, dark green and beautiful. It was just grass. Her arms in the water looked pale and strange, not hers but arms in the shadow world as real as the one she was in. She cupped her hands and brought some water up into her world to drink, feeling the spill of it through her fingers and down her arms. The water tasted of cold earth and leaves and moss. She tasted the roots of all the trees that stood in it and the bark and wood of the fallen ones. She swallowed it, cool and sweet in her throat, and took more, still drinking long after she wasn't thirsty any more.

The forest is larger than the world, though those who live outside it think the opposite.

She was Maroussia Shaumian still. Nothing of that time was forgotten, nothing was lost, though she was more now, more and less and different and changed and far from home. Like the water in the rain she was fresh and new, and as old as the planet, both at once.

You don't know where home is until you're not there any more.

She waded out deeper into a wide pool loud under the rain to where a beech tree lay on its side, its rain-darkened bark smooth and wet to the touch. The beech had fallen but it wasn't dead; it was earth-rooted still, and its leaves under the water were green. She let her hands rest on it and felt the tree's life. She wished she could speak to it but she didn't have the words, and what would she say? *Help me*, perhaps. *Help me to get home.* But that wasn't right. It wasn't what you should ask, and no help would come.

Wolves plashed under tree-shadow, distant and silent and indistinct as moths. One turned his face towards her, wolf eyes in the rain, unhurried, considering. She returned his gaze and he looked away.

*

Some while later she came on the wolf kill. It was an aurochs, huge and bull-like, lying on his side in a shallow pool of bloodied water, his rough fox-coloured hair matted with mud and rain-sodden. From a distance he looked drowned, but when she got close half of him was gone, a rain-washed hole of raw meat. Rain-glistening flies sipped at his eyes and crawled on the grey flopped rain-wet slab of his tongue. The noise of the rain beat in her ears like the rhythm of her own blood, too close and too ceaseless to attend to.

Sudden and uncalled, the killing moment closed its grip on her and she was in it. It was still there, still happening, and she was the happening of it, not outside and watching, not remembering, but being there. She was aurochs not hearing the splashing charge of wolf above the rain, not seeing wolf behind him, not smelling wolf through rain and water and the rich scent of rain on leaf. She felt the appalling shock of the boulder-heavy collision and the clamp of the tearing mouth at her throat. Heard with the aurochs' own strange clarity the small snap deep inside her neck. Felt the wordless sad dismay of ruminant beast, the surge of fear and panicked stumble, the attempted burly sweep of a neck that didn't respond – delivered nothing, moved nothing, connected with nothing. The loneliness of that.

She saw with hopeless aurochs eye the wolf that made the first charge turn and come splashing back through mud-swirled blood-swirled water. Then other wolves were on her back and she fell. Pain and the acceptance of pain. Aurochs could not rise and could not stand. Her leg wouldn't go where she wanted it to go, her beautiful leg was lost. Aurochs grieved for it. Maroussia lived the last long moments when wolves ripped aurochs belly open and pulled the stuff there out and tore and swallowed bits from her beautiful twitching leg and slowly and softly minute after minute aurochs grew tired and far away and died.

And that wasn't all.

She was the death of aurochs but she was also the hunting of the wolves. She was salt on the wolf's tongue and the dark hot taste of blood. She was the sour breath of the aurochs' dying and the glad teeth in the neck of it. She was the crunch of the killing bite and the thirsty suck and tearing swallow of warm sweet flesh.

And that wasn't all.

She was the life and growth and connected watchfulness of every

46

tree and every leaf and every small creature and every water drop in the pool and the rain, its history and the possibilities of what was to come.

And that wasn't all.

Nothing was *all*, because there was no end to the fullness of what she could perceive. Because this was what she had become, this overwhelming surprise of plenitude.

She was Maroussia Shaumian still – Maroussia Shaumian, who had made her choice in Mirgorod and followed her path to its end in Novaya Zima – but she had been inside the Pollandore when the temporary star ignited around it. The Pollandore had imploded and exploded and changed and brought her here, and now it was gone. It was inside her now, if it was anywhere: inside her, new and strong, volatile and unaccommodated. The Pollandore and what she could be ran ahead of her and overwhelmed her until she hardly knew what was her and what was not, because sometimes she was everything.

Time wasn't a river; time was the sea, layered and fluid and malleable, what was past and what was possibly to come all intricately infolded and vividly present inside the rippling horizons of now. Nothing of Maroussia was lost, but she was more. She was changed and become *this*. All *this*.

The seeing faded. (She called it seeing though it wasn't that, but there was no word.) Seeing always came uncalled and surprised her. She suspected she could learn to call it up at will, but she was afraid of learning that. Once she went through that door, there would be no coming back, and she hadn't chosen that and did not want it. She hadn't chosen anything of this, not *this*, but here it was.

She was as lonely in the rain as the dying aurochs and as far from home.

Time to move on.

The meeting place was not far, and they would be waiting.

2

There were three of them at the place on the White Slope, Fraiethe and the father and the Seer Witch of Bones, and Maroussia Shaumian was the fourth.

The father spoke, as he always did, the phrases of beginning.

'And so we are met again under wind and rain and trees and the rise and set of sun. We are the forest; the forest is everywhere and everything, and the forest is us.'

'No,' said Maroussia. 'We are something but not everything.'

The father made a barely perceptible movement of his head, acknowledging the justice of that, but frowned and said nothing. *An antagonist then*, Maroussia thought. *Well, there it is then. So it is.*

The father was not actually present at the meeting on the White Slope. After the first time he had not come in bones and blood and flesh but as a fetch, a spirit skin, while he kept himself apart and somewhere else. The fetch had come as a man with woodcutter's hands and forearms, hair falling glossy-thick across his brow and shoulders. A rank aroma, and burning green eyes that watched her openly. Maroussia thought the fetch crude and suspected a deliberate slight aimed at her. *This is the form*, it said, *that seduced your mother and made her sweat and cry in a timberman's hut in the woods. This the form that fathered you. Like some too?*

But Maroussia didn't believe it. Whatever artifice seduced her mother at Vig would have been more subtle than that, more complex and thoughtful and elegant and patient and kind, to console her for the wasteland of her marriage to Josef Kantor and draw her out of it into the shadow under the trees. It was imagination that seduced her mother, not this unwashed goat. The goat was provocation only.

Then she realised that the father knew this, and knew that she knew it, and in fact the burly woodcutter was not a provocation but a complicitous tease. A wink. A father–daughter joke to be shared.

She didn't resent the father for fathering her. Not any more. When she was growing up in Mirgorod she'd lived with the pain of the consequences of that, but now and here she understood. For the father there was a pattern to be woven, things to be done, opportunities to be taken and prices paid. What he had done to her mother and her wasn't personal. It wasn't even human.

She turned away from him to the other two.

Fraiethe had come in the body. She was really there. Though Fraiethe had guided the paluba that reached Maroussia in Mirgorod, that spoke to her and half-lied and half-bewitched and set her on the course that brought her here; though Fraiethe was part of the deception – if deception was what it had been (which it was not, not a deception but an opening-up) – Fraiethe did not like spirit skins. She stood now under the trees, shadow-dappled like a deer, rain-wet and naked except for the reddish-brown fur, water-sleek and water-beaded, that covered her head and neck and shoulders and the place between her breasts. Fur traced the muscular valley of her spine, and a perfume of musk and warmth was in the air around her. Her skin was flushed because of the rain and cold, and her eyes were wide and brown and there were no whites in them.

The third, the Seer Witch of Bones, was neither body nor fetch, but something else, a shadow presence, a sour darkness, the eater of death, the mouth that opened with a smile of dark leaves and thorns, rooted in neither animal nor tree but of the crossing places, muddy and terrible.

And Maroussia Shaumian, who had sewn uniforms at Vanko's factory and pulled Vissarion Lom out of the River Mir and lain beside him in the bottom of a boat to bring him back with the warmth of her body; Maroussia Shaumian, who had sliced a man's head off with a flensing blade and crossed the snow of Novaya Zima to the Pollandore; Maroussia Shaumian, who forgot none of that but remembered everything: Maroussia Shaumian was the fourth at the White Slope, and she claimed an equal place.

The three of them had drawn her to the Pollandore in the moment of its destruction. Because of them she had been there at that moment and absorbed it – been absorbed into it – and become what she was. Because of them the Pollandore was gone from the world beyond the forest and she was here. It was their stratagem against the living angel in the forest. The forest borders were sealed and she, Maroussia, by her presence here, was what held them so. But the three had no sense of the consequences of what they'd done, none at all; only Maroussia had that, and even to her it came only in broken glimpses, fragments that were dark and bleak and hopeless.

She didn't know if there was a better thing they could have done than what they did, but if there was, they hadn't done it.

The fetch of the father spoke again, the man with green eyes: 'The forest is safe. The living angel is contained and we will deal with him. Already he is growing weak and slow. He subsides and grows mute. His ways out of the forest are closed and he no longer draws strength from the places beyond us. The trees are growing back. He has no influence beyond the forest, and here we are stronger than he is.'

The human woman, dark-eyed Maroussia, answered him, and the voice she spoke with was her voice but not only hers but the Pollandore's also, and sounded strange to her ears.

'Yet the angel *lives!*' she said. 'Whatever you say, it is not yet destroyed, and it is not clear that we alone have the strength to do it. And we must look to the world beyond the forest. The years there are moving hard and fast, the Vlast is resurgent, the last slow places are closing, the giants and rusalkas are driven out.'

'What happens beyond the edge of the trees doesn't concern us,' the fetch of the father said. 'It is outside. That's what outside means.'

'The world beyond the forest is growing steel fists,' said Maroussia. 'There's no balance there, no breathing of other air. They will not rest content with what they have; they want it all. They will come here, they'll cut and burn. There are winds the forest cannot stand against. I've seen—'

'They've come here before,' said the fetch of the father, the green-eyed man of muscle, the rich deep voice. 'And always we have always driven them out. It's not even hard.'

'But nothing is the same now, because of what you did. The Pollandore is gone from that world. There is no balance there, and the Vlast will come in numbers, they will drive and burn and burn and drive. There is a man that leads them. Josef Kantor, called Rizhin now. I know something of him and so do you. You know how far he's gone already and how fast he moves.' The human woman, dark-eyed Maroussia, paused and looked at all of them, not just the father. 'And we all know what he is throwing into the sky. We have all heard the hot dry thundercrash and smelled the burning stink of dead angel flesh cutting open the sky. We know the force and speed of what is passing overhead and looking down on us. It makes the forest small. And that's just the beginning of his ambition. How can you say this doesn't concern us?'

The fetch of the father moved to speak, but Maroussia dark-eyed paradigm shifter, the unexpected outcome and maker of change, held up her hand to stop him.

'You must listen to me,' she said, 'or why did you do this? Why make me as I am and bring me here – which I did not ask for, which I did not choose – why do this and not listen now to what I say?'

The fetch fell into silence. Maroussia realised that the father, wherever he was, had finished his testing of her.

The Seer Witch of Bones said nothing. It didn't matter to her. Whatever came there would be a fullness of death at the house of bleached skulls.

But Maroussia felt the pressure of Fraiethe's attentive examination. Fraiethe knew everything: the heaviness and smell of her wet muddy clothes, the hot sweat of her palms and the beating of her heart, her anger at the trickiness of the father, that she was lonely and didn't like the forest and wanted to go home. It was Maroussia not Fraiethe who was naked on the White Slope.

'What would you have us do?' said Fraiethe.

The human woman dark-eyed Maroussia Shaumian opened her mouth to answer Fraiethe. She felt again the dark earth roots and the watchful sentience of rain. A wind stirred the leaves and moved across her face.

'Nothing,' she said. 'I would have you do nothing. There is another way. '

3

Mailboat Number 437 chugged down the mighty mile-broad River Yannis. Vissarion Lom sat in the stern and watched the low wooded hills roll by. The river was slow and quiet here, taking a wide turn to the south, its green waters a highway for tugs, ferries, excursion boats and barges riding low under the weight of ore and grain and oil. Mailboat Number 437 was a dogged striver. The vibration of her engine defined Lom's world: the gentle rhythmic shocks, the slap of small waves against her iron skin. It was a world that smelled of diesel engine and pine planking and rust. Wet rope and mailbags.

Sora Shenkov, master and sole crew of Mailboat Number 437, was a big man with hard brown hands and eyes the colour of ice and sky. He wasn't a talker. Every day Lom sat in the stern and watched him work, unless it rained: then he would go below and watch the river through the specks and smears of his little cabin window. And every day Shenkov's boat made slow headway: her engine churned the screw, and her forward speed through the water exceeded the south-west slide of the Yannis by a certain number of miles, and the marginal gain accumulated. Not that Lom was keeping count. He'd earned some money and taken passage with Shenkov. He'd paid his way. This boat-world time belonged to him. Lom had never owned a time before, but he owned this one and did not wish for it to hurry to an end.

The last six years had changed him. He had travelled far, keeping himself to himself, taking rough work where he could find it, never staying in one place long. His wanderings had taken him into the forest margins, and he had found the endless forest simply that: an endlessness of trees. There were sounds in the night and pathways that went nowhere. Above all, he had not found Maroussia. Of her no trace at all. When he came out of the forest again, months had passed by, seasons come and gone, and he had imagined much but found nothing. He was heavily bearded now, muscular, wiry and weather-darkened, with shaggy wheat-coloured hair. The hole in the front of his skull was nothing but a faint thumbprint visible in certain slanting lights, sun-browned and almost healed. And slowly, slowly, day by day, he was being carried down the river in Shenkov's boat. He enjoyed these days, which required no decisions, required nothing from him at all. He wasn't going anywhere in particular. His adventure was over and time had moved on. Once giants rode the timber rafts west on the Yannis, but now it was women without husbands or sons, and it seemed on the wide quiet river that it had always been so.

Swinging round a headland, the boat came up on two huge timber rafts sliding side by side downstream on the current. Rather than waste time and fuel going out into the middle passage, Shenkov, in the little wheelhouse, gunned the engine and nosed skilfully though the channel between them. Lom reached instinctively for the boathook, not that it would help if the rafts chose to drift together and crush the boat between them. Each raft was as big as an island and carried a cluster of plank huts with smoking chimneys and fenced paddocks for goats and chickens. The logs were red pine, and though they were boughs and branches only, never the trunks, they were thicker and heavier by far than whole trunks of beech or oak. As the boat eased through the gap, a woman was milking a cow and speaking in a soft easy voice to her neighbour on the next raft, who was hanging out clothes to dry. Shenkov gave the women a courteous nod. The air was thick with the resinous red pine scent.

It was early evening when Mailboat Number 437 came to the timber station at Loess. Shenkov grunted in surprise. The wharves were crowded with military vessels: cruisers in brown river camouflage, crane-mounted barges loaded with stacked pontoons, a requisitioned paddle-wheel ferry painted stem to stern and smokestack in dull sky grey.

Shenkov managed to find a berth in front of the excise house, tucked in under the looming steel hull of a cruiser, and began to unload mail-bags onto the steps. Lom left him to his work and wandered off to have a look at what the troops were doing. Sitting on a bollard at the railhead, he watched a captain of engineers supervising the unloading of vehicles from an armoured train. The engine noise was deafening. The stink of diesel fumes. Heavy grinding tracks churned the mud, splintered the boardwalks and cracked the paving. There were half-tracks and troop carriers, but also tractors and cherry pickers and things Lom hadn't seen before that looked like immense hooks and chainsaws mounted on caterpillar tracks. The sapper platoon was marshalling them off the train and onto waiting barges whose decks were already stacked high with oil drums. The sappers struggled with three Dankov D-9 battle tanks, each towing what looked like a hefty spare fuel tank. Instead of a gun, the tank turrets were equipped with a short and vicious-looking nozzle. Lom knew what they were. He'd seen flame-thrower tanks in newsreels. Seen spouts of burning kerosene ignite buildings and flush trenches. Seen the enemy run. Screaming. Burning.

The captain of engineers saw him watching and came across. Took in Lom's weathered face and thick untidy crop of beard, his mud-coloured clothes and boots.

'You came down the river with the mailboat,' he said. 'Were you ever in the forest?' He was a decent-looking man, efficient and practical, more engineer than soldier. It was a question not a challenge.

Lom nodded. 'Off and on,' he said. 'A little.'

'What's it like there?' said the captain of engineers.

Lom gave a slight shrug. 'Trees,' he said. 'Trees and rivers and lakes. Valleys and hills. Miles and miles of nothing much.' He gestured towards the fleet of machinery, the barges and the armed boats. 'You going in there? With that?'

'That's right. No secret about that.'

'It's been done before. Always got nowhere.'

Once a generation the Vlast mounted incursions against the forest. It was one of the futile repeating rhythmic spasms of the Vlast's history. Patrols wandered, ineffectual and lost, doing a bit of damage till they got bogged down in mud and thorn and disease. Lom's own parents had lived in the forest edge. Soldiers came and killed them and razed their village to the ground. The soldiers had carried him out, an orphaned infant, and left him at the Institute in Podchornok. Lom remembered nothing of that forest time and nothing of his parents: presumably they were buried in there somewhere. Bones under the leaf mulch.

So it was to happen again.

'It'll be different this time,' the captain said. 'This time we're going to do it right. We're going in in numbers, whole divisions on a broad front, with heavy machinery and air support. Three salients along the three big rivers. What you see here is just the tip of the iceberg. We're going to cut and burn all the way through to the other side. We're going to break the myth of the forest once and for all.'

'Guess you people need something to do,' said Lom, 'now the war's over.'

'I was hoping you might give me some advice. The benefit of experience? On-the-ground knowledge? Let me buy you dinner and pick your brains.'

'Not a chance,' said Lom. 'Not a chance in a million fucking years.'

4

Lom went back to the mailboat moored at the jetty but Shenkov
wasn't there; he'd gone into Loess for supplies. Lom settled
himself on the bench in the stern to wait. There was twilight
and silence on the air, and a faint smell of woodsmoke. The lapping of
the river's edge against the side of the boat. Tiny white moths coming
to the newly lit lamp. Not many, not yet, just a few: there was still
some life in the western sky. Time was quiet and hardly moving: like
the broad deserted river in gathering darkness, all islands and further
shores hidden, it seemed to rest and breathe. Huge. Secretive. Watchful.

Maroussia came to him then in the cool of the evening.

Lom knew she was there before she spoke. Before he turned to see
her, he felt her as a presence emerging. Resolving out of the periphery
of things. She was watching him from out of the silence and the twilight and the shoals of time.

He turned his head to look at her full on, thinking as he did so that
she might not be there if he did that. But she was still there, except it
was impossible to say exactly where she was. She was on the jetty and
on the deck of the boat and on the river shore and on the water. She
was very precisely *somewhere*, but the frame of reference that located
her was not the same as his. She was solid and real but she was made
from air and shadow, woven out of the river twilight. Not flimsy, but
he could not have reached out and touched her; the space between
them wasn't crossable. He didn't try. For a long time he looked at her.
Studying. She was different: older, wiser, changed and strange. She saw
things now that he didn't see.

Lom found he was waiting for her to speak first, but she didn't. He
wasn't sure if it was possible to speak, anyway, if sounds and words
could cross the space that separated them. If language itself could
survive that crossing.

'I went into the forest,' he said at last. 'I was looking for you.'

There was a moment when he thought she hadn't heard. He wasn't
even sure he'd actually said anything aloud. And then she spoke. It was
her voice, the shock of her real voice speaking. He thought he'd kept

the memory of it but he had not. The appalling uselessness of memory, how drab and inadequate it was. The sudden raw and open pain of six lost silent years

'I know,' she said.

Lom felt an overwhelming sudden surge of anger and despair. It ambushed him from within. He thought he'd moved beyond all that, he thought he'd acclimatised to loss and living on, but it was all there, unchanged since the day he'd lost her. Since she'd gone where he couldn't follow.

'You knew?' he said. 'But you didn't ...'

'I couldn't,' she said. 'I'm sorry.'

He pushed the anger aside. That hurting was old business, to be dealt with another time, not now.

'Still,' he said, 'you're here. You came back.'

'No,' she said. 'I can't stay here. I can't come back. It isn't possible. Not yet. Perhaps not ever.'

'But—'

'Listen to me,' she said. 'I need you to listen. I need you to understand. What I'm doing now, somewhere else, not here, is I'm holding the forest closed. The angel is shut in and the intermixing of the worlds is separating out. Time runs at different speeds. My time will become, in your world, small fragments of stillness, areas where there is no time at all. I can't come back; I can't come home.' She stared at him, dark eyes wide and urgent in the twilight. They were made of the twilight and the air of the river breathing. 'Can you understand that? Can you?'

'How long?' he said. 'How long have we got?'

'I don't know,' she said. 'There's no measure. How can I say—'

'I mean today. Now. How much time have we got now?'

'Oh,' she said. 'Today? I don't know. I shouldn't have come here at all. Even being here makes a hollowing, a gap for the angel to come through. If that starts to happen, I must go.'

'I could come to where you are,' said Lom. 'You could show me how.'

'No.'

'I would come gladly. I would want that. There's nothing here for me now.'

She looked away sadly in the gathering river darkness.

'It's not possible. The barrier mustn't be broken.' She paused. 'I don't have a choice. I didn't choose this. But if I had a choice, I would choose it. You have to understand that. If I could choose this, I would.'

'Then why come at all?' he said. 'Why are you here?'

'You did something for me once, and I've come to ask you again. I'm sorry. You should be left in peace, but I'm not doing that.'

'What do you need?' said Lom. 'I will do it if I can. Of course I will.'

'This world is going too fast and too hard. The future here is ... I see it, I see glimpses sometimes, and it's too ... The fracture is deeper and wider and harder ... It was unexpected ... It could bring everything down—'

Sealed inside endless forest, Archangel grinds slowly on. Look away from him now; he is nothing. He feels the desolation of despair and self-disgust. Cut off from history, his futures slow and fade. Time is failing him. He cannot breathe. He is weak. He is dying. Once he was Archangel, strongest of the strong, quickest of the quick, most powerful of soldiers, quintessence of generalissimos, Archangel nonpareil, but those memories burn and torture him. So does the encroaching of the slow grass.

Archangel probes the boundaries of his enclosure, but they are blank to him, utterly without information and closing in. Archangel hurls himself against the borders ceaselessly, searching for a chink, a crevice, the faintest possible thinning in the imperceptible wall, but all the time the roots of forest trees dig deeper, the grass grows back, and every tiny root-hair is a burning agony to him. He is succumbing to frost and the erosion of rain and wind. They will wear him away to insensate dust.

But then something happens.

It is only a beat of quietness in the roar of the storm, only the fall of a twig on the river. None but an archangel could hear it. None but an archangel could sense the flicker of a shadow in the face of the sun. The quick thinning of ice. The opening of a moment's gap in the wall of his cage.

With a scream of desperate hope Archangel launches his mind towards the hollowing.

Maroussia flinched and looked over her shoulder as if she had heard a loud noise.

'Not yet!' she groaned. 'Not so soon!' She looked at Lom in alarm. 'There's no more time. I have to go now.'

'Wait! Tell me what you need me to do.'

'Stop Kantor,' she said. '*Stop* him.'

'You mean kill him?'

'No! Not kill. Not that. If you only kill him, the idea of him will live, and others will come and it will be the same and worse. Don't kill him; bring him down, destroy the idea of him. Ruin him in this world, using the tricks of this world. Ruin this world he has created.'

'But ... how? I'm just one person.'

'You have to find a way. Who else can I ask, if not you? Who will listen to me if you don't listen? There is no one else.'

'And if I can do this,' he said, 'then afterwards ... '

'No,' she said, 'there's no *then*. No *afterwards*. No consequence. No reward. I can't see *then*. I can only see what will happen if this doesn't. Do you understand?'

'No,' said Lom. 'I don't understand. But it doesn't matter.'

She was looking at him across a widening distance, and he knew that she was leaving him.

'I have to go now,' she said. 'I've already stayed too long. I wanted ... Oh no ...'

There was a ripple, a shadow-glimmer, and Maroussia was gone.

In the forest it takes Archangel time to react and time to move, and time in the forest is recalcitrant. Slow. Even as he gets close to the gap, it is closing. By the time he reaches it, the tear in the wall has snapped shut. He is too late.

This time.

But now for him there is hope.

And on the quiet River Yannis it was moonless dark and long after midnight and the stars were uncountably many, scattered like salt across darkness, bitter and eternal. She was gone, and Lom felt they hadn't said anything at all, not really – nothing *adequate*, nothing *enough*. She'd come to him and spoken to him, but he didn't know anything, he didn't understand more; in fact he understood less than ever, and all the terrible loss and solitude of the last six years was open and fresh and raw once more: the bleak ruination, the need and the grief and the necessity of acting, of doing something, of finding her again. Perhaps that was the point of her coming. Perhaps that was what she had done.

Lom packed his bag and left the mailboat without waiting for Shenkov to return.

5

The Vlast Universal Vessel *Proof of Concept* circles the planet at tremendous speed, outpacing the planetary spin, passing by turn into clean sunlight and star-crisp shadow. The cabin's interior days and nights come faster and last for less time even than the rapacious advancing days of Papa Rizhin's New Vlast, but aboard the *Proof of Concept* there is no perceptible sense of forward motion.

Cosmonaut-Commodore Vera Mornova, tethered by long cables to her bench, drifting without weight and having nothing much to do, presses her face against the cabin window. The air she breathes smells of hot rubber, charcoal and sweat. The spectacle of the stars unsettles her: they burn clean and cold but seem no nearer now, and all she sees is the infinities of emptiness that lie between. It is her lost, unreachable home that captures her loving attention: the continent, striated yellow and grey by day, the glitter of rivers and lakes, the sparse scattered lamps in inky blackness that are cities by night, the dazzling reflection of the sun in the ocean, the green chain of the Archipelago, the huge ice fields spilling from the poles towards the equator and the edgeless forest glimpsed under cloud.

Misha Fissich drifts up alongside her, accidentally nudging her so she has to grab the edge of the window to stop herself spinning slowly away. He offers her a piece of cold chicken.

'Hungry?' he says. 'The clock says lunchtime. You should eat.'

She shakes her head.

'No, not now, Misha. I'm not hungry. Thanks.'

'You should eat,' he says again. 'The others are watching you, Vera. If you don't bother, neither will they.'

'OK,' she says. 'Thanks.' She smiles at him and takes the chicken and chews it slowly.

When she's finished, it's time for the radio interview: a journalist from the Telegraph Agency of the New Vlast, her voice on the loudspeaker sounding indistinct and far away.

Commodore Mornova, she says, *the thoughts of all our citizens are with you. You and your crew are the foremost heroes of our time. Parents are naming their newborns after you. Will you tell us please what it's like to leave the planet? What do you see? How does it feel? How do you and your comrades spend your time?*

'We feel proud and humble, both at once,' says Vera Mornova. 'It is humankind's first step across the threshold: a small first step perhaps, but we are the pioneers of a great new beginning. History is watching us, and we are conscious of the honour. Space is very beautiful and welcoming. We test our equipment and make many observations.'

Such as? Please share your thoughts with us.

'Well, from orbit one can clearly discern the spherical shape of the planet. The sight is quite unique. Between the sunlit surface of the planet and the deep black sky of stars the dividing line is thin, a narrow belt of delicate blue. While crossing the Vlast we see big squares below – our great collective farms! Ploughed land and grazing may be clearly distinguished. During the state of weightlessness we eat and drink. It is curious that handwriting does not change though the hand is weightless.'

And do you have a message for your loved ones left behind?

'Tell them,' says Vera Mornova, 'tell them we love them and remember them in our hearts.'

Part II

Chapter Four

We have raised the sky-blue sky-flag –
the flag of dawn winds and sunrises,
slashed by red lightning. Over this planet
our banners fly! We present ...
ourselves! The Presidents of the Terrestrial Globe!

Velemir Khlebnikov (1885–1922)

1

The sky above Mirgorod was a bowl of luminous powdery eggshell blue, cloudless and heroic. Enamel-bright coloured aircraft buzzed and twisted high in the air, leaving trails of brilliant vapour-white. The loudspeakers were broadcasting speeches and news and orchestral music at full distorted volume. The production of steel across the New Vlast exceeded pre-war output by 39 per cent. The cosmonaut-heroes continued to orbit through space.

Citizens! Today is Victory Day! Congratulate yourselves!

From all across the city hundreds of thousands of people were making their way towards Victory Square on buses and trams and trains for the celebration parade. Hundreds of thousands more were coming on foot. Already an inexhaustible river of people was moving up the wide avenue of Noviy Prospect (newly paved and freshly washed before dawn that morning). Half the population of Mirgorod must have been there, going in a slow tide between the towering raw new buildings of the city centre. Vissarion Lom, less than twenty-four hours back in Mirgorod, sat at a café table under a canopy on a terrace raised above the sidewalk, nursing a cooling birch-bark tea, and watched them pass: more people in one place than all the people he'd seen in the last six years put together. Sunlight glared off steel and glass and concrete fresh out of scaffolding; glared off the flags and banners that lined Noviy Prospect; glared off the huge portraits of Papa Rizhin and the lesser portraits of other faces Lom could not name.

Lom disliked crowds. Even sitting somewhat apart and watching them made him uneasy. Edgy. Even anxious. The noise. The faces. He couldn't understand how it was that most people could merge into a throng so readily, so gladly even. To him it felt like submersion. Surrender. Drowning. He couldn't have done it even if he'd wanted to. But he saw the woman with the heavy canvas bag on her shoulder.

He almost missed her. She was moving with the crowd, one small figure in the uncountable mass, going in the same direction as everyone else. Someone else might not have noticed her or, if they had seen her, wouldn't have understood what it meant. It would have been a coincidence, nothing more. But because he was Lom, not someone else, he saw her, and recognised her, and knew what she was doing.

She was just another slight ageing woman in shabby sombre clothes: there were dozens like her, hundreds, shuffling along among the uniformed service personnel, the families, the classes shepherded by harassed teachers, the young women workers in blue overalls and sneakers, the salaried fellows in shirtsleeves and fedoras, the limping veterans, the veterans in wheelchairs and the tight little groups of short-haired and pony-tailed Young Explorers in their blue shorts, grey shirts, red neckerchiefs, knee-length woollen socks and canvas shoes. The women in dark clothes walked alone or in twos and threes. They had their special place that day: they were the widows, the childless mothers, come to watch and remember on bittersweet Victory Day. Lom's gaze passed across the one with the canvas bag on her shoulder and moved on. But something about her caught his attention and he looked again.

People in a large slow crowd surrender themselves to it. They all have the same purpose, all heading for the same destination. Simply being part of the crowd is itself the occasion and the only reason for being there. There's no rush. They have no need to do anything except move along at the crowd's speed and take their cues from the crowd. So they look around and take in the sights and talk, or absorb themselves in their own thoughts. Some bring drink and food and eat as they go. They won't miss anything. They're already where they need to be.

But this one woman was different. There was a tension and separateness about her. Something about the way she held her head and looked around: an obsessive, exclusive watchfulness that snagged his attention, raw and jangled as his nerves were by the numbers of people everywhere. She was making her way through the crowd, not moving with it, and she was alert to her surroundings as those around her were not. She knew where the security cordons and the crowd watchers were, and kept away from them. She tracked her way forward, intent on some private purpose.

And then there was the bag. A drab and scruffy canvas bag, nothing remarkable except Lom could tell by the way she carried it that it was heavy, and the object inside was long and protruded from the top. The thing in the bag was wrapped in a bright childish fabric, which was clever because it attracted attention but also disarmed suspicion. It looked like something that belonged to a child, or used to. The kind of thing an older woman might carry for her grandchild. Or keep with her for ever and never lay down, to remember the dead by. Only this woman seemed a little too young and a little too strong, and it wasn't easy to guess what sort of childish thing this long heavy object was. It scratched at Lom's crowd-raw nerves.

As she passed near where Lom was sitting, the woman with the bag glanced sideways at something, and as she turned Lom glimpsed her face in profile. And recognised her. Six years had changed her. She was leaner, harsher, a stripped-back and sanded-down version of the woman who'd once given Maroussia and him shelter in the Raion Lezaryet, but still he knew instantly that this was Elena Cornelius: Elena, who used to have two girls and live in an apartment in Count Palffy's house and make furniture to sell in the Apraksin Bazaar.

He watched her move on through the crowd. She was good but not that good. Intent on her work, she was just a little too interesting. Too noticeable. Too vivid. She made use of sightlines and available cover for protection. She made small changes of pace. She was moving instinctively as a hunter did. Or a sniper. But snipers move through

65

empty streets, not crowds. In a crowd she was conspicuous. If he could spot her, so could others. Like for instance the security operatives, who were no doubt even now scanning Noviy Prospect from upper windows, though he could not see them.

Lom got up from the café table and followed. He moved up through the crowd to get closer to her, working slowly, cautiously, so as not to be noticed himself and above all not draw the attention of other watchers to her. He felt her vulnerability and her determination. He wanted to protect her, and he owed her his help, but he couldn't let her do what she was going to do. She had to be stopped.

She made a sudden move to the right, picking up speed and making for the ragged edge of the moving crowd. Lom tried to follow, but his way was suddenly blocked by a knot of loud-voiced broad-backed men. They had just spilled out from a bar and stood swaying unsteadily and squinting in the glare of the sun. They smelled of aquavit. By the time Lom got past them, Elena Cornelius had disappeared from view.

2

The meeting room of the Central Committee of the New Vlast Presidium was painted green. The conference table was simple varnished ash wood. There were no insignia in the room, no banners, no portraits: only the smell of furniture polish and new carpet. *There is no past; there is only the future.* Each place at the table had a fresh notepad, a water jug, an ashtray and an inexpensive fountain pen. A single heavy lamp hung low above the table, a flat box of muted grey metal shedding from its under-surface a muted opalescent glow. The margins of the room where officials and stenographers sat were left in shadow.

On the morning of the Victory Day Parade the Committee gathered informally, no officials present, to congratulate their leader and President-Commander General Osip Rizhin, whose birthday by happy chance it also was that day. At least, according to the official biography it was his birthday, though of course the official biography was a tissue of fabrication from beginning to end.

All twenty-one committee members were present: twelve men and eight women, plus Rizhin. Sixteen were makeweights: bootlickers, honest toilers, useful idiots, take your pick – placeholders just passing through. Apart from Rizhin there were only four who really mattered, and they were Gribov, Secretary for War; Yashina, Finance; Ekel, Security and Justice; and Lukasz Kistler. Above all, Lukasz Kistler.

Kistler was a shaven-headed barrel of a man, boulder-shouldered, hard not fat, his torso straining at the seams of his shiny jacket. Kistler liked money, drank with workers and didn't care about spilling his gravy. His shirt cuffs jutted six inches beyond his jacket sleeves. But the intelligence in his small creased eyes was sharp and dangerous as spikes. Kistler was never, ever tired and never, ever got sick and never, ever stopped working. His energy burned like a furnace. He had made huge amounts of money before he was thirty out of iron and oil and coal, anything big and dirty that came out of rock and was hard to get. He was a digger and a burrower and a hammerer. When Rizhin found Kistler he was turning out battle tanks from a factory that had no roof. It had been bombed so often Kistler had stopped rebuilding and left it a ruin in the hope the enemy would piss off and bomb something else. Within half an hour of their first meeting Rizhin put him in charge of producing battle tanks for the whole of the Vlast. Since the war ended, Kistler had expanded into oilfields, gasfields, hydro turbines, petroleum refineries, atomic power. Energy. Energy. Energy. Lukasz 'Dynamo' Kistler made Papa Rizhin's Vlast burn brighter and run louder and faster every day.

And Lukasz Kistler was a clever, subtle, observant and far-sighted man. He saw that Rizhin knew how to spend money and people but had no idea where such resources actually came from. Rizhin didn't know how to turn dirt into cash or people into workers. Rizhin grabbed and stole to spend, and spent what he could not make, and in the end he would spend the whole of the world until he had nothing left. Kistler suspected that one day he and Papa Rizhin would come to blows.

Kistler was watching Rizhin now. Rizhin was on his feet and prowling behind the seated committee members in his soft leather shoes. He liked to walk behind them. It made them uncomfortable. And today Rizhin was wielding a sword. He gripped it in his swollen fist and made experimental swipes at the air as he prowled. (Rizhin's hands fascinated Kistler: hard, thickened, stub-fingered hands, butcher's hands, raw-pink hands that looked like they'd been stung by bees. Long rough work on stone in ice and cold could make such hands. Many years in labour camps. That was something not in Papa Rizhin's official biography.)

The sword was ridiculous. *The Severe Sword.* The Southern Congress of Regions had presented it to him that morning as a birthday gift. Its blade was inscribed on one side SLASH THE RIGHT DEVIATION! and on the other SLASH THE LEFT DEVIATION! and on the hilt it said PUMMEL THE CONCILIATOR!

'They give me a *sword*?' Rizhin was saying. 'And what are we to make of *that*? I give them jet engines and atomic space vessels and they give me a sword. What am I to do with a sword? What does a sword say? You see how riddled we are with aristocrats and peasants still? Fantasists. Nostalgists. Am I to ride out on a fucking horse like a khan? Do they mean me to butcher my own people? Well, if there is butchery to be done, let us start with the Southern Congress of Regions.'

'The sword is an emblem, Osip,' said Yashina. 'That's all.'

'Everything is an emblem,' said Rizhin. 'A generator is an emblem. A sky rise is an emblem. Those fuckers need to get better emblems.'

Rizhin laid the sword on the table and sat down, slumping back in his chair. He picked up a pen and began to scrawl doodles on his notepad.

'The people call me Papa and sing hymns about me,' he said. '"Thank you Papa Rizhin. Glory to our great commander." It's laughable. I'm not Papa Rizhin; I'm a simple man. I am Osip, a worker and a soldier just like them.'

He paused and looked around the table, fixing them one by one with his smiling burning eyes.

'Even you, my friends,' he said, 'even you do this to me. You want me to walk out there today on that platform and let you make me Generalissimus. Do I need this? No. Does Osip the simple industrious man need such empty titles? No, he does not. I do not. I will not accept it. I give it back to you. Take it back, I beg you, and make someone else your Generalissimus, not me.'

There was silence in the room. Everyone froze. Everyone looked down. Secretary for Agriculture Vladi Broch stared glassy-eyed at the sword on the table in front of him as if it would leap up and stab him in the neck. Rizhin doodled on his pad and waited.

For one horrifying moment Lukasz Kistler thought the idiots were going to accept. *It's a test!* he screamed inwardly. *A loyalty test!* If someone didn't speak soon he would have to do it himself, and that would be no good. He wasn't on trial – everyone knew he was Rizhin's dynamo – but if he had to step in and repair the situation it would be the end for some of them.

It was Yashina who rescued them in the end. Smooth, calm, cultured Yulia Yashina.

'We're nothing without you, Osip,' she said quietly. 'No one else could step into your shoes. It is unthinkable.'

They all swung in behind her then. General acclamation, a clattering of fists on the table. Rizhin sighed and straightened himself up in his chair.

'Very well, then,' he said. 'If you insist … I do not like it, you hear me. I protest. Let the record show that. Well … let's get this over with, and get back to our real work.'

Lukasz Kistler glanced down at Rizhin's notepad as they filed out of the room. There was a jagged black scribble in the corner of the top sheet: the scrawled angular face of a wolf glaring out at him from a wall of dark trees. The wolf's jaw was open, showing its teeth.

3

E lena Cornelius climbed the concrete stairwell in near-darkness, counting floors as she went. Five. Ten. Fifteen. Twenty. The light filtering through fluted glass panes in the landing doors was enough to climb by, but too dim to read the floor numbers. It didn't matter. She could count. She knew how many storeys up she needed to go. The key to the service entrance of the New Mirgorod Hotel was in her pocket. Vesna Mayskova, a floor attendant at the New Mirgorod, had got it for her, and she'd left a bucket of dirty water and a mop in the alley outside, the signal that the area was clear of militia patrols.

On the twenty-second floor of the New Mirgorod Hotel, Elena

Cornelius stopped climbing and shoved open the door onto the second-tier roof. The sudden daylight was blinding: the shock of air and sky and the noise of the city after the dim stairwell. Elena held the door open with her foot, swung the canvas bag off her shoulder and rummaged in it for a small sliver of wood. Panic rose for a moment when she couldn't find it, but there it was. Putting the bag on the ground, she let the door almost close and slipped the wooden sliver between the edge of it and the jamb. From the stairwell it would look shut, but there was just enough edge left proud of the surround to wrench it open again from outside with the tips of clawed fingers.

She turned and looked out across the roof. Taking stock. Considering. Checking. She had been here before – a rehearsal run – but nothing must be taken for granted. Check and check again. That's what had kept her alive in the siege.

She was trembling from the effort of the long climb, but that was OK: she knew that it would pass and her hand would steady. There was plenty of time. The impersonal oceanic murmur of the crowd in Victory Square twenty-two floors below was oddly restful. It didn't sound human but like the power of waterfalls or the wind in forest trees.

There was no chance of being seen from below as long as she kept back from the edge. Only the newly built Rizhin Tower on the other side of Victory Square was tall enough to overlook her, and that was still unoccupied. If she were in charge of security, she'd have posted an observer with binoculars in one of the deserted rooms high in the Rizhin Tower. Maybe somebody had, but the architect who designed the three-tiered edifice of the New Mirgorod Hotel had set thirty-foot bronze allegorical figures at the roof corners of every stage. He hadn't worried that he was giving cover for shooters.

The final tier of the New Mirgorod Hotel rose dizzyingly high behind her, casting a deep shadow all the way to the parapet. There was a risk of being seen from one of those upper windows, but she'd checked the angles when she scouted the location. The danger was only when she crossed the roof. Once she was in firing position the hut-like lift mechanism housing would hide her, as long as she kept low.

The roof crossing was only half a dozen paces. Crossings were always a risk, and there was no point in waiting. Elena Cornelius picked up her bag and went. In the cover of the lift housing she crouched low.

Knelt. Lay flat, stomach to the ground, face inches from the mix of rough gravel and tar that coated the roof. The waist-high parapet was five yards in front of her.

During the siege she had crawled on her belly every day. Now she crawled again, hauling herself, knees and elbows and belly across the rough surface, dragging the canvas bag, until she was in the shelter of the parapet. Then she moved right until she was tucked in under the plinth of the bronze statue in the corner.

The statue was a woman in military uniform facing out across the city, a rifle held at an angle across her breast. Above her huge bronze military boots her calves swelled, shapely and muscular. Elena scrabbled into a sitting position and pressed her back against the parapet wall. She was in a safe high place, a vantage point to hide and watch from and not be seen. She knew how to do this. It was familiar. It was a kind of home. She didn't think about why she was there, what had led her to this point. All the decisions were already taken. When you were at work, you worked. That was how you survived.

She unwrapped the Zhodarev rifle, checked the magazine and banged it into position with the heel of her hand. Found the telescopic sight at the bottom of the bag, polished the optics with her sleeve and pushed it onto the rail, easing it forward until it clicked solidly. Then she folded the faded pink towel with the lemon-yellow tractors into a thick sausage, reached up and laid it on the parapet for a barrel rest. Raising herself into a kneeling position, she propped her left elbow on her left knee and raised the rifle, made sure the barrel sat good and solid on its towel rest, settled the stock into her shoulder, pressed her eye to the scope and adjusted the focus.

The VIP viewing platform jumped into view, crisp and clear, down and to the left of her firing position. Tiers of empty seats. They hadn't started to arrive yet.

It was a long shot. She could have done with a more powerful scope, but she didn't have one. She checked the adjustment of the graticule. It was unchanged from how she'd set it that morning before she left home. The range was six hundred and fifty yards – she'd paced it out a week ago plus some simple geometry to allow for height.

The warm morning air rested gently against her cheek. Windage, zero.

Nothing to do but wait and watch.

4

Lom had lost sight of Elena Cornelius at the top of Noviy Prospect just before it opened into Victory Square. He tried to find her again, but it was hopeless: there were any number of alleys and doorways she might have taken, or she could have switched direction and ducked past him back down the avenue against the flow of people without him seeing. He hesitated. Considered abandoning looking for her. After all, it was possible he was wrong about what she was doing. Maybe she'd just come to see the parade.

But he didn't believe that.

He made his way out onto the fringe of Victory Square. The open space, laid out on what had once been the much smaller Square of the Piteous Angel, was staggeringly vast. Block after block of streets and buildings (Lom remembered them) had been demolished to make room for it. Rivers and canals had been covered over, the city completely reoriented. And now it was completely filled with people come for the Victory Parade. It was impossible to estimate how many were there: half a million? A million? There were high terraces for seating, and crowds of people standing shoulder to shoulder in the gaps between. He could see across to the raised platform where Rizhin would take his place. The VIP seats were beginning to fill up.

Not far from the platform the Lodka still stood, the dark and many-roofed headquarters of the old Vlast, no longer on an island between river and canal, occupying one small corner of the square. The Lodka had survived siege bombardment and aerial bombing raids, but now – eviscerated when Chazia removed the great archives and burned most of the contents, overtopped by the surrounding sky rises of concrete and granite and glass with their wedding-cake encrustations and monumental bas-reliefs – the huge cliff of a building looked isolated and diminished. Smartened-up but mothballed. A museum piece.

And next to the Lodka, dwarfing it, climbing higher – far higher – than any other building in the city, rising tier upon tier of stark grey stone, fluted, slender and almost weightless against the sky, was the Rizhin Tower, which was to be formally declared open that day. The top of the tower, constituting one tenth of the total height of the building, was an immense and gunmetal-grey statue of Papa Rizhin. He was in civilian clothes, standing bare-headed, his long coat lifting behind him slightly in a suggestion of wind. He was stepping forward towards the city, his back to the sea, his right arm raised and outstretched to greet and possess. The statue's civilian clothing puzzled Lom. Not the military tunic and shoulder boards of the standard Rizhin portrait, it struck an odd note.

Then the truth struck him. This dizzying and mighty behemoth was not a statue of Rizhin at all; it was a statue of Josef Kantor. Kantor the agitator, the plotter, the revolutionary orator, the killer, the master terrorist.

Josef Kantor had transformed himself into Papa Rizhin at the siege of Mirgorod. He kept his origins secret, hidden, suppressed. All hints of his former self were ruthlessly obliterated. But here in Victory Square in the heart of Mirgorod – in plain sight, in the most visible, most spectacular place of all, full in the face of the whole of the Vlast – Rizhin thrust the truth of himself at them all, and nobody could see it, or if they did they dared not say. The Rizhin Tower was an act of the most astonishing hubris: a challenge, a yell, a dare, a spit in the eye of the world.

At that moment a strange noise started to swell and grow in Victory Square. Lom had heard nothing like it before. It began as a low clatter and hum and grew to a great roaring, deafening buzz. It was the sound of the crowd rising to greet the arrival of Papa Rizhin, who had stepped out onto the raised platform. It wasn't cheering. It was a vibration of excitement like the agitation of a billion bees. The extraordinary noise reverberated around the square and echoed, magnified, off the surrounding buildings.

Lom turned his back on it. He shoved and threaded his way back into Noviy Prospect, which was almost deserted now, its flags and banners and portraits of Rizhin stirring in a gentle rising breeze. Everyone who was going to Victory Square had found their place; the parades and speeches were about to begin. But where was Elena Cornelius?

5

Eligiya Kamilova walks once more the five level miles, the long straight stony road south out of Belatinsk and back to Nikolai Forshin's dacha. The dacha of the Philosophy League. Keeping her eyes down, no longer even consciously hungry, she walks with slow and fierce determination. One step. One step. One step. All her attention is fixed on her dust-yellowed boots and the pale stalks that are her shins.

To either side of her, electricity pylons march away across bare earth and dried yellow grass, level to the encircling blued horizon. Grey wooden sheds and grey corrugated-iron roofs. Dust and bone sunlight. The pylons carry no cables. The pylons are built, but the gangs that bring the cables have not yet come.

Kamilova notices none of this. Not any more. Every day the same. Nothing changes.

One step. One step.

She has done this walk every day for a week. Five miles out and five miles back. She wonders how much longer she can.

Her legs are so thin it frightens her. These fleshless wasted sticks are not hers; they are the legs of one who died long ago. How do they carry her without the shifting contour of muscle? Dried knots and tendons only, visibly working. Her knees are crude obtrusions, like the stones in the unmade road. Her own hands startle her: demonstration pieces of skeletal articulation for the instruction of anatomists.

My face is gone. I have transparent skin. I have forgotten how to be hungry.

All day Eligiya Kamilova has stood in line in Belatinsk, Galina's ration card in her pocket. (Galina has found a job running messages at Lorschner's. The wage is pitiful but the ration card is more valuable than platinum and silks.) She didn't know what she was queuing for. People in line in Belatinsk hold tight to the belt of the one in front to keep their place. Too weak to stand alone, they lean against strangers and do not speak.

All day Kamilova's line waited and did not move. In the afternoon the shopkeeper closed up.

'Fuck off now,' he screamed at them. 'Fuck off. Fuck off. There's nothing here.'

So Kamilova turned away and walked back out through the town.

Belatinsk was everywhere silent, subsided under dugouts, shacks and shanties of rusty iron, planks, cardboard, wire, glass and earth. There was no water, no electricity, no sewerage. Paved streets were dug up for scraggy allotments where nothing properly grew. Everything wood – benches, hoardings, fences, boardwalks – had been ripped up and burned. Vermin everywhere and no repairs to anything.

She passed a scrap of municipal garden behind iron railings. Sign on the gate: DIG NO GRAVES HERE.

No cars or trucks on the road out of Belatinsk to Forshin's dacha. On the verge a mare had died, her body swollen hard. Black lips stretched off yellow teeth in a snarl. Black jewel flies were sipping at her eyes and crawling over the blue fatness of her tongue. Kamilova wanted to sit in the dust and lean against her like a couch, just for a while.

One step. One step. One step.

She does not know how many more days she can do this. Hunger is not the absence of food. It is a big black rock you carry that fills the sky. It crushes you while you sleep.

Yet things are better now at Forshin's dacha than they were on the road.

The evening after they buried the twice-killed soldier, Kamilova stole a boat from the village at Yamelei. She still felt bad about the boat, but the village would survive and the girls could not walk. Not so far, not all the way. The equations of necessity.

So Kamilova had taken the boat, and in her they crossed the lake above the sunken city. Still purple waters at twilight and the sound of a distant bell.

The soul of the people is forever striving to behold the sunken city of Litvozh.

Kamilova knew boats. All night she let the chill wind take them west, and in the dawn they followed the shore to where the westward river flowed out.

'What river is this?' said Yeva.

'I don't know,' said Kamilova, 'but it's going the right way.'

Low wooded hills and scraps of cool dawn mist. The girls slept under dewy blankets in the shelter of the gunwales, and the river took them into strange country. Unfamiliar hunting beasts called to one another across the water. Dark oily coils surged and rippled, and the backs of great silent fish broke the surface of the river. Kamilova sat in the stern with the gun across her knees and steered a course clear of the black bears that swam slow and strong and purposefully from shore to shore. They passed through a city ruined in the war. Nobody was there. Not anybody at all.

The end of day brought them across the sudden frontier out of slow memorious places into the hungerland.

In the deep past and in remoter places even now families and villages might fall into hunger and all of them die. That was one thing. In the towns and cities of the Vlast a wretched person sick and alone without a kopek might starve in a gutter. That was another thing. A ragged inconvenience. But when entire regions, millions of people, conurbations and suburbs and the penumbra of organised rural production, plunged into sudden and total desperate famine, that was something else. That was something never seen before.

That was the hungerland.

The boat came to a weir. A tremendous white-water fall. Nothing for it but to sleep and in the morning leave the boat and walk.

Kamilova, thinking the house on the edge of the nameless town empty, broke in the door. The family was gathered in darkness, curtains drawn against the day. The smell was bad. There were puddles of water on the floor.

Two chairs were pushed together, and across them lay the corpse of the boy. He might have been fourteen but starvation aged you. You couldn't tell. The baby was propped in a pram, head to one side on the pillow, dead. The mother on the bed was dead. The daughter sat beside her on the stained counterpane, rubbing at the mother's chest with a linen towel.

'Where is your father?' said Kamilova. 'Did he go for help? For food?'

The girl glanced up at her without expression and carried on rubbing the dead woman's chest. The smell of embrocation.

Kamilova took from her bag a piece of hard dry bread and a handful of potatoes brought from Yamelei and laid them on the bed. The girl didn't look. The food just lay there on the counterpane.

When Kamilova reached the door she stopped and turned back, picked the food up again and put it back in her bag. The equations of necessity.

The girl didn't glance up when Kamilova left the room.

Days rose dark in colourless sunshine and set in bleakness. The hungerland walk was one long unrelenting road. Aftermath, aftermath. Deadened days after the end of the world.

Slowly they realised how late they were. The distortions of slow time in the memorious zone. Here in the hungerland six years had passed, the war was over and this was Rizhin country now.

'Mother will think we forgot her,' Galina said. 'She must think we are dead.'

'She is waiting,' said Yeva. 'She would never stop waiting.'

'I will take you home,' said Kamilova. 'I promise. We're going there as quick as I can.'

The girls wrote letters and posted them when they came to towns. *We are OK, Mother. We are alive and fine. Not long now. We'll be with you soon.*

Silence, horrible silence, settled across the hungerland. Livestock, cats and dogs, all dead. Birds and wild things all hunted or driven away. The only sound in the early morning was the soft breath of the dying. The footfalls of carrion eaters on patrol.

A woman in a garden held up her baby as they walked by.

'Please. Take him, take him. I beg you take him. I cannot feed him. They will eat him when he dies.'

The child had an enormous wobbling head. A swollen pointed belly. He was already dead.

They studied starvation and became connoisseurs of hunger. Darkened faces and swollen legs were the symptomology of famishment. Corpse faces with wide and lifeless eyes, skin drawn skull-tight and glossy and covered with sores.

First your limbs grew weak, then you lost all physical sensation. The body became a numb and burdensome sack. The circulation of the blood grew sluggish until the unnourished muscles of the heart, unable to shift their own weight any more, simply failed to beat. By then you no longer had the energy to care.

People died working at their desks. They died as they walked the streets.

There was a shape to it, a pattern of progression. The speed of it surprised them. A few weeks was all it took before the people started dying. Those died who refused to steal or trade their bodies for food. Those died who shared their food with others. Parents who made sacrifices for their children died before them, and then their children died. Those died who refused to countenance the consumption of the most forbidden flesh. In the end it made no difference because everyone who didn't escape the hungerland died.

The hungerland was spreading westward, and Kamilova and the girls walked in the same direction. Sometimes they took a lift in a truck and sometimes they got ahead of the hungerland wave. Behind them the cannibal bands were coming. Mobile platoons of mechanised anthropophagi grinding their butchering knives.

Kamilova shot two men with her gun to save the girls. The equations of necessity. Five shells left.

All three of them were growing weak. Kamilova knew the signs.

A cart brought them to Belatinsk one morning, and there they were stuck. Yeva and Galina could walk no more.

'How far to go to Mirgorod?' Kamilova enquired.

'Twelve hundred miles,' said the post office clerk. 'Fifteen maybe.'

The only way out was the railway.

'Sixty-five roubles,' said another clerk at another window. 'Third Class. One way. Each.'

Kamilova had money, scavenged from the bodies of the roadside dead. Money didn't help in the deep hungerland, not unless you ate the paper. She had a sheaf of roubles in her pack. It was not enough.

She sat on a bench by the station in Belatinsk with Yeva and Galina. She had simply reached the end. She didn't know what to do.

And then she saw the gleaming domed brow and wild flowing hair of Nikolai Forshin, six foot three and swinging an opera cane, come to the station to enquire about the arrival of a parcel of journals expected from the printers at Kornstadtlein.

'Eligiya? Eligiya Kamilova?' he called across the road. "Is that you?'

Not all the members of Forshin's Philosophy League were happy at the arrival of three extra mouths. Some of the wives were the worst. But Forshin decided, boom-voiced disputatious Nikolai Forshin of the purple bow tie and the hard bright visionary eye. Forshin led. Forshin prevailed. It was Forshin's dacha and Forshin's crazy hopeless League.

At the dacha there was a clear stream for water, a few scrawny chickens that didn't lay and a meagre vegetable patch. Potatoes were coming on. It was something but not enough. Not nearly enough. Kamilova gave her share to Galina and Yeva, though the girls didn't know it.

Forshin's League was growing fearful. They looked to their defences. There were rumours of gangs in Belatinsk and a trade in human flesh. Starveling packs had already approached the dacha more than once. Stick-people stood in the road and looked. The hungerland was coming, and the walls of Forshin's dacha were not strong enough to hold it back.

Eligiya Kamilova reaches the end of the road and turns into the track to the dacha.

This is the last return. I cannot do that fruitless walk again. It will kill me.

Forshin himself is standing on the veranda smoking his pipe and watching her come. He is excited. He steps out to meet her, waving a piece of paper in his hand.

'A letter, Eligiya! A letter from Mirgorod is come! The winds are changing. Rizhin himself has made a wonderful speech. "Times of Enlightenment", that's what he calls for. We are invited back! The League is to go home, I'm sure of it. We are to have a meeting this evening to resolve the matter. Come with us, Eligiya Kamilova, and bring your bright wonderful girls. Come! It will be a treat for them. Would they not *adore* to see the streets of Mirgorod again?'

6

Elena Cornelius couldn't get a clean shot. The head of the woman sitting next to Rizhin – Secretary for Finance Yulia Yashina, long neck, aquiline nose, grey hair pulled tight back off a long pale face – floated in the centre of the scope's optic, and behind her Rizhin's nose and shoulder.

That was OK. Eventually he would stand and come forward to the microphoned lectern to speak. Elena Cornelius could wait.

Marching formations and rumbling military vehicles were passing interminably under the viewing platform. A huge cheer – the kind that used to greet the earth-shaking trudge of the old Novozhd's platoon of forty-foot war mudjhiks – rose at the sight of atomic bombs on wide flatbed trucks. To Elena they looked ridiculous, like elephantine boiler-plated pieces of plumbing equipment.

The fresh-painted weaponry of the Vlast – battle tanks, mobile artillery and radar vehicles, rocket launchers – was followed by a display of captured enemy war machines looking battered and drab. Then came the March of the Heroes of Labour. Smiling blond men in overalls. Women in skirts and white ankle socks, waving. To pass the time, Elena let her telescope sight climb the endless rising walls of the Rizhin Tower. Since she could not see Rizhin himself, except one shoulder, she scanned the statue instead. It wasn't stone or bronze but steel, constructed by armaments engineers from the melted-down ships and guns and shell casings of the enemy. In her scope she could see the polished, shaped sections riveted together. The welding scars like patchwork.

She got the eye of the statue in her cross hairs.

Lom had lost time and found nothing. It was hopeless. He couldn't find her by wandering and randomly looking, not if he had a week. He wondered if he was wasting his time and taking an unnecessary risk by lingering here. He was beginning to feel visible, and if something was going to happen he was probably already too late to prevent it. Elena Cornelius had most likely just joined the crowd to see the parade. But that's not what he'd sensed when he watched her, and he'd learned to trust feelings like that.

If I was a sniper, he thought, *where would I choose? Where would I go?*

The only way to find her was to think like she thought. Work it out from first principles. Narrow down the options and make a throw of the dice. It was fifty-fifty: choose right or choose wrong. Except it wasn't fifty-fifty. How many high buildings looked across Victory Square? How many rooftops? How many windows? There were a thousand options, and all of them wrong except one.

Think it out. Narrow the odds. You're a lucky man. Things work out for you. Yeah, right.

The criteria were: a clear shot, access to the shooting position, inconspicuousness, an escape route.

The first was useless. It didn't narrow the field. Any building on three sides of the square would give a clear shot from the fourth floor up. The last was useless too: he had no information. And maybe she didn't intend to escape. That was possible. So he was left with access and inconspicuousness. Access. That was the key. That had to come first. She'd choose a building she could get into, then look for a shooting position, and she'd only abandon it and move on to the next one if there wasn't a place to fire from.

But that was no good either. Access to anywhere in the vicinity today was a nightmare. Places were either locked down tight and shuttered, or they had people crowding every window to get a view of the parade. There were police and militia everywhere. Regular sweeps and patrols. There *must* be a way in somewhere – he knew that because he knew she'd found it – but there was no possibility that he could spot it or guess. Not today.

Not today.

Of course not today. But it wasn't today that mattered. Today she'd have come already knowing where she was making for. She must have scouted the place out beforehand, on another day. She must have poked into corners, looked for vantage points, worked out lines of sight and ways in and out. Preparation. Planning. That meant that, wherever she was now, she'd have had to go there at least once before with plenty of time to look around. The access that mattered wasn't today but any other day. Any normal day.

81

He was getting somewhere. Maybe. He could rule out offices and residential buildings. You couldn't wander around places like that without attracting attention – not unless you worked or lived there. Well maybe she did. But if so he was defeated: he had no chance. So rule all those buildings out anyway. Which left public places: shops, hotels, museums. And say the place she'd chosen wasn't too far from where he'd lost her. There was no reason to think that, except that when he'd noticed her she was in the open, visible and vulnerable, and he could assume she'd expose herself as little as possible. It was likely he'd lost sight of her because she'd ducked in somewhere. Not certain, but the odds were in his favour. And this was all about odds.

He looked around, scanning the buildings. There were three good possibilities: two hotels and the Great Vlast Museum. The museum was closed. She might be in there, but if so he couldn't follow. Not quickly. Perhaps not at all. That left the two hotels. He was back to fifty-fifty.

He chose the bigger, which was also nearer to where he'd last seen her. It was a thirty-storey three-tier granite cake. The entrance was guarded by two militia men and cast iron bas-reliefs of steelworkers with bulging forearms and collective farmers brandishing ten-foot scythes.

Lom took stock of himself. When he arrived yesterday he'd had a shave and a haircut and bought himself a suit. In his pocket he had a thickish wad of rouble notes and ID papers in the name of Foma Drogashvili, which he'd been using on and off for several years. So how did you get to look around inside the New Mirgorod Hotel? You went up to the desk and asked for a room.

Elena Cornelius watched the aircraft fly past low in the brilliant early-afternoon sky. The bass rumble of slow ten-engined bombers. The screaming of new-made jets trailing coloured vapour. Parachutists spilled from a lumbering transport plane and drifted down under brilliant blossoming canopies of red and yellow, alighting with perfect precision in the space in front of the viewing platform.

Twisting, ducking fighters enacted dogfights against the warplanes of the Archipelago. One enemy bomber spouted oily smoke and flame and sank lower and lower as it limped from view. When it was out of sight behind the Rizhin Tower there was a loud flash and a white pall rose into the sky as if it had crashed. Perhaps it had. Elena remembered no such dogfights during the siege of Mirgorod. Then, the bombers had come day and night unopposed.

Gendarmes had thrown a cordon across Karolov Street. On the other side of it a battered old delivery truck was propped up on a jack at the kerb, one wheel off. Two bearded young men lay on the ground, spreadeagled, rifles pointed at their heads. The back of the truck was open, being searched. And beyond the truck was the side entrance to the New Mirgorod Hotel. Lom had a choice: wait, or retrace his steps and try the front entrance on Victory Square.

He didn't want to keep going over the same piece of ground. If there were watchers – and there surely were – he would be noticed. He made a quick calculation. Something would be found in the truck or it would not. Either way, within five minutes the situation here would change. But for ten long edgy minutes he waited and nothing was different. He turned back the way he had come.

The dark-panelled lobby of the hotel, when he finally reached it, was almost deserted. Ornate gilt-framed mirrors. Empty leather sofas under glowing chandeliers. The doorman was settled at a low marble table, cap off, drinking tea. Lom rang the bell at the desk. Waited. Rang it again. He could feel the eyes of the doorman on his back. From the room at the back came a radio commentary on the parade unfolding outside. He wished the doorman would just step outside and take a look.

Finally the reluctant clerk appeared.

'A room?' he said, raising his eyebrows sceptically. It was as if no one had ever asked him for such a thing before. 'Regrettably, that is not possible. Naturally for Victory Day all our rooms are taken.'

'All of them?' Lom laid a stack of roubles on the table. The clerk scowled at him.

'Of course all of them. Tomorrow you can have a room. Today, not.'

'Then perhaps someone could just bring me coffee.'

'Now?'

'Now. Yes, now. Thank you. And a newspaper.' Lom indicated a low sofa against a pillar near the entrance to the lifts. 'I'll be over there.' He went across and sat down to wait. The clerk, scowling, spoke into the telephone on the counter then returned to his back room.

Minutes passed and Lom's coffee did not come. He knew he should get out of there. He'd drawn attention to himself. If the clerk hadn't been calling for tea, who had he been talking to on the phone? And Elena had already had plenty of time: if anything was going to happen it would have happened by now. But he stayed and waited. Eventually the doorman stood up with a sigh from his table by the window, set his cap on his head and went out through the plate-glass doors to take up his position outside on the steps.

Lom moved.

Elena Cornelius heard a roar from the crowd twenty-two floors below. An amplified voice was crashing out across the city, carried not only by the loudspeakers in Victory Square but also by every tannoy and radio in Mirgorod. Rizhin had come to the lectern and was speaking.

The vast crowd hushed, but the hush had its own noise, like waves over shingle. Rizhin's amplified speech bounced off the wall behind her. The echo confused sense. She could only make out fragments.

'... life has become better, friends, life is happier now... remember yesterday's sacrifices, yes, but look to tomorrow ... a greater victory to come ...'

She re-settled the rifle. Pulled back the bolt with the outside of her hand to drive the first cartridge into the breech. One should be enough, but there were nine more in the magazine. She let the cross hairs move along the line of faces on the platform. You. You. You. The graticule came to rest clear and steady in the middle of Papa Rizhin's head.

'... our vessels explore the cosmos, but we must master our own planet also ... inevitably the Archipelago will crumble and fade ... the force of history will do our work ... the forest ... no more dark areas of super-stition and myth ... this time we will not be prevented, we will take a strong grip ...'

In the siege she had shot without thought or conscience. The whole city then was filled with a loud dinning noise that made everyone always deaf. Sleepwalkers. The invaders wore blank masks. This, today, was different: the face in the cross hairs the focus of all the world and more familiar than her own. A killing imagined a thousand times. Long sleepless years. Her heart beat faster. Perspiration on her forehead. In the roots of her hair.

She breathed in and breathed out slowly, emptying her lungs.

Calling up calm. She reached back to wipe her hand dry on her skirt. Cocked her wrist into the firing hold she had practised till it came easy and smooth. Began to squeeze her obtuse finger gently. Taking up the slack. A breath of wind kissed her sweat-damp cheek.

Lom pushed open the door onto the hotel roof and stepped out into dazzling glare. The rooftop was empty. There was nobody there and nothing to see but parapet and sky.

He heard the sound of a single rifle shot. It was unmistakable. And it had come from somewhere above him.

Not the first-stage roof, the second.

Shit.

He spun round, went back inside and ran up the darkened staircase, taking the steps three at a time.

Elena Cornelius saw the bullet strike the cushioned seat of the chair behind Rizhin. It must have passed his skull by inches, but he didn't react. Didn't pause. Didn't flap a hand at the zip and crack by his ear, like she'd seen people do. He'd heard nothing above the amplified echoes of his own speech.

Lukasz Kistler was staring, puzzled, at the hole that had been punched in the seat beside him. In a second it would dawn on him what it meant.

She lined up the cross hairs on Rizhin again, took a deep slow breath, exhaled and fired again. Rizhin's face disappeared in a puff of soft pink. The energy of the bullet snapped his whole body backwards. He went down as if someone had smashed him full force in the temple with a baseball bat.

Even in the dim stairwell Lom heard the horrified moan of the crowd. It was like the lowing of a stricken herd. He pounded on up the stairs, floor after floor.

He almost ran smack into Elena Cornelius coming down, the rifle held delicately in splayed fingers, pointing at the floor.

'It's me, Elena. You know me. Vissarion. Vissarion Lom.'

Her eyes were wide and unblinking, glassy bright in the shadows.

'I've killed him,' she said.

It was like a punch in Lom's stomach. All the air went out of him.

Less than a day in Mirgorod and he had failed. Mission over.

He took the rifle from her awkward grasp and propped it against the wall.

'You have to lose this,' he said. 'Leave it. The bag too. Lose it. We need to get out of here.'

She didn't resist. She didn't move. He took her by the arm and led her down the stairs.

7

On a broad front the divisions of the New Vlast army entered the endless forest. Fleets of barges up the wide slow rivers and under the trees.

The forest is woods within woods, further in and further back. It has an edge but no central point and there is no end to going on. Deeper and deeper for ever. Strange persons live there. It is not safe.

As long as the divisions kept to their barges on the rivers they made progress, but five yards back from the bank all was impassable: layers of dead wood, luxuriant undergrowth, lake, bog and hill. Oak, ash, elm, maple and linden tree. Thorn and fir. A trackless catalogue of all the forests of northernness and east. Disoriented compass needles swung. Radios sucked in static. Green noise.

The forest removed irony. It was the place itself. Woodland and shadow and the lair of wild beasts. Every divisional commander was on his or her own. One by one each hauled up on some bend of their nameless river and disembarked and began to burn. Petrol-driven chainsaws ripped resinous raw avenues. The noise echoed down the river valleys. Trundling battle tanks pissed arcs of singeing ignition, the soldiers' smut-grimed sweat-shone faces gleamed dull and lurid orange, and every day the churned and stinking ash-carpeted swathes extended deeper into the interior of the forest. Fingernails scraping at the heart of green silence. A war against the world.

The rivers became supply lines for the beachheads. Barge trains shuttled fuel day and night from New Vlast base camps at the forest edge.

In a week the black smoke had darkened the midday sky.

Divisions encountered waterlands that would not burn, marshes that sucked at the tracks of wallowing tanks. Engineers sank to the waist in bog and floundered. Horses drowned. Methane pockets burst and burned behind them. Divisions came to sudden rising cliffs and turned aside. Divisions reached the brink of mile-wide bottomless mist-rimmed holes in the ground. Trolls blundered out of the thickets, roaring, hair on fire and blackened blistering skin.

The advancing swathes of engine-driven desolation drifted left and right, circling round to rejoin themselves, beginning to lose direction, tracing mazy aimless scribbles on the margins of elsewhere under the trees.

Chapter Five

Skulking along behind the revolution's back
the petty functionaries stuck out their heads …

From the motherland's farthest corners they assembled,
hurriedly changing their clothes and settling in
at all the institutions,
their chair-hardened buttocks
solid as washbasins.

Vladimir Mayakovsky (1893–1930)

1

Dead shock pulsed out across Mirgorod from the head of Papa Rizhin obliterated in a pink flower. His poleaxed fall punched the city in the face.

There was a spontaneous attempt to put a roadblock across Noviy Prospect, but the tide of dazed and weeping spectators rolled down out of Victory Square and swept on through, and nobody seriously tried to stop them. Militia patrols gathered in stricken leaderless huddles. Officers with panic in their eyes jogged between them barking orders no one seemed to hear.

Elena Cornelius pulled herself together quickly. She dropped her dark coat in an alleyway. In a white short-sleeved blouse she was taller and ten years younger, narrow shoulders and pale muscular arms, almost unrecognisable as the woman of the morning crowd. From six years back Lom remembered a rounder, fuller face, but she was all bone structure now. Nose pushed askew and night-blue eyes. The lines of a mouth long kept pressed tight shut to keep words back. Lom noticed her damaged hands. Fingernails not grown properly back.

'What are you *doing*?' she said.

'Helping you,' said Lom. 'Two are less visible than one.'

They walked among the stricken, the shocked, the wandering. Not fast, not slow, catching no one's eye. Gendarmes were hauling people from the crowd. Pushing them against the wall. Spilling the contents of pockets and bags onto the pavement.

'I don't need you,' said Elena. 'I'm better alone.'

'I'm good at this kind of thing.'

Bright banners fluttered in the strengthening wind. Rizhin's huge smiling face watched over them. Rizhin's face – Josef Kantor's face – the man Lom had known, become a monstrous bullying avuncular god. The death of him left the world strangely deflated and pointless. *Not the world*, thought Lom. *Only me.*

'Were you following me?' said Elena. 'Were you looking for me?'

'Later,' said Lom. 'We'll talk later, when we're clear.'

'What were you *doing* there? How could you *know*?'

'I didn't know. I saw you in the street. You were pretty obvious. But I lost sight of you, and by the time I found you again it was too late.'

'Too late? For what?'

'Too late to stop what you did.'

She left him then. Turned on her heel into a side alley, a narrow chasm between high windows and steep blank walls. Lom thought of hurrying after her. Catching up. *What happened to you? How are you become this?* But he let her go and watched her until she reached the far end of the alley and turned to the right. She didn't look back.

Then he followed.

2

Elena Cornelius was going east. The streets were almost empty. She took a low underpass beneath the thundering Rizhin Highway: a urinous pillared human culvert.

She was easy to follow. Lom trailed her across waste and cratered rubble-lands and through pockets of still-standing bullet-pitted soot-grimed war damage. She led him into a wilderness of elephantine newness: concrete apartment buildings hastily thrown up among the ruins, already stained and dispirited and bleached colourless in the watery afternoon desolated sun. Lom logged the meaningless street names and recognised nothing at all, but he always knew where he was: wherever you went in Mirgorod you could tell your position by the Rizhin Tower. The skied statue of dead Josef Kantor was a beacon. A steering star.

He remembered the old city, the shifting rain-soft city, layered with glimpses, haunted with strange perceptiveness, turnings and doorways alive with contending futures, but now the triumphant future was here, and if the city was littered with shards and broken images, they were dry bone fragments of the past. Angels and giants were gone, rusalkas also: the waters had closed over them and people behaved as if they had never existed.

The blank blinding sky on concrete and asphalt made him squint. He was thirsty, and heavy with obscure guilt. He had made a mistake somewhere, taken a wrong turning, this future now and in Mirgorod his fault. His intentions were good, but history judged only results, and all his choices so far had been bad. The world around him had come out wrong. One day back in Mirgorod and here he was, trailing across wasted ground after a damaged and solitary woman who had killed a monster and made things worse. He didn't know why he was here, except there was nothing better to do.

He kept following Elena Cornelius. She entered an apartment block indistinguishable from the others except by a name. KOMMUNALKA SUBBOTIN NO. 19.

Lom waited in a doorway across the square to see if she would come out again, but three hours later she had not. He turned away then, back towards the clustered sky rises under the reaching steel arm of the Rizhin statue.

3

General-Commander Osip Rizhin held himself rigidly upright in the chair while the doctor leaned in close and did his work. Papa Rizhin stared at the desk in front of him and focused his mind on the pain. He held himself open to it and felt it to the full.

His right eye was swollen shut but his left eye was good. Water streamed from it, not tears but cleansing salt burn, and when the doctor offered him morphine Rizhin cursed him. He had borne worse, in other chairs in other rooms, chairs with straps in rooms with barred high windows. Pain was a good harsh friend. An honest friend. Pain was strength and focus. Everyone who had ever leaned over him in a chair and caused him pain was dead now, and he was still here, the survivor, the indestructible.

The whole of the right side of his face was a swollen, shifting, stiffening map of numbness and pain. Every fresh insertion of the needle, every tug of thread, every application of the burning antiseptic pad, brought its own unique and individual new agony. Rizhin paid attention to the particularity of them all, the thing that made each pain different from every other pain he had ever felt. Pain magnified the right hemisphere of his head until it was bigger than the whole of the rest of the world, but Rizhin knew all the intimate topography of it. Carefully, attentively, he traced across it every new event in the intricate history of hurting.

The collar and back of his dress-uniform tunic were drenched with cold sticky blood. Fragments of human meat and bone. Most of the blood and all of the fleshy mess was not his but Vladi Broch's. The sniper's bullet had deeply furrowed Rizhin's cheek as it passed on by and entered the seated Broch on a downward trajectory, finding the soft gap between left shoulder and neck. A trajectory that took the top of Broch's spine out through a hole in his back.

The doctor straightened up and dabbed at his handiwork on Rizhin's cheek with an iodine cloth. He washed his hands in a bowl of soap and then took a clean handkerchief from his pocket to polish his round-rimmed spectacles. The doctor had soft subtle hands. He wore his thinning hair combed back.

Trust no doctor, that was Rizhin's iron rule. Doctors were the cunning eunuch viziers of the modern world. Mountebank snake-oil alchemists. Obfuscating cabalists of a secretive knowledge. Master superciliists. All surgeons and physicians played you false. In comfortably upholstered rooms they wove their mockery and plots.

Doctor, respected doctor, fear your patient.

'There will be a scar, I'm afraid,' the doctor said. 'There's nothing I can do about that. I've been as neat as I can.'

He began to prepare a dressing pad.

'A battle scar is a source of pride,' Rizhin growled at him through lopsided tongue and uncooperative mouth. 'A million of our veterans bear far worse than this, and they're the lucky ones.'

4

Nikolai Forshin convenes a conference of the Philosophy League at eight in the evening to consider the letter from Mirgorod.

'Of course you must come to our meeting, Eligiya Kamilova,' he says. 'You are one of us, and I may need your support.'

They gather in the principal room of the dacha, part salon, part library: a room of divans and cretonne and canework chairs, threadbare rugs on a parquet floor. Forshin has left the doors to the veranda open, admitting sullen lilac evening. The birch avenue flimsy and skeletal.

Everyone is there: Forshin himself, standing tall and wild-haired at the fireplace, brimming with enthusiasm; the economist Pitrim Brutskoi; Karsin the lexicographer; Olga-Marya Rapp, novelist of the woman's condition; the historians Sitzenvaldt and Polon; Likht the architect and tiny birdlike Yudifa Yudifovna, one-time editor of the short-lived *New Tomorrows Review*. Wives and husbands and lovers are crammed into the room too, squeezing onto sofas, propping cushions on the floor. Here are all the members of Forshin's odd ad-hoc league of the self-exiled and self-appointed intelligentsia, withdrawn into obscurity when the air of the Writers and Artists Union began to chill against them. One by one they got out before the cycle of denunciation, ostracism and arrest got an unbreakable grip. Forshin recruited them. Encouraged them. Gathered them in. Told them they were awaiting better times. At Forshin's dacha they could work and write and plan. There were schemes and journals to be prepared for publication when the wheel turned.

All are thin now, gaunt, their clothes worn thin and polished with age and overuse.

We are the last of the last of the cultured generation, Forshin had said to each of them tête-à-tête over tea and petit-beurre biscuits in a quiet corner of the Union. *Confronted by horrors on such a scale, such a massiveness and totality of alien attitude, our cultured souls can have no response. There is no place for us here. We are numbed. We are enfeebled. We are without resources. We are exiled from the world itself. Our own country no longer exists, so we must learn to breathe in a vacuum and float three feet above the earth. We must withdraw from the world and wait for other times, until the call comes – as one day it will – for us to return.*

But now – this very day – that call has come. So Forshin believes. Pacing in front of the mantelpiece he reads to them once more extracts from Pinocharsky's momentous letter.

'*Come back to the capital, Nikolai! The times are changing, and much for the better. Now is the moment for the Philosophy League to step into the light.*'

Pinocharsky told in his letter how Rizhin himself had commissioned him to found a great new institution, the House of Enlightened Arts!

'*We are to have our own new building,*' Pinocharsky wrote. '*A splendid and beautiful place. A true monument of modernity! The plans are already drawn. I have seen them, Nikolai! Rizhin himself had a model before him on his desk when he spoke to me. Oh, you should have heard him speak, Nikolai. He is a surprisingly cultured man. Not crude at all. He speaks our language. I did not expect this at all. I remember his exact words. "Get me writers, Pinocharsky!" That's what Rizhin said to me. "Get me musicians. Artists. Intellectuals. Build me a palace of culture. What we need now is people who will look at life clearly and show us its* truth. Intellectuals will produce the goods we require most of all. Even more than power plants and airplanes and factories, we must forge strong new human souls."

'I must confess I was reserved at first. I played my cards close to my chest, as you can imagine. Factories are important too, I said wisely. But Rizhin leaned towards me and touched my arm. "I myself," he said, "I myself wrote verse in my youth. You doubt me but I did. I respect poetry. I respect art. I am myself a creative man. I am your brother and your friend."

'I declare, Nikolai, that Papa Rizhin had tears in his eyes! "Do you mean this?" I said to him. (I wanted him to see I was a canny operator. A fellow with something about me.) "Let there be an amnesty," that's what Rizhin said then. "A great homecoming welcome for our finest minds, and past disagreements forgotten: that was then, this is now; we had to be tough, but now it is time to be kind."'

Forshin finishes reading the great letter aloud, stuffs it in the pocket of his jacket with a flourish and pauses to light his pipe.

'And there you have it, friends,' he says, effortless powerful voice booming. 'We have no choice; our duty is clear. Our country and our people need us now and so we must return to Mirgorod. And the call has come none too soon, for frankly the conditions here are worsening. Belatinsk is no longer safe for us.'

'I agree,' says Brutskoi. 'We can do more for Belatinsk in Mirgorod than here. We can speak up for the provinces in the capital. We can protest against the inefficiency of this neglect.'

'Indeed,' says Forshin. 'If Pinocharsky is right, we will have the ear of Rizhin himself.'

'Colleagues,' says the miniature, frail Yudifa Yudifovna quietly, 'I cannot believe you are falling for this transparent shit. Do you not know a trap when you see one?'

'No, no, Yudifa!' Forshin protests. 'This is no trap. What about that speech of Gzowski's that Pinocharsky enclosed?' He quotes a part of Gzowski's speech from memory. 'We are in danger of destroying the spiritual capital of our people. We risk breeding a new crop of brutal and corrupt bureaucrats and a terrible new generation of cruel and lumpen youth. The New Vlast needs poetry and culture and art fit for our great aspirations. The people themselves call for it. Such words could never have been printed without sanction from the very top. It's is as if

Rizhin himself had spoken directly in public to us. This is no trap. This is enlightenment.'

'Well I'm too old to fall for that crap again,' says Yudifovna. 'I'd rather take my chances here with a temporary shortage of beans than risk ending up in a VKBD cell. I've been there already. I'll wait here and see how you get on.'

'I think Yudifa is right,' says Sitzenvaldt. 'Pinocharsky is overexcited and misled. What he describes will never be permitted. We should stick together. If you leave us here we are too few to defend ourselves, and I for one know nothing of chickens.'

'But how much longer do you think we can hold out here?' says Polon. 'One day the mob from Belatinsk will come for us, and what can people like us do then? We cannot fight.'

'These shortages are a natural corrective mechanism,' says Pitrim Brutskoi. 'There will be a rebalancing before too long, you'll see. The human soul is basically sound, and economic society is naturally efficient. I'm sure our fellows in Belatinsk will sort themselves out soon enough: all they need is systematic collective organisation.'

'Well I've had enough of hiding in the country!' cries Olga-Marya Rapp. 'Personal safety is secondary. We must see what is happening and write about it. My duty as an artist requires me to share whatever faces the women of the capital and report on it fearlessly!'

'Are there no women in Belatinsk?' mutters Yudifovna. 'Is what's happening here not worth writing of?' But only Kamilova hears her.

And so, to Forshin's dismay, the League divides. Some are for Mirgorod, and some are for staying at the dacha and waiting out the famine.

'And what about you, Eligiya Kamilova?' says Forshin at the end. 'Will you and the girls come with us to Mirgorod? Surely you will? You'd be safe with us. You'd be travelling under the protection of the League.'

Kamilova hesitates.

'All we want to do is go home to Mirgorod, Nikolai,' she says, 'only we cannot afford the tickets.'

Yudifa Yudifovna leans across and puts a hand on Kamilova's arm.

'How much do you need, Eligiya?' she says.

'Ninety roubles. But—'

'I will give you all of that,' says Yudifovna. 'I'll give you a hundred if you will sell me your gun.'

L om spent a broken night between unclean sheets in his room in the Pension Forbat overlooking the Wieland Station and rose late and ill slept to the news that Papa Rizhin had survived the attempt on his life. He stared at the newspaper headline blankly, too stupid-tired and slow to take it in. His mind was still stuck with the noise of night trains shunting. The clank of points and signals. The echo of klaxons. Porters calling. An arc light splashing bone-sharp shadow across his wall. The empty wardrobe with the door that wouldn't close.

Unshaven and only half awake he went out into the morning and bought black coffee and cigarettes in a railway workers' café-bar on the corner by the pension. Laid the paper out on the table in front of him. Lit a cigarette with a cardboard match from a match book on the bar marked LOCOMOTIVE STAR. The unaccustomed smoke tasted bad and caught in his throat. His chest clenched. He ground the unfinished cigarette into the ashtray and lit another. Scooped sticky sugar into his coffee and swallowed the whole cup to take the taste away. Got another. That was breakfast.

The paper still said the same thing, which wasn't much. Some minister for agriculture was dead and Rizhin was not. There was a photograph of Rizhin at his desk and in command, a wad of cotton stuck on where the bullet had grazed his face. Rizhin glared straight into the camera, purposeful, confident. Burning with determination undimmed. No day's work lost for the man they couldn't kill. Lom felt that the picture was meant for him personally: the dark energy of Rizhin's gaze locked eyes with him. It was a challenge. *See what I am? See what I can do? Did you think I could be stopped? Then think again. What's it like to be alone?*

Lom got a third coffee.

In the sleepless watches of the night he'd lit the dim bedside lamp and read again the official biography of Osip Rizhin. There was a copy in every guest house, pension and hotel room across the whole of the New Vlast. It went with the head-and-shoulders portrait on the wall. In the night the book had been an obituary, the shadowed Rizhin face above the dresser a funerary mask, but in the morning the man had climbed out of his grave, fresh and ready for the day.

You couldn't kill a man who wasn't there.

When Lom read the biography of Rizhin, what he saw was nothing. Gaps. Elisions. Lacunae. Imprecision covering emptiness. The testimony of witnesses who were not there. It was a life that had not happened. All the hardness and roaring industrious speed of Mirgorod and the New Vlast were a tissue of words laid across nothing at all.

And two other simple words, one name spoken out loud, a double trochee on a single breath of air – *JO-sef KAN-tor* – would scatter the whole construction and blow it all away.

Don't kill him, Maroussia had said. *Bring him down. Destroy the idea of him. Ruin him in this world, using the tricks of this world, and ruin this world he has created.*

For centuries the Vlast had wiped histories away. The stroke of a bureaucrat's pen created unpersons out of lives and made ruined former people the unseen, unheard haunters of their own streets.

So there it was.

Turn the weapon on the wielder of it. One name spoken would turn Osip Rizhin into another empty unperson.

JO-sef KAN-tor.

Lom's heart was beating faster. He shifted in his seat with excitement. He wanted to be moving again. He had seen the way. He could do that, and he would.

What was needed was proof.

6

President-Commander Osip Rizhin had at his disposal the entire security machinery of the New Vlast. Two million police and militia men and women, their agents and informers and surveillance systems. Interrogators, analysts, collectors and sifters of intelligence. Torturers, assassins and spies. Rizhin had all of that, but trusted none of them because he of all people knew what kind of thing they were, and knew they must themselves be watched and kept in fear.

And so Rizhin had created the Parallel Sector. The Black Guard. The Streltski.

The Director of the Parallel Sector was Hunder Rond, and Rond was Rizhin's man. Narrow-shouldered and diminutive, Rond had the cropped grey hair and brisk featureless competence of a senior bank official. In the brief civil war against Fohn and his crew, Rond – then a colonel of militia – had shown himself assiduously and unflamboyantly effective as an eliminator of the less-than-committed within Rizhin's own camp. As an interrogator he was imaginatively destructive. He had certain private desires (which he gratified) that Rizhin disliked and documented, but in Rond he overlooked them. He needed someone, and Hunder Rond met the requirement as no one else. When Rond entered a room he brought darkness with him.

'Keep that doctor locked up for now,' Rizhin told Rond. 'I want no blabbing from him.'

(Did Rizhin trust Hunder Rond? He did not. But he was sure Rond had no involvement in yesterday's sniper attack. Rond had no friends, no allies because Rond hurt everyone – Rizhin made sure of that. Rond had no independent means of support and wouldn't survive a week with Rizhin gone. Rond would not have tried to cut off the branch he sat on.)

'Grigor Ekel's outside,' said Rond. 'He's been sitting there for two hours in a pool of his own piss and sweat. As secretary for security he is *most distraught* at this failure on the part of others outside his control. He wishes to abase himself and name the negligent.'

'Have the fucker sent away,' said Rizhin. 'Tell him he's lucky he's not already under arrest. And tell him he's got better things to do than lick my arse. Like find the fucker who shot me.'

Rond nodded. If he noticed that Rizhin spoke more slowly and emphatically than normal, through swollen lips that barely moved – if he observed Rizhin's tunic soaked with blood, Rizhin's face half-hidden under bandages, the slight tremor in Rizhin's right hand – then Rond gave no sign. He was reassuring efficiency, only there to serve.

'And there has been nothing?' Rizhin was saying. 'No further moves? No claims of responsibility?'

'Nothing,' said Rond. 'Nobody seems to have been prepared for this. Everybody is watching everybody else and waiting to see what happens. The situation is drifting. Perhaps we should make a public statement? You could make an appearance. Reassert control. Vacuum is the greater risk now. Nerves are shot. We need to worry about the whole continent, not just Mirgorod.'

'Not yet,' said Rizhin. 'Keep it vague a few more hours. And watch. Someone may still make a move.'

Rond made a face.

'I think the time for that's gone,' he said. 'We'd have seen something by now. The more time passes, the more likely it is that this was a lone wolf.'

Rizhin looked at him sharply.

'A *wolf*? You say a *wolf*?'

'Someone working alone,' said Rond. 'A grudge. A fanatic. A private venture. It was always a possibility. It's the hardest threat to see coming and protect against.'

'Nothing comes from nowhere,' said Rizhin. 'I want to know who did this, Rond. Find the shooter. Find them all. I want them dis-embowelled. I want them swinging in the wind and screaming to be let die.'

7

L om passed the morning in a ProVlastKult reading room among stacks of newspapers six years old. The whole of the story was there if you knew how to read it.

There was the assault on Secretary Dukhonin's residence in Pir-Anghelsky Park: Dukhonin and all his household butchered by a terrorist gang who then themselves all died at the hands of the militia, including their leader the notorious agitator Josef Kantor. The papers gave a surprisingly full account of Kantor's history: his involvement with the Birzel plot; his twenty-year confinement in the labour camp at Vig; his death in a hail of bullets as he tried to escape the Pir-Anghelsky charnel house. There was no photograph of Kantor though, not even a prison mug shot. Of course there wasn't.

And then the very next day after Dukhonin's death, the Archipelago bombers had come for the first time and Mirgorod began to burn. The government withdrew and it seemed the city would quickly fall. But there was Colonel-General Osip Rizhin, suddenly come from nowhere, an unknown name (there were no prior references in the index, none at all) to lead the city's defence. To stem the enemy advance and hold the siege. To conjure out of nowhere atomic artillery shells, a whole new way of killing, and turn the tide. Step forward Papa Rizhin, father and begetter of a new and better Vlast. *Times are better now, citizens.*

What Rizhin stood for was never made clear. If there were principles they were not spoken of. It was all about racing ahead. Dynamism. Taking the future in hand. A fresh beginning. Victory and peace and a bright widening tomorrow. *Papa Rizhin works on the people*, an editorial read, *as a chemist works in his laboratory. He builds with us, as an engineer builds a great bridge.*

In the early weeks and months after Rizhin's first appearance in the world the papers had carried vague and inconsistent accounts of who he was and where he'd come from. Stories came and went, made little sense and did not stick until the publication of the little pamphlet *An Account of the Life of Osip Rizhin, Hero of Mirgorod, Father of the New Vlast.* Ten million copies of a little book of lies.

But who knew the truth? Hundreds must have known. Thousands. People who would have seen the portraits of Osip Rizhin and recognised Josef Kantor. For a start there would be those who knew him from his childhood among the families of Lezarye. Lom turned cold. He went back to the newspapers from the first days of the siege and read again a passage he had seen there. The whole of the Raion Lezaryet had been cleared and every last person of Lezarye 'relocated in the east'. There was no reference to Lezarye in the journal index after that. No account of the place or its people ever again. He felt dizzy. Sick.

Of course there would have been others who could identify Kantor as Rizhin. Fellow inmates in the camp at Vig, for a start. But how easy it would be to reach out from Mirgorod and silence them if you had already removed an entire city quarter.

Josef Kantor knew who knew him, and Osip Rizhin could kill them all.

Lom went through the list in his mind. Under-Secretary Krogh (who knew because Lom had told him) was dead: his obituary was there in the paper, a eulogy to a lifetime's service cut short by heart failure in his office a week before war came to Mirgorod. Raku Vishnik was dead. Lavrentina Chazia was dead (not killed by Kantor because Lom had saved him that trouble). Kantor's wife, Maroussia's mother, was dead: Lom had seen her shot down in the street in front of him. They had come to kill Maroussia herself more than once. And they had tried to kill him, Lom, as well.

Who else? Who else? Was there anyone left at all, apart from Maroussia and himself, who had been so comprehensively lost to view that Rizhin could not find them?

Lom racked his brain. There was one more face he remembered, a wild-eyed prophet of the new arts, standing green shirt half un-buttoned in the rain in the alley outside the Crimson Marmot. The painter Lakoba Petrov. He knew Josef Kantor. He was one of Kantor's gang. *Kantor the crab*, Petrov had called him. *Josef Krebs. Josef Cancer. Nothing but shell, shell, and lidless eyes on little stalks staring out of it, like a crab.* Lom remembered Petrov swaying drunk in the red glow of the Marmot's sign, oblivious of the rain in his face. *And shall I tell you something else about him?* Petrov had said, speaking very slowly and clearly. *He has some other purpose which is not apparent.*

Lom went back to the index and searched for Lakoba Petrov, painter.

For the second time he turned cold. Sick and dizzy with disbelief. Following a couple of references to reviews of Petrov's paintings, there was one last entry: 'Petrov, Lakoba: assassination of the Novozhd; death of.' Petrov had blown himself up and taken the Novozhd with him. The papers presented it as some mad kind of anarchist artwork, the ultimate product of a degenerate corrupted mind. But Petrov's act had paved the way for Chazia, and ultimately Kantor, to seize the Vlast, and Petrov was Kantor's man.

Lom ripped the page from the newspaper, stuffed it in his pocket and walked out of the library in a daze. Sat on the steps in the early-afternoon sunshine and lit a cigarette. There were still a couple left in the packet.

The story was there in the archive to be read if you knew what to look for, but everyone who could have known even part of it … Papa Rizhin had raked the Vlast with a lice comb and killed them all, every one, as he would kill anyone who came forward with a rumour or began to ask around. There was no proof. And what would proof look like anyway? What were the chances of finding a police file with Josef

Kantor's photograph and fingerprints neatly tagged and docketed?

But there had once been such a file. Lom had held it in his own hands. He'd stolen it from Chazia's personal archive in the Lodka: the file that contained Chazia's account of her recruitment of Kantor as an informant and conspirator, and of her contact with the living angel in the forest. That file was proof enough to bring Rizhin down. But it was gone. Lom remembered how he'd left it hidden in the cistern in the bathroom of Vishnik's apartment, but he knew the militia had searched the building when they killed Vishnik. *They looked all over*, the dvornik had told him. *The halls. The stairwell. The bathroom. They pulled the cistern off the wall.*

That surely meant they had found it, and the file was gone. But it had gone *somewhere*. Where? Back to Chazia presumably. The efficient paper handling of the old regime.

It came back to him now. There had in fact been two files in the folder he hid in the cistern: Chazia's folder on Josef Kantor, and Lom's own personnel record, which he'd also lifted from Chazia's archive and brought away to read. Lom remembered the manuscript note on the second file from Krogh's traitorous private secretary, who'd extracted it from Krogh's office and passed it to Chazia.

Lom felt a sudden waking of excitement and hope. The private secretary. He was Chazia's man, and he'd known something, perhaps a lot. He'd certainly known all about Lom's mission to track down Kantor. But Kantor almost certainly would not have known about him.

Lom could still see the private secretary's face.

His name? What was his name?

It was there somewhere, neatly lodged away in his long-unused policeman's brain.

Find it. Find it.

Pavel!

Pavel. First name only, but it might be enough.

Lom raced back up the steps and into the library again. In the reference section next to the newspaper index he'd seen the long rows of annual volumes of the *Administrative Gazette Yearbook*, which among much other turgid information listed the ministers and senior officials of the Vlast. Including details of their private offices. Heart pounding, Lom pulled down the volume of the *Gazette* he needed and flipped through the pages until he found the one he needed. And there it was, in small italic typeface under the name of Krogh himself: '*Private Secretary: Antimos, Pavel Ilich*'.

It was a lot to hope that Pavel Antimos had survived: survived the siege, survived the war, survived Rizhin's lice comb; survived it all and continued to work for the government of the New Vlast. A lot to hope for but perhaps not too much. Men like Pavel did survive. They even kept their jobs. He might still be there.

The long unbroken run of the *Administrative Gazette Yearbook* had gold lettering on blue spines fading to grey as the years receded to the left. Tucked in at the right-hand end of the last shelf were five volumes with the same gold lettering, but the spines were green and shining new. *Administrative Gazette Yearbook, New Series*. Lom took the last one, the most recent volume. Antimos, Pavel Ilich had not only survived but his career had flourished. He was an under-secretary now, in the Office for Progressive Cultural Enlightenment, with a private secretary of his own.

Lom didn't want to approach him in his office. Better to do it in the evening, at home. Pushing his winning streak for one last throw, he scouted around for a Mirgorod residential telephone directory. He found it. And Pavel Antimos was in it. Lom memorised the address. It was a tenuous lead but the only one he had.

Pull on a thread. See where it takes me.

Just like the old days.

8

Maroussia Shaumian feels small beyond insignificance. The trees spread around her in all directions, numberless, featureless and utterly bleak. A still, engulfing, unending tide of blankness. The skin between her and the forest is permeable: she wants to spill out into it, a scent cloud dispersing under the branch-head canopy. The forest tugs and nags at the edges of her. Pieces of her snag on the trees and pull free.

She is walking again. Walking.

When it rains the rain clags the mud and makes the forest hiss and whisper. Mud clumps and drags and weighs on her boots. Every time it rains the rain gets colder and there are fewer leaves on the trees. Winter seems coming too soon, but she has boots and blankets and she will be OK.

Towards the end of the day she finds a dry rise of ground and a heavy oak tree, half fallen, its root mass torn from the earth. With her axe she hacks off some branches, props them against the fallen tree's side and weaves thinner stem-lengths through to make strong, shallow, sloping walls. When the walls are solid she heaps leaves on top, pile on pile, until it swells, a natural earthy rising of the ground, skinned with leaves an arm's length deep, at one end a low dark mouth. She rests another layer of branches across the outside, for the weight of them, to hold the leaves in place, and crawls inside, dragging more leaves after her, the driest she has found. Spreads them deep across the ground and packs the far end until she has a narrow earth-smelling tunnel scarcely wide enough to lie in. With more leaf-heavy branches she makes a door to pull in place behind her.

She works quickly but the light is failing.

The forest is too dark to see beyond the fire circle but she feels its presence. Trees rolling without end or limit, their roots under the earth all touching and knotting together, root whispering to root as branch brushes against branch. Connected, watchful, they merge and make one thing, the largest animal in the world. Night-waking. Watchful. It knows she is there.

There are stars in the gaps between branches, and a deeper purple-green shining blackness.

Maroussia crawls into the enclosing darkness of her leaf-and-branch cocoon. Her hiding, her little burial, her dream time, her forgetting. Deep beneath her in the earth the fine tangled roots sift and slide and touch each other. They whisper.

The shelter has its own quiet whispering too, a barely audible shifting and settling, the outer layer flickering and feathering in the night breeze. She hears the rustle and tick of small things – woodlice, spiders, mice – burrowing in the canopy. The shelter absorbs her, mothering, nurturing. Hiding her away.

The blanket is wrapped tight around her, rough against her face. Knees pulled up tight against her belly, feet pressed against the solid weight of her pack, head pillowed on her arms, she breathes with her mouth, shallow, slow breaths. Breathing the warmth of her own breath. The smell of leaves and earth and moss. Woodsmoke in the blanket and in her clothes and hair.

This isn't right. This isn't what I meant at all.

She is a rim of troubled consciousness encircling immensities without and immensities within. Sustaining it hurts. Her fragility and capacity for fracture terrify her.

A hand of fear in the darkness covers her face so it is hard to breathe. Fear grasps her heart inside her chest and squeezes out breath. Everything inside her is tight. Tight like wires. The trees she cannot see in the night prickle with the same fear. She wants to dig herself into the ground and be buried.

One break and I could lose myself for ever.

The Pollandore speaks its presence softly all the time, a voice inside her that sounds like it is outside, whispering dangerous promises. It swells and grows. The spaces inside her are as measureless as the forest and less human. Maroussia-Pollandore holds the green wall shut: the forest is withdrawn from its borders and does not leak. It holds no traffic with the human world, not any more. She feels the human world grow hard and quick and dying, and she is the engine of that. She is the separation and the holding back. She is the border patrol.

I wanted the opposite of this. I chose to open the world not close it. This is not me. My name is Maroussia Shaumian. When the angel in the forest is gone, then I can go home.

All she has to do is keep on walking. Keep it clear and simple, that is all she has to do. Be hard and strong and clever, and somehow she will keep the darkness from her. Somehow she will do that.

Trees in the forest walk, but slowly, year by year. Inching.

She will outrun them yet.

9

Lom had never heard birdsong in Mirgorod before. Never smelled new-cut lawn.

The lindens on the street where Pavel Ilich Antimos lived must have been planted fully grown. The fragrant asphalt, the raked gravel, the clipped laurels, they were all fresh out of the box, but those late-afternoon-sun-kindled shade-breathing linden trees would have taken fifty years to reach the height they were. They cast a kind of quiet privacy over Voronetsin Heights that made you feel like an intruder, just being in the road.

Atom House, the residence of Pavel Ilich Antimos, was a low-rise apartment building in walled grounds. A pleasant low-key fortress. The gate in the wall was wrought iron, painted to a gleam like broken coal. Lom watched the block for fifteen minutes. He saw domestic staff and deliveries checking in and out; wives coming back from shopping; children being driven home from school. The gate opened for them and closed behind them, and no way was the woman in the kiosk going to open that gate, not unless she knew you or you had an appointment and you were in her book.

Thus lived the List – the managers, the lawyers, the officials, the financiers and architects and engineers of Rizhin Land – spending different currency in different stores.

Lom went round the corner out of sight of the kiosk, jumped to hook his fingers on the coping ridge, hauled himself up till he could scrabble over the wall and dropped on the other side. The soft earth of a rose bed. A quiet formal garden in the slanting sun.

Pavel's apartment was at the end of a short corridor, top floor back. It felt like an afterthought in the building. Single occupancy, one of the less expensive units, not a family home. Lom hoped so. He didn't want to find Pavel's wife at home. Or children. That would complicate things. The only other door in the passage was a cleaner's storeroom. Lom checked it. Empty. Smelling of bleach and musty mops.

He knocked on Pavel's door, brisk and businesslike. The door felt solid. His knocking sounded dull and didn't carry. There was no bell push.

He knocked again.

'Hi!' he called. 'Residence Antimos! Is someone at home? Open please!'

Nobody came. No matter how long he stared at it, the door stayed shut. It had a solid Levitan deadbolt lock, heavier than was normal for domestic use and fitted upside down to make it more awkward to pick.

Lom had spent his time productively since leaving the ProVlastKult library that morning. From a dusty shop by the Wieland Station (broken clocks and watches on velvet pads in the window) he'd bought a basic lock-picking kit: a C-rake, a tension wrench and short hook, all wrapped in a convenient canvas roll. He'd also acquired a neat small black rubber cosh in a silk sheath, with a plaited cord lanyard. The cosh was expensive but the proprietor sewed an extra pocket for him in his jacket sleeve. No extra cost. You had to know how to ask.

He popped the Levitan deadbolt without too much trouble. The door was solid hardwood a couple of inches thick. It took weight to open it.

'Hi,' he called again quietly. 'Pavel, old friend? Are you there?'

The place was cool and dim and still and obviously empty. Lom stepped inside, pulled the door shut behind him and relocked it. On the inside it was fitted with two heavy bolts and a chain. Lom looked around. It was a single man's apartment: kitchen, bathroom, sitting room with one armchair and a desk, a bedroom with a single bed. Pavel didn't get many visitors obviously. Didn't seem to spend much time at home at all.

Lom moved from room to room. Everything was neat. Possessions carefully put away. There was a phonogram cabinet in the sitting room, the lid closed. A shelf of recordings arranged in alphabetical order of composer. On a low glass-topped table with splayed tapering legs Pavel had stacked some literary magazines – *New Cosmos*, *The Forward View* – and three days' worth of newspapers, crisply folded. In the bedroom there were books, also carefully arranged, the spines unbroken, on a low shelf under the window. The food in the kitchen was brightly coloured packages and tins – fruit juice, condensed milk, rye bread, caviar – all high quality List Shop brands.

There was something about Pavel's apartment that was odd. It took

Lom a moment to realise what it was. Nothing in the whole place was personal: nothing was old or well used or could possibly have had sentimental value. The pressed dark suits, the careful ties, the white shirts folded in drawers, the carpets, the curtains, the coverlet on the bed, the gramophone recordings of new composers singled out for favour by the Academy of Transformational Artistic Production (chairman, Osip Rizhin). Pavel had kept nothing that was made before the inception of the New Vlast. Nothing that deviated from post-war cultural norms. Pavel had accepted Rizhin's world utterly, immersed himself in it, acquired with the obsessiveness of a connoisseur the top-rank artefacts of its material culture and surrounded himself with them. This was the apartment of an exemplary fellow, New Vlast Man to the core, from whose life all vestiges of the past had been removed with surgical thoroughness. Pavel was a chameleon, a caddis fly. He raised the art of blending in to new pinnacles of ruthless ostentation.

In a drawer of Pavel's desk Lom found a travel agent's confirmation of a booking for one – two weeks at the Tyaroga Resort Hotel on the Chernomorskoy Sea, single-berth rail sleeper included. He also found a carton of small-calibre shells and a diminutive pistol. A Deineka 5-shot Personal Defender. It looked like it had never been fired.

Lom loaded the gun, slipped a round into the chamber and put it in his pocket. Then he went into the kitchen, opened a packet of Pavel's Oksetian Sunrise coffee, filled Pavel's coffee pot and put it on Pavel's stove. When the pot hissed and bubbled he poured himself a cup, picked up a book from the kitchen counter and went back into the other room to wait for Pavel to come home. The window was slightly open, letting in a stir of warm early-evening air. The quiet sound of distant traffic. Liquid blackbird song.

The book from Pavel's kitchen was the Mikoyan Institute's *Home Course of Delicious and Healthy Food*. Lom flicked through the pages to pass the time. Monochrome photographic plates displayed smiling family faces and crowded tables: meat loaf canapés filled with piped mayonnaise; bottles of sparkling Vlastskoye Sektwine and shining crystal goblets; a platter of pike in aspic decorated with radish rosettes. There were recipes for crab and cucumber salad; vinaigrette of beetroot, cabbage and red potato; crunchy pork cutlets; mutton aubergine claypot. Papa Rizhin himself had provided a foreword. 'The special character of our New Vlast,' it began, 'is the joyousness of our prosperous and cultured style of life.' There were no grease spots on the herb-green cloth binding. No spills. No stuck-together pages. Pavel didn't have any favourite recipes then. Pavel Ilich Antimos would eat them all with equal relish. *Anything that Papa Rizhin recommends.* Lom looked at his watch. It was well past six o'clock. He hoped Pavel wasn't working late or dining out.

Lom got another coffee and occupied himself with the pictures on Pavel's walls. The pictures people put on their walls told you as much about them as their books – more, because they were meant to be seen. *This is what I like. This is my mind. This is who you should think I am.* Pavel's visual world was framed prints advertising exhibitions of art promoted by the Office for Progressive Cultural Enlightenment. He'd probably picked them up free at work. There was a jewel-bright painting of a Mirgorod Airways Skyliner over snow-capped mountains. Dancers in a town square. The storm-beset factory ship VV *Karamazov* riding glass-green churning foam-flecked waters under a purple thunder-riven sky (*Recall Our Heroic Sailors of the Merchant Marine!*). Pride of place went to a large colourised photograph of the Vlast Universal Vessel *Proof of Concept* climbing on a column of fire into a cloud-wisped sky.

Three hours later it was getting dark outside when Pavel Antimos let himself into his own apartment with his own key. Lom heard him lock the door behind him, drive the bolts home top and bottom, safe and sound, and hook the chain in place for the night. He let Pavel find him in the sitting room. In his armchair. Reading his books. Drinking his coffee. From his mug.

'Pavel,' he said, 'it's been too long, old friend. How're you doing? Working late tonight? You're looking well. You haven't changed.'

And Pavel hadn't changed, hardly at all. Some thickening at the neck and shoulders, maybe. A suggestion of jowl under the chin. A darkening around the eyes, the pallor of long office days.

He blinked. But only once.

'You,' he said. 'You're Lom.'

'You remembered.'

'I'm efficient. What do you want?'

Lom saw his eyes flick to the desk. To the drawer left open where the gun had been. A small loss of hope. You had to know it was there to see it.

'I want a talk,' said Lom. 'About Josef Kantor.'

Pavel's eyes widened. Not so missable this time.

'Who?'

'Please don't spoil it,' said Lom, 'the memory thing. Let's talk Papa and Joe. The Rizhin–Kantor nexus. Identities.'

'You're insane.'

'He never knew about you, did he?' said Lom. 'You were never on his list. You've been lucky. It's been a long time now, and you're in the clear unless somebody mentions you to him. An anonymous note would be enough; a phone call would be better. He might even remember your name then, and if he didn't he might check it out, but probably he wouldn't bother. It wouldn't make any difference. He'd err on the safe side. That would be bad for you. And I can make that happen, Pavel. Maybe I will.'

Pavel didn't flinch. No bluster. No threats. No visible emotion of any kind. He absorbed the position and adapted to it. Instantly. It was a masterclass in how to survive.

'This is wasting time,' he said. 'I understand you perfectly. You have information dangerous to me, and you come to my home to threaten me because you want something in return for your silence. I do not like this but I accept the inevitability of it. Well, I am listening. So what do you want?'

'I want proof,' said Lom. 'I know that Rizhin is Kantor, but I want evidence. Photographs. Police files. Intelligence reports. Identification.'

'Like I said, you're insane,' said Pavel. 'You really are. Fortunately for both of us, what you're asking for is impossible. The Lodka archive is long gone. Most of it was burned when the Archipelago came, before the siege.'

'Only most of it?' said Lom.

'Some papers were sent to Kholvatogorsk, but Rizhin has been there. He's been everywhere. You won't find any files on Josef Kantor; they're all gone, and everybody who might have dealt with such information is dead or disappeared into a labour camp.'

'Has he been to Vig too?' said Lom. 'The courts? Provincial stations?

There must have been a lot of paper on Kantor. A lot of people who would recognise his face.'

'All of it,' said Pavel. 'He's been everywhere, you can be sure of that. He's a thorough man.'

'Even Chazia's personal archive?' said Lom.

Pavel missed a beat. 'What?'

'Chazia had her own private papers,' said Lom. 'She kept them in a room in the Central Registry. I saw them. And they wouldn't have been burned or shipped off to Kholvatogorsk. No way. Chazia would have made arrangements to keep them separate and safe.'

'I know nothing about this,' said Pavel.

'Don't you?' said Lom. 'Well you should. Chazia had papers there with your name on, Pavel. Papers that you passed to her from Krogh's office, including papers about me and how Krogh wanted me to find Kantor. I saw them, Pavel, and you don't want Rizhin finding them, do you?'

Pavel sat down. He looked suddenly diminished.

'What do you want from me?' he said.

'I want the same thing you want for yourself. I want you to retrieve those papers.'

'For fuck's sake!'

'I'll tell you what you're going to do, Pavel. You're going to find out what happened to Chazia's archive, then you're going to find it and you're going to get the file on Kantor from it and bring it to me. It's there. I've read it. What you do with the rest is up to you.'

'What if I can't do this?' said Pavel. 'The archive could have been lost or destroyed by now. And even if it still exists, who will know where it is? I can hardly ask.'

Lom shrugged.

'I don't care how you do it. These are your problems, not mine. They're administrative problems, the kind you're good at solving. If you bring me the Kantor file, you won't hear from me again. If not, well ... I don't like you, Pavel. I don't like the kind of person you are, and I remember how you pissed me about when I was working for Krogh. I'm not your friend.'

'Look,' said Pavel, 'OK. I'll try to find it, but it may not—'

'I'm not interested in intentions,' said Lom. 'Only outcomes. I'll come back for it this time tomorrow. Have it ready.'

'No,' said Pavel. 'One day isn't enough. And you are not to come to my home again. Not ever again.'

'Two days then,' said Lom. 'But no more.'

Pavel nodded. He looked sick.

'There's a konditorei on the lake in Kerensky Gardens,' he said. 'If I can get what you want, I'll be there. I will arrive at 10 p.m. and I will wait till eleven.'

10

Night in the city, and Mirgorod celebrates the survival of Papa Rizhin the unkillable man. Lamps project the immense face of Rizhin all ruby-red against the underbelly of broken scudding cloud. Moon-gapped, star-gapped, streaming, he fills a quarter of the sky and floods the city with dim reflected redness.

In the rebuilt Dreksler-Kino, Ziabin's greatest work, *The Glorification of Time Racing*, makes its triumphant premiere before an audience of twenty thousand. Oh, the ambition of Ziabin! Two thousand performers fusing music, dance and oratory! He will unify the arts! He will raise humankind to the radiant level! New instruments constructed for the occasion emit perfumes and effusions of vaporous colour in accordance with Ziabin's score, and the auditorium reverberates to wonderful sounds previously unheard. Towers and mountains rise from the floor and cosmonauts descend thunderous from the sky, waving and smiling as they join the chorus in polyphonic harmony. Across the enormous cinema screen roll images of Rizhin country against a backdrop of galaxies. And all in glorious colour! The roars of wonder of twenty thousand watchers echo across the city, new gasps of rapture in perfect time with the long under-rhythms of Ziabin's scheme. A synchronised crescendo every seventh wave.

Rizhin himself is there at the Dreksler-Kino, seated in a raised box. The wound on his face is agony but his chair is gilt, the walls of his box padded and buttoned velvet. *Like a brooch in a jeweller's box*, he says to Ziabin. It is not a remark intended to put the great artist at his ease. *Haven't we shot you yet?*

11

The Vlast Universal Vessel *Proof of Concept* tumbles slowly, describing twenty-thousand-mile-per-hour corkscrew ellipses of orbiting perpetual fall. The cosmonauts ride in silence, having nothing to do. Sweeps of shadow and light. Cabin windows crossing the sun. Nightside passages of broken moon. The internal lighting has failed.

The frost of their breath furs the ceiling thickly.

Hourly they flick the radio switch.

'Chaiganur? Hello, Chaiganur? Here is *Proof of Concept* calling.'

Universes of silence stare back from the loudspeaker grille.

In Mirgorod the twenty-foot likenesses of cosmonauts in bronze relief carry their space helms at the hip. In bright mosaic above the Wieland Station concourse they look skyward with chiselled confidence, grinning into star-swept purple. *Our Starfaring Heroes. Mankind Advances Towards the Radiant Sun.*

On the giant screen in the Dreksler-Kino wobbling smoky rockets descend among rocks and oceans out of strange skies. Bubble-cabin tractors till the extraplanetary soil, building barracks for pioneers. The audience roars and stamps its forty thousand feet. All children know their names from the illustrated magazines.

Our Future Among the Galaxies.

The Vlast Universal Vessel *Proof of Concept,* two-thousand-ton extraplanetary submarine, makes a shining white mote against the nightly backdrop of the stars. It slides on smooth invisible rails across the sky. You can set your clock by it. It is clean and beautiful and very sad.

Silent the cosmonauts, eyes wide and dark-adapted, having nothing to do.

The turning of the cabin windows pans slowly across vectors of the lost planet, blue-rimmed, beclouded, oceanic. Shadow-side campfire towns and cities glitter. Ant jewels. The shrouded green-river-veined darkness of forest. Lakes are yellow. Lakes are brown. The continent is a midriff between ice and ice. Glimpses of the offshore archipelago.

Complex geometries of turn bring the snub nose of the *Proof of Concept* round to face the world. It's a matter of timing. Her fingers stiff with cold and lack of use, Cosmonaut-Commodore Vera Mornova engages console mechanisms. The distant tinny echo of whirr and clunk. The magazine selects a charge.

Her companions observe unspeaking with heavy-lidded eyes and do not move.

'I'm going home now,' she says and pushes her thumb into the rubber of the detonation button.

The response is a distant bolt sliding home.

A half-second delay.

The tiny silent star-explosion of angel plasma smashes them in the small of the back. They do not blink.

Vera Mornova jabs her finger into the rubber button again and again.

Her aim is true. *Proof of Concept* surges forward into burning fall. The world in the window judders and bellies and swells.

The melting frost of their breath on the ceiling begins to fall on them like rain.

12

After leaving Pavel's apartment, Lom took a night walk on the Mir Embankment. The Mir still rolled on through the city, carrying silt and air and the remembering of lakes and trees, but it was silent now and just a river. Everything was hot and open under the Rizhin-stained sky. He didn't want to go home, not if home was a room in the Pension Forbat.

He was looking for something. Shadows and trails of what used to be. Old wild places where the forest still was. Giants and rusalkas and the dry ghosts of rain beasts in a wide cobbled square. There must be something left, something he could work with. But he was the only haunter of the new ruined city, caught between memory and forgetting, listening to the silence of dried waters. The city had turned its back on the Mir, and he was on the wrong side of the river.

In the very shadow of the Rizhin Tower, almost under the walls of the Lodka, he crossed into a small field of rubble. Mirgorod was aftermath city yet, and the heal-less residuum of war still came through. Stains under fresh plaster.

Lom stepped in among roofless blackened walls propped with baulks of timber. Night scents of wild herb and bramble. The smell of ash and rust and old wood slowly rotting. A grating in the gutter and running water down below – moss and mushroom and soft mud – the Yekaterina Canal paved over and gone underground.

Follow. Follow.

Gaps and small openings into blackness everywhere. Subterranea.

He kicks aside a fallen shop sign. CLOVER. BOOKS AND PERIODICALS.

Down he goes into old quiet tunnels and long-abandoned burrowings. There is no light down there, no lurid Rizhin glow, but he is Lom and needs no light to find his way.

Chapter Six

The sisters all had silent eyes
and all of them were beautiful.

Velimir Khlebnikov (1885–1922)

1

The Lodka, sealed up and abandoned by Papa Rizhin – New Vlast, new offices! Sky rise and modern! Concrete and steel and glass! – stands, a black stranded hulk on Victory Square, doors locked, lower windows barred and boarded, the silent and disregarded River Mir at its back. Papa Rizhin refuses to use it at all. *It is a mausoleum*, he says. *A stale reliquary. It stinks of typewriter ribbons and old secrets and the accrual of pensions. Four hundred years of conferences and paper shuffling and the dust of yesterday's police. Will you make me breathe the second-hand breath of unremembered under-secretaries? Titular counsellors who died long ago and took their polished trouser seats with them to the grave? Fuck you. I will not do it.*

And so the panels of angel flesh were removed from the Lodka's outer walls to be ground up for Khyrbysk Propellant, and the vast building itself – its innumerable rooms and unmappable corridors, its unaccountable geometry of lost staircases and entranceless atria open to the sky, its basement cells and killing rooms – was hastily cleared out and simply closed up and left.

Inside the Lodka now an autumnal atmosphere pervades, whatever the external season. Time is disrupted here, unforgetting and passing slow. Many windows are broken – shattered bomb-blast glass scattered on floors and desks – and weather comes in through opened oriels and domes. Paint is flaking off leadlights. In the reading room the great wheel of the Gaukh Engine stands motionless, canted two degrees off centre in its cradle by an Archipelago bomb that fell outside. Animals have taken up residence – acrid streaks and accumulations of bird shit – bats and cats and rats – but they do not penetrate more than the outermost layers, leaving undisturbed the interior depths of this hollowed-out measureless mountain. Only shadows and paper dust settle there, little moved by slow deep tides of scarcely shifting air.

In the inner core of the Lodka, unreached by traffic noise and the coming and going of days, the silence of disconnected telephones drifts along corridors and through open doorways, across linoleum, tile and carpet. Nowhere here is ever completely dark: bone moonlight sifts and trickles eventually through the smallest gaps. Dim noiselessness brushes against walls painted ivory and green and the panels of frosted glass in doors. Quietness drifts along empty shelving and settles like ocean sediment inside deed boxes, cubbyholes, lockers and filing cabinets, the drawers of desks. Chairs still stand where they were left, pushed back. Abandoned pens rest on half-finished notes and memoranda. Jackets hang on coat stands in corners. Spare shoes are stowed under cupboards. Muteness insinuates itself into the inner mechanisms of typewriters, decryption machines, opaline desk lamps and heating boilers. Tiny fragments of angel flesh, inert now, lie where they fell on workroom floors. Obscurity preserves in grey amber the strangely intimate and homely office world of government. The Lodka is an ungraspable archaeology of administration. Surveillance. Bureaucracy. Interrogation. Death. Suspended and timeless. An unfathomable edifice. A sanctuary. An abysm.

Vissarion Lom found his way into the abandoned Lodka by subterranean ways. Following passages till recently used by only the most secretive of confidential agents of the secret surveillance police, he crossed the barely tangible time-slow frontier into memorious residuum, and long hours he wandered there, a warm attentive ghost. There was endless freedom in the Lodka now. It was the one free place in Rizhin's new city. Free of everything but memories and a strange nostalgia for faded old oppression. It suited Lom better than the Pension Forbat.

But about one thing he was wrong.

The abandoned Lodka is not empty.

The vyrdalak sisters are light and fragile, almost weightless. They dress in brittle patchwork fabrics of subtle colour unlike anything in Rizhin world, and they have wide nocturnal lovely eyes. Inside them is very little body left at all. They are not of the forest but older and stranger than that.

Lom, entering the Lodka, spilling bright perfumed pheromone clouds of forestness all unawares, drew the hungry vyrdalak sisters to him like a warm candle flame.

'He's beautiful,' said Moth. 'I'd almost forgotten the good smell of trees.'

'But he stinks of angel also,' said Paper. 'Violence is coming back.'

'We should go to him,' said Pigeon. 'One of us must go.'

'Let it be me then,' said Moth. 'Let me. I will go.'

2

Under-Secretary Pavel Ilich Antimos had a natural talent for dealing with complex administration, matured by years of experience. He was subtle, clever, far-sighted, cautious and patient, and he grasped the elegant beauty inherent in meticulous precision and detail. He had been around a long time in large institutions and knew instinctively how to make his way.

Lom's appearance in his apartment had put Pavel in an uncomfortable place, caught between risk and risk. Through a long evening and sleepless night he weighed up options, measured the balance of danger and reward, and by the time he rose in the morning he had decided to do as Lom suggested. He would find the private Chazia archive. It was a dangerous project, but who could tackle it better than he could, and do it without attracting notice? He knew the ways of government offices: the harmless word in the corridor, the enquiry hidden inside the request, the flicker of reaction, the silent tell. The oblique and traceless passage through a filing list.

By the first afternoon Pavel was beginning to feel he was getting somewhere. There was a book of cancelled requisition slips in a box under a counter at the former address of the Ministry of Railways, a building located out towards the old Oxen Quarter and now occupied by an outpost of the Catering Procurement Branch. If certain papers were not there, if a certain circuit of communication had not been closed, he would be several steps nearer the missing archive, which he was increasingly certain did actually exist.

He made a good job of it, a brilliant job actually – Pavel Antimos was a genius at that kind of thing. But Hunder Rond was better, and Rond had had years to prepare, so Pavel had no way of knowing that, when he put in a chit for a particular registry number, a tag on the file triggered a clerk to marry a pink perforated slip with its other half and slide them both into a manila envelope addressed only to a box number. The arrival of the same envelope some hours later in a post room halfway across the city led to a telephone call, which led to another call, to the Parallel Sector, to the office of Hunder Rond.

'It could be nothing,' the caller said. 'A random coincidence.'

'We have anything on this Antimos?' said Rond.

'No. Nothing at all. He has an exemplary record.'

Rond took a decision.

'Let's pick him up,' he said. 'Collect him now.'

'Shall I talk to him?'

Rond looked at his watch.

'No,' he said. 'Leave him to me.'

And so, at the end of the day, when Pavel called in at the Catering Procurement Branch on his way home from work, two women in the black uniform of the Parallel Sector emerged from a side room and took him into custody with little fuss. Pavel showed no rage. He was not distraught. It was a moment he had prepared himself for, many years before, and when it happened he went along with them, numb and automatic. The only thing that really surprised him was how little his arrest actually mattered to him, now that it had finally come. He hated his life. He hated his apartment. He wouldn't miss anything at all.

'You don't need to hurt me,' Pavel said to Rond in the interrogation room. 'I will tell you anything you want. I will say whatever you ask me to say. Let me be useful to you. I help you, and you keep me alive. Yes?'

He was half right anyway. One out of two.

3

Lom encountered the vyrdalak Moth in the reading room of the Central Registry. She came down silently, weightlessly, out of the moon-dim lattice, the glass-broken rust-scabbed ceiling dome, the strut and gondola shadows of the Gaukh Engine. (The Gaukh Wheel! Stationary and permanently benighted sun wheel, ministering idol of information now burned, ash-flake-scattered, released to rain.) Out of the wheel Moth came to him, face first, noiseless and beautiful. Her presence brushed across his face like settling night-pollen. Quiet vortices of neck-prickling wakefulness. She was young with the freshness of ageless moonlight. Youngness is the oldest thing there is.

Close she came and tipped at the air near his face with a quick dry tongue.

'You smell sweet,' she said, wide dark eyes shining. 'Foresty. Earth and trees.' Her sunless skin was warm, her wide mouth purple-dark. 'I'm Moth,' she said. 'Who are you?'

'My name's Vissarion.'

She sniffed.

'No, it isn't,' she said. 'What do you want?'

'I thought no one was here,' said Lom. 'The giants and rusalkas have left, the river's gone silent, but you're still here?'

'The forest is closed, but we're not of the forest. We've always been here.'

'We?'

'Three sisters, all nice girls. I'm the one that wanted to come. My sister Paper thinks you're dangerous, name's-not-Vissarion. She says you stink of angel like Lavrentina. I say you stink of angel like nothing else does now, but not like Lavrentina; you're also sweet. I say you're liminal compendious duplicitous. I say you're beautiful but violent and you've hurt and killed much in your time but you're not dangerous. Which is right, name's-not-Vissarion? Say whether Moth or Paper.'

'Lavrentina?' said Lom when finally she took a breath.

'Changing the subject?' said Moth. 'That's an answer of a kind. Do you know Lavrentina? She said she was coming back but she hasn't come back yet. Do you know where she is?'

'What do you have to do with her?'

'Oh, she knew us! There were more of us then and some of us she *used* for purposes and missions and death. Some liked it. It was purpose. Bez liked it a lot but he hasn't come back either. The word that Lavrentina liked was coterie but we didn't like all that my sisters and me. We kept from Lavrentina far away. Keep to the rafters when Lavrentina's about! Come down when she's gone! The rest of us have gone away but not the three sisters we like it here. Is Lavrentina ever coming back?'

'I don't think so,' said Lom.

'So answer the question then name's-not-Vissarion are you a danger thing?'

'Are you?'

'Not to you.'

'Then Moth,' said Lom. 'The answer is Moth.'

She laughed.

'I like you name's-not-Vissarion even if I don't believe you even if you bring us fire and death.'

'No,' said Lom. 'I don't.'

She frowned.

'We're not stupid,' she said. 'Listen this is how it is. The days pass slowly here it's quiet and cool there's shade and moonlight and the sun doesn't reach in here. There are other places like this across the city. But no giants, no rusalkas. No wind walkers. They've all left the city and gone far to the east under the trees. The Pollandore drew things to itself while it was here including us but all those ways are closed now. We consider ourselves abandoned the new city has no time for us they would hate us if they knew. This red man Kantor has no time for us Kantor you know Kantor? Has a new name but still the same we know we're memory. Ask us what we do here all the time I'll tell you what we do here all the time we read a lot. They took much but they didn't take it all away there's lots still here to read.'

She leaned in confidentially to whisper something in his ear, as if it was a secret.

'The libraries,' she said, 'have libraries in them.'

She paused.

'Do you understand anything I'm talking about?' she said. 'Anything? Anything at all?'

'Yes,' said Lom. 'I do. I understand it all.'

'I think you do,' said Moth. 'There's noise and fire in the city anxiousness hunger bombs it has not stopped yet it goes away but it doesn't it never stops. We go out sometimes to the city to forage. That's better now. More for us. No! Not killers idiot! The bins at the back of the market. You can stay here with us if you want. You'll find plenty to read. Stay out of the basements though the corpses in the mortuary make a lot of noise they thrash about but they can't get out and anyway there's nowhere else for them to go.' She paused again and gazed deeply into his eyes. Hers were warm dark waters. 'I'd like to kiss you, name's-not-Vissarion, you smell good.'

'What?'

'Weren't you listening? I thought you were listening. I want to kiss you. Can I do that? Only once to see what it is like. You're very fierce and warm.'

'If you want,' said Lom. 'If you want to, yes.'

Moth's mouth on his was dry and cool and dark as a well and tasted faintly of fruit. Something inside her was buzzing lazily like a wasp in a sunlit afternoon window.

'What time is it now?' she said.

'I don't know,' said Lom.

'No you don't because the clocks don't work any more. Clocks tell you something, but it's not the time.'

Lom stayed in the Lodka, walking and thinking, long after Moth had left him alone. There was water in the basins and when he tired he went back to the reading room and slept. Better than in the Pension Forbat. Morning sun flooding the broken dome woke him. He didn't want to go back out into the city, but he went.

4

There were three of them in Rizhin's office: Rizhin himself, Hunder Rond, Director of the Parallel Sector, and Secretary for Security and Justice Grigor Ekel.

'We are making good progress, Osip,' Ekel began. He opened a folder and consulted his notes. 'All my best people are working on this. Nothing is more—'

Rizhin held up his hand. 'Rond,' he said. 'Rond first.'

'The rifle that was used to shoot you,' said Rond, 'was a Zhodarev STV-04. Military sniper issue. It was found in the stairwell of the Mirgorod Hotel.'

Ekel jerked forward in his chair. 'You *have* it?' he said. 'You have the weapon? Why wasn't I told of this?'

Rond ignored him. 'Two sets of fingerprints,' he continued, speaking without notes. 'The majority belong to a woman. Name, Cornelius. Trained as a sniper by the VKBD but deserted. Operated as a lone shooter during the siege. History of involvement with dissident elements. Arrested. Deep interrogation. Two years in the Chesma Detention Centre.' He glanced at Ekel. 'Released. Disappeared. Presumed to have left Mirgorod. Evidently did not. This is your shooter, Generalissimus.'

'We must find this woman!' said Ekel. 'Why have the militia not been informed?'

'They have the name, Grigor,' said Rond. 'Didn't they tell you?'

'Two,' said Rizhin quietly. 'You said two sets of prints,'

'Yes. The other gave us a little trouble, but we tracked them down. They belong to a former senior investigator of the Political Police. A career in the eastern provinces. Effective but insubordinate, made no friends, under investigation for antisocial attitudes when he came to Mirgorod six years ago and immediately got into trouble with Chazia. There's been no trace of him since. The assumption was, he was killed on Chazia's orders. His name—'

'Lom,' said Rizhin. 'Vissarion Yppolitovich Lom. From Podchornok.'

Rond looked at Rizhin in surprise. 'You know of him?'

Rizhin was sitting upright and leaning forward intently. 'Is he back, Rond?' he said. 'Is it him?'

'He was in the Hotel Mirgorod at the time you were shot. A clerk and a doorman identified his photograph. The same man took a room at the Pension Forbat the night before Victory Day under the name of Foma Drogashvili. He took the room for a week, stayed there two nights but has not returned since.'

Ekel's face was chalk. Neck flushed pink. The sheaf of papers in his hands trembled. A leaf in the breeze. He glared at Rond.

'None of this was shared—'

'There is more,' Rond said to Rizhin, taking no notice of Ekel. 'I had a conversation recently with an under-secretary in the Office for Progressive Cultural Enlightenment. Antimos. A man with a hitherto blame-free record who suddenly upped and started to search for some old files. Highly sensitive old files. During my conversation with Antimos he mentioned this same Lom. There was a history between them.' Rond glanced at Ekel meaningfully. He was about to enter into topics which Ekel must guess nothing of. 'It concerns a certain six-year-old mission that Lom has apparently reactivated. A certain former intelligence target.'

Rizhin nodded. Expressionless. 'I understand,' he said. 'Please go on.'

'Lom was blackmailing my friend Under-Secretary Antimos,' said Rond. 'He wanted Antimos to find and bring him files that were closed long ago.'

'Thank you, Rond,' said Rizhin. 'That's enough for the moment. I congratulate the Parallel Sector again.' He turned to Ekel. 'And now, Grigor, what do you have for me? Your report please? Tell me, what have the VKBD, the gendarmes, the militia and the secret police done to clear up after the attempt on my life you failed to prevent?'

Ekel was quivering with frustration and rage. Also fear. Primarily fear. He addressed Rizhin but he could not tear his eyes from Hunder Rond.

'This is a stitch-up! My people have done their best, Osip!' Ekel's voice was becoming more high-pitched and nasal. 'I have done my best! But you see what I am up against? Obstruction … hiding evidence … deliberate betrayal! Fuck!' He turned to face Rond. 'I will not let you do this to me! I will not be hung out to dry!'

'Someone must be,' said Rond quietly. 'In circumstances like this, it's an inevitable necessity. You know that, Ekel.'

'But not me, you fucker! Not *me*! You see, Osip, see how he's trying to protect himself, that's all! But I know you see through him, like I do.'

'No, Grigor,' said Rizhin. 'It is you. I smell conspiracy on you. It's on your breath. You stink of it.' He put his right hand – five fat fingers – on his heart. 'You hurt me, Grigor, here. Just here. I gave you all you have. I gave you my trust, and you repay me how? You are complicit in this attempt on my life. There is no other explanation.'

'No! Osip, please! I have been more than just loyal. I *like* you, Osip. I'm not like the others. I *love* you. As a man I am your *friend*.'

'We will have the names of your gang out of you, Grigor. Then we will see.'

'The thing is,' Rond said to Rizhin after Grigor Ekel had been taken away, 'we think the archive Lom is looking for may actually exist. But we don't yet know where it is.'

'Archive?'

'Lavrentina Chazia kept her own personal files, and it seems they have not been destroyed. They are still out there somewhere. Antimos was on their trail but he hadn't found them yet. They're likely to contain compromising material.'

'Of course they'd be *compromising*. That mad old vixen Lavrentina Chazia was a cunning poisonous bitch. Find what she kept, Rond, and bring it all to me.'

'Of course,' said Hunder Rond. 'We'll find the Cornelius woman too.'

Rizhin shrugged. 'Naturally, but she won't be anything much. Find Lom. He's the one that matters. Him I want alive. Him I want to talk to.'

5

The railway station at Belatinsk is crowded for the departure of the Mirgorod train. Forshin's Philosophy League has booked an entire carriage. They struggle with chests and suitcases full of books and papers. The atmosphere is grim determination under a bleak grey sky. Dusty wind whips at their clothes.

'I put on a mask of good cheer for the others,' says Forshin to Kamilova, 'and perhaps above all for myself, but I do not underestimate the task ahead.'

There are forms to be filled out in triplicate. Municipal officials search their luggage for what they can confiscate. Brutskoi's wife weeps and protests at the loss of all her roubles and silver. A gendarme ruffles Yeva and Galina's hair in search of hidden jewels.

'Let us exult in leaving this place, comrades,' says Forshin, waving his cane at the lowering sky. 'We carry with us the flame of our people's future. No customs officer can confiscate that!'

Kamilova and the girls climb aboard at last. They have no baggage. Yeva and Galina huddle together, looking out of the window. The locomotive trembles. Steam is up.

'Don't worry, Galina,' says Yeva. 'You know we'll see our mother soon.'

6

Lom reached Kommunalka Subbotin No. 19 early and ran up the steps two at a time in fresh midsummer Rizhin-morning sunshine. There was a fresh efficient woman in the glassy walled lobby cubicle: patterned cardigan, horn-rim spectacles, blond hair tied back, young and cheerful, not unsmiling, ready for the day.

'What is the number of the apartment of Elena Cornelius, please?' he asked her.

'I'm sorry,' she said. 'There is nobody of that name. Not here.'

'Perhaps she left recently?'

'I've worked here ever since the building opened. Eleven months. I know all the residents. There is no Cornelius here and there never has been. I'm afraid you have the wrong address.'

It was not yet eight o'clock. Lom waited on a bench with a view of the exit. Perhaps she was using another name. Perhaps she had married again. It was possible.

Forty minutes later he saw her come out alone, in her dark clothes again, intense and purposeful, not looking around. She was coming his way. When she got near he rose to meet her.

'Can we talk?' he said. 'Not here. Is there a place?'

'I have to be at work.'

'Say you were sick.'

'I'm never sick.'

'Then they'll believe you.'

She hesitated.

'Please,' he said.

'All right then. OK.'

She took him to a workers' dining hall. Long wooden benches and sticky chrome-legged tables. Yellow-flecked laminate tabletops. The floor was sticky too. The place was crowded with people taking breakfast – young women mostly, girls in sneakers and overalls with tied-back hair. Sweet smells of make-up and scent at war with the black bread and apricot conserve, tea and coffee and steam. The din of cutlery and crockery, the chatter of women with the workday ahead.

Lom and Elena found a space at the end of a bench, near a wide window which looked across an empty paved square to an identical dining hall on the other side.

'Where's Maroussia?' said Elena. She held her cup awkwardly in clawed, broken hands.

'I lost her.'

Elena nodded. In the aftermath of war, when half the world, it seemed, was lost, you didn't ask. People told you or they did not. The stories were always more or less the same.

'I lost my children,' Elena said. 'Galina and Yeva. You remember them?'

'Of course,' said Lom.

'The building they were in is gone, built over now, but I go there every day, and when they come back they'll find me waiting. They're not dead, I know that at least. Of course I'd know if they were killed. A mother would feel that, wouldn't she? In her bones? They were taken away but nobody would tell me who took them or where. They all denied knowing anything about it – *Taken away? Nobody was taken away* – but some of them were lying, I could see. There's a post office box in my name, so when Galina or Yeva writes me a letter it should go there. The system is very reliable and good, everyone says that.'

'Is that why you want to kill Rizhin?' said Lom quietly. 'Because of what happened to Galina and Yeva?'

'Not his fault,' said Elena. 'Before him, that. That was others. Rizhin came later.'

'What happened to your hands, Elena?' said Lom.

'These?' She shrugged.

'Did they do that in the camps? Did they interrogate you?'

'These are nothing, not compared to what they did to others … not compared to …' She stopped. Looked out of the window.

'They hurt someone you knew?' said Lom.

'What good is this doing? Talking never does any good. None at all.'

'Who was he?'

'He was trying to make a new start,' she said, still looking out across the sunlit concrete square. 'New ideas. A better world after the war. Some of us believed in that. We tried … We wanted to … Why would I tell *you* this? You wanted to stop me killing Rizhin. You were trying to save him. Weren't you?'

'Yes,' said Lom. 'And now I'm trying to stop you trying again.'

'But … why?'

'Because simply killing Rizhin is no use at all. It's worse than useless: it would be disastrous. It's the idea of him that needs to be destroyed. Killing the man will only make the idea of him stronger. Things will only be worse if you kill him. Much, much worse.'

'No,' said Elena. 'You're wrong. Why do you think that?'

'I don't think it,' he said. 'I know it.'

'What do you want from me? Why are you here?'

'I want your help. I want to bring Rizhin down. Not kill him, but worse than kill him. Destroy him. Ruin him. Ruin his memory. Make it so people will hate all his plans and all he wants to do, and never do any of it simply because it was what he wanted.'

'How? How would you do this?'

'With information. With proof of what he really is.'

'And you have this?'

'Not yet. I should have it tomorrow. But I'll need help to use it properly. That's why I came to see you. I thought you might know people. You could put me in contact—'

'What kind of people?'

'Like you said. People with new ideas. Do you know people like that? People I could talk to?'

'Maybe. Perhaps they would talk to you. You could show them what you have.'

'I'd need to meet them first, before I brought them anything.'

Elena looked hard at Lom. Her thin dark face. Her broken nose. Eyes burning just this side of crazy.

'I don't know,' she said. 'But Maroussia trusted you.'

'And this is Maroussia's work I'm doing. Unfinished business.'

Elena moved her head slightly. That connected with her.

'Is it?' she said.

'Yes, it is.'

She took a deep breath. 'OK. Come with me. I'll take you there now.'

7

Maroussia Shaumian walks in the forest and as she walks she picks things up. Small things, the litter of forest life that snags her gaze and answers her in some instinctive wordless way. Smooth small greenish stones from the bed of a stream. Twigs of rowan. Pine cones. Galls and cankers. Pellets and feathers of owl. A trail of dark ivy stem, rough with root hairs. A piece of root like a brown mossy face. The body of a shrew, dead at the path-side, a tiny packet of fur and frail bone, the bright black drupelet of an open eye. She stops and gathers them and tucks them in her satchel.

When she rests she tips the satchel out and sorts through them. Holds them one by one, interrogates them, listens, and shapes them. Knots them together with grass, threads them on bramble lengths, fixes them with dabs of sticky mud and resin smears. She is making strange objects.

Each one as she makes it becomes a tiny part of her, but separated off. Each one is an expression, a distillation, a vessel and an awakening: not the whole of her, but some small and very specific part, some particular and exact feeling, one certain memory that she separates from herself and makes a thing apart. Some don't work. The investing doesn't take, but slips through the gaps and fades. Those, the emptied ones, the ones that die, she buries under earth and moss and leaves. But many do take, and she knows each one and gives it a name. Lumb. Hope. Wythe. Frith. Scough. Carse. Arker. Haugh. Lade. Clun. Mistall. Brack. Lund. In the evenings she hangs them at intervals around her camp. They dangle and twist and open themselves to the night, to watch and listen while she sleeps.

No one showed her how to do this, not Fraiethe or the father or the Seer Witch of Bones. She found her own way to it.

She comes to where a wide shallow beck crosses the path, running fast and cold, spilling across mounded rocks. Trees on either side lean across it, leaf-heads merged, darkening the water. She drinks a little from the stream and sits a while on the bank. Makes a leaf boat, pinned in shape with thorns, weighted with pebble ballast.

When the leaf boat is ready she reaches for one of the figures she's made. Brings it close to her eye and studies the tiny striations on the twig bark, the exact complexity of grass-stem knots, the russets of moss, the lichen maps like moth wings. She tries to feel her way into it, curious to find what part of herself it is that the object holds. But it is opaque now and keeps its own counsel. She puts it in the boat.

Holding the boat in one hand, carefully, raising it high, she makes her way out into the beck to a dark wet flat of rock. Downstream of the rock the stream has dug a pool, dark brown, slower turning. She crouches and leans out to set the leaf boat on the water and let it go. It turns a while, uncertain, listing, testing the way, then settles and rights itself. The water carries it clear of the matted litter on the bank. It wobbles and turns, tiny under the trees, until it goes beyond where she can see.

It is not a message, not even a messenger, but an explorer: a voyager sent ahead where she can't yet go.

All morning the ground climbs under her feet and the trees grow sparser, lower, more widely spaced, until in the middle of the day she crests a rise and finds herself on a scrubby hilltop among hazel and thorn, looking across a wide shallow valley. The grey-brown canopy of leaf-falling woodland spreads out at her feet. Solitary hunting birds circle below her on loose-stretched flaggy wings. A range of low hills on the further side rises into distance and mist. Without trees above her she can see the sky.

Smirrs of mist hang over thorn and bramble scrub, pale and cold, motionless and patient, like breath-clouds: the trees' breathing. The finger-touch of damp air chill is on her face. Her hands are bunched in her pockets for warmth. She is walking on a thick mat of fallen leaves and wind-broken tips and twigs, bleached of colour. It crunches underfoot. There is winter coming in this part of the forest. Every edge and rib of leaf has a fine sawtooth edge of frost.

The body of the lynx lies on its side in a shallow pool as if it has drowned. Maroussia crouches beside it to look. The pool is dark and skinned with ice: forest litter is caught in it, and tiny bubble trails. The lynx is big like a large dog: sharp ears, a flattened cat-snout, ice-matted fur. She puts out her hand to touch its side. It feels cold and hard. She closes her eyes and reaches out with her mind, groping her way, and touches a faint distant hint of warmth. A last failing ember. A trace. Life, determined, hanging on.

She isn't dead. She isn't gone. Not yet.

Maroussia feels her way cautiously into the cold-damaged body. The sour smell of death is there: an obstacle, an uneasy darkness she has to push through. She feels the death seeping into her and pushes it back, trembling with revulsion.

'Get out,' she whispers aloud. *Get away from me.*

She is feeling her way inside the lynx, looking for the core of life, reaching out to it. *Here*, she is saying. *I am here. Where are you?*

The lynx barely flickers in response, so faintly that Maroussia doubts at first that it is there at all. But it stirs. She catches a weak sense of lynx life.

Who are you? she says to the lynx life. *Who are you?*

Leave me. I am death.

No. Not yet. Not quite.

I am tired and death. I am the stinker. The rotting one.

Not yet. Take something from me. I want to share.

It is too much and I am death.

I have life. Share some.

I am lynx and do not share.

The lynx is faint and far away. Drifting. Maroussia pushes some of her self into it, shoving, forcing like she did with the objects she made, but stronger. Harsher. Until it hurts to do it.

Who are you? she says again to the lynx.

Leave me alone.

Who are you? Remember who you are.

Maroussia pushes more of herself into the lynx, feeling the weakening of herself, the draining of certainty, the forest around her grow fainter. The sound of death is like a river, near. She will have to be careful. But the lynx is stronger now. Maroussia can see her, as if the lynx is at the back of a low dark cave. There is something behind her that she cannot quite see. A shadow moving fast across the floor.

Who are you? says Maroussia again.

Plastered fur and soaking hair.

More than that, says Maroussia.

Weakness and all-cold all-hungry and wet and full of dying cub. All strength gone.

More than that!

I am shadow-muzzle, dark-tooth, wind-dark and rough. Faintness and lick and dapple, and pushing, and bloody hair. I am mewler and swallower and want, the shrivelled one, the suckler. I do not need to share.

Take it then. Because you can. Maroussia pushes again. *Who are you?*

Meat-scent on the air at dusk. Salt on the tongue and the dark sweet taste of blood. I am the eater of meat. I do not share. I do not need to share.

No, you don't.

I am shit in the wet grass. Milk on the cub's breath and the cold smell of a dead thing. I am the bitch's lust for the dog I do not need. I am the abdomen swollen full as an egg, the pink bud suckler in the dark of the earth den.

Yes.

I am the runner hot among the trees. Noiseless climber. Sour breath in the tunnel's darkness and teeth in the badger's neck. The crunch of carrion and the thirsty suck and the flow of warm sweet blood-or-is-it-milk. Shrew flesh is distasteful, and so is the flesh of bears. I am shit and blood and milk and salty tears. I do not share!

No. But you can take.

I am the lynx in the rain with the weight of cubs in my belly. Cub-warm

sleep under the snow, ice-bearded. I am life and I am called death. I am
the answer to my own question, and if you look for me, I am the finding.
Leave me alone now. I am not dying but I want to sleep.

Eat something first. Then I will carry you and you can sleep.

My teeth are sharp. My claws are sharp.

Don't bite me.

I do not share.

OK.

Maroussia sits on the ground and lifts the animal into her lap. Holds
a piece of pigeon to its mouth. Lynx glares at her but takes it and chews
at it warily. Resentfully. Maroussia sees the needle-sharp whiteness of
teeth.

The Pollandore inside her gives an alien grin. The growing human
child in her belly stirs and kicks. She is alone and very far from home.

8

The place Elena Cornelius took Lom to was a wide field of
broken concrete and brick heaps and hummocks of dark
weed-growth. It rolled to a distant skyline of ragged scorched
facades.

Such landscapes were everywhere in Mirgorod. Lom had seen other
war-broken towns and cities that were all burned-out building shells
and ruined streets – grids of empty windows showing gaps of sky
behind – but during the siege of Mirgorod the defenders had pulled
the ruins down and levelled the wreckage, creating mile after mile of
impassable rubble mazy with pits and craters, foxholes and rat runs
and sniper cover, all sown with landmines, tripwire grenades, vicious
nooses, shrapnel-bomb snares and caltrops. Trucks and half-tracks
were useless. Battle tanks beached themselves. The enemy had to
clamber across every square yard on foot, clearing cellar by cellar with
flame-throwers and gas. Artillery and airborne bombardment could
not destroy what was already blasted flat.

Elena led him through pathless acres of brick and plaster and dust.
A girl emerged from one of the larger rubble piles and passed them

with a smile, neat and clean and combing her hair. Two men in business suits came up a gaping stairwell. A woman in a head cloth with a market basket. Patches of ground had been cleared for cabbage and potato. There was woodsmoke and the smell of food cooking. Soapy water. The foulness of latrines.

'People *live* here?' said Lom.

'They must live somewhere,' said Elena. 'There aren't enough apartments, not yet, and what there is is far away, and there are so few buses ... For many people, this is better.'

She pulled aside a sheet of corrugated iron and went down broken concrete steps. Knocked at a door.

'Konnie? Konnie? It's Elena.'

The door opened. A woman in her early twenties, vivid red hair straight and thin to her shoulders, green eyes in a pale freckled face. A clever face. Bookish. Intense. Interesting. She looked like a student. When she saw Elena her eyes widened.

'Elena! Shit!' She grabbed her by the arm and pulled her forward. 'Come in quickly. Maksim is here. We can help. Maksim!' she called over her shoulder. 'It's Elena! Elena is here!' Then she saw Lom and frowned. 'Who's this?'

'A friend,' said Elena. 'It's OK, Konnie. He's a friend.'

'Oh.'

'I trust him,' said Elena. 'I want you to help him.'

Konnie hesitated.

'OK,' she said 'Then you'd better come in.'

Lom followed the women through the entrance into a low basement space. Bare plaster walls lit by a grating in the ceiling with a pane of dirty glass laid across it. The room was divided in two by a tacked-up orange curtain. It smelled of damp brick. The part this side of the curtain had planks on trestles for a table. There were two chairs, a sagging couch, a single-ring gas stove on a bench in the corner.

'You have to get away, Elena,' Konnie was saying. 'The militia have your name. They know it was you that shot Rizhin. They're searching for you. You have to leave the city.'

'No,' said Elena. 'I'm not leaving. Never. My girls—'

'Maksim!' Konnie called again.

There was a stack of books on the table. Lom glanced at them. Drab covers with ragged pages and blurry print. Wrinkled typescripts pinned with rusting staples. Dangerous thinking, circulated hand to hand. He scanned the titles. *The Ice Axe Manifesto. Bulletin of the Present Times. Listen, We Are Breathing.* Someone – Konnie presumably, it was a woman's handwriting – had been making pencil notes in a yellow exercise book. Lom picked it up. '*ALL GOVERNMENT,*' she had written, '*rests on possibility of violence against own citizens. Cf Jaspersen! – Principles of Interiority Chap 4. Apeirophobia.*'

'Hey!' said Konnie. 'Put that down.'

'Sorry.'

Maksim came out, buttoning his shirt, from behind the orange curtain, where presumably there was a bed. His hair was long and tangled. He was tall, taller than Lom. He looked as if he'd just woken up.

'Elena?' he said. 'What's happening?' He saw Lom and Konnie glaring at him. 'Who is this?'

'It's OK, Maksim,' said Elena. 'He's a friend.'

'What's he doing here?'

'I'm looking for advice,' said Lom. 'Maybe some information. Elena said you might—'

'What's your name?' said Maksim. He was trying to get the situation under control. An officer, used to command.

'Lom.'

Konnie frowned.

'I know that name. They're looking for you too.'

Lom looked at her sharply. 'Who is?'

'The militia. They have two names for the shooting of Rizhin: Cornelius and Lom.'

'No!' said Elena. 'Not him. He wasn't there.'

'How do you know this?' Lom said to Konnie.

Konnie shook her head. 'We know.'

'I was on my own,' Elena was saying. 'He only came later.'

'I let them see me in the hotel. I put my prints on the gun.'

'You did that deliberately?' said Elena.

'Yes.'

'Why?'

'To make things happen. To get their attention. To get involved.' *Pull a thread. See where it leads.* 'They've done well. I thought it would take them longer.'

'That's insane,' said Maksim.

'It was quick,' said Lom. 'I can't do what I do from the outside look-ing in.'

'And what exactly is it you do?' said Maksim.

Lom looked him in the eye. 'I'm here to bring Rizhin down.'

Maksim pulled the outside door shut.

'You've put us in danger coming here,' he said.

'I'm sorry,' said Elena. 'I didn't know. About the militia. The names. I'd never have come here if I'd known.'

'You have to get out of the city quickly,' said Maksim. 'Both of you. We have a car. Konnie, you will drive—'

'No,' said Elena. 'I'm staying. I'm not going anywhere. I can't leave Mirgorod. It's impossible. I must be here when Galina and Yeva come home.'

'Elena, it's not safe,' said Konnie.

'They won't find me at the Subbotin. I am Ostrakhova there.'

'They'll come for you. They always find you in the end.'

'The VKBD will hunt you down,' said Maksim. 'You cannot imag-ine. You cannot begin to imagine how they will hunt you now.'

'You have no children, Maksim. I will not abandon my girls.'

'Six years, Elena, it's been six years. I hope they survived the bomb-ing, but even if they did … They're not coming back. You must know that.'

'My girls are not dead. They were taken but they will find their way back.'

'You must disappear now,' said Maksim. 'If they capture you, if they question you … you will endanger us all, Elena.'

Konnie put a hand on Maksim's arm. 'Please. Enough.'

'You don't need to leave the city,' Lom said to Elena. 'You can come with me. I know a place. They won't find you there, and you can stay as long as you want. You'll be safe.'

'With you?' said Maksim. 'Who the fuck are you anyway? Where did you come from? We don't know you.'

'I trust him, Maksim,' said Elena. 'I want you to help him. That's why we're here.' She turned to Lom. 'Maksim is an old friend,' she said. 'A comrade. He was in the army, an officer, a good fighter. After the war he was one of the ones who wouldn't go back to the old ways.'

'You're right to be cautious,' Lom said to Maksim. 'I would do the same. But I just need some advice, that's all. We're on the same side.'

'Side?' said Maksim. 'What side is that?'

'The side that Rizhin's not on.'

Maksim studied him. Weighing him up. 'Were you in the army?'

'No,' said Lom. 'I was with the Political Police.'

'The *police?*'

'It was a long time ago.'

'Maksim,' said Elena, 'I'm only asking you to listen to what he's got to say.'

'But …' Maksim let out a long slow breath. 'Oh shit. OK. You're here now. So what do you want?'

'If you had proof of something that could bring Rizhin down,' said Lom, 'if you had documentation which, if it was used properly, would expose him and empty him out and turn the world against him, would you know what to do with it?'

'What kind of proof?' said Maksim. 'Proof of what?'

'Later,' said Lom. 'Say there was such proof, what would you do with it? How could it be used? Do you have the means? Are you prepared for this?'

Maksim thought for a moment.

'It's good, is it?' he said. 'This proof? It's something dangerous? Something big?'

'Yes. It would be explosive. It would make Rizhin's position impossible. Everyone would turn against him. Everyone. He'd be finished. He would fall.'

Maksim's eyes gleamed.

'That would be a great thing indeed,' he said. Then he frowned. 'But no. We couldn't use it. We wouldn't have a chance. We haven't the means. We are too few.'

'We know journalists,' said Konnie. 'The newspapers—'

'The papers wouldn't print it,' said Maksim. 'Never.'

'The Archipelago then. We have friends at the embassy.'

'If it came from the Archipelago, who would believe it? It would be dismissed as propaganda and lies.'

'Then wouldn't you need …?' Konnie began and trailed off.

'Yes?' said Lom.

'Someone in the government. Someone big, with power and influence, who isn't afraid of Rizhin. Someone who could step in and push him out.'

'They're all Rizhin's creatures,' said Maksim. 'They're all terrified of him, and anyway whoever ousted Rizhin would be just as bad, or worse.'

'All of them?' said Lom. 'Is there no one?'

'Well.' Konnie paused. 'There's Kistler. You hear things about him. There are rumours. He has connections … Kistler could be worth a try. Maksim?'

'Maybe,' said Maksim. 'Maybe Kistler. Possibly. He's stronger than the others. He has an independent view – sometimes, apparently.'

'Do you have a link to this Kistler?' said Lom. 'Are you in communication with him?'

'No,' said Konnie. 'Nothing that firm, but there is talk about him. Like I said, you hear things.'

'How would I reach him?'

'I'm not sure about this,' said Maksim. 'I wouldn't trust Kistler more than any of the others. But … we have the address of his house. We have all of them. We know where they live.'

'Give it to me, please,' said Lom. 'I'll go and see what this Kistler has to say.'

He was flying blind. Throwing stones at random, hoping to hit something. But he didn't know another way.

'Like I said, it's just a rumour,' said Konnie. 'A feeling. You shouldn't place any weight on what I say.'

'It's the best lead I've got,' said Lom. 'The only one.'

'Do you have this proof, then?' said Maksim as Lom and Elena were leaving. 'Really?'

'No,' said Lom. 'Not yet. But tomorrow, I hope so. I should have it on Wednesday.'

Maksim looked puzzled. 'But today is Wednesday,' he said.

'Is it?' said Lom. 'Is it?'

The clocks tell you something, but not the time.

9

Rizhin had not yet appointed a successor at the Agriculture Ministry for the unfortunate Vladi Broch, killed by the assassin's bullet meant for another, so Broch's deputy, an assiduous man named Varagan, was summoned in his place to the weekly meeting of the Central Committee.

For Varagan this was a once-in-a-lifetime opportunity. His chance to step out from the shadows and demonstrate his quality. Poor Varagan. A man of prodigious administrative capacity and earnest zeal, he had profoundly mistaken his purpose, having got it firmly (and regrettably) fixed in his head that it was his job as Under-Secretary for Food Production to identify and address the causes of growing starvation in the eastern oblasts of the New Vlast.

When Rizhin called on him to speak, he rose and hooked his wire spectacles behind his ears, cleared his throat nervously and began to introduce his report. He was a freshly washed sheep among wolves.

'Everywhere the population shows the demographic impact of war,' he began. 'Six hundred men for every thousand women, and worse among those of working age. The rebuilding of our factories proceeds far too slowly. Water, electricity and sewerage everywhere are in an abysmal condition. Above all the prices for agricultural producers are ruinously low, though the prices in shops still rise—'

Rizhin raised a hand to interrupt. 'Is it not your own ministry, Varagan, that fixes these prices?'

'Precisely, sir. I have recommendations which I will come to. I am sketching the background first. The rural populace has fled to the cities. They eat dogs and horses and the bark of trees. In many of our towns we see black-marketeering. Gangsterism. Bribery. The rule of this committee in such places is nominal at best.'

Rizhin sat back in his chair, doodling wolf heads as he listened with half-closed eyes.

'Steady, Varagan,' said Kistler quietly. 'Remember where you are.'

But Rizhin waved Varagan on. 'Let the man speak,' he said. 'Let us hear what he has to say.'

The committee looked on in silence as Varagan methodically ploughed his furrow.

'Grain is exported to the Archipelago even as our own people starve,' he said. 'Our errors are compounded by poor harvests. Famine is widespread and growing. Deaths are to be counted in hundreds of thousands, perhaps millions, and—'

'But surely,' said Rizhin, raising his eyelids and looking round the table, fixing them one by one with a stony gaze, 'this is not right? Did not our old friend Broch tell us just the other week that this talk of famine was a fairy tale? Am I not right, colleagues? He said so often. And you are telling us now, Varagan, that Vladi Broch's reports were false?'

Varagan looked suddenly sick, as if he had been punched in the stomach.

'I ...' he began. 'I ...'

'Who drafted Vladi's reports for him?' said Rizhin. 'Who produced those false statistics?' He made a show of riffling back through old papers in his folder. 'Come, Varagan, I want the name.'

Poor Varagan was shaking visibly now. He was beginning to understand what he had done. The pit he had dug for himself with his own honest shovel. His face was blood-red. His mouth opened and shut soundlessly. Kistler wondered if he might collapse.

Varagan snatched at a glass of water and drank it down.

'But people are *dying*,' he said, struggling to speak. Mouth dry, voice catching. 'I have ideas for saving them. I have drawn up a programme ...'

'And yet,' said Rizhin, 'week after week we have had reports to the precise contrary. Tables of figures. I have them here.' He lifted a file from his pile. 'Figures from the Secretariat of Food Production. Signed by your own hand, Secretary Varagan. How do you account for this? How do you explain?'

'I ...' said Varagan again, eyes wide in panic, and snapped his mouth shut.

Rizhin threw the file down on the table.

'There is no famine in the New Vlast,' he said. 'It is impossible. What there is, is pilfering and theft. Corrupt individualism! Starvation is the ploy of reactionary and deviationist elements. Our enemies hate our work so much they let their families die. The distended belly of a child is a sign of resistance. It is good news. It confirms we are on the right track that our opponents grow so desperate.'

'Yes,' whispered Varagan, casting desperately around the table for support, but no one caught his eye. 'Of course. I see clearly now. I have misinterpreted the data. I have made a mistake. An honest mistake.'

Rizhin was suddenly trembling with anger.

'Mistake?' he said. 'Oh no, I think not. This is a power play, Varagan. Transparent viciousness. You wriggle now, oh yes, you squirm. That is always the way of it with men like you. First you come here and throw accusations at your own dead boss, yes, and at others around this table, honest hard-working fellows, and now you row backwards. I know your type, my friend. You are ambitious! You would rise! You ache for preferment, and you cover your tracks. You are at fault and blame everyone but yourself. Well I see now that there is someone to blame, and it is you.'

'No,' whispered Varagan. 'I wished only—'

Kistler leaned across to him. 'Leave the room, man,' he said quietly. 'This agenda item is closed.'

Varagan nodded. Wordless and methodical, shaking like a leaf, he collected his papers. Unhooked his wire spectacles from his ears and popped them into the top pocket of his jacket. Rose, turned, pushed back his chair and went out slowly into the lonely cold.

10

After sundown in the balmy nights of summer the well din-nered families of the List, Rizhin's plush elite, take to the paths of the Trezzini Pleasure Gardens in the Pir-Anghelsky Park. Entering the blazing gateway of crystal glass – lit from within by a thousand tiny flickering golden lights – they move among pagodas and boating lakes. Arched bridges, tulips and water lilies. Straight-haired girls walk there with mothers sleekly plump. Awkward boys with arro-gant blank eyes wince as father calls to father with penetrating voice. There is music here. Sugared chestnuts and roasting pig and candyfloss. Take a pedalo among enamel-bright and floodlit waterfowl! Visit the

Aquarium and the Pantomime Theatre! Ride the Dragon Swing! The Spinner! See the pierrot and the dancing bear!

The List regarded their pleasures coolly, with the assurance of natural entitlement. They were the experts. The competent ones. You would not know that a handful of years ago none of them was here. No old money in Papa Rizhin country! But the polished faces of the List reflect the coloured lamps strung among wax-leaved dark exotic trees. Their soaps and perfumes mingle with evening-heavy blossom.

Lom stayed in the darkness under the trees. Pavel had chosen this meeting place to make a point – *This is the coming world. Here it is. I'm at home and familiar among these people. I belong here, and you, Lom, you ghost, you do not* – but also because the konditorei was on an island in the shallow lake reached by a causeway. Light blazed from the filigreed iron glasshouse and blazed reflections off dark waters. Within, the List at white-linen-covered tables ate pastries from tiered plates and drank chocolate from gleaming china jugs. The gilt-framed mirror behind the central counter showed the backs of master patissiers and konditiers: their crisp white tunics, shaved necks, pomaded hair.

The narrow causeway was the one way in and the one way out.

Pavel Ilich Antimos was achingly visible, sitting alone at a table in the window. Lom had watched him for half an hour and he had not moved. He might as well have been under a spotlight. *Here I am. See me. Come to me.* He stared at the untouched chocolate in front of him, twisting a knotted napkin, his injured right shoulder hunched up against his neck. He never looked up. Never looked around.

The konditorei was crowded but the tables near Pavel were empty. Perhaps the customers had been warned away; more likely they shunned him through instinct: the unerring sense of the List for avoiding the tainted. The untouchable. The fallen. Even from across the lake Lom could detect the sour grey stink and sadness of the already dead.

Ten feet from Lom, in the dark of the lakeside trees, a corporal of the VKBD was also observing Pavel Antimos. From time to time he scanned the brightly lit approach to the causeway through binoculars. There were three other VKBD at intervals in the shadow near Lom, and no doubt there were more on the other side of the lake. Probably they had a team in the konditorei as well. Lom couldn't see them but they would be there.

Poor Pavel. He wouldn't have gone to the VKBD with his story

– he'd have known that was suicidal – so they must have caught him with his fingers in the drawer. And they'd taken the trouble to keep him alive and use him as bait. So they wanted Lom too. That told Lom something. That was information.

He could have simply slipped away, back in under the rhododendron trees, and left the VKBD to their watching, but the corporal ten feet from him had a pistol on his hip and Lom wanted that. He needed to broaden his options.

He waited till the brass orchestra in the bandstand reached the finale of 'We Fine Dragoons'. They made a lot of noise. The corporal didn't hear him coming.

11

An hour later, with no secret Rizhin file from Pavel Antimos but a VKBD pistol in his pocket, Lom re-entered the Lodka by underground ways. He came up past empty cells and interrogation rooms into the tile-floored central atrium. There was no moonlight. He felt the corridors, the stairwells, the doorways, the ramifications of office and conference room as spaciousness and slow currents in the air. Opened up, arboreal and dark-adapted, Lom scented out his way. Forest percipience. He knew the difference between solid dark and airy dark. He felt the invitation of certain thresholds, the threat beyond others; he heard the echo of entranceless passageways on the far side of walls, and the restless shuffling of the basement mortuary dead.

This forest-opened world was not like *seeing*; it was *knowing* and *feeling*. Everything – absolutely everything – was alive, and Lom shared the life of it. Raw participation. The boundaries of himself were uncertain and permeable. Shifting frontier crossings. He felt history, watchfulness, weight and presence.

And there was something else. Another spectrum altogether. Liminal angel senses came into play, the residuum of the coin-size lozenge of angel flesh fitted into his skull in childhood and gouged out by Chazia; the residuum also of Chazia's angel suit, its substance seared into him and joined with his by Uncle Vanya's atomic starburst at Novaya Zima. Angel particles and angel energies had soaked through him to the blood-warm matter at the heart of bone. Synapses sparkled with alien angel speed and grace. By the faint afterglow of the Lodka's radiating warmth, Lom saw with a crisp and prickling non-human clarity that needed no more light.

Always at some level he was these two things: the heart of the forest and the heartless gaze of the spaciousness inside atoms, the spaciousness separating stars. He saw further and better in the dark. Darkness simplified.

In the Lodka's cool central atrium (a huge airy space lined by abandoned reception desks, a plaza of echoing linoleum, a node for wide staircases heavily balustered and swing-door exits, surfaces dust-skinned and speckled with the faeces of small animals) Moth was waiting for him. She had sensed his perfumed brightness coming, and he knew she was there: from several floors below he had felt her agitation.

'Men are here!' she hissed. 'They have lamps and guns. We know the black uniforms they wear, my sisters and I. They are *Streltski*!' She spat the word. Anger and hatred. 'They have your friend. Some threaten her; others look for papers.'

Lom had brought Elena Cornelius to the Lodka before he went to look for Pavel in Pir-Anghelsky Park. *She is my friend*, he'd said to Moth. *She's here under my protection*. He'd thought she would be safer here than at her apartment.

'It's bad the black Streltski are here,' Moth was saying. 'We remember them from long ago, but Josef Kantor who is Papa Rizhin brought them back. Streltski burn us! If they find us they burn! Two of us they roasted in the Apraksin. My sisters blame you for bringing them here and for bringing this woman here, and they blame me for this because of you. There will be a bad end of things now.'

'How many men and where?' said Lom.

'Two with the woman in the reading room under the wheel and two in the locked corridor nearby where they look for Lavrentina's private archive. I heard them say that.' She grinned, a wide dark gaping slash of mouth. 'But they will not find what they want it is not where they look.'

'Lavrentina's archive?' said Lom. 'I want that too. I need that very much.'

Was it possible the papers he needed were still in the Lodka? That Chazia hadn't moved them before she left for Novaya Zima with the Pollandore? In the chaos of the withdrawal and burning of that day, it could have happened.

'My sisters are right,' said Moth. 'It's because of you the Streltski are come here where we were forgotten and safe.'

'Moth?' said Lom 'Do you know where Lavrentina's papers are?'

Her wide nocturnal eyes flashed in the darkness.

'The black uniforms will not find them,' she said. 'However long they search. We took them to be safe. Lavrentina will want them when she comes back.'

'Lavrentina isn't coming back,' said Lom. 'She's dead. It's Rizhin who wants her archive now. He must know I'm looking for it, and that's a danger to him. He wants to find it first. ' *Poor Pavel. And Chazia's papers here all the time.* 'That's why he sent the Parallel Sector here – I mean the Streltski.'

'Oh?' said Moth. 'Lavrentina is dead?' She reacted to that with the incurious indifference of the non-human who measure their lives in centuries. Then he felt her gaze in the darkness harden and grow colder. Dangerous. 'And now you want to take Lavrentina's papers away from us? You didn't say.'

'One file, Moth. Only one file. Lavrentina had papers about Josef Kantor that I need to find. I didn't tell you before because I didn't think the papers were still here.'

'Kantor papers? Papers that endanger *Kantor*? Kantor whose Streltski drive us out and burn us '

'Yes.'

Lom felt Moth smile. A malevolent smile. A playful smile with rows of pin-sharp blade-edge venomous teeth.

'I could take you there,' she said. 'My sisters, though …'

'Elena first,' said Lom. 'The men with the guns.'

12

Hunder Rond swept his torch across empty shelves.
'Well?' he said.
'This is the correct room,' said Lieutenant Vrebel. 'There's
no mistake.'

'So where are the fucking papers?'

'According to the register they should still be here. Permission to remove them was issued to a Captain Iliodor but the completion slip was
never matched. He did not come for them. They were never released.'

'This Iliodor,' said Rond. 'Who is he?'

'He was Commander Chazia's aide,' said Vrebel. 'He went missing
the first day of the withdrawal, and he was presumed killed in the first
bombing raids though no body was found. The paperwork is clear.
Chazia commissioned him to remove her archive to some other place
but he never did. That's what Pavel Antimos was on to when we took
him.'

Rond played his torch over the emptied shelving again. 'So where
are Chazia's files now?'

'I cannot say, Director Rond. I do not know.'

'Do you understand,' said Rond, 'how dangerous those papers could
be? Who knows what poison that woman stored away for her own
use and protection. If such an archive falls in the hands of antisocial
elements, or rivals for the Presidium ... This archive must be found,
Vrebel. It has to be destroyed. Our lives depend on this now. Rizhin
knows of its existence, and if we can't bring it home—'

He broke off suddenly and spun round, his torch skipping wildly.
'What the fuck!'

From somewhere down the corridor behind them came the sound
of gunshots. A man screaming and screaming in terror. Pain. Screams
without hope.

Lieutenant Vrebel pulled out his gun and ran.

'Vrebel! Wait!' called Rond.

Too late. Vrebel was disappearing down the corridor towards the
reading room.

'Idiot,' said Rond quietly. Hunder Rond was no kind of coward but he understood caution. Circumspection. Explore and comprehend your position, test your enemy, discover your advantage, then exploit it with surprise and overwhelming deadly force. Survival is the first criterion of victory, and in the end the only one. He switched off his torch, drew his pistol and began to follow Vrebel's jerky flashing beam.

Lom watched the attack of the vyrdalaks on the Parallel Sector men from an upper gallery of the Lodka reading room.

Moth had led him there. Together they had crept out onto a balcony from where, by the starlight spilling through the broken panes of the dome, he could look down on the rows of reader's desks that radiated out from the insectile bulk of the motionless great wheel. He'd seen Elena Cornelius sitting at one of the desks, upright and fierce. Men in black uniforms were sitting on desks either side of her, swinging their legs. Relaxed. Waiting for the others to return.

'Let me take them,' he had whispered to Moth. 'I'll do it quietly. No fuss.'

'Too late,' she'd hissed. 'See! My sisters are vengeful. Blood for the burnings at the Apraksin!'

Two dark uncertain shapes were swarming head-first at silent impossible speed down the gantry of the great wheel. White mouths in the moonlight. Lom felt the fluttering shadow-memory of vestigial papery wings brush against his face. Liminal whisperings. He remembered Count Palffy's collection in the raion. The glass cases mounted on the wall, the pinned-out specimens, some drab, some gaudy. *My specialism is winter moths. Ice moths. Strategies for surviving the deep winter cold.*

The Parallel Sector men had also felt movement above them and looked up, swinging their torch beams. They saw what was coming.

'Elena!' Lom had yelled. 'Run! They don't want you. Get clear! Run!'

He'd started to run himself then, racing for the iron spiral stairway down to the reading room. But before he reached the head of the stairs there were shots and then the screaming began.

When the vyrdalak sisters attacked her guards, Elena Cornelius had backed away, retreating to the edge of the room. Lom made his way across to her between the desks.

'Keep back out of the way,' he said. 'This isn't for us.'

There was a flash of light in the frosted pane of the doorway behind her. Lom sensed someone was coming fast. Another one of the Streltski. He felt the man's fear. He was coming for a fight.

Lom pulled from his pocket the VKBD pistol he'd acquired in Pir-Anghelsky Park. There was no time to think. Just react. The door crashed open and Lom fired.

The shot probably hit the man in the chest, but Lom never knew for certain because Moth swept past him noiselessly, knocking him aside, and took the man's head off with a slash of a pale-bladed hand. The detached head thudded against the wall as the body collapsed. Moth leaped over it and flew on into the darkened corridor beyond.

In the reading room the vyrdalak sisters were making thin papery screams of triumph and delight.

Hunder Rond got only a vague impression of what had destroyed Vrebel before the lieutenant's head flew off and his torch fell to the floor, but it was enough. He knew what it was. He knew it was coming for him next.

He emptied his entire magazine in the direction of the approaching vyrdalak. Seven blinding muzzle flashes in the dark. Seven deafening explosions. Somewhere among the noise he heard a high-pitched shriek and a stumble. Then he turned and ran back into the corridors of the private archives.

13

Moth, struck by seven bullets from the pistol of Hunder Rond, collapsed in a heap on the corridor floor. Lom crouched over her. Moved her hair aside to clear her face.

She hissed and pushed his hand away.

'Hole in my chest,' she said. 'Harmless. Piece gone from my leg. I'll be a limper for a while.'

'Is there pain?' Elena was there. 'Let me see. You must be bleeding. I can try to stop it.'

Moth began to haul herself upright. Lom put a hand under her arm to help her. There was almost no weight at all.

'No bleeding,' she said, leaning her back against the wall. 'No blood to bleed. As for pain, there is pain sometimes. Existence hurts. This will pass.'

'Can I leave her with you?' Lom said to Elena. 'I need to go after the one that escaped.'

'Leave the Streltski for my sisters,' said Moth. 'When they have finished with the others they will hunt him. Pigeon and Paper will bring him down. You come with me and look at Lavrentina's papers.'

It was ten minutes before Moth was ready to move. The vyrdalak sisters had gone into the shadows, leaving the torn and ruined bodies of the dead Parallel Sector men where they lay. Lom collected their torches and switched them off to save the batteries, all but one for Elena's benefit.

'This way,' said Moth when she was ready, and set off limping towards the lobby. She was halting and slow. 'We will have to go by corridors and stairs.'

For twenty minutes at least they climbed, slowly and circuitously. Lom recognised the backwater corridor where his brief office had been, buried among cleaning cupboards and boiler rooms, when he was Krogh's man. His typescript card was still tucked into the slot on the door, yellowing and faded now. INVESTIGATOR V Y LOM. PODCHORNOK OBLAST. PROVINCIAL LIAISON REVIEW SEC-RETARIAT. He stuck his head inside. The same desk and coat rack were still there but the placard on the wall had gone.

Citizens! Let us all march faster
Through what remains of our days!
You might forget the fruitful summers
When the wombs of the mothers swelled
But you'll never forget the Vlast you hungered and bled for
When enemies gathered and winter came.

Someone had remembered the old Vlast well enough to take that away. Lom wondered if it had been Pavel.

*

In the mazy unlit corridors behind the reading room there was no panic for Hunder Rond, though he knew he was vyrdalak-hunted. There was fear – there was horror in the dark – but he knew that panic would kill him. The vyrdalaks would come fast; they would not lose him in the passageways; they would not give up. They would come and come, quick and silent and relentless in the darkness. Out of shadows and ceilings and lift shafts they would come. He had seen the remains of vyrdalak kill. He had heard the screams.

He had also seen vyrdalaks burn. He knew how that sounded. How it smelled. How it felt.

Hunder Rond moved on at a slow even pace and put aside terror for later. Stored it up for a better time and place. This was his forte, his talent, advantage and pleasure: clinical self-restraint – ice and iron – primitive emotions under unbreakable control to be retrieved for private release *when he chose*. The trembling hot sweat, delirium, anger and screaming could be brought to the surface then, and satisfied *in his way*. Not now. Later. There was energy and pleasure to be had from it then. A heightening.

He smiled grimly in the dark as he cleared and focused his mind and considered his situation from every angle with dispassionate accuracy. He had one spare magazine for his pistol, which was now empty. That was not sufficient, but then no number would have been. Bullets rarely killed a vyrdalak, though a lucky shot might give it pause. Seven cartridges were better than none. He ejected the empty magazine, inserted the spare and loaded the first round into the breech.

And he had a map.

That was foresight. That was efficiency. Cool administrative imagination.

There was no point blundering around in the dark and getting lost. He switched on his torch and unfolded the floor plan of the Lodka.

Century by century the interior of the Lodka had evolved to meet the needs of the day. Corridors and stairways were closed off and new ones opened. Cables and heating were installed. Angel-fall observatories, and radio antennae in attics. Rooms knocked together and repartitioned and requisitioned for new purposes. Subterranean railway access opened and abandoned. A vacuum-pipe internal postal system. Every few years the superintendent of works sent expeditions into the building to update the master survey, but the results were obsolete before the work was complete, and the edges and margins, the heights and depths, remained ragged and obscure. For the core areas and the zones in regular use, however, the map was reliable enough. The Gaukh reading room and the layout of the main archives hadn't changed much. They were near the public door that used to open onto the Square of the Piteous Angel, now Victory Square.

Rond studied the map and chose his way out. It wasn't far. Ten minutes in the passageways and across two wide hallways should do it. He refolded the map and jogged forward at a steady sustainable pace, vyrdalak-horror and primal prey-animal fear tucked away in a closed interior filing system of his own.

Moth led Lom and Elena higher, up narrower stairwells. There was more light up here: more windows, and the yellow moons were shining, nearly full, low and sinking towards the western skyline. Lom switched off the dimming torch. There was no need for it now. They were passing along some kind of high covered gangway. Narrow windows to their right looked across the Lodka's tumbled inner roofscape – slopes of lead and slate, dormers and gables and oriels, downpipes and guttering, naked abandoned flagpoles – and through to their left Mirgorod spread out towards the sea. Dawn was breaking pink and green. Traffic was moving slowly along the eight-lane Rizhin Highway. The sun-flushed thousand-windowed sky-rise towers – the Rudnev-Possochin University, the Pavilion of the New Vlast, the Monument to National Work – heaved up from the plain. Warm-glow termite nests.

'Here,' said Moth at last. She stopped and pushed open a door. The sudden wave of cloying enclosed air that escaped from the room made Lom take a step back. Elena Cornelius put her hand across her mouth.

'Oh god,' she muttered under her breath. 'Oh god, what have they been doing?'

Hunder Rond was within sight of the threshold, the door he'd left open, when the two vyrdalaks rose at him from the shadows of a downward stair.

The light of early morning spilled through the doorway, and the sound of the waking city. *Day already?* Rond had thought. It was barely an hour since he'd come this way the evening before with Lieutenant Vrebel and the others now dead.

The vyrdalaks closed on him with impossible speed. He heard a gasp of pleasure and smelled the age and mustiness of rags. The sickly sweetness of unhuman breath.

Rond's panic box broke wide open then. He felt the shriek from his own throat, the hurt of it; it wasn't his voice but it was him. He turned into the attack and pulled the trigger of his gun, and as he spun he slipped on dusty polished marble and fell. The charge of the day-blinded vyrdalaks missed him. He felt a slicing tear across his upraised forearm and that was all. The crash of his shot echoed impossibly loud in the airy space as the bundle of screeching vyrdalaks skittered across the floor. Rond scrabbled to his knees and jabbed at the trigger again and again until the mechanism clicked empty, and then he hurled the gun at them and threw himself headlong scrambling towards the door into air and sunshine, and he was outside and he was safe and free.

Rond's car was where he'd left it the previous evening (scarcely an hour ago). He was trembling. *Focus. Focus.* His left arm was numb, the jacket sleeve ripped open and wet with blood, his forearm opened above the wrist, an oozing superficial tear. *Drive one-handed then. How hard is that?* He needed to clean himself up. Get the wound dressed quickly. Vyrdalak strikes fester.

But then, when he'd done that, he would come back and he would burn them. Burn the vyrdalaks. Burn the foulness. Burn their nests. Burn whatever archives were still inside that should have been burned years ago. Burn the whole fucking Lodka to the ground.

14

Moth led Lom and Elena into the broad interior of some kind of tower. For five or six floors it rose above them, but wide jagged holes were broken through all the floorboards and plaster ceilings so they could see all the way to the roof. Dust-ridden daylight splashed in through pointed-arch windows. The tower was some kind of library. It was also a beautiful attic nest.

The vyrdalak sisters lived among chambers of sweetness. The whole of the inside of the tower was hung with great webs and pockets and caverns of chewed paper and fruit. Rotting-fruit-and-paper extrusions. Files and books and sea charts, centuries of memoranda and reports – diplomatic letters, records of surveillance, interrogation and betrayal – they ate them all. Masticated and regurgitated them to make hundreds of comfortable translucent compartments the colour of ivory and bone. The floor was uneven papier mâché, matted and lumpy with stalagmites of eaten newsprint and maps and confessions under torture, and all crusted with a yellow-brown craquelure of age.

The whole construction had a perfect, proportioned elegance. It was like standing inside dried egg casings. The sea-worn honeycombed interiors of bone. Wasps' nests like lanterns under eaves. It was the work of centuries and it was beautiful.

'We read and read,' said Moth with quiet pride, 'and as we read we chew.'

Half-eaten fruits – long ago dried to leathery sweetness – and rotting foraged stores were tucked away in cavities and corners.

Hunder Rond returned to the Lodka with men in trucks. They threw a safety cordon around the building and Rond sent in six two-man burning teams, one for each of the half-dozen main public entrances. Pressurised fuel tanks strapped to their backs, they penetrated as far as they dared, leaving themselves escape runs, and began to spray arcs of fire.

The Lodka burned. Oh yes, it burned. The desks, the chairs, the conference tables, the books and files and carpets, the pictures on the walls, the beams, the floor boards, the staircases, all tinder-dry and hungry for combustion.

At the first licks of flame up the walls, the firestarters turned and ran. They took up fallback positions outside the doors, flame-throwers ready for anything that tried to escape.

Moth led Lom and Elena into side rooms off the main tower. There were libraries within libraries, collections and cabinets of curiosities, some small as cupboards with cramped connecting ways, some large as salons. Dormers and airy roof constructions. Moth swept ahead, motley fabric train swishing bare floorboards and fading patterned rugs. Lom and Elena followed more slowly, lingering by items shelved, ranged and museumed with their own mysterious logic.

The sisters had picked up and hauled back home things they had found in tunnels and the city and the Lodka itself: detached fragments of the old Vlast and its predecessors. Flotsam from the wreckage of forgotten worlds. They had gathered furniture and papers, pieces of porcelain and pottery, broken and not, astronomical instruments, components electrical and mechanical. There was a whole wing for works rescued from Vlast storerooms of confiscated art.

Lom paused over aquatints and engravings and photographs of vanished cities. He glanced through the correspondence of margraves, landgraves, electors and county palatines. Accounts of coats of arms, lineages and uniforms. Canvas bags still bearing the brittle broken seals of the *corps diplomatique*. Orders of battle for campaigns of which he'd never heard. The Yannis River Advance. Battles on frozen lakes. Cavalry charges against artillery. The repulsion of the northern dukes. *A Model Village Prospectus on the New Rational Principle. Schools Not Guns Will Feed Our People.* Displayed under glass were ancient undated maps of the continent. Small countries Lom had never heard of remained like ghosts, a stained patchwork of counties and princedoms. All maps ended in the east with forest.

The sisters had hung their collection with tiny pieces of other people's privacy: combs and portrait lockets; the headcloths and bast shoes and tin cups of the nameless. The more Lom lingered there, the more aware he became of beginnings that had had no continuation, lines cut off and possibilities unrealised. Ways and places these beginnings might have gone but never did. It was a museum that told no story except absence.

A circular window gave a view across the sky-rise city: Rizhin Highway, Rizhin Tower. It was perpetual zero hour – null o'clock – in the real world outside. *All the things that might have happened (some of them good, some bad, some beautiful) did not happen. They did not happen because this happened instead.*

Moth came bustling worrisome back for him.

'This way,' she said. 'This way. Hurry.'

The sisters had lovingly recreated Lavrentina Chazia's private archive in every detail. The green-painted walls. The empty desk. Floor tiles lifted from downstairs and relaid. Rows of steel-framed racks holding files and boxes of papers. Every shelf brought up, placed and labelled as it had been; every file and box exactly where it should be according to the former commander of the secret police's own scheme.

'We took them away and hid them,' said Moth. 'We kept them safe for when Lavrentina came back.'

Lom found what he wanted, exactly where he had found it once before. The lavender folder for Josef Kantor was in its place on the *K* shelf. It was fat and full. He took it and pushed it inside his jacket.

At that moment the echo of shrill distant screeching reached them. It found them even here, even in this quiet archive of an archive.

'What's that?' said Elena.

Moth stiffened and screamed. Her sisters crashed in through upper windows, flew down and scuttled, rattling, in circles around them.

'Fire! Fire! They are burning us! Fire!'

Throughout the Lodka the fires were roaring now, blinding vortices of flame and heat. Flames crawled along the walls and floors of corridors, meticulous and thorough, spilling into every room. Floor by floor, shaft by shaft and stair by stair, ignition spread. Rooms unopened for centuries popped into sudden combustion. Thick worms and blankets of smoke flowed across ceilings. Whirlwinds of burning paper. Billowing flakes of fire. Caves of red heat. Explosions and backdrafts sucked whole floors in. Fire smouldered against locked doorways and burst through, searing irruptions, sucking whole annexes into the hot mouth.

Paint blistered. Pigments boiled off canvases and the canvases burned with their frames. Countless linoleum acres bubbled and stank to sticky residual ash. Inkwells boiled dry in burning lecterns. Typewriters buckled and twisted, their ribbons burned, the enamel licked away. The immolation of code books and cipher machines. A fire-clean forgetting of four hundred years of lost secrets.

A column of fire surrounded the leaning skeleton of the Gaukh Engine, heat and smoke pouring with the hurtling updraft through the broken dome and into the outside air.

In the basement mortuary the restless corpses thrashed and subsided. Fire tongues licked the cell-floor bloodstains clean.

Rats and bats and cats and mice and birds escaped or died. Shelves of forgotten files burned unread. Fire touched the hem of the vyrdalak sisters' beautiful galleried nest and it exploded. Libraries within libraries, their long careful centuries' archives and collections, the last secret memories of absence and what did not happen, burned.

Moth and her sisters took Lom and Elena across rooftop gangways and down through the most central heart-stone stairwells and unopened passageways of the Lodka where the fire had not yet reached.

The burning was a distant roar, a smell of searing, heat on the face and the thickening of smoke clogging the chest. The vyrdalaks skittered and jumped and flew short distances on vestigial fabric wings. At lift shafts they carried them down: Moth scooping up Lom in her weightless bone-strong arms, one of her siblings with Elena. They jumped into space and leaped from stanchion to bolt, barely touching, barely slowing their plunge. Dull orange glowed far below and a cushion of heat rose from it.

Somebody screamed. Lom wondered if it might have been him, but he doubted it. He kept the lavender folder grasped tight to his chest: the truth he saved from the burning building.

Down and down they went into the closing heat, racing against it.

The outer walls of the Lodka were a crumbling sooty crust enclosing cubic miles of roaring roasting heat. Quiet crowds gathered at the cordon to watch the ancient building burn.

The Lodka's thousand exterior windows glowed baleful red. Panes burst and shattered and rained glass on the margin of Victory Square. Fragments splashed into the River Mir. Smoke cliffs, orange-bellied and flecked with whirling spark constellations, billowed above the collapsing roofscape and darkened the eggshell sky. Smuts and ash scraps drifted and fell far across Mirgorod. The whole city smelled of burning.

The Lodka – for four hundred years the dark cruel heart and flagship memory ark of the Vlast, the crouching, looming survivor of bombs and siege – the Lodka was ceasing to be, and that was a good thing happening.

Part III

Chapter Seven

Man will make it his purpose to master his own feelings, to raise his instincts to the heights of consciousness, to make them transparent, to extend the wires of his will into hidden recesses, and thereby to raise himself to a new plane, to create a higher social biologic type, or, if you please, a superman ... Man will become immeasurably stronger, wiser and subtler; his body will become more harmonised, his movements more rhythmic, his voice more musical. The forms of life will become dynamically dramatic. The average human type will rise to the heights of an Aristotle, a Goethe or a Marx. And above this ridge new peaks will rise.

Leon Trotsky (1879–1940)

There is no substance which cannot take the form of a living being, and the simplest being of all is the single atom. Thus the whole universe is alive and there is nothing in it but radiant life.

Konstantin Tsiolkovsky (1857–1935)

1

Engineer-Technician 2nd Class Mikkala Avril receives the letter that will change her life. It is waiting for her in the morning. Breakfast at the Kurchatovgrad Barracks.

Today is her twenty-fourth birthday, but she isn't counting years;

what matters is the accumulation of knowledge, the contribution she can make, not the piling-up of finished days you don't get back again. Only achievement is notable. Next week she takes examinations that will lead to her promotion, and she has a report to finish: her paper on the dynamics of volatile angel plasma under intense shearing pressures. There are efficiencies to be gained by scoring microscopic fresnel grooves in the face of the pusher plate. So she believes. The equations are beautiful: they click into place inevitably, like good engineering.

Mikkala Avril dreams of making universal vessels that are less crude and primitive and brutal. More *evolved*. She has had her hair cut short to save time in the mornings.

Citizen women! Race ahead of the lumbering carthorse years! Consecrate yourselves to speed!

Every day she devotes forty-five minutes to the gymnasium. A good worker is healthy and strong.

The envelope waiting for Mikkala Avril on the morning of her twenty-fourth birthday is flimsy and brown and bears no official crest. A crinkly cellophane window shows the typed address within. She has smoothed it and read the address three times. It is for her. On the gummed back flap there is a purple ink-stamp, slightly off centre – PERSONAL & CONFIDENTIAL – and a manuscript addendum neatly capitalised: *RECIPIENT ONLY. POST ROOM DO NOT OPEN*. She notices that the flap has not been slit. The envelope is unopened, its peremptory instruction to the surveillance office (remarkably) obeyed. They must have known where it was from. But who communicates confidentially with an engineer-technician 2nd class at the Kurchatovgrad Barracks and has the weight to give the censors pause?

Mikkala's heart runs faster: wild momentary anxieties show themselves, and crazy hopes she didn't know she had. It's probably nothing. Some error over her pay. A rebuke for some omission in the weekly returns. She leaves the envelope unopened on the tray and finishes her coffee.

Mikkala Avril is eking out the last empty moments of her old life. She is hesitating. She is wasting time. The letter stares back at her from the brink.

She rips it open and hooks out the single sheet.

FROM THE DIRECTOR, PROJECT PERPETUAL SUNRISE
PROFESSOR YAKOV KHYRBYSK

Technician Avril!

Please be informed, you have been selected for participation in Project PERPETUAL SUNRISE. You are to present yourself for duty at the Yarkoye Nebo Number 3 Institute immediately on receipt of this communication. Personal effects are not required and none should be brought. All necessary items will be provided. Onward travel will be arranged.

This is a secret appointment which you should discuss with no one. Conversation with your current colleagues and officers must be avoided. You are now under my command, and all other instructions are herewith superseded and void. The nature of your new duties will be explained to you at the institute.

I congratulate you, Technician Avril. You will be contributing to special and challenging tasks of tremendous significance for the future of the New Vlast.

You should know that your name was brought to my attention as a candidate for this task by President-Commander Rizhin himself, acting personally. Your courageous determination and clarity of thought at the launch of *Proof of Concept* has been recognised by the award of Hero of the New Vlast . This is of necessity a secret decoration, of course. No medal can be given. Your promotion is confirmed without examination. I look forward to knowing you better.

Yakov Khyrbysk, Director

2

Lom sat at the desk in the guardhouse at the entrance to the drive that led to Lukasz Kistler's house. The guard was slumped in the corner, unconscious. He'd have a headache but he would recover: nothing a few days' rest wouldn't put right. Lom was wearing the guard's cap. The interior light was dim: his profile would pass muster. Casual inspection from a distance, anyway. There was always risk.

There were two telephones on the desk: one an outside line, the other connected to the house's own internal system. A typed list of extension numbers was pinned next to it. LOBBY. GARAGE. HOUSE-KEEPER. SWITCHBOARD. SECURITY. STUDY. BEDROOM. Lom took a guess and chose the bedroom. It was almost midnight. He dialled the three-digit number.

And seven miles away in a windowless basement in the headquarters of the Parallel Sector a lamp on a switchboard console winks into life. The night duty operator stubs out her cigarette, puts on her head-phones, flicks a switch and begins to type.

Kistler Residential – Internal
23.47 Transcription begins

Kistler: Yes?
Unknown caller: I wish to speak with Lukasz Kistler.
Kistler: This is Kistler. Who the fuck are you?
Caller: You don't know me.
Kistler: Where are you calling from? How the hell did you get this
    number?
Caller: I have information for you and I am told you are someone
    who might make use of it. I am told you are a person of courage
    and independence. Was I told right?
Kistler: Who is this? What are you talking about? What kind of
    information?
Caller: Information of consequence. Documentary proofs.
Kistler: Proofs? Proofs of what?
Caller: Proofs that a certain person is not who he says. Proofs of
    conspiracy. Deception. Assassination. The seizure of power
    by a revolutionary terrorist operating under a false name with
    the collusion of certain very senior elements within the official
    security services.
Kistler: When would this happen?
Caller: It has happened. It has already happened. I am talking
    about the greatest power there is, and I am talking about
    incontrovertible documentary proofs.

162

Kistler: [*Pause*] Why are you telling me this?

Caller: I want to give these proofs to you. I want you to use them. I am told you are a person who could do this. You have strength of will. You have influence and you are independent of mind. You are also perhaps a decent man. I offer you these proofs, which in the right hands are dangerous – I would say deadly – to the utmost power.

Kistler: Who are you working for?

Caller: Nobody.

Kistler: This is a trap. A loyalty test. Or you are a crank. Either way, I cannot speak to you. Fuck off and leave me alone.

Call disconnected

23.50 Transcription begins

Kistler: Hello?

Unknown caller: I am not a liar. I am not a crank. This is not a trap.

Kistler: Then you are a most dangerous kind of man. You should not have this number.

Caller: I'm offering you a chance to act. To make a change. Perhaps to take power yourself if that's what you want. The utmost power in the land is a deception. A plot. A man who is not what he seems. See my proofs, Kistler. Let me bring them to you. I will come to your house. See what I have, Kistler. Listen to me, then decide.

Kistler: [*Pause*] When?

Caller: Now. I am at your gate. All you need do is tell your door security to let me in. [*Pause*] I'm coming now, Kistler. Five minutes. Tell them to let me in.

Kistler: They will search you.

Caller: That is reasonable. I expected that. I am unarmed. I'm coming now.

Kistler: Wait. Who are you? What is your name?

Call disconnected

23:51 – Transcription ends

The transcription operative pulls the sheet from the platen, slides it into an envelope, adds it to the pile in her tray and lights another cigarette. She gives no thought to what she has heard. No reaction at all. Nothing she ever hears leaves any trace: she listens and types and then she forgets. She is a component in a transmission mechanism only, an instrument with no more capacity for retention than the headphones and the typewriter she uses. That's the safe way, the survivor's way, and she has been in her job for many years. If she happens to see the consequences of her transcripts later in the rise and fall of magnates and the newspaper reports of arrests and trials, she takes no notice and never says anything. Even to herself she makes no remark.

It's for others to read the transcripts in the morning and make of them what they will.

3

L om walked the length of Kistler's gravel drive in darkness, waiting for the sudden flood of light, the harsh call of a challenge, a bullet in the back. But there was nothing, only the restless animal calls from Kistler's menagerie in the summer night: the grunting of monkeys, the growl of a big cat. The air was heavy with the scent of orchids and roses. A peacock, startled, disgruntled, stalked away across the starlit lawn.

What am I doing here? Blundering on. Butting my head in the dark against trees to see what fruit falls, and every moment could be my last.

Kistler received him in his study, a dressing gown over his pyjamas. He sat on the couch, chain-smoking, and listened in silence as Lom outlined the facts against Rizhin. Told him the story of the rise of Josef Kantor, the list of his terrorist acts, Lavrentina Chazia's connection with him, their involvement in the assassination of the Novozhd by Lakoba Petrov. Lom made no mention of the living angel in the forest, Maroussia or the Pollandore.

'But you haven't brought me these papers from Chazia's archive?' said Kistler when Lom had finished. 'They're not with you now?'

'No.'

'Then you misled me.'

'I have them,' said Lom. 'They're nearby but safe, where you will not find them. If I don't emerge from here in another hour, they will be destroyed.'

'Perhaps that would be for the best.'

'They are as I have said.'

'But who are you? You ask me to take your word on trust, yet I don't even have a name. You attack my guard and force yourself into my house, and tell me this wild story, which if it's true—'

'It is true,' said Lom. 'I told you: I have authentic documentary proofs.'

'If it's true, for me to even hear it is lethal. Even if it's not true, look at the position you put me in by coming here. How am I to react? I should make a report immediately, but if I do that Rizhin will feed me to Hunder Rond anyway. You tell me others have died to keep this rumour silent, and I don't doubt that, even if all the rest of this is horse shit. The only thing I can safely do is have you shot myself, here and now. Get rid of your carcass quietly and forget you ever came. There are a half a dozen VKBD men in the house. It would be straightforward enough to arrange.'

'You'd have done it long before now, if you were going to,' said Lom. 'You wouldn't have let me reach the door. Though I'm not so easily killed.'

'Maybe I was curious,' said Kistler. 'Maybe I'm not afraid of a little risk. You're an impressive fellow. You intrigue me. But I need to know who I'm dealing with.'

'My name is Lom. I used to be a senior investigator in the Political Police. Six years ago I was commissioned by Under-Secretary Krogh to pursue the terrorist Josef Kantor. This is what I have found out.'

'Used to be?' said Kistler. 'And what are you now?'

'My official career came to an end. I'm freelance now.'

'You work for no one? Really?'

'I work alone,' said Lom

'You're one of Savinkov's experiments, I think?' said Kistler. 'That I can see for myself.'

Lom's hand went to his forehead, reaching for the indentation in his skull where the angel piece had been before Chazia gouged it out.

It was an involuntary movement. He caught himself and pulled his hand away. Too late. It was a weakness shown, but there was nothing to be done.

'That's gone now too,' he said.

'I see,' said Kistler. 'OK. Let's say I accept all this. Let's say I take you for what you say you are. Let's say you're a good fellow and your heart's in the right place. My advice to you is to destroy these proofs of yours. Burn them. Forget it. Get on with your life and find something else to do.'

'You're not interested then. You will do nothing. You will not take my proofs.'

'Nobody will take them, man! What you have is useless. Worthless. Rubbish. It is no good, no good at all. Oh it's good police work, surely, but police work will not bring Rizhin down.'

'But—'

'Listen. I'll tell you something about Rizhin—'

'Kantor. Josef Kantor.'

Kistler shrugged.

'Rizhin or Kantor,' he said. 'It makes no difference. It's just a name.'

'No!'

'Listen to me. I sympathise with you, Lom. I should not say so, but I do. Osip Rizhin is a terrible man. He bullies, he intimidates, he kills. He diverts resources to the military and to idiotic pet projects like the fucking space programme. He sells our grain to our enemies while our people starve by the million. The ordinary economy is collapsing and he has no idea at all. Industrially the Archipelago walks all over us. We have no chance. You can't run a modern nation on the labour of convicts and slaves, for fuck's sake. It's not sustainable. In ten years this Vlast of Rizhin's will be history's forgotten dust. I see this and it pains me. I do what I can—'

'You do nothing,' said Lom.

'I do what I can. Here's the truth about Rizhin. Not the story, the truth. The public fiction is maintained that Papa Rizhin runs his New Vlast alone. He sits in his plain office and smiles, bluff and avuncular, and through the haze of his pipe smoke he sees everything that happens. He intervenes everywhere. Nothing is done without Rizhin's permission and every decision is his. He is the authority on all subjects. Politics. Culture. History. Philosophy. Science. Works in his name are

166

published in their millions and studied by millions. That is the fiction for the people. Recognise it?'

Lom said nothing.

'It's shit,' Kistler continued. 'Of course it's shit. The New Vlast is huge, complex and technical. One man couldn't possibly direct the government, the armed forces, the security services and the economy. Rizhin needs support. He needs lieutenants. People with the expertise and competence to make decisions of their own. Yes?'

'Go on,' said Lom.

'Have you never wondered,' said Kistler, 'what kind of person works for Rizhin? Does it not astonish you that people will do this, knowing what they do? They tolerate the bullying and the humiliation and worse; they accept terror and purges; they know the fate of their predecessors and still they step forward, still they accept appointment to the Central Committee, still they do Rizhin's work, assiduously and as well as they can. Don't you wonder why?'

'You should know. You're one of them.'

'Not really. You do not know me yet. Rizhin's lieutenants are a special sort of person. Iron discipline and faithful adherence to the norms of thought. They continuously adapt their morality, their very consciousness, to the requirements of the New Vlast. Without reservation, Lom. Absolutely without reservation. But above all – you must understand this, it is the key – they are *ambitious*. For *themselves*. They don't support Rizhin because they believe in him, but because they believe in *themselves*. They want the power and prestige he gives them, and the gratification of their nasty little needs. Half of them will be imprisoned or dead within the year, but everyone thinks it won't happen to *them*. They all believe, in the face of all the evidence, that they're different from the rest, that they can hang on and survive the purges and arrests. Blind ambition. They support Rizhin because he is their security, their leader and the feeder of their desires. It's a very distinctive cast of mind.

'And Rizhin understands this. Perfectly. He is the greatest ever player of the game. In the early days, when he was still fighting the civil war against Fohn and Khazar, he used to shoot his commanders at a rate of one a week, but he learned he couldn't shoot everyone. The people around the President-Commander must be effective, not paralysed. Terror is still the most powerful tool but he's more subtle now. He purges sparingly. He lets others do the intimidation for him. I've watched him learn. It's been a masterclass.'

Kistler paused to light another cigarette.

'So you see why your plan won't work?' he continued. 'To bring down Rizhin, you must win the Central Committee. There's no other way. But if you tell the Central Committee he's not Rizhin but Josef Kantor, they'll say – like I do – what's in a name? Tell them he killed the Novozhd and owes his position to Lavrentina Chazia, and they'll say – like I do – where are the Novozhd and Chazia now?

'You see, Lom? You can't shake the Central Committee's faith in Rizhin's integrity of purpose, because they've no thought of it anyway. They simply couldn't give a flying fuck. Everyone has skeletons in the cupboard, and personal ambition is everything. Nobody in Rizhin's New Vlast wants to rake up memories. What's past is nothing here.'

'You're saying, do nothing, then,' said Lom, 'because nothing can be done. This is the counsel of despair. Like I said, you're one of them. You are ambitious too.'

'Perhaps. But my ambitions are of a different quality. I see further. I want more. I want better.'

'It makes no difference.'

'You know,' said Kistler carefully. 'A man like you might dispose of Rizhin if he wanted to. Nothing could be more straightforward. A bomb under his car. Seven grams of lead in the head. No Rizhin, no problem.'

'No good,' said Lom. 'Someone else would take his place. It's not the man that must be destroyed, it's the idea of him. The very possibility has to be erased.'

Kistler's eyes widened. He studied Lom carefully.

'This isn't just squeamishness?' he said. 'It's not that you're afraid.'

'I've killed,' said Lom, 'and I don't want to kill again, not unless I have to. But it's not squeamishness. Call it historical necessity if you like. It doesn't matter what you think.'

'I see. You really are more than a disgruntled policeman with a grudge.'

Lom stood to go. 'I made a mistake,' he said. 'I shouldn't have come. You're not the man I was told you might be. I'll find another way.'

'Wait,' said Kistler. 'Please. Sit down. I have a proposition for you. Perhaps I could use a fellow like you.'

'I'm not interested in being used.'

'Sorry,' said Kistler. 'Bad choice of word. But please hear me out.'

Lom said nothing.

'I share your analysis,' said Kistler. 'To put it crudely, Rizhin's way of running the show is a bad idea. It's effective but not efficient. History is against it. Frankly, I believe I could do better myself, and I want to try, but for this I need a weapon to bring him down. You have the right idea, Lom, but the wrong weapon. To make my colleagues on the Central Committee abandon Rizhin and come across to me, I need something that convinces them that his continued existence is against their personal interests *now*. If you can make them believe it'll go worse for them with him than without him, then he'll fall. But they *all* have to believe it, all of them at once, and they have to strike together; if not, Rizhin will just purge the traitors and his position will be stronger than ever. I need to convince them he's a present danger. A terrible weakness. A desperate threat. That's what I need evidence of, not your tale of forgotten misdemeanours and peccadilloes in the distant past.'

'But—' Lom began.

Kistler held up a hand to silence him.

'There is a way, perhaps,' he said. 'Let me finish. There's something going on that my colleagues and I have sensed but cannot see. It makes us uneasy and afraid. Rizhin has created a state within a state. The Parallel Sector. We are blind to Hunder Rond and his service, but it is vast, its influence everywhere. And Rizhin has secrets. A plan within a plan. Resources are still being diverted, just like in Dukhonin's day. Funds. Materials. Workers. The output of the atomic plants at Novaya Zima is far greater than we see the results of. Whole areas on the map are blank, even to us.

'A man in my position can't ask too many questions. I have my resources but I can't use them: the Parallel Sector's reach is too deep and the penalty for being caught is, well, immediate and total. But for you, Lom, it's different. I think you might just be the man for the job. I'll tell you where to look. I'll give you money. Whatever you need. If you fail, if you're caught, I'll deny all knowledge of you. No, I'll have you killed before you can implicate me at all. But if you find me something I can really use, then we'll be in business. You bring me back the weapon I need, Lom. This will be our common task.'

'I don't work for anyone but myself,' said Lom. 'I'm not a police-man. Not any more.'

'Ego talk,' said Kistler. 'I'm offering you an alliance, not fucking em-ployment. Call it cooperation in the mutual interest. Call it a beautiful friendship. A meeting of minds. Call it whatever soothes your vanity – I don't care. I don't need you. I was going along just fine before you came, but now I see an opportunity that's worth an investment and a risk. That's what you came here for, isn't it? What the fuck else are you going to do?'

4

Lieutenant Arkady Rett of the 28th Division (Engineers) left his division behind and led his men deeper into the forest. The division had become hopelessly bogged down. They were going in circles.

'Take a small party, Rett, and scout ahead,' the colonel had said. 'Three or four can travel more quickly. Find us an eastward path. Find us solid ground and somewhere to go.'

Rett chose two men, Private Soldier Senkov and Corporal Fallun, and walked out of the camp with them. Behind them the sky was black with the smoke of burning trees, and ahead lay woods within woods, always further in and further back, deeper and deeper for ever. There was no end to going on.

Rett had thought that entering the deeper woods would mean disappearing into darkness. He'd imagined a densely packed wall of trees. Impenetrable thorn-thicket walls. Endless columns of tall trunks disappearing up into gloom, and beneath the canopy nothing but silence. But the reality was different: open spaces filled with grass and fern and briars and pools of water; occasional oak and ash and beech, singly or in small groups; hazel poles so slender he could push them with one hand and they would bend and sway like banner staffs. Ivy and moss and sticky mud and fallen branches underfoot. The forest was the opposite of pathless; there were too many paths, and none led somewhere.

'Paths don't make themselves,' said Senkov.

The compass was useless. After the first day he didn't get it out of his pack.

On the second day Rett woke feeling small. The world was inexhaustible and he was one tiny thing alone. There was no human scale: hostile, featureless, relentless, the forest defeated interpretation. Rett was a constructor of bridges, a worker with tools, a rational man: he looked for pattern and structure and edge, and found none here. His mind filled the gaps, the spacious lacuna of unresolvable chaotic plenitude, with monsters. There were faces in the trees. Movement in the corner of the eye. Presences. Watchfulness. The nervous child he no longer was returned and walked alongside him.

Senkov and Fallun fell silent, sour, but the invisible child talked. The child saw the shadow-flanks of predatory beasts between the trees: witches and giants and forgotten terrors returning; the fear of being forever lost and never finding home again; men that were bears, stinking eaters of flesh. Trolls crowded at the edge of consciousness, importuning attention at the marginal twilit times. Dusk and dawn.

The 28th had crossed the edge into the trees at the start of summer, but it was chill and autumnal here. Mushrooms and mist and the damp smell of coming winter. There was always a cold wind blowing in their faces. The wind unsettled them: they didn't sleep well, tempers were short, always there was a feeling something bad was about to happen.

As they penetrated deeper into the trees Rett saw signs of ancient construction: overgrown earthworks; lengths of wall and ditch built of huge boulders, shaped by hand and smooth with moss and age, collapsing unrepaired; broken spans of bridge; tunnel entrances; empty lake villages rotting back into shallow green waters. Shaggy-haired grazing beasts, wisent and rufous bison, faded into further trees at their approach.

On the fourth day they came to the edge of an enormous hole in the earth's crust: not a canyon or a rift but a gouge, dizzyingly immense, approximately circular, about half a mile across. It was like a great throat, a punched hole, a core removed from the skin of the world. It was terrifying to stand at the brink and lean over, staring down into bottomless darkening depths. It seemed to Rett that there were faint distant points of light down there. It was as if they were stars, and he was seeing through to the night on the other side of the world. More than anything else he wanted to jump off and fall for ever. It cost him tremendously to tear himself away.

Rett and his men skirted the edge of the great gouge and pressed on. Deeper into the inexhaustible forest. They hacked white strips in the bark of trees to mark their way back out. On the eighth day Rett woke early, before the others. He woke in confusion out of stupefying dreams, a thick heavy pain in his head, his mouth dry and fouled.

Hard frost had come in the night. Mist – damp, chilling, faint, insidious, still – brushed against his face, filled his nose and lungs, reduced the endlessness of the surrounding trees to a quiet clearing edged by indeterminacy. His boots crunched on brittle, whitened grass and iron earth. The sound was intrusive. Loud and echoless. The trees seemed suddenly bare of leaves, sifting a dull and diminished light through the monochrome canopy of branches.

The intense cold made his fingers clumsy. Breath pluming in small clouds, he fumbled the tinder, dropped it, couldn't make his stiffened blue-pale hands work to get a fire started. The water was frozen in the bottle and the pan felt clumsy, and fell, spilling chunks of ice across the hearth. It took an age to coax a meagre, heatless flame into burning. There were a few dusty grains, the last of the coffee. He scattered them across sullen water. It didn't boil. He built up the fire with thick stumps of log and put a neat pile of others ready. The heat chewed at the wood, smouldering, strengthless, with occasional watery yellow licks of flame the size and colour of fallen hazel leaves. Smoke hung over it, drifting low, thickening the mist. Clinging to his hair.

Rett left Senkov and Fallun to sleep and climbed the shallow rise they'd chosen last night for shelter. The trees were awake. The many trees, watching. The weight of their attention pressed in on him, sucking away the air. It was so cold. His ankle was hurting. His limbs were stiff from too much walking.

Ten minutes later he was on a scrubby hilltop among hazel and thorn, looking across a wide shallow valley. Without trees above him he could see the sky, the grey-brown canopy of leaf-falling woodland spread out at his feet. A range of low hills on the further side climbing into distance and mist.

There was a new hill above the treeline. It hadn't been there the day before. A fingernail clot of dark purple-red, the rim of a second sun rising.

Rett hurried back down the slope to rouse the others.

All that day they walked in the direction of the red hill rising. The sky settled lower with thickening cloud banks and strange copper light. Trees spread around them in all directions, numberless, featureless and utterly bleak, a still, engulfing, unending tide of reddening blankness. Hour followed hour and always they passed between trees, and always the trees were replaced by more trees, and always the trees were the same. They were moving but getting nowhere because the forest was without boundary or finish or variation. Its immenseness was beyond size and without horizon. Walking brought them no nearer and no further away. Motion without movement. Everything unchanging copper and grey except the red hill. That was coming closer. They walked on towards it until it was too dark to move, and then they camped without a fire. Rett felt small beyond insignificance and absolutely without purpose or hope.

In the morning the red hill was nearer. It had moved in the night. Its lower slopes were ash-grey. Rett started towards it. The air prickled, metallic. The trees were looking ill. They had no leaves.

Fallun hung back. 'I don't want to,' he said. 'It's not right.'

The sky was low and copper again. The air tasted of iron, the fine hairs on their skin prickled.

'We must,' said Rett. 'Orders. I think that's what we've come to find.'

Fallun stared at him. 'Orders?'

'"Find a hill that might be moving,"' said Rett. 'It's the primary objective of this whole thing. Burning the forest is secondary. The icing on the cake. The colonel told me before we left.'

'A hill?' said Senkov? 'A moving *hill*? What the fuck's it meant to be?'

'An angel,' said Rett. 'But alive.'

Fallun took a step backwards. Hitched his pack off his shoulder and dropped it. 'No. No way. Not me.'

Rett stared at him. He didn't know what to say. He was an engineer. 'It's an order.'

'Fuck orders.'

'An *order*, Fallun.'

Fallun looked at Senkov. Rett felt sick, like he was going to throw up again. Senkov blushed and looked at his shoes.

'Fuck orders,' said Fallun again, 'and fuck you both. I'm going home.'

Rett hesitated. Then he shrugged. 'Wait here,' he said. 'We'll pick you up on the way back.'

Shreds of low bad-smelling mist drifted across the ground. A sour sickening smell under the copper sky, the light itself dim and smeary. The earth in places a crust over smouldering embers – the roots of trees burning under the ground – but there was no heat.

The wind brought the smell of burning earth and something else, something edgy, prickling and dark. Like iron in the mouth.

'Something bad,' said Senkov. 'Careful.'

'We have to see,' said Rett. 'We have to go there.'

'OK,' said Senkov. 'But be careful.'

The red hill was hundreds of feet high. Rounded, fissured, extending shoulder-slopes towards them. Rett felt the pressure of its gaze.

A mile before they reached it, the earth was a brittle cinder crust that crunched and broke underfoot. Boots went through ankle-deep into smouldering cool blue flames. The ground was on fire without heat and the air sang with electricity. Ahead of them were pools of colourless shimmering. Small lakes but not water. The undergrowth and the trees were white as bone. Ash-white, they snapped at the touch.

A grey elk struggled to get to her feet and run from their approach but couldn't rise. She had no hind legs. She gave up and collapsed to her knees and watched them with dull frightened eyes. Milky blue-grey eyes. Like cataracts.

Rett felt dizzy and almost fell.

'I can't feel my feet,' said Senkov. 'Please. This is far enough.'

'Just a bit further,' said Rett. 'Then we'll turn back.'

Five more minutes and they came upon the bodies of the giants. The giants weren't simply dead; they were destroyed, their bodies eroded and crumbling like soft grey chalk. Parts of the bodies were there and parts were not. Broken pieces were embedded with fragments of hard shining purple-black skin. Flinty bruises.

Objects crunched underfoot.

Senkov picked up an axe from the ground. The iron was covered with a sanding of fine grainy substance, a faintly bluish white, as if the metal had sweated out a crust of mineral salt. When he tried it against a tree the axe head broke, useless.

'What did this?' he said quietly

The copper was draining from the sky, leaving it the colour of hessian. Darker stains seeping up from the east. A hand of fear covered Rett's face so it was hard to breathe. Everything inside him was tight. Tight like wires.

'They're moving,' he said. 'Oh god, they're moving. They're not dead.'

The ruined giants were shifting arms and legs slowly. Scratching torn fingers at the air. Eyes opened. Mouths mouthing. Wordless. The eyes were blank and sightless and the words had no breath: they were parodic jaw motions only. One body was twisting. Jerking. A hand seemed to grasp at Rett's leg. He recoiled and kicked out at it, and the whole arm broke off in a puff of shards and dust. Gobbets of bitter stinking sticky substance splashed onto his face. Into his mouth. Rett made a noise somewhere between a groan and a yell, leaned forward and puked where he stood.

'They're dead,' said Senkov. 'The poor fuckers are dead, they just don't know it.'

'We need to get out of here,' said Rett. 'We need to move. Now.'

Senkov stumbled and fell, twitching, shuddering, struggling to breathe. White saliva bubbles at the corner of his mouth. Thick veins spreading across his temples, the muscles in his neck standing out like ropes. His back arched and spasmed. He fell quiet then but his chest was heaving. His eyes stared at the sky. They were dark and intent, unfocused inward-looking whiteless bright shining black. Senkov's mouth began to speak words but the voice was strange.

'Tell him,' he said monotonously and forceful and very fast, over and over again. 'Tell. Tell. Tell I am here. Tell I am found. Come for me. Come for me. Nearer now. Nearer. Tell him to come.'

5

Engineer-Technician 1st Class Mikkala Avril, secret Hero of the New Vlast, personally selected for a glittering new purpose and destiny by Papa Rizhin himself, freshly uniformed, all medicals passed A1, tip-top perfect condition in body and mind, ready and willing to hurl herself into the shining future, takes a seat across the desk from Director Khyrbysk himself. In his own office. A welcome and induction from the very top. She is conscious of the honour, flushed and more than a little nervous. She must work hard to concentrate on what he is saying, and the effort makes her frown. It gives her an air of seriousness that belies the trembling excitement in her belly. She holds her hands together in her lap to stop them fidgeting.

Here she is, twenty-four years and two days old, a thousand miles north-east of Kurchatovgrad and Chaiganur, in a place not shown on any map, on the very brink of what it's really all about. This is Project Perpetual Sunrise. This is Task Number One.

Khyrbysk is a cliff of a man, a slab, all hands and shoulders and clipped black curly hair, but his voice is fluent and beautiful and his pale eyes glitter with cold and visionary intelligence. They burn right into Mikkala Avril and she likes the feeling of that. Director Khyrbysk sees deep and far, and Mikkala Avril is important to him. He wants her to hear and understand.

'All known problems –' Khyrbysk is saying in that voice, that fine beguiling voice '– all known problems have a single root in the problem of death. The human lifetime is too brief for true achievement: personality falls away into particulate disintegration before the task at hand is finished. But this will not always be so. Humanity is not the end point of evolution, but only the beginning.

'Now is the telluric age, and our human lives are brief and planetary. Next comes the solar age, when we will expand to occupy our neighbour planets within the limits of our present sun. But that is merely an intermediate step on the way to the sidereal age, when the whole of the cosmos, the endless galactic immensities, will be ours. This is inevitable. The course of the future is fixed.'

Director Khyrbysk pauses. Mikkala Avril, brows knotted in concentration, wordless in the zero hour and year, burning with purpose and energy, nods for him to continue.

I understand. I am your woman. Papa Rizhin was not wrong to pick me out.

'You see immediately of course,' says Khyrbysk, 'that the contemporary human body isn't fit for such a destiny. Active evolution, that is the key: the extension of human longevity to an unlimited degree; the creation of synthetic human bodies; the physical resurrection of the dead. These are the prerequisites for the exploration and colonization of distant galaxies. The living are too few to fill the space, but that is nothing. The whole of our past surrounds us. Everybody who ever lived – their residual atomic dust still exists all around us and holds their patterns, remembers them – and one day we'll resurrect our dead on distant planets. We will return our ancestors to life there! The whole history of our species, archived, preserved, will be recalled to live again in bodies that have been re-engineered to survive whatever conditions prevail among the stars. And when that time comes the whole cosmos will burn with the light of radiant humankind.'

Mikkala Avril, astonished, excited, confused and strangely disturbed, feels it incumbent upon her to speak. She opens her mouth but no words come.

'You doubt the practicality of this?' says Khyrbysk. 'Of course you do. These ideas are new to you. But there is no doubt. We have already seen the proof of it. What do you think the angels were, but ourselves returning to greet ourselves. It is a matter of cycles. The endless waves of history. The great wheel of the universe turns and turns again.'

Mikkala Avril is puzzled by this reference to angels. It stirs vague troubled memories. Uncertain images of large dead forms. Dangerous giants walking. She thinks she might have heard talk of such things long ago, but nothing is certain now. She can't remember clearly. Rizhin's New Vlast burns with such brightness, the blinding glare of it whites out the forgotten past.

'Of course,' says Khyrbysk, 'our science is far from being able to do this yet. The success of *Proof of Concept* was a great step forward, but there are technical problems that may take hundreds, even thousands of years to overcome. Yet surely if all humanity is devoted to this one single common purpose then it will be done. And that, Mikkala Avril, is what the New Vlast is for. Rizhin himself appointed me to this task, as he appointed you to yours. "Yakov," he said to me then, "devote all your energies to this. Abandon all other duties. This, my friend, this is Task Number One.'"

6

When Mikkala Avril had left him, Yakov Khyrbysk reached for pen and paper. A man of many cares and burdens, he had a letter to write.

Secretary, President-Commander and
Generalissimus Osip Rizhin!

When you entrusted me with the responsibilities of Task Number One, you invited me to come to you if ever I needed your help. 'I am a mother to you,' you said (your generous kindness is unforgettable), 'but how may a mother know her child is hungry, if the child does not cry?' Well now, alas, your child is crying.

Our work progresses better than even I might have hoped. We have had technical successes on many fronts, and our theoretical understanding of the matters under consideration advances in leaps and bounds. I claim no credit for this: our scientists and academicians work with a will. Your trust and vision inspire us all daily. Building on the success of the Proof of Concept *(which came to an unfortunate end, but the fault there lay with the human component not the ship herself, and we have stronger human components in preparation now), we are well ahead in production of the greater fleet. Both kinds of vessels required are in assembly. The supply of labour continues to exceed attrition and our mass manufacturing plants outperform expectations (see output data enclosed).*

But we have struck an obstacle we cannot ourselves remove. Our reserves of angel matter are exhausted. We simply do not have a supply sufficient to power the launch of the numerous ships envisaged. All known angel carcasses have been salvaged and there is no more.

Helpless, I throw myself at your feet. Find us more angel matter and we will deliver you ten thousand worlds!
Yakov Khyrbysk, Director

Three days later he received a scribbled reply.

Don't worry about the angel stuff, that's in hand. Forget it, Yakov – soon you'll have all you can imagine and ten thousand times more. Drive them on, Yakov, drive your people on. Make the clocks tick faster. O. Rizhin.

7

Kistler had given Lom an envelope with a thousand roubles in it and a place name.

I hear whispers, Lom. Phrases. Vitigorsk, in the Pyalo-Orlanovin oblast. Post Office Box 932. That's all I can give you. Make of it what you can

A thousand roubles was more than Lom had ever held at one time in his life. He bought an overnight bag, some shirts and a 35-millimetre camera (a Kono like Vishnik had, but the newer model with integral rangefinder and a second lens, a medium telephoto). He also bought ten rolls of fast monochrome film and an airline ticket to Orlanograd. From there he took buses. Four days and several wasted detours found him set down at a crossroads in a blank space on the map. He shouldered his bag and began to walk west into the rhythmic glaring of the late-afternoon sun.

Grasslands and low, bald, rolling hills.

Lom measured his progress by the heavy pylons and the rows of upright poles that stretched ahead of him: high-tension power cables and telephone wires. If the wires and cables were heading somewhere, then so was he.

The road was straight and black and new, a single asphalt strip edged with gravel. Wind hummed in the wires, slapped his coat at his knees, scoured his face with fine dry sandy dust. He'd never felt so alone or so exposed. He was the only moving thing for miles. Whether he was going forwards or backwards he had no idea. There was no plan. He put no trust in Kistler, except that Kistler's demolition of his proofs had the compulsion of truth, and Kistler had shown him a different tree to shake.

One tree's as good as another in that regard.

The world's turned upside down, and I'm the terrorist now and this is Kantor's world. Everything is changed and gone and new, and I am become the surly lone destroyer, opening gaps into different futures by destruction, ripping away the surfaces to show what's underneath.

One target's as good as another when everything is connected to everything else.

Maybe I'm just a sore loser, and this is nothing but resentfulness and grudge.

I never saw Maroussia on the river. Trick of memory. Didn't happen.

Six years. I've been alone too long.

A huge truck thundered up the road behind him. He had to step off into the grass to let it pass. Three coupled sixteen-wheeled containers in a cloud of diesel fumes and dust, the wheels high as a man. There were no markings on the raw corrugated-steel container walls, just fixings bleeding streaks of rust. The driver stared down at him from the elevation of his cab, a blurred face behind a grimy window. Lom nodded to him but the driver didn't respond.

Time to get off the road.

The forty-eight-wheel truck dwindled into the horizon and silence, leaving him alone under the weight of the endless grey sky. Lom turned and left the asphalt behind him. The grass was coarse under his feet, tussocky and sparse.

For the first time in far too long he opened himself to the openness around him. There was a hole in his head. A faint flickering drum-pulse under fine silky skin. A tissue of permeable separation.

He let the wind off the hills pass through him. The soil under the grass was thin. A skimming of roots and dust. He ignored it and felt for the rock beneath, the bones of the living planet. Beneath his feet were the sinews of the world, the roots of ancient mountains, knotted in the slow tension of their viscid churn. The low surrounding hills were eroded solid thunderheads.

Lom's heart slowed and his breathing became more quiet and easy.

He kept on reaching out, down into the dark of the ground, till he touched the heart rock of the world: not the sedimentary rocks, silt of seashell and bone, but the true heart rock, extruded from the simmering star stuff at the planetary heart. Layered seams of granite and lava, dolerites, rhyolites, gabbros and tuffs, buckled, faulted, shattered and upheaved under the pressure of their own shifting. Rock that moved too slowly and endured too long to grieve. He felt the currents of awareness moving through it, eddying and swirling, drifting and dispersing: sometimes obscure and indifferent and sometimes watchful; sometimes withdrawing inwards to collect in pools of deep dark heat, and sometimes sharpening into intense, brilliant, crystallised moments of attention.

There was life in the air. The ground wore a faint penumbra of rippling light like an electrostatic charge, the latent consciousness of the stone fields. He let the currents play across his skin. Felt them as a stirring of the fine small hairs of his arms and the turbulence of his blood. He was alive to the invisible touch of the deep planetary rock. It reached into his body to touch the chambers of his heart.

This is who I am. I will not lose sight of this again.

The grasslands were not empty. Everywhere, invisible vivid small animal presences burrowed and hunted. Bright black eyes watched him from cover. The high-tension power lines were black and sheathed in sleeves of smoke. When he opened his mouth to breathe, their quivering tasted metallic on his tongue.

Rizhin's new world was thin and brittle. Translucent. Lom reached up into the sky and made it rain simply because he was thirsty and he could.

Beyond the skyline was the place he was going to. He knew the way.

Walking in the endless forest, Maroussia Shaumian feels the stirring of the trees and the cool damp touch of moving air against her cheek. The faintest ragged edge of a distant storm.

Chapter Eight

See him – rescuer, lord of the planet,
Wielder of gigantic energies –
In the screaming of steel machines,
In the radiance of electric suns.

He brings the planet a new sun,
He destroys palaces and prisons
He calls all people to everlasting brotherhood
And erases the boundaries between us.

Vladimir Kirillov (1880–1943)

1

Vacation season came early for the Central Committee that year. A motion was tabled in plenum in the name of Genrickh Gribov, Secretary for War: 'To grant Osip Rizhin a holiday of twenty days.' It was a formality, preserving the fiction that Papa Rizhin worked for them; naturally the motion was approved by acclamation.

The wound on Rizhin's face was healing more slowly than he'd have liked: the assassin's bullet had reawakened the old problem with his teeth. He wanted southern sunshine, a change of food and good dentistry, so it was with some relief that he settled into his personal train for Dacha Number Nine in the mountains overlooking Zusovo on the Karima coast. Lobster and citrus trees.

VKBD detachments secured the route, six men per kilometre. Sixteen companies guarded the telephone lines and eight armoured trains continually patrolled the track.

And where Rizhin went the Central Committee followed. Holidays were serious business in Rizhin's New Vlast. Gribov and Kistler, Yashina, Ekel and the rest packed hastily and piled into their cars and trains. They all had dachas in the Zusovo heights. Hunder Rond flew on ahead to be there when they came.

2

Engineer-Technician 1st Class Mikkala Avril works fourteen hours a day in a windowless room in the basement of a nine-floor block in the centre of the Vitigorsk complex, pausing only to bolt food and sleep in her one-room apartment in the House of Residence: bed, bookshelf, desk and chair.

They've given her a bank of von Altmann machines, six of them wired in linear sequence. Each machine has six cathode tubes, and a tube is 12,024 bits of data in 32 x 32 array. Each phosphorescent face is read, written and refreshed a hundred thousand times a second by electron beam. The smell of ozone and burning dust thickens the air. At the end of every shift her skin and clothes and hair stink of it. The odour pervades her dreams.

Her task is calculating pressure, force and trajectory. The vessels under development at Vitigorsk are larger and heavier than *Proof of Concept* by orders of magnitude – crude sledgehammer monsters – and the question presented to her for consideration is, one pressure plate or two? It's a matter of running the models again and again. Mikkala Avril is trusted to work alone, unsupervised, in silence, with her von Altmann array. She works through the models diligently. Progress is ahead of target.

But something is going wrong. Day by day Mikkala Avril's wide-eyed joy at the greatness of her purpose, her privilege, the task she's been selected for, is growing hollow. The sustenance it gives her is getting thin. The song of the New Vlast wearies her heart and jangles her nerves, even as her skin grows chalky-grey and her cropped hair loses its lustre.

The power of the detonations required to haul such behemoths crawling up the gravity well is terrifying: the ground destruction would gouge city-wide craters in the rock, obliteration perimeters measured in tens of miles. Mikkala Avril understands the numbers. She knows what they mean. But that's not the trouble: the continent is wide, the atmosphere is deep and broad.

In her rest periods she has ventured out into the Vitigorsk complex. She's seen the glow on the skyline at night from the forging zone, and she knows convict labour works there. The children sleeping on concrete. She's seen the people trucks come in. Yet that's not the trouble either: the labourers reforge their consciousness as they work; they welcome it and leave gladdened and improved. An efficient system that brings benefit to all.

No, it's the double mission parameter that corrodes her confidence. She doesn't understand it. It has not been explained.

She has not one model to work with, but two. Vessel Design One must hold propellant bombs sufficient to take it out of planetary orbit and speed it on its way across the cosmos into the sidereal age, and it will carry a store of empty casings to be fuelled on the moons of the outer planets. Staging posts. But Vessel Design Two, even more massive and with a payload provision twice that of Design One, needs no more power than to lift it into near orbit. A fleet of several hundred platforms, each dwarfing any ocean-going ship, lifted into orbit two hundred miles above the ground and settled stable there? What is the reason for this? It has not been explained. The variable is unaccounted for, and that's a lacuna of trust, a withholding of confidence that tugs at the edge of her and begins to unravel conviction.

She isn't fully conscious of what's happening. She doesn't have the right words, and if she ever did she's forgotten them now, the vocabulary of doubt eroded by the attrition of continually reset clocks, the accelerating repetition of year zero. What she feels is the uneasy itch of curiosity and upset at a distressing flaw in the machine. She takes it as a shortcoming in her own comprehension and sets about rectifying the fault, but her superiors frown and brush her off with critical remarks and the repetition of familiar platitudes. It never occurs to her that they don't know either.

Unhappy and alone, Mikkala Avril lingers in the refectory over the evening meal. Having no circle of companions (the theoretical mathematicians exclude her, so do the engineers of the von Altmann machines), she attaches herself to other groups and listens. She gets to know the bio-engineers – the humanity-synthesisers, the warriors against death – and picks up fragments of their talk. There are rumours of strange zones where clocks run slow and the dead climb from their graves. Quietly she joins the groups that gather around people returned from expeditions to find such places, which they say are shrinking fast and will soon be gone. She listens to the news of specimens collected. Samples of earth and air. But nobody knows or cares about the parameters of vessel design.

A chemist called Sergei Ivanich Varin, eager to seduce her, invites her to see the resurrectionists' laboratory after hours.

'Come on,' he says. 'I'll show you the freak shop.'

Strip lights flicker blue. The sickly stench of formaldehyde. Shelf after shelf of human babies in jars: misshapen foetuses and dead-born homunculi with bulging eyes, flesh softened and white like they've been too long under the sea. A boneless head, creased, flattened and flopped sideways. A torso collapsed in flaps of slumped waxy skin, diminutive supplicating arms raised like chicken wings. A lump with two heads and no internal organs, its shoulders ending in a ragged chewed-up mess.

Mikkala Avril coughs on choked-back sickness. Varin comes up close behind and nuzzles his face into her neck.

'No need to be frightened of the fishes. Big Sergei's here.'

She feels his hand sliding inside her jacket and blouse to cup her breast.

3

The lurid sleepless glare of the arc lamps and foundries and waste gas burn-off plumes of the Vitigorsk Closed Enclave was visible from two hours' drive away. A billboard on the approach road celebrated the shattering of the Vlast record for speed pouring concrete. TAKE SATISFACTION, LEADING WORKERS OF VITIGORSK! THE ENGINEERING CADRES SALUTE YOU! YOU HAVE RAISED A NEW CITY AT A PACE HITHERTO THOUGHT POSSIBLE ONLY FOR DEMOLITION! The entire ten-mile sprawl was enclosed by barbed wire and observation towers.

Lom brought the truck to a halt at the checkpoint, turned off the engine and swung down from the cab into a wall of noxious chemical fumes, plant noise, the smell of hot metal and the brilliance of floodlights bright as day. A guard in the black uniform of the Parallel Sector came over to check his papers. Two more hung back and covered him with automatic weapons.

The guard frowned.

'You're three hours late.'

Lom shrugged.

'Brake trouble,' he said. 'Fixed now.'

He shoved the sheaf of documents towards the guard. They were creased and marked with oily finger marks. Lom was wearing the truck driver's scuffed boots and shapeless coat. His hands were filthy.

'I could do with a wash,' he said. 'And I haven't eaten since breakfast.'

The guard glared at him.

'The transport workers' kitchen's closed. You're late.' He went through the papers slowly and carefully and took a slow walk around the truck, checking the seals. Comparing serial numbers with his own list. Kicking the tyres for no reason. Making a meal of it. *Bastard.*

Lom's heart was pounding. He smeared a greasy hand across his face, rubbing his eyes and stifling a yawn. There was a tiny sleeping compartment at the back of the cabin. The truck driver was in there, hidden under a blanket, trussed up with a rope, his own sock stuffed into his mouth.

The guard came back and handed Lom the signed-off papers. He looked disappointed.

Lom had wanted to come in late to avoid other drivers and catch the night-shift security: less chance they'd know the regular drivers by sight, that was the calculation. He hadn't reckoned on a guard who was bored and looking for trouble.

'What was the trouble with the brakes?' the guard said, still reluctant to let him go.

'Hydraulics leak,' said Lom. 'I patched it up. It should hold till I get back.'

He knew nothing about trucks and hoped the guard didn't either. *Please don't look in the cab.*

The guard signalled to the kiosk and the first barrier lifted.

'OK,' he said. 'Bay Five. Follow the signs. Check-in won't open till six but you can park there, and if you walk over towards the liquid oxygen generators there's a twenty-four-hour rest room for the duty maintenance. You might be able to get something to eat there. Maybe someone'll look at those hydraulics for you.'

Lom nodded. 'Thanks. Appreciate that.'

The gates of Bay Five were closed. No one was about. Beyond the chain-link fence was a row of dark containerless cabs. Lom checked on the driver. The man glared back at him with hot, frightened angry eyes. He pulled against the ropes and grunted through the sock in his mouth.

Lom hauled him up and propped him in a sitting position.

'Someone will find you,' he said, 'but not before morning. Don't try to call out; you'll make yourself throw up and that'll be very bad for you. You'll choke on it. Sit tight and wait.'

The man grunted again. It sounded like a curse.

Lom left the truck on the unlit apron in front of Bay Five, locked it and dropped the keys through a drainage grating. He reckoned he had seven hours before anyone would investigate. Maybe another half-hour before the alarm was raised.

So what the fuck do I do now?

He shouldered his bag and walked. The gun he'd taken from the VKBD man in Pir-Anghelsky Park was a comforting weight in his pocket.

He wandered among vast hangars and metal sheds. Chemical process-ing plants. Yards stacked with enormous pieces of shaped steel: curved components for even larger constructions. There was a river running thick and green under lamplight and a poisonous-looking artificial lake: scarfs of mist trailed across the surface and the acrid rising air warmed his face. Klaxons blared and gangs of workers in overalls changed shift. Parallel Sector patrols cruised the main roads in unmarked black saloons. It was easy to see them coming: he stepped into the shadows to let them pass.

For an hour he walked steadily, keeping to one direction as far as he could: east, he thought, though there was no way of telling. Vaporous effluent columns from a thousand vents and chimneys merged overhead in a low dense lid of cloud that shut out the night sky and reflected Vitigorsk's baleful orange glow.

A cluster of signs at an intersection pointed to meaningless numbered sectors but one caught his attention: PROTOTYPE – ASSEMBLY. Cresting a low hill, he found himself looking out across a floodlit concrete plain. From the centre rose a huge citadel of steel capped with a rounded dome. It resembled a massively engorged grain silo with stubby fins at the base. The trucks parked at the foot of it gave some sense of scale: if it had been a building, it would have been twenty or thirty floors high. Lom had seen pictures of the *Proof of Concept* – everyone had – and this thing was the same but much larger: a parent to a child.

From the cover of a low wall he took a couple of photographs just for the sake of it – he couldn't see what use Kistler could make of them, even if the facility was being kept secret from the Central Committee – and slipped away.

He glanced at his watch.

Almost 1 a.m.

He felt like he was playing at espionage.

What he needed was someone to talk to. Human intelligence.

PROJECT CONTROL. INSTITUTE OF RESEARCH. RESIDENTIAL CAMPUS.

It was a labyrinth of office blocks and apartment buildings, all crammed in and pressing against one another cheek by jowl: ramps and bollards and courtyards, walkways and flights of shallow concrete steps. Scrappy shrubs in concrete containers. Unlit ground-floor windows, service roads and areas of broken paving. A yard for refuse bins. Lom could see into uncurtained corridors. A few lights still burned in upper rooms.

Steps led up from a square with benches and flower beds to a revolving door. He heard voices, hushed but urgent. A couple standing in the splash of yellow light at the foot of the steps, arguing.

'No, Sergei. Please. I have to go now. I must go in.'

The woman was young. Slight and not tall, with cropped hair. Neat, sober office clothes. The man was bigger, older. Aggressive. Standing too close.

'Why not, Mikkala? What's wrong with me?'

'Nothing's wrong with you, Sergei. It's just … It's late. I have to go.'

He grabbed her arm. 'Come on, Mikkala,' he said. 'You'll like it. I'm good. I'm the best.'

She pulled her arm away and stepped back. 'I said no.'

'You fucking bitch. All evening you've been … What's a man supposed to think? You can't just turn round and say no, you cold fucking…' He reached out and pulled her towards him. Moved his head to hers. She turned her face away.

'Please, Sergei.'

Lom stepped out of the shadows.

'Hey,' he said. 'What's happening? Is this man bothering you?'

Sergei turned. 'Who the fuck are you?' He was swaying on his feet. Squinting. Lom smelled the aquavit thick on his breath.

'You should leave her alone,' said Lom.

'It's nothing to do with you, arsehole. Piss off. I'll break your fucking neck.'

Lom ignored him. 'Is this where you live?' he said to the woman. 'Come with me. I'll take you inside.'

'I said piss off, fuck-pig,' Sergei growled. 'You can't push me around.'

'Sergei,' said the woman. 'Don't.'

Sergei made a shambling lunge and swung a fist at Lom. He was big but soft and clumsy, and there wasn't much speed or power in the punch. Lom could have stepped out of the way. But he didn't. He raised his arm awkwardly as if to ward off the blow but he let it through. Turned his head slightly to take it on the side of the nose.

It hurt. A lot. He rocked back and put his hands to his face. Felt the warm blood flooding from his nostrils.

'You hit me!' he said to Sergei. 'I'm bleeding.'

'You were lucky, pig. Next time I'll break your fucking spine. And yours, bitch. I'll see you again. I'll ruin your fucking career. I'll ruin your *life*. People will listen to me.'

He turned and walked away, swaggering, unsteady. Lom tried to staunch the bleeding with the sleeve of the driver's coat. Smeared it around. It made quite a mess. His whole face felt stiff and sore.

'Are you all right?' said the young woman. She was thin and pale. Narrow shoulders. Her eyes glistened blurrily. She had been drinking too. 'Did Sergei hurt you? 'I'm sorry.'

'Not much,' said Lom. 'Not really. I'll be fine in a moment.' He pressed the back of his hand to his nose and brought it away covered in blood. Red and gleaming in the light from the doorway. 'I could do with a little cold water. And perhaps a towel. Is there somewhere ...?'

The young woman hesitated. Made up her mind.

'Come with me,' she said. 'I'll find you something.'

4

Lom sat on the bed in Mikkala Avril's room. She brought a bowl of cold water and a couple of rough grey towels. He dipped the end of one in the bowl and dabbed at his face.

'I'm sorry,' she said. 'I haven't got a mirror. There's one across the way, in the bathroom, but it's women only. Actually we're not meant to have men in this building at all.'

'Don't worry,' said Lom. 'I'll manage. You tell me how I'm doing. Is there much blood?'

She sat down next to him on the bed and studied his face. Her face was very thin, her eyes unnaturally wide.

She hasn't been eating. Pushing herself too hard.

'There's still blood coming from your nose,' she said. 'There's some in your hair, and it's all over your coat.'

He wet the towel again and pressed it against the side of his nose.

'I don't even know your name,' he said. His voice was muffled by the cloth. 'I'm Vissarion.'

'Mikkala. And ... thank you. For what you did just now.'

Lom waved it away. 'It was nothing.'

'But I feel awful,' said Mikkala. 'I was so *stupid*; I should never have gone with Sergei and got drunk like that, it's not the kind of thing I do. Ever. I'm not ... I wasn't good at it. I didn't handle it. It all went wrong. Everything's gone wrong here. I was so proud when I came, but nothing's going right ...'

She was really quite drunk. Words tumbled out.

'Is Sergei your boyfriend?' said Lom.

'No!' She shook her head fiercely. 'No, no, not at all – nothing like that. I've met him two or three times, that's all. It's just ... I don't know many people here. I work on my own; there's no one I can talk to, and the resurrectionists are more friendly than the others. They drink and talk and they're not so cold and stuck-up. I started spending evenings with them. It was ... a mistake.'

'How long have you been here?' said Lom. 'At Vitigorsk?'

'Not long.'

'Same here,' said Lom. 'It's an odd sort of place. It's hard to know what it's all here for. It's not easy to fit in.'

Mikkala nodded. Her cheeks flushed.

'Yes!' she said. 'Yes! That's it exactly. That's how I feel too. I thought I could be friends with the resurrectionists. I thought they liked me, and it made me feel part of something, not just on my own.'

Lom put down the towel and showed her his face.

'How is it now?' he said.

Mikkala frowned and squinted.

'Your nose has stopped bleeding,' she said. 'It looks a bit sore though, and I think you're going to have a black eye. Oh, there's still blood in your hair. You poor man, I'm so sorry.'

Lom dipped his hands in the water and pushed them through his hair.

'So what went wrong tonight?' he said. 'I mean, if you don't want to talk about it ...'

'Oh it was awful,' said Mikkala. 'Sergei took me to see the resurrectionists' building, where they work. He showed me the freak shop and it was *horrible*. It made me really upset. I was sick on the floor, and afterwards ... Sergei had a bottle of aquavit and we went somewhere and drank it. He said it would make me feel better but it didn't. I drank too much – we both did. I don't normally drink at all. But after what I saw ...'

'At the freak shop?'

'Yes.'

'How's my hair, Mikkala? Do you mind just checking?'

'What? Oh, yes, it's fine now – I think so – but your coat …'

'That's nothing.' Lom took it off and began to dab at the sleeve. 'What did Sergei show you at the freak shop?'

She shuddered. 'Dead babies. In *jars*. Ruined babies. Deformed foetuses.'

She went quiet.

Keep going, thought Lom. *Don't stop now.*

'Dead *babies*?' he said gently.

'It's not right,' said Mikkala. 'What they're doing. I don't think it's right. Of course they have their duty. It's their part of Task Number One, they're working to solve the common problem and that's a good thing, but … they're experimenting with the effects of exposure to different isotopes, and it goes wrong all the time. It *feels* wrong. They have old bodies too. From graves.'

'Why are they doing that?'

'It's the resurrection programme, learning to grow artificial bodies and bring people back from death, making it so people can live for ever and not die any more. So we can make the long journey to planets around other stars. The Director told me himself, one day we'll be able to bring someone back to life if you have even just a few atoms left from their bodies, because atoms have memories and they're alive. Sergei said they're thinking now that you don't need living people on the ships at all, only a few crew: you could maybe just send out small pieces of the dead and bring them back to life when you get there.'

Lom remembered Josef Kantor's strange invitation to him, six years before, alone in Chazia's interrogation cell in the Lodka. Looking into Kantor's dark brown eyes was like looking into street fires burning.

Humankind spreading out across the sky, advancing from star to star!

Impossible, Lom had said, and Kantor slammed his hand on the table.

Of course it's possible! It's not even a matter of doubt, only of paying the price! Imagine a Vlast of a thousand suns. Can you see that, Lom? Can you imagine it? Can you share that great ambition?

It had seemed like an invitation. Lom had turned him down without a thought.

'But you must know this already,' said Mikkala. 'Everyone here knows about the resurrectionists.'

'Not me. I'm just a grease monkey. Rivets and bolts. I do what I'm told. I haven't been here long. Still learning the ropes.'

Mikkala got up from the bed and moved to the chair at the desk.

'I shouldn't talk so much,' she said. 'I feel giddy. I've had a lot to drink.'

'It's fine, Mikkala,' said Lom. 'You're fine. That thing with Sergei was a shock, but you'll be OK.'

'I'm sorry,' she said, 'I can't remember your name. I don't know what you do. I've never seen you before.'

'Vissarion. I'm a construction engineer.'

'What are you working on?'

Lom thought fast. 'Prototype assembly.'

'Yes? Really? Then maybe you can tell me about the—'

She stopped.

'I don't think I'm supposed to ask,' she said. 'I ought to know, for my work, but nobody will say. They don't trust me; they keep me in the dark and they expect me to work alone. I don't like it. I don't feel comfortable here; it doesn't feel *right*.'

'I'll tell you what I can, Mikkala. We're all in this together. Working for the common purpose. That's what Vitigorsk is all about. What do you want to know?'

'Oh, nothing.'

'What?'

'It's just … the vessels, the planetary ships … I'm supposed to be working on launch calculations, only there are two kinds, and one kind is meant to leave this planet and make the long voyages, but the other only needs to reach a low orbit, and I think there are going to be more of those. But that makes no sense, does it? It doesn't fit in and I don't know why. Which kind is it you're building? I've never even seen it.'

She was looking at him, hot and staring eyes. He could see the wildness there. She was on the edge.

'I don't know,' said Lom.

'Oh.'

'Like I said, I just build what I'm told.'

'You mean you wouldn't tell me,' she said fiercely, 'even if you knew.'

'Of course I would.'

Her shoulders slumped.

'I don't feel well,' she said. 'I'd like to sleep now.'

'I would tell you if I knew, Mikkala. I tell you what: I'll help you to find out.'

She got up unsteadily from the bed.

'I think you should go,' she said. 'You're not meant to be here, you know.'

'Of course.' Lom stood and started putting on the truck driver's coat. There was blood soaked into the sleeve.

'Who would know?' he said.

'Know what?'

'Who knows about the plans for the different ships? Where could we find out about that?'

'Some people know, but they won't say.'

'So who knows? Who could we ask, if we wanted to?'

'I … Oh, lots of them know. The von Altmann programmers, the supervisor of mathematics, the chief designer. And the Director of course. Khyrbysk knows everything.'

'Khyrbysk? Yakov Khyrbysk?'

'Of course.'

'Khyrbysk is here? Where?'

'What do you mean, where?'

'I mean where's his office?' said Lom.

'Why?'

'We're old acquaintances. I'd like to go and see him. Where's his office?'

Mikkala slumped down again on the bed.

'In the Administration Block,' she said. 'But …' She stared up at him. Her face was drawn and chalky. Dark tears behind her eyes. 'Oh god. I've made another mistake. I thought you were my friend.'

'I am your friend. Of course I am.'

'I don't think so.'

'You're a good person, Mikkala. I don't mean you any harm. I'm glad we met.'

'Please go now.'

'Get some sleep,' said Lom. 'Everything'll be fine.'

5

I t was almost 2.30 a.m. when Lom found the Administration Block. Parallel Sector security patrols had slowed him up.

The building was dark and locked. He took a small torch and the roll of lock-picking tools from his bag, let himself in and locked the door behind him. Made his way up the stairs and started from the top. Fifteen minutes later he was in Khyrbysk's office. He extinguished the torch, drew the curtains and switched the desk lamp on.

He should have at least three hours before someone found the driver in the cab of his truck. Unless Mikkala raised the alarm, but he didn't think she would.

He felt bad about Mikkala.

There was a row of steel cabinets along the wall of Khyrbysk's office. Locked, but the locks were flimsy. No obstacle at all. He went through them methodically one by one, taking the most promising files across to the desk to read.

Piece by piece the story came together. Some of it he knew, but the rest ... There were plans within plans. The *ambition*. Some of it was flat-out insane. He thought about trying to take photographs of the documents, but the light was poor and he had the wrong kind of lenses. He'd seen too many blurred and badly exposed copies of documents. He started pulling out pages and stuffing them into his bag. Whole files if need be. It wasn't ideal – Khyrbysk would know he'd been burgled – but it couldn't be helped.

By 4.30 a.m. he had the whole picture. It was lethal. All that Kistler needed to work with, and more. Except that nothing tied it for certain to Rizhin, and he was running out of time.

There was a green steel safe behind the door. He hadn't touched it yet because of the combination lock. He didn't know how to open those. But everyone wrote their combination somewhere.

Lom went through the drawers of Khyrbysk's desk. Nothing. Checked the blotter but it was no help. Looked inside the covers of the books on his shelves. There was nothing that looked remotely like a combination to a safe.

Think. Think.

He went out into the corridor. There was a card on the door of the next office, tucked into a holder by the handle: ASSISTANT TO THE DIRECTOR.

Secretaries always knew the combinations to their boss's safe. Lom went into the room. There was an appointments diary next to the telephone. He flicked through the pages rapidly. On the inside back cover was a sequence of numbers. Four groups of four. In pencil.

Why would pencil be more secure than pen?

So you could erase it later.

He took the diary back into Khyrbysk's office and tried the numbers, but they didn't work. The safe didn't open.

Shit.

Then he tried them backwards.

The tumblers fell into place and he heard the lock click open.

On the bottom shelf of the safe was a small stack of brown folders. Not official files. Titles printed carefully in manuscript. Black ink.

Private Correspondence.

Conference – Byelaya Posnya.

There was no time to look inside: grey light was beginning to show behind the curtains in the window. Lom pushed the folders into his overloaded bag and switched off the desk lamp.

When he came out of the Administration Block there was a dull band of light across the eastern sky. Dawn came late and dark to Vitigorsk under the livid permanent cloud. In the plush quiet of Khyrbysk's office Lom had forgotten how the air stank. His bag was bulging. The sleeve and lapels of his coat were stained with his own dried blood. He looked a mess.

There was another truck loading bay a few blocks away. He'd noticed it in the night. He hustled, half-walking, half-running. The alert could come any moment now. He had to get clear of the checkpoints and on the road.

The gate of Bay Nineteen was open. An early driver unlocking his containerless cab. Lom circled round behind it.

The driver was lean, compact, energetic; long nose, flashing white teeth, thick black moustache; glossy black curls under a shiny leather cap. The kind of fellow that carried a knife. Bright black eyes narrowed viciously when he saw Lom's gun.

'Keep your hands out of your pockets,' said Lom. 'I'll be in the back of the cab. All I want is a ride out, no trouble for you at all. But I'll be watching you. I'll have the gun at your head. You say anything at the checkpoint, you make any move, any sign at all, and there'll be shooting. Lots of it. And you'll be caught in the crossfire, I'll make sure of that. You'll be first. I'll splatter your brains on the windscreen.'

The driver spat and stared at him. Said nothing. Didn't move.

'And I've got five hundred roubles in my pocket,' said Lom. 'It's yours when we're fifty miles from here.'

'Show me.'

Lom reached into his inside pocket with his left hand. Showed him the thick sheaf of Kistler's money.

'Pay now,' the driver said.

'Fuck you,' said Lom. 'We're not *negotiating*. It'll be like I say. Nothing different. Move. Quickly.'

The driver spat again and nodded. Stood back to let Lom climb aboard.

'You first,' said Lom

The driver swung up and slid across behind the wheel. Lom followed and squeezed into the sleeping compartment. Crouched down behind the driver's seat.

The engine roared into life.

6

Investigator Gennadi Bezuhov of the Parallel Sector, Vitigorsk Division, arrested Engineer-Technician 1st Class Mikkala Avril at three the next afternoon, less than ten hours after the discovery of the intrusion into Director Khyrbysk's office. Bezuhov presented her with his evidence: the statement of assaulted truck driver Zem Hakkashvili; the accusation of assaulted chemist Sergei Varin; the reports of communications operatives Zoya Markova and Yenna Khalvosiana, who overheard a male voice in Avril's room in the small hours of the night; the damp towel under her desk, stained with blood and engine oil. Suspect descriptions provided by witnesses Hakkashvili and Vrenn were undoubtedly of the same person.

The interrogation was brief. Suspect Avril, in a condition of marked emotional distress, immediately made a full confession and provided a detailed account of her encounter with the terrorist spy, whom she knew as 'Vissarion'. She admitted discussing with him restricted information concerning the work of Project Continual Sunrise. She had provided guidance and assistance in breaking into the Director's office and stealing Most Secret papers.

Engineer-Technician Avril's attitude under interrogation demonstrated poor social adjustment, psychological disturbance and instability, personality disorder, pathologically exaggerated feelings of personal importance, severe criticism of senior personnel and opposition to the purposes of her work and deep-seated internal deviation from the norms, aims and principles of the Vlast. Investigator Bezuhov permitted himself to observe that the subject had been promoted to her current rank without passing though normal processes of assessment, and had been allowed to work unsupervised on tasks for which she lacked the necessary intellectual capacities and technical credentials.

Bezuhov's superiors – Major Fritjhov Gholl, commander, Parallel Sector, Vitigorsk, and Director Yakov Khyrbysk himself – saw the broader perspective. They were acutely aware that Mikkala Avril was a Hero of the New Vlast, recruited and promoted on the instruction of Osip Rizhin himself, and she was in possession of information which must not be permitted to escape the confines of the project. Also they were not blind to the fact that the supervision of Mikkala Avril at Vitigorsk was not above criticism.

In the light of these additional considerations it was clear to Bezuhov's superiors that the Avril case required sensitive and flexible treatment. Embarrassment must be avoided. Their own careers were at stake, and surely Rizhin himself would prefer to know nothing of this. A judicial trial followed by a period in a labour camp was out of the question.

'Special handling, Gholl,' said Khyrbysk. 'In the circumstances? Don't you think?'

Gholl accepted the Director's judgement was sound, as ever.

Special handling. Seven grams of lead in the back of the head and the body dumped in the Cleansing Lake to dissolve.

'But retain a sample of body tissue, Gholl,' said Khyrbysk. 'Mikkala Avril had promising qualities. Death is temporary and she will be recalled, not once but millions of times, to walk for ever in perfected forms under countless distant suns.'

It was a comforting thought. The Director was not a harsh man. He looked to the radiance of humankind to come, and in dark days he lived by that.

'You understand, Director, I will have to report back to Colonel Rond?' said Gholl. 'I must do that.'

'Naturally.'

'You need not be concerned; the colonel is always discreet.'

7

The 28th Division (Engineers), guided by Lieutenant Arkady Rett, arrives at the edge of the living angel's cold-burning anti-life skirt where the trees are dying. They build walkways across the cold smouldering embers, the flimsy crusts of ground. The red hill advances and they retreat before it. Observations suggest it is picking up speed.

The commanding officer wrestles with many practical problems. Prolonged contact with the hill's margin is troublesome. The metal of his machines grows weak and brittle, and his people fall sick. Their limbs and faces and bodies acquire strange patches of smooth darkness. Their extremities grow numb, whiten and begin to crumble. An hour a day is the safe limit, all they can stand. But the commanding officer makes progress. Now he has lines of supply, he puts the sappers on rotation. The excavation gear arrives. They reach the lower slopes and begin to dig.

Corporal Fallun, who refused an order and abandoned his comrades, was never seen again. Rett didn't find him on his way back, and Fallun is assumed to be lost in the woods. The commanding officer classifies him a deserter and thinks of him no more. Fallun's comrade, Private

Soldier Senkov, who returned with Rett but never regained his senses and babbles relentlessly, never sleeping, is sent back out of the forest on a returning barge. He did his duty and the commanding officer recommends a sanatorium cure.

A piece of Archangel rides Senkov's mind down the river and out of the trees. Quiet and surreptitious, all hugger-mugger, he slips the green wall and squeezes a tenuous blurt of himself through the gap into Rizhin world.

It is the merest thread of Archangel. A wisp of sentience. But he is through. He inhales deeply and shouts defiance at the sky.

This – this! – this is what he needs!

The impossible slow forest behind the green wall was killing him. There was no time there. There was no history.

But he finds Rizhin world different now. Hard. Quick. Lonely. There is no place for living angels here: the whole world stinks of barrenness and death.

Desperately he scrabbles for purchase and purpose.

Archangel! Archangel! I am beautiful and I am here!

And a tiny distant voice answers from the west. A shred of shining darkness from the space between the stars.

Chapter Nine

My age, my predatory beast –
who will look you in the eye
and with their own blood mend
the centuries' smashed-up vertebrae?

Osip Mandelstam (1891–1938)

1

Vasilisk the bodyguard, six foot three and deeply tanned and sleek with sun oil, naked but for sky-blue trunks, runs five springing steps on his toes, takes to the air and executes a long perfect dive. Enters the pool with barely a splash, swims twelve easy lengths, hauls out in a single smooth movement and lies stretched out on a towel – blue towel laid on perfect white poolside tiles – in the warmth of the morning sun.

He lies on his back with eyes half closed, arms spread wide to embrace the sun, the beautiful killer at rest, empty of thought, breathing the scent of almonds. His slicked yellow hair glistens, his firm honey-brown stomach is beaded with water jewels. Through damp eyelashes he watches blue shimmer.

The pool is filled with water and sunlight. The surface glitters.

A warm breeze stirs the fine pale hairs on his chest.

A dragonfly, lapis lazuli, fat as his little finger, flashes out of the rose bushes, disturbed by a quiet footfall in the garden. The chink of glass against glass.

A housemaid with a tray of iced tea.

Vasilisk the bodyguard, blond and beautiful, half asleep, listens without intent to the bees among the mulberries, the shriek and laughter from the tennis court, the *pock pock pock* of the ball, the sway of trees on the hillside that sounds like the sea.

The sky overhead is a bowl of blue. Brushstroke cloud-wisps. Vasilisk closes his eyes and watches the drift of warm orange light across trans-lucent skin.

Far away down the mountain a car drops a gear, engine racing to attack a steep climb. The sound is tiny with distance.

2

Lukasz Kistler's sleek ZorKi Zavod limousine took the corniche along the Karima coast, purring effortlessly, a steady sixty-five, glinting under the southern sun. Two and a half tons of engine power, bulging wheel arches, running boards, mirrors and fins.

The road was a dynamited ledge, hairpins and sudden precarious fallings-away. The mountains of the Silion Massif plunged to the edge of the sea: bare cliffs and steep slopes of black cypress; sun-sharpened jagged ridges and crisp high peaks, snow-capped even in summer. And always to the right and hundreds of feet below, the white strip of sand and the sea itself, discovered by glittering light, a tranquil and brilliant horizonless blue.

This was the favoured country: sun-warmed Karima rich in climate and soil, with its own little private ocean. Karima of the islands and the hidden valleys. Karima of the flowering trees, hibiscus, tea planta-tions, vineyards and orange groves. Karima of the white-columned sanatoriums in the wooded hills and on the curving quiet of the bays. Rest-cure Karima. Union-funded convalescent homes for the para-gons of sacrificial labour in olive and lemon and watermelon country: the bed-ridden propped under rugs in their windows to watch the sea, the ambulatory at backgammon and skat under striped awnings.

Secluded private hotels with balcony restaurants (LIST ROUBLES ONLY ACCEPTED). Resort Karima. Twenty-mile coastal ribbons of pastel-blue concrete dormitories for the ten-day family vacations of seven-day-week leading workers. War never touched Karima. The Archipelago never got there, neither bombers nor troops nor cruisers nor submarines. Civil war was fought elsewhere. Karima was never hurt at all.

The municipal authorities of Karima made the most of the annual Dacha Summer of the Central Committee. The road to Rizhin's Krasnaya Polyana, Dacha Number Nine at Zusovo, was remade fresh each year: the velvet shimmer of asphalt, the gleam of undented steel crash barriers.

The limousine tyres hissed quietly. The driver dropped a gear and slowed into a hairpin switchback, and the turn brought Kistler suddenly face to face with the biggest portrait of Papa Rizhin he'd ever seen: two hundred feet high, surely, and the benevolent smiling countenance outlined with scarlet neon tubes, burning bright against the cliff face even in the noonday light.

ALL KARIMA LOYALLY WELCOMES OUR GENERALISSIMUS!

Lukasz Kistler had his own dacha, a white-gabled lodge in the Koromantine style tucked in among black cypresses a mile or so from Krasnaya Polyana. They all did – Gribov, Yashina and the rest – all except Rond, who travelled with his staff and had rooms in Rizhin's place. No vacation for the assiduous Colonel Hunder Rond.

Studded timber gates opened at Kistler's approach. The car entered a rough-walled unlit tunnel cut through solid mountain and ten minutes later emerged into sunlight and the courtyard of Krasnaya Polyana, a sprawling low green mansion on the brink of a sheer cliff.

The sun-roofed verandas of Dacha Number Nine looked out across the sea. Some previous occupant had planted the gardens with mulberry, cherry, almonds and acacia. Tame flightless cranes and ornamental ducks for the boating lake. Rizhin had added tennis courts, skittles, a shooting range. Papa Rizhin holidayed seriously.

Kistler found Rizhin himself in expansive mood, rigged out in gleaming white belted tunic and knee-length soft boots, Karima-fashion, paunch neat and round, hair brushed back thick and lustrous in the sunshine. He seemed taller. Mountain air suited him. The bullet scar on his cheek, still puckered and raw, gave his long pockmarked face a permanent lopsided grin. A show of white ivory teeth.

'Lukasz! You came!' Rizhin clapped him on the shoulder. 'So we haven't arrested you yet? Still not shot? Good. Come and see Gribov playing tennis in his jacket and boots, it's the most comical thing – everyone is laughing. But he wins, Lukasz! He plays like a firebrand. What a man this Gribov is.'

They linked arms like brothers and walked around the edge of the lake.

'Zorgenfrey came up yesterday from Anaklion,' said Rizhin, 'and completely fixed my teeth. No pain at all. Why can't we have such dentists in Mirgorod? The Karima sanatoriums get the best of everything. Yet he tells me he can't get his daughter into Rudnev-Possochin. He wants her to study medicine but the university puts up no end of obstructions. We must do something there. Talk to them for me, Lukasz. Iron the wrinkles out.'

'Leave it with me, Osip,' said Kistler. 'I'll take care of it.'

There were twenty-four at dinner: the Central Committee, Rizhin's bodyguards Bauker and Vasilisk, uncomfortable and self-conscious ('Come,' said Rizhin. 'We're all family here.') and silent, watchful Hunder Rond. They ate roasted lamb in a thick citrus sauce. Sliced tomatoes, cherries and pears. Red wine and grappa. Rizhin kept the glasses filled, and after dinner there was singing and dancing.

Bauker and Vasilisk pushed the table to the side of the room and rolled back the carpet. Rizhin presided over the gramophone, playing arias from light operas and ribald comic songs. He led the singing with his fine tenor voice. The bodyguards circulated, refilling glasses.

'Dance!' said Rizhin. 'Dance!' He put on 'Waltz of the Southern Lakes' three times in a row, loud as the machine would go. The men danced with other men or jigged on the spot alone. Yashina, tall and gaunt, twirled on her spiky heels, arms upraised, face a mask of serious concentration. Gribov went to take her in his arms, and when she ignored him he pulled out a handkerchief and danced with it the country way, stamping and shouting like the peasant he used to be. He lunged at Kistler, breathing grappa fumes. Kistler ducked out of his way.

'Osip!' shouted Gribov. 'Osip! Put on the one with dogs!'

'What's this about dogs?' said Marina Trakl, the new Secretary for Agriculture, red-faced. She was very drunk. 'Are there dogs? I adore dogs!'

'These are dogs that sing,' said Gribov. He started to dance with her.

'Then let us have singing dogs!' Marina Trakl grinned, snatching Gribov's handkerchief and waving it in the air.

'Of course,' said Rizhin. 'Whatever you say.' He changed the record to Bertil Hofgarten's 'Ball of the Six Merry Dogs'. When the dogs came in on the second chorus Rizhin started hopping and yelping himself, face twisted in a lopsided beatific smile. Kistler hadn't seen Rizhin so full of drink. Normally he left the aquavit and the grappa to the others and watched.

'Come on, you fellows!' called Rizhin, dancing. 'Bark with me! Bark!'

One by one, led by Gribov, the members of the Central Committee pumped their elbows and put back their heads and howled like hounds and bitches at the broken moons.

'Yip! Yip! Yip! A-ruff ruff ruff! Wah-hoo!'

'Come on, Rond!' yelled Rizhin. 'You too!'

Peller, the Secretary for Nationalities, slipped on spilled food and fell flat on his back, legs stuck out, laughing. He wriggled on his back in the mess.

'Yap! Yap! Yap!'

When the music stopped Gribov slumped exhausted and sweaty on a couch next to Kistler, undid his jacket, put back his head and began to snore. Kistler jabbed him when Rizhin, face flushed, eyes suddenly on fire, drained his glass and banged the table. It was time for Rizhin's speech.

'Look at ourselves, my friends,' he began. 'What are we?'

He paused for an answer. Somebody made a muffled joke. A few people laughed.

'What was that? I didn't hear,' said Rizhin, but no one spoke. The atmosphere was suddenly tense.

'I'll tell you what we are,' Rizhin continued. 'Nothing. We are nothing. Look at this planet of ours: a transitory little speck in a universe filled with millions upon millions of far greater bodies.' He gestured towards the ceiling. 'Out there, above us, there are countless suns in countless galaxies, and each sun has its own planets. What is any one of us? What is a man or a woman? We are, in actual and literal truth, nothing. Our bodies are collections of vibrating particles separated by emptiness. The very stuff and substance of our world is nothing but light and energy held in precarious patterns of balance, and mostly it is nothing at all. We are accidental temporary assemblages in the middle of a wider emptiness that is passing through us even now, at this very moment, even as we pass through it. Emptiness passing through emptiness, each utterly unaffected by the other. The energies of the universe pass through us like Kharulin rays, as if we are not here at all. We are our own graves walking. We are handfuls of dust.'

Several faces were staring at Rizhin with open dismay. Gribov leaned over in a fug of grappa to whisper in Kistler's ear, 'What the fuck's the man talking about? What's all this crazy shit?'

Kistler winced. 'You're too loud,' he hissed. 'For fuck's sake, keep it down.'

Every time Kistler glanced at Hunder Rond the man was watching him. Their eyes locked for a second, then Rond turned away.

One day, little prince, thought Kistler. *One day I'll snap your fucking thumbs.*

'But what a gift this nothingness is, my friends!' Rizhin was saying. 'It is the gift of immensity! Once we see that this world, this planet, is *nothing*, we realise what our future truly holds. Not one world, but all the worlds. The universe. The stars like sand on the beach. The stars like water, the oceans we sail. Our present world is trivial: it is merely the first intake of breath at the commencement of the endless sentence of futurity.'

Rizhin poured himself another glass, the clink of bottle against tumbler the only sound in the room. He fixed them with burning eyes. It was Rizhin the poet, Rizhin the artist of history, speaking now.

'I have seen this future! Red rockets, curvaceous, climbing on parabolas of steam and fire. making the sky seem small and wintry-blue. Because the sky *is* small. We can take it in our fists! I have seen these rockets of the future rising into space, carrying a new human type to their chosen grounds. Individuals whose moral daring makes them vibrate at a speed that turns motion invisible. There are new forms in the future, my friends, and they need to be filled with blood. We are the first of a new humankind. Where death is temporary a million deaths mean nothing.'

After the dinner and the dancing, Rizhin led the way to his cinema. Blue armchairs in pairs, a table between each pair: mineral water, more grappa, chocolate and cigarettes. Rugs on the grey carpet. They watched an illicit gangster film, imported from the Archipelago: men in baggy suits with wide lapels fought over a stolen treasure and a dancing girl with silver hair. Then came a Mirgorod Studios production, *Courageous Battleship!* Torpedoed in the Yarmskoye Sea, a hundred shipwrecked sailors line an iceberg to sing a song of sadness, a requiem for their lost ship.

Halfway through the film, Rizhin leaned across and gripped the elbow of Selenacharsky, secretary for culture.

'Why are the movies of the Archipelago better than ours?'

Selenacharsky turned pale in the semi-darkness and scribbled something in his notebook.

Dawn was coming up when they filed out of the cinema into the scented courtyard. Kistler was going to his car when Rizhin appeared at his elbow.

'I shoot in the mornings at the pistol range. Join me, eh, Lukasz? We'll have a chat, just you and me. Man to man.'

Kistler groaned inwardly. His head hurt.

'Of course, Osip.'

'Good. Nine thirty sharp.'

3

Kistler managed a couple of hours' sleep and returned to Rizhin's dacha stale and depressed, unbreakfasted, the dregs of the wine and the grappa still in his blood, a sour taste of coffee on his tongue. The dinner of the night before weighed heavy in his stomach. He felt queasy.

He followed the sound of gunfire to Rizhin's shooting range, a crudely functional concrete block among almond trees. Vasilisk the bodyguard, six foot three, blond and beautiful, was lounging on a chair by the door, white cotton T-shirt tight across his chest. He was wearing white tennis shoes and regarded Kistler with sleepy expressionless sky-blue eyes.

Kistler nodded to him and entered the shooting range.

Vasilisk rose lazily to his feet and padded in behind him. Closed the door, leaned against the wall and folded his arms. Kistler watched the muscles of the bodyguard's shoulders sliding smoothly. His thickened honey-gold forearms.

Rizhin was alone inside the building, bright and fresh in shirtsleeves, firing at twenty-five-yard targets with a pistol. Three rounds then a pause. You could cover the holes in the target with the palm of your hand.

He paused to reload. The gun was fat and heavy in his swollen fists but his fingers on the magazine were lightning-quick. Nimble. Practised.

'Do you know firearms, Lukasz?'

'Not really.'

'You should. Our existence depends on them. The powerful should study and understand the foundations of their power. This, for instance, is a Sepora .44 magnum. Our VKBD officers carry these. Heavy in the hand, but they shoot very powerful shells. Very destructive. They tend to make a mess of the human body. The removal of limbs. The bursting of skulls. Large holes in the stomach or torso. Butchery at a distance. Not a pretty death.' He turned and fired seven shots in rapid succession. The noise was deafening. An unmistakable acrid smell.

Rizhin offered the gun to Kistler.

'Would you like to shoot, Lukasz? It's important to keep one's skills up to scratch'

'No,' said Kistler. 'Later perhaps. I drank too much grappa last night.'

Rizhin shrugged.

'Your hand's trembling,' he said.

Kistler couldn't stop himself looking down at his hands. It was a sign of submission. He cursed himself inwardly.

Careful.

He held his hands out in front of him, palms down.

'I don't think so,' he said.

Rizhin ejected the magazine from the pistol and reloaded, taking a fresh magazine from his pocket.

'You enjoyed our evening then?' he said. 'I hope so.'

'Of course! It's good to know one's colleagues better. The holiday season is valuable. Time well spent.'

'I thought you were bored. You seemed bored. Gribov can be over-powering.'

'Not at all. A little tired perhaps. I'd had a long journey.'

Rizhin raised his arm and squeezed off three rapid shots. 'But you keep a distance – I see you doing it – and that's sound. I admire it in you. Music and feasting are excellent things, Lukasz; they reduce the bestial element in us. Song and dance, food and wine, good company: they calm the soul and make one amiable towards humanity. But we aren't ready for softness yet, you and I. Today is not the time to stroke people's heads. Of course, opposition to all violence is the ultimate ideal for men like us, but you have to build the house before you hang the pictures. Your attitude last night was a criticism of me, which I accept.'

'No. Not at all, Osip. I only—'

'But yes, it was, and I accept it. I've sent the others home, you know. I've packed them all off back to Mirgorod, back to their desks. There is work to be done and they must get to it.'

'What? All of them?' said Kistler.

'I thought you'd be pleased. Our colleagues bore you, Lukasz, isn't that so? Be honest with me. I'll tell you frankly, they bore me too. For now I must use people like them, but they're narrow, they have limited minds. Not like you and me. We see the bigger picture.'

Where is this going?

Vasilisk the bodyguard moved across to a wooden chair. The neat brown leather holster nestled in the small of his back bobbed with the rhythm of his buttocks as he walked. Vasilisk settled into the chair, crossed legs stretched out in front of him, and absorbed himself in studying his fingernails.

Rizhin was turning his pistol over with thick clumsy-looking fingers.

'What I was trying to say last night,' he continued, 'but I was drunk and over-poetical … what I was trying to say is that this – *this*, all around us, our *work* and our *diplomacy* and our *cars* and our *dachas* – this is not the point to which history is leading us. This is only the beginning: the first letter of the first word of the first sentence of the first book in the great library of futurity. You see this as well as I do.'

'There's a lot more to be done,' said Kistler cautiously. 'Of course. Certainly. Our industry...'

Rizhin fished out three more shells from his pocket, ejected the magazine and pressed them into place one by one. Replaced the magazine in the pistol.

'I'm talking philosophically,' he said. 'The moral compass is not absolute, you see. It has changed and we have a new morality now. A new right. A new good. A new true. Our predecessors were scoundrels; the angels were an obfuscation, the things of the forest bedbugs. Leeches. A distortion of the moral gravity. Whatever serves the New Vlast is moral. That's how it must be, for now. Where all death is temporary then death is nothing. Killing is conscienceless. A million deaths, a billion deaths, are nothing.'

'But we need people,' said Kistler. 'Strong healthy people, educated, burning with energy. We need them to work. And we need steel. We need oil. We need power. We need mathematics and engineering. We need to be clever, Osip, or the Archipelago will—'

Rizhin brushed him off with a gesture. 'The Archipelago will be ground to powder under the wheels of history, Lukasz,' he said. 'You underestimate inevitability.'

He raised the pistol and levelled it at Kistler's head, the ugly blackness of the barrel mouth pointing directly between his eyes.

'History is as inevitable and unstoppable as the path of the bullet from this gun if I pull the trigger. Effects follow causes.'

Kistler made an effort to take his eyes from the pistol. His gaze met Rizhin's soft-brown gentle look.

'Osip...' he began.

Rizhin turned away and fired a shot at the target. The raw explosion echoed off the concrete walls. Kistler realised his hands were damp. The back of his shirt was cold and sticky against his skin.

'I had hopes for you, Lukasz,' said Rizhin. 'I was going to *involve* you. You're a man of fine qualities. An outstandingly useful fellow. I was going to take you with us. But I find you are also a sentimentalist. Your belly is soft and white and you aren't to be trusted. You've let me down. Badly.'

'I don't understand this,' said Kistler. 'What's happening here, Osip? Where is this going to?'

'Tell me about Investigator Vissarion Lom.'

'Who?'

'Feeble. Feeble. Where is the famous Kistler fire in the guts? Where is the energy?' Rizhin pulled a crumpled typescript from the back pocket of his trousers and pushed it towards him. Kistler read the first few lines.

Kistler Residential – Internal
23.47 Transcription begins

Kistler: Yes?
Unknown caller: I wish to speak with Lukasz Kistler.
Kistler: This is Kistler. Who the fuck are you?

'I know this is Lom,' said Rizhin. 'He's a man I know. He circles me, Lukasz. He buzzes in my ear. I can't shake him off.'

'So shoot me.'

Rizhin shook his head.

'I want you to extend your vacation, Lukasz. Another week or two maybe. I've had enough of this bastard Lom. I want to trace him. I want to tie him down and finish him. And he's not doing this alone; there are conspiracies here, Lukasz, and you're deep in the whole nest of shit, and I'm going to know the extent of it. The whole fucking thing. Names. Dates. Connections. Circles of contact. You'll stay here and spend some time with Rond and his people. We're going to be seeing a lot more of each other. We'll have more talks.'

4

Back in Mirgorod again after the long journey from Vitigorsk, Lom wasted no time. He dialled from a call box at the Wieland Station. The contact number Kistler had given him rang and rang. He hung up and tried again.

Eventually someone answered. A woman's voice. Cautious.

Yes? Who is this?

'I want to speak with Lukasz Kistler.'

Name, please. Your name.
'I will speak to Kistler. Only Kistler. He is expecting me.'
Secretary Kistler is unavailable.
'I'll call back. Give me a time.'
The Secretary will be unavailable for some considerable time, perhaps days, perhaps longer. You may discuss your business with me. What is your name?
Lom cut the connection.

He took a cab across the city and walked the last few blocks to the war-levelled quarter of the rubble dwellers, to the cellar Elena Cornelius had led him to. His link to the Underground Road. Konnie and Maksim were there. So was Elena, looking strained. Hunted.
'I can't reach Kistler,' said Lom. 'I've got something he can use. Devastating material. Dynamite. In Kistler's hands it will bring Rizhin down. Definitely. But Kistler is out of contact. His number's no good. I thought you could—'
'Kistler has been arrested,' said Maksim.
Lom felt the warmth drain from his face.
'No,' he said. 'No. When?'
'He went to Rizhin's dacha. He's being held there under interrogation. Rizhin is there with him, and so is Rond. Nobody else.'
'How do you know this? How can you be sure.'
'We have somebody there,' said Konnie. 'On the dacha staff. There is no doubt.'
'But Kistler is alive?'
'Oh yes,' said Maksim. 'For now he is alive, though what state he's in …'
'Is there anybody else?' said Lom. 'Anyone else who could use the material I have, like Kistler could?'
'In the Presidium? No. Not a chance.'
'Then I have to get Kistler out of there and back to Mirgorod,' said Lom.
'That's impossible,' said Maksim. 'He's being held by the Parallel Sector in Rizhin's own fucking dacha.'
'Nothing's impossible,' said Lom. 'I need Kistler. Tell me about this dacha. Tell me about your contact there.'
'No,' said Maksim. 'It's out of the question.'

'This material,' said Konnie. 'It's as big as you say? It's that dangerous for Rizhin?'

'Absolutely,' said Lom. 'Poisonous. Lethal. In Kistler's hands it will
bring him down.'

'What is it?' said Maksim.

'No,' said Lom. 'First you tell me about Rizhin's dacha.'

'But what you've got is really that good?'

'Yes. If we can get Kistler back to Mirgorod, free, and arm him with
what I have, he can turn the Central Committee against Rizhin and
he will fall.'

Konnie glanced at Maksim.

'We won't tell you where Rizhin's dacha is,' she said. 'You'll need
help. We'll take you there. We'll go with you.'

'Konnie...' said Maksim.

Konnie ignored him.

'You can't get Kistler out of there all by yourself,' she said. 'We have
some resources, not much maybe, but better than one man on his own.'

Lom considered. 'Thank you,' he said. 'Yes. That would be good.'

Konnie turned to Elena.

'You're welcome to stay here,' she said. 'You'll be safe. You won't be
found. Someone will bring you food. It won't be more than a week.'

Elena Cornelius bridled. 'I'm coming. I'm tired of hiding. I've got a
job to finish and none of you can do what I can do. Get me a rifle and
I will come.'

5

Every day in the first pale pink and violet flush of another new
morning Vasilisk the bodyguard runs in the hills above Dacha
Number Nine. Ten easy miles on yellow earth tracks before
breakfast, taking the slopes through fragrant thorny shrub with cardio-
vascular efficiency, the early warmth of the sun on his shoulders. He
sees the soft mist in the valleys. Sees the black beetles crossing the
paths and the boar pushing through thickets. Watches the big hunting
birds, high on stiff wings against the pale dusty blue, circling up on the

thermals. Miles of rise and fall unrolling smoothly and effortlessly.

No words. No thoughts.

He knows the routes of the security patrols and the places they watch from and he does not go there; he prefers to drink the mountain solitude in, like cool sweet water. The watcher doesn't like to be watched. Doesn't like the feel of a long lens on his back. Ten miles of nobody in the morning sets him up for the day.

Two hundred push-ups, breathing steady and slow, two sets of fifty per arm, and a downhill sprint between pine trees – jumping tussocks and stony glittering streams – and Vasilisk the bodyguard steps out onto the road, corn-yellow hair slick with sweat. Sweat patches darkening his singlet.

The guards at the gatehouse phone him in through the gate, as they do every morning. He glances at them lazily, indifferent small blue eyes blank and pale behind pale-straw eyelashes. He goes to his room, picks up a towel and heads for the pool.

6

The streets of Anaklion on the Karima coast were wide and shaded by trees. Many of the houses were modern, every fifth building a guest house or hotel. Women at the roadside and in the squares sold figs and watermelons and clouded-purple grapes. Warm air off the sea disturbed the palms and casuarina trees.

Konnie, Lom and Elena took the funicular up to the Park of Culture and Rest. Gravel paths between long plots of enamel-bright flowers. Statues of dogs and soldiers. Wrought-iron benches for the weary and the convalescent. At the Tea-Garden-Restaurant Palmovye Derevya they took a table some way from the other customers, at the edge of the cliff, shaded by waxy dark green leaves against the low morning sun. A hundred feet sheer below them youths swam in the river, and across the gorge balconied houses recuperated: quiet lawns, striped awnings.

A waiter materialised at their table. Tight high-waisted trousers, a pouch at his hip for coin.

'Tea,' said Konnie. 'With lemon. For four. And some pastries.' Her long fine hair was burnished copper in the flickering splashes of sunlight between leaves. Her eyes flashed green at the waiter. A hint of a conspiratorial smile. 'You decide which ones.' A beautiful young woman with friends, on vacation. A husband or boyfriend would join them soon.

They'd arrived the night before. Lom used the last of Kistler's roubles for rooms at the guest house Black Cypress. Maksim hadn't appeared at breakfast.

'He went up the mountain before dawn,' said Konnie. 'He wanted to have a look for himself.'

Lom said nothing. Since they had left Mirgorod, Maksim had changed subtly. His face cleared. No longer pent-up and clouded with frustration, he was self-contained, competent and direct. Back in the military again, he was a man at his best with a mission. A simple purpose. Lom liked him. He'd started to trust him too.

'We can do this,' said Maksim when he arrived. 'It is possible. There is a way. But it's all about timing. Everything has to work precisely right. Absolute discipline.'

'OK,' said Lom. 'Go on.'

Maksim glanced at him. The two men had never quite resolved the unspoken question of who was in charge.

'The dacha is a fortress,' Maksim began. 'A compound surrounded by steep hills. The only way in is a tunnel through the mountain. There's a gate at the entrance from the road: wooden but three inches thick and reinforced with iron. There's a gatehouse – always two guards, with binoculars and a view for miles down the mountain. They'd see any vehicle coming ten minutes before it reached them. The gate is kept closed and barred from within. It's opened at a signal from the gatehouse, when they're expecting company. But nobody comes and nobody goes, except the domestics make a shopping trip once a week. A couple of guards go with them.'

'And inside?' said Lom.

'VKBD security. Plus Rond is there, and he's got Parallel Sector personnel with him. And Rizhin has his own personal security. Two bodyguards. Part of the family. Very dangerous. Say, twenty in all.'

'Not so much,' said Lom.

'There's a militia company in the town, an armoured train five miles away, a cruiser in the bay. They think they're safe enough.'

'Patrols in the hills?'

'No information,' said Maksim. 'But assume so. Yes.'

'So what's the plan?' said Lom.

'We must have the gate open at eleven tomorrow morning. Eleven o'clock exactly, to the second. No sooner and no later. Kistler will be coming out in a car.'

'A car?' said Konnie.

'Rizhin's personal limousine. It's the most powerful and heavily armoured they have. Bullet-proof glass in the windows. Thick steel panels underneath too. Hell, even the tyres are bullet-proof.'

'And all we have to do,' said Lom, 'is open the gate tomorrow?'

'Yes.'

'How?' said Konnie.

Maksim's face clouded. 'It can't be unbarred from outside, so we'll need explosives.'

Konnie looked around at the Park of Culture and Rest, at the teen-age boys and girls in the river and stretched out on flat slabs of rock, lazy under the sun.

'Where do you get explosives in a place like this?' she said.

'Every construction project here has to start with blasting rock,' said Maksim. 'There's got to be a supply somewhere. A builder's merchant. An engineering yard.'

'That won't be necessary,' said Lom. 'You can leave the gate to me. I'll take care of it. And the guards in the gatehouse too.'

Maksim looked at him doubtfully.

'How?' he said.

Lom hesitated. Maksim's expression was soldierly. Sceptical. He couldn't begin to explain. Explaining would make it worse.

'It'll be fine,' said Lom. 'Please. I know what I'm doing. Leave it to me. If you can get Kistler to the gate at eleven, it'll be open.'

Maksim bridled.

'I must know what you intend,' he said. 'I will not lead my people blind. Lives depend on me.'

Lom shrugged. 'Stay here then. I'm grateful for what you've done, and from here I will go on alone.'

'Maksim,' said Elena Cornelius quietly, 'I think we should trust Vissarion. He has brought us this far. Without him we would be no-where. We owe the chance we have to him.'

'Chance!' Maksim began, but thought better of it. 'OK,' he said. 'But I'll be at the gatehouse with you.'

'Good,' said Lom. 'Thank you.'

He took a long draught of hot sweet tea and considered the plan. It was terrible. A really shit plan. But it would be fine.

Just keep blundering on. Plough through the obstacles as they come. Way too late to back off now.

7

Weary after weeks of frustrating travel – delays over paperwork, failed and diverted trains, fuel shortages, their carriage attacked by a hungry mob – the Philosophy League arrived at the Wieland Station. Penniless – all their money spent on unexpected expenses along the way – but back in Mirgorod at last.

They'd hoped for more of a reception. Forshin had wired ahead to Pinocharsky to warn him of their arrival. They'd expected journalists and prepared the lines they would take: Forshin had the text of a speech in his pocket, and Brutskoi had written an article for the *Lamp*, a manifesto of sorts, a call to intellectual arms. But there was no one to meet them. The League stood together in a disgruntled huddle on the platform, surrounded by their suitcases and chests of books, their luggage much battered and repaired.They all looked to Forshin for answers.

'Well?' said Yudifa Yudifovna. 'So what are we to do?'

Eligiya Kamilova stood somewhat apart from the rest with Yeva and Galina Cornelius. The girls were restless and unhappy.

'Do we have to stay with these people any more?' said Yeva. 'Can't we go home now?'

Home? thought Kamilova. *What is home?*

'Ha!' said Forshin, visibly relieved. 'Here's Pinocharsky at last.' He waved. 'Pinocharsky! I say, Pinocharsky! Here!'

Pinocharsky came towards them, arms open in a mime of embrace. He was wreathed in smiles but looked harassed, his wiry red hair wisping.

'Well then!' he said. 'Here you are; you have come at last! But you're late. I was expecting you two hours ago. You have to hurry. Your train is waiting on the next platform.' He gestured for porters. 'What a lot of luggage you have. But no matter, there's no doubt plenty of room.'

The members of the League were looking at one another in dismay. Forshin took Pinocharsky by the arm.

'Train?' he said. 'What train? We've only just arrived, man. We need a hotel. We need a meeting. Editors. Publishers. We need a plan. We have much to say to the people.'

'Ah,' said Pinocharsky. 'Well, no, not exactly. Not yet. There's been a change of plan. Unfortunately I wasn't able to contact you.' He was looking shifty.

'A change of plan?'

Yes. The House of Enlightened Arts … Rizhin decided Mirgorod wasn't the place for it after all. He has a new plan, a better plan. You'll see the advantages when you understand.'

'What?' said Forshin. 'No. This is unacceptable.'

'I'm to take you there directly,' said Pinocharsky. 'The train's waiting—'

'This is outrageous,' said Forshin. 'I protest. On behalf of the League. There must be consultation.'

'These are the instructions of Rizhin himself,' said Pinocharsky stonily.

'At least let us have some time to rest and recover from the journey. The ladies—'

'I'm sorry, that won't be possible.'

'Then tell us where we are going, man,' said Olga-Marya Rapp. 'At least tell us that.'

'A new town in the east,' said Pinocharsky. 'A pioneering place. Leading edge. A city of the future. A place called Vitigorsk. There's a great project under way there. I don't know much about it yet myself.'

The League muttered and grumbled and cursed under their breath but there was no rebellion. They were too weary, too inured to disappointment; they knew in their hearts the limits of their true worth. Porters picked up their baggage and moved along the platform, and they followed in a subdued huddle.

Eligiya Kamilova caught up with Forshin.

'Nikolai …'

Forshin looked at her, puzzled. She and the girls had slipped his mind in all the fuss.

'Oh, Eligiya, of course …'

'I wanted to thank you, Nikolai. You've been very kind to the girls and me. You've done more than we had any right to hope for.'

'Oh. You're not coming with us? No, of course not. But do. Come with us to this Vitigorsk place, Eligiya. See where all this excitement leads. The future is opening for us, I feel sure of it.'

'I can't, Nikolai. I must take Galina and Yeva to look for their mother.'

'Of course you must do that.' He held out his hand and she took it. 'Well, goodbye then.'

'Thank you, Nikolai. And good luck.'

Eligiya Kamilova watched Forshin walk away purposefully, hurrying to catch up with Pinocharsky. She never saw or heard of him, nor any other member of the Philosophy League, ever again.

'Eligiya,' said Yeva, 'can we go now, please? We have to go and find our mother.'

Two hours later they were standing in the street where their aunt's apartment building had stood, the place where the Archipelago bomb had fallen: six years before in Mirgorod time, but for them it was a matter of months.

Everything was different. Everything was changed.

Of their mother Elena Cornelius there was of course no sign at all. They waited a while, pointlessly. It was futile. They were simply causing themselves pain.

Eligiya Kamilova wondered what to do. It was only now she was here that she realised she had no plan for what came next, no plan at all.

'We'll come back again tomorrow,' said Galina to Yeva. 'We'll come every day.'

8

The next morning, early, Lom went up into the mountains with Maksim, Konnie and Elena. Konnie had rented a boxy grey Narodni with a dented near-side wheel arch. The interior smelled strongly of tobacco smoke. There was a heaped ashtray in the driver's door. The streets climbed steeply out of Anaklion into scrub and scree and dark dense trees. No sun yet reached the lower slopes.

They drove in silence. Lom, squeezed onto the scuffed leather bench-seat in the back next to Elena, watched out of the window. The Narodni struggled on the steep inclines and Konnie swore, fishing for the second gear that wasn't there. The back of Maksim's head sank lower and lower between his shoulders.

After forty-five minutes Konnie pulled off the road onto a rough stony track. Out of sight among boulders and black cypress she killed the engine.

'This is it,' she said. 'You walk from here.'

Maksim, Lom and Elena left her with the car and started up a steep narrow hunting trail. Elena carried a rifle slung across her back. When they crested a ridge and clear stony ground fell away to their right, she broke away on her own. Two minutes later Lom couldn't see her at all.

It took him and Maksim another hour to work their way around to the thick woodland above and behind the gatehouse of Dacha Number Nine. Maksim picked his route carefully, stopping to look at his watch. He seemed to know what he was doing. Once he had them crawl on their bellies in under thick green spiky vegetation.

'Patrol,' he hissed.

The sun was higher now, kindling scent from crushed leaves and crumbling earth. Slow pulses of purple and blue rippled across the cloudless sky. A liminal solar breathing.

Lom's every move and step was a startling noise in the thin motionless air.

They crouched in the shadow of a pine trunk. The roof of the gatehouse was fifty feet below them, and beyond it the closed gate itself. Maksim checked his watch again and put his face close to Lom's ear.

'Now we wait,' he whispered. 'I will tell you when.'

9

Lukasz Kistler was lying on a low cot bed in his cell. Every part of him was in pain. He followed the passing of days and nights by the rectangle of sky in the high window, but he didn't count them. Not any more. He divided time between when he was alone and safe and when he was not, that was all.

When the key turned in the lock and the door opened he wanted to open his mouth and scream but he did not. He knotted his fingers tight in his grey blanket and pulled the fabric taut: a little wall of wool, a shield across his chest. A protection that protected nothing at all.

Vasilisk the bodyguard stepped inside and padded across to the bed. Looked down on Kistler impassively with sleepy half-closed eyes.

'Please,' said Kistler. His mouth was dry. 'Not any more. There is no more. It's finished now.'

'You've got friends outside the dacha,' said Vasilisk. 'They're coming to take you away.'

Kistler tried to focus on what he was hearing. He couldn't get past the fact it was the first time he had heard Vasilisk speak. His voice was pitched oddly high.

'They're going to try to blow up the gate,' he said. 'Stand up. You have to come with me.'

'I refuse,' said Kistler. He pressed himself deeper into the thin mattress. The springs dug into his back.

'You refuse?' Vasilisk looked at him with faint surprise, like there was something unexpected on his plate at dinner.

'I refuse,' said Kistler again. 'Absolutely I refuse. No more. I will not come again. Not any more. I'm finishing it. Now.'

Vasilisk bent in and hooked a hand under Kistler's shoulder, iron fingers digging deep into his armpit, hauling him up. Kistler resisted. Pulled away and tried to fall back onto the mattress.

Vasilisk leaned forward and jabbed him in the solar plexus.

Kistler screamed and retched and tried to bring his knees up, curling himself into a protective ball, but the last of his strength had gone. Rizhin's bodyguard yanked him to his feet and held him upright, though his legs failed him and he could not stand.

Kistler heard a strange sound and realised it was himself sobbing.

'Shut up,' said Vasilisk and jabbed him again.

On the slope above the guardhouse Maksim nudged Lom in the ribs and gestured with his chin.

Go! Go!

Vasilisk the bodyguard half-carried, half-dragged the unresisting semi-conscious Kistler through the rose garden and past the swimming pool. There was no one there. From half past ten to half past twelve there was tennis.

Iced tea at half past eleven.

Rizhin's car was parked in the courtyard and Vasilisk had the keys in his pocket. He checked the time on his watch: 10.51.

He opened the rear door and bundled Kistler inside. Pushed him down into the footwell. Kistler groaned and retched again, spilling sour vomit down the front of his shirt.

Vasilisk took his place in the driver's seat and settled down to wait.

Lom eased open the door of the gatehouse. Maksim entered first, pistol in his hand. The guards swung round in surprise: one reached for his holster, the other made a grab for the telephone receiver.

Maksim fired twice. Neat and precise.

Lom ripped the phone cable from the wall.

At 10.55 Rizhin himself came round the corner of the veranda into the courtyard. Vasilisk followed him in the rear-view mirror. Saw him glance across at the car and see his bodyguard in the driver's seat. Puzzled, Rizhin started to come over.

Vasilisk turned the key in the ignition and the engine purred into life. He slipped the car into gear and headed for the tunnel entrance. A cool dark mouth in the rock. In his mirror he saw Rizhin standing in the middle of the courtyard watching him go.

Vasilisk increased the weight of his foot on the accelerator pedal.

The car roared forward. The barrier was down but the car weighed nearly three tons.

As the barrier splintered it occurred to Vasilisk in an abstract way that he was probably beginning the final two minutes of his life.

Lom walked up to the massive gate across the tunnel and pressed the flat of his hand against it, feeling the dry solid wood. Its grain and fine flaws. The bars of iron within it. The blackened studs. The wide sunlit air. The scent of cypress and resinous southern pine. Feeling and remembering.

In the dark time, after Maroussia went, Vissarion Lom moved fast across ice fields and raced through the snow-dark birch trees. Part man, part angel, part something else, body and brain saturated with starlight and burn, all the dark months of winter he ran the ridges of high mountains.

He pushed his fists deep into solid rock just to feel it hurt.

Ten days and more he had stood without moving on the thick frozen surface of a benighted lake. Cold dark fishes slid through darkness far below him and bitter black wind scoured his face with particles of ice.

Lom-in-burning-angel counted the needles on pine trees and ignited them one by one with an idle thought. Little bright-flaring match flames.

He had forgotten who he was and he didn't care.

But slowly he had been moving south, and slowly the star-fire faded from the angel skin casing Lavrentina Chazia had made. In the early sunlight of that first spring five years ago Vissarion Lom shed his angel carcass and pushed it off a rock into the river.

He squirrelled the recollection of that dark inhuman time deep in the secret fastnesses of the heart where bitterness festers, and guilt. Kept it there, locked under many locks, along with the memory of all the winter slaughtering Lom-in-burning-angel did, or could have done and thought he might have. The iron smell of blood on ice.

After that long inhuman winter in the north without the sun, Vissarion Lom wanted to be nothing more than simply human again, but secretly he knew he never could be quite that. Possibly he never entirely had been: the earliest roots of himself were buried in oblivion and inexhaustible forest. As everyone's are.

*

'Turn your back and cover your face,' Lom said to Maksim. 'Splinters.'

Lom focused. Tried to drive all other thoughts and memories from his mind. Tried to calm the rising anxiousness and the beating of his heart.

There was only him and the gate.

He probed. Pushed. Nothing happened.

Changing direction, he gathered all the urgency, the growing white panic inside him, squeezed it all into a tight ball and forced it out from him. Hurled it into the timbers, deep into the corpse limbs of forest trees.

Burst open by the pressure of tiny air pockets – the desiccated fibrous capillaries suddenly and violently expanding – the heavy wooden planks of the gate exploded loudly from within, split open and shattered.

The rock tunnel behind the broken gate was dark and silent. It smelled like the mouth of a well.

'What the fuck?' said Maksim. 'What the fuck did you *do*?'

'Later,' said Lom.

Where the hell was Kistler's car?

They stood side by side for thirty long slow seconds.

'Where is he?' said Lom. 'He's not coming.'

Engine roar echoed, and the sound of gunfire.

The long black limousine was racing towards them. Lom glimpsed a face behind the thick windscreen as he scrambled aside. A tanned impassive handsome face. Cropped yellow hair.

The limousine slowed to a crawl. Maksim pulled open the front passenger seat.

'Get in the back!' he yelled at Lom.

Lom slid in alongside the collapsed form of Kistler, who was crouched on the floor. Dirty shirt and soiled trousers. Unshaven face grey. He looked up at Lom with glassy eyes. No recognition. There was a smell of urine and vomit in the car.

The driver didn't look round but gunned the engine and raced off down the mountain.

The heat of the sun, now high in the sky, beat against the side of Elena Cornelius' face. She could feel her skin burning. Insects buzzed and clattered in the grass, crawled across the back of her neck, sunk tiny probes into her arms and her ankles. She fought back the urge to scratch. All movement was dangerous.

She was still. She was nothing but eyes watching. She was part of the rock.

From five hundred yards she saw the gate shatter and the limousine emerge, slow to pick up Maksim and Lom, and hurtle away down the hill, jumping culverts, taking the hairpin too fast, scraping its side along the crash barrier.

The racing of the engine and the squeal of tortured metal echoed off cliffs and scree.

Elena Cornelius waited. Less than a minute later two vehicles came charging out of the tunnel mouth: a black Parallel Sector saloon and an open VKBD jeep with three men cradling sub-machine guns on their knees.

Elena moved the rifle slowly, sliding the graticule smoothly along the road, catching up with the windscreen of the leading pursuit car. The driver's head was a shadow. She moved the scope with the saloon for a moment, matching speed for speed, then shifted her aim three car lengths ahead and lifted it half an inch.

Squeezed the trigger gently.

Half a second after she fired, the glass in the windscreen shattered. From where she was it seemed to collapse and dissolve. The Parallel Sector saloon swung wildly to the left, crashed against the rock face and spun twice.

The jeep, following close behind, had nowhere to go and no time to stop. It crunched sickeningly into the side of the saloon. The men in the back of the jeep were thrown out. They landed badly.

Elena shifted the scope back to the driver. He was folded into the jeep's steering wheel, his head pushed through broken glass in a mess of blood.

She watched a man stagger from the back of the saloon. Limping. He pulled at the driver's door. It wouldn't open. None of the men from the jeep was moving at all. The two crashed vehicles together completely blocked the road.

She shouldered her gun and slid backwards away from the ridge, stood up and began to move, half running, half sliding down through the trees. This route would cut off a mile of road. In seven minutes she would be back at the track where Konnie would be waiting with the boxy grey Narodni.

10

*A*rchangel hurls himself across the continent, Rizhin world. He is a fisted pocket of certainty crashing from mind to mind – land and pause and look and leap again – leaving a crumb trail of sickness and fall. Hunting the only angel trace still left in Rizhin's New Vlast.

Brother, I am racing to you! Brother, call again and I will come!

He has scarcely the strength for it. Mile by mile the connecting cord back to his rock-lump-grinding-carcass in the forest lengthens and thins. The thread grows weak and spider-fine.

In the deep concrete cistern under the Mirgorod Sea Gate, Safran-in-mudjhik pummels the imprisoning wall with shapeless fists. His mind is dark with anger at his fall.

Lom pushed him in there.

He cannot get out.

Six years.

The endless surging weight of water, the whole force of the River Mir, pins him on his back. The noise of it fills his head and deafens him. The lost mind of Safran huddles in a silent corner, curled and foetal, wanting only the sound and the shouting and the hopelessness to cease.

Hairline fractures are opening in the concrete.

Two thousand days ago an aircraft of the Archipelago returning from a raid emptied its bomb bay, dumping its unspent load across the White Marshes. Two bombs fell against the dam. No visible damage done, but in the secret places, in the dark interior of immense solid walls, weakened bonds began to shear and slip.

Predator-Archangel plummets from height, daggering into the mind of Safran-in-mudjhik and taking possession with a shriek of triumph.

Instantly he expands to fill the space. Scoops the remnants of the weaker mudjhik mind from their runnels and crannies with a spoon and eats them all.

Sorry, brother.

Archangel glows with satisfaction and joy. He has a worthy body now in Rizhin world. He flexes. He samples. He trials his goods.

In a dark corner he finds Safran cowering and hauls him out wriggling and retching by the ear.

What use are you? he wonders briefly, rummaging with clumsy fingers through the maddened Safran mind before crushing it for ever out of existence.

Deep in the endless forest the Seer Witch of Bones is the first to discern the gap in the wall. She shrieks in dismay, 'Close it! Close it! The angel is through!'

Maroussia Shaumian walking under the trees, preoccupied with the child in her belly and Vissarion Lom, reluctantly turns her attention to the call. She traces the fine connecting threadway. It is weak and she is strong, invested with the Pollandore. It costs her no more than a tussle with the weakened and attenuated angel mind. She pinches her fingers and the cord is cut.

The forest is secure.

But the archangel fragment in the mudjhik, isolated from the depleted mother hill, clings on to life and purpose. In the mudjhik carcass he is strength and fire and brilliance like nothing has been in a donkey work-horse mudjhik ever before.

Slowly Archangel-mudjhik rises to his feet against the power of the crushing river and puts his shoulder to the wall. Shoves and batters and kicks against the weakening concrete.

Brute force does it. Boulders come tumbling down, the river is unleashed and Archangel-mudjhik is swept out, twisting and floundering in a torrent of broken concrete and white water, out into the deeper colder darkness of the bay.

Chapter Ten

They all believed their happiness had come,
That every ship had reached harbour,
And the exhausted exiles and wanderers
Had come home to bright shining lives.

Aleksander Blok (1880–1921)

1

They changed cars at a small fishing port ten miles east along
the coast from Anaklion, ditching the Narodni for a spacious
pre-war Tsvetayev with cloth-covered seats, more tractor
than automobile, and drove back to Mirgorod. By the direct north-
east route it was only nine hundred miles, but it took them five days
of doubling back and taking less-used circuitous routes. They assumed
they were being searched for. Trains and flights were out of the question, even if they'd had the money for that.

There were five of them in the car: Lom and Elena, Maksim and
Konnie and Kistler. They left Vasilisk at the fishing port, where Maksim
had arranged a place for him on a boat. He would work his passage
south and disappear. As they were leaving, Vasilisk shook hands with
Maksim and snapped a military salute.

'He was in my unit,' was all Maksim would say afterwards. 'In the
war.'

They drove long hours on ill-made roads, sharing the driving and sleeping in the car, picking up food where they could and stopping as little as possible. North of the Karima mountains they skirted the hungerland. What they saw was bad and the rumours were worse. Ruined and abandoned farmland, the people of the towns gaunt, grey-faced, weak, watching them pass through with sullen hopeless eyes. Villages where there was nobody at all, only crows and pigeons and packs of dogs that circled, heads down, ribcages, dirty lustreless coats.

'I didn't know,' said Konnie. 'None of us knew about this.'

They ran into a roadblock in a birch wood: a tree across the road and five men in rags with staves and a shotgun rising from a ditch. An attempt to steal the car: fuel and food and a way out. Maksim had to shoot two of them. The rear window of the Tsvetayev was broken.

Maksim had been wary of Lom since the incident of the gate. Lom felt himself watched. By Konnie too. Maksim tried to ask him about it once, but Lom didn't answer. Where to begin and what to say? The atmosphere was strained.

Elena Cornelius just wanted to get back to the city. She'd been away too long, She was terrified that her girls had come home and she had missed them.

Kistler recovered slowly. They cleaned him up and fed him, found him fresh clothes and let him sleep most of the day. He had lost weight in Rizhin's interrogation cell. His eyes were dark, blank and anxious, and for long hours he sat in the back of the car next to Elena, pressed up against the door, leaning forward, hands on his knees, staring at nothing. Every few minutes he would open his mouth to speak but say nothing. On the second day tears came, silent tears soaking his face. He didn't wipe them away.

Lom feared he was permanently gone, that they'd lost him for ever in Rizhin's interrogation cell, but slowly with the passing of the days some of Kistler's fire and energy returned, though not like before. When Lom had first seen Kistler he was a master of the world, filled to the brim with confident assurance. The smooth sheen of real power. It had been there in his voice, in his gaze, in the way he moved. Now he was coming back, but darker, more determined, altogether more dangerous. His hurt and his fall, the shock of his humiliation and psychic destruction at the hands of Rizhin and Hunder Rond were raw and near the surface and he was vengeful. His face was thinner and he glared at the world through dark-hooded eyes.

'I should thank you,' Kistler said on the third day. 'All of you. I know what I owe, and I will not forget.'

'We came because we need you,' said Lom. 'I went to Vitigorsk as you suggested. I've got information you can use. If you want it. If you feel you still can.' Lom paused. 'Or my friends can help you get far away, if that's what you want. To the Archipelago, even. That is possible. It can be done.'

'Yes,' said Konnie from the front seat. 'We can arrange that. We've done it before, for others. It's what we do.'

Kistler said nothing. He looked for a long time out of the window: there was dry grass out there, dull grey lakes and low wooded hills in the distance.

'We would understand,' said Lom, 'if you decided to go. No shame in that.'

Kistler didn't look round.

'Liars,' he said. 'You people didn't risk yourselves just to let some sick old fucker go free. Certainly not a bastard and a criminal like me.'

Kistler's eyes followed a young girl leading a horse across a hill, until they left her far behind. Lom thought he wasn't going to say any more. Long minutes passed before Kistler spoke again.

'I'm going to bring the fucker Rizhin to his knees,' he said. 'And I will do whatever it takes, *whatever it takes*, to make that happen. I want to see him *broken*. I want to see him *hurt*. I want to see him *crawling* on the floor in his own *shit* and *piss* and *puke* and *blood*. I would *die* to make that happen and be *glad*. I would *suffer* and *howl* till the end of fucking *time*, as long as it was him and me there *together*. So tell me. What have you got?'

'Pull over,' said Lom to Maksim, who was driving. 'I'll get my bag from the back.'

As they drove on, Lom told Kistler about the vast construction plants at Vitigorsk. The plans for a fleet of atomic-powered vessels to go to the planets. The experiments in resurrection and synthetic human bodies. The aspiration to abolish death.

'Insane,' said Kistler, 'insane, but—'

"That isn't all,' said Lom. 'It's just the beginning.'

He opened his bag and brought out the papers from Khyrbysk's office.

'They are building vessels of two kinds,' he said. 'There was a conference a couple of years ago. A hotel on a lake. Rizhin was there, and Khyrbysk, and the chief engineer. Others too. Some names you know. Papers were circulated and minutes taken. All most efficient, and Khyrbysk kept a copy.'

He spread a folder open on his knee.

'They are constructing two kinds of vessel,' he said again. 'One, a fleet to go to the planets and the stars. Five years, they think, ten at the most before they are ready. Resources are no obstacle. Rizhin promised them whatever they need. They will be arks. Transport ships to carry pioneers and the equipment they will require. It's all planned. They'll select the people carefully. Even two years ago they'd begun to draw up criteria and candidate lists. They are gathering scientists, artists, writers, athletes. The best of the armed forces and the finest workers.'

'Let me see,' said Kistler. 'Show me the names.'

'They need huge amounts of angel matter to power the craft,' said Lom. 'More than all the carcasses can supply. But there is a living angel in the forest and Rizhin says it's huge. Immense. An angel mountain. He's going to find it and excavate its living flesh. Army divisions are already in the forest searching.'

Kistler was still looking at the lists. The people at the conference.

'I don't recognise these names,' he said. 'None of the Central Committee is here. No one from the Presidium or the ministries. Only Rond.'

'They don't know,' said Lom. 'None of them know about it because they're not going. They're not invited to the stars. But the arks are just part of it. There's another kind of vessel design. These are for low planetary orbit only, and there are to be thirty of them. They're also building bombs. Huge atomic bombs. *Emperor Bombs*. The power of these weapons can't be understated, it can't even be imagined: a single one would have the power of sixty million tons of high explosive, big enough to flatten entire cities and destroy half a province on its own. They expect them to set the air itself on fire. The orbital craft, the second design, will be artillery platforms. Flying gunships, each one equipped with twenty Emperor Bombs. That's six hundred of them. The dust will blacken the skies for years. Five years of darkness and winter. Clouds of poisonous elements will cover the continent, raining disease and death. The atmosphere of the world will burn away.'

'Even if they could build such weapons,' said Kistler, 'they could never use them. We know the Archipelago has its own atomic weapons now. We would destroy each other.'

'No need for the Archipelago to do that,' said Lom. 'Rizhin's orbiting gunships are intended to do it all. Burn the Archipelago, burn the Vlast, burn the endless forest too. Burn it all. Scorched earth. Leave the planet a smoking cinder.'

Kistler stared at him. Lom saw growing understanding in his eyes.

'I see,' said Kistler. 'Rizhin and his arks will leave the planet and destroy it behind them so no one can follow, so no such ships are ever built again.'

'That's part of the reason,' said Lom, 'but also so that no one who goes with Rizhin to the stars can ever dream of coming home again.' He took the note of the conference and found the page he needed. 'Rizhin's own words were recorded verbatim.'

He handed the paper to Kistler.

'We must leave nothing behind us. No before-time. No happy memory. No nostalgia for golden age and home. And above all, no one to come after us. We will be the first and the last. There is no past, there is only the future.'

Kistler read it over several times. Shaking his head.

'A single man might think this,' he said, 'but that others should follow, and help him, and do his work ...?'

'Khyrbysk for one didn't care,' said Lom. 'Nor did the chief engineer. There are letters between them that Khyrbysk kept.'

Lom quoted a passage. He had it by heart.

'"Where death is temporary, a million deaths, a billion, ten billion, do not matter. When we have mastered the science of retrieving memory from atoms we can come back here for the dust, if we have need of the ancestral dead to fill the planets we find."

'I'm not sure if Rizhin believes the resurrection stuff himself,' he added. 'You can't tell that from these papers.'

'But,' said Kistler, 'can they really do this? Could they actually build these things? Could they truly hope to travel to the stars?'

'For our present purposes,' said Lom, 'that doesn't really matter, does it? It hardly makes any difference at all. Rizhin intends it. He has

232

corresponded with Khyrbysk – I've got letters in his own hand here. The project has begun.'

Kistler stared at him.

'Fuck,' he said. His face flushed. 'Fuck. You're right. Hah!' He reached across and put his hand on Lom's knee. Squeezed it affectionately. 'Of course you're right, you marvellous fucking marvellous man. It doesn't matter at all.'

'So did I get you what you need?' said Lom.

'You did,' said Kistler. 'You bloody well did. Get me back to Mirgorod and I'll tear the bastard down. I'll bury him.'

2

As soon as he was back in Mirgorod, Lukasz Kistler went to work. It took time. There were no phone calls. No letters. No traces. Kistler travelled across the city only by night, with the assistance of Maksim and the Underground Road, and by day he lay up in hiding and slept and prepared himself for the next night. He visited every single member of the Central Committee. In secret he came to them, unannounced and unexpected, when they were alone and at home. Each one was shocked by the thinness of his body, the new lines in his face, the black energy burning in his eye.

But you were dead, Lukasz. We all thought you were dead.

He sat with them, whispering into the early hours of the morning in studies and bedrooms while the households slept, and told them his story. He showed them the documentary proofs that Lom had brought back from Vitigorsk. The notes of meetings. The lists. The letters to Khyrbysk in Rizhin's own scrawl.

And as he spoke, they saw the intact intelligence in his face. They understood the clarity of vision, the urgent determination: this was not Kistler broken and made mad by fear and detention and loss of power; this was Kistler commanding. Kistler on fire. Kistler the leader they had been waiting for.

And one by one in the watches of the night each man and woman of the Central Committee made the same response to what he told them, as Kistler knew they would. He knew his colleagues. He knew the stuff of their hearts.

What shocked and horrified them most was not the plan Rizhin had put into effect; it was that they were not in it. They were not included.

I am not on the list! He was going to leave me behind. I was to burn. My husband, my wife, my children, all were to burn.

One after another Kistler reeled them in. Stroked their vanity, fed their fear, bolstered their courage and swore them to secrecy. And when he had them, he convened a secret meeting at two in the morning at Yulia Yashina's house, and presented them with his proposal.

'We must all be signed up to this,' he said. 'Absolute and irreversible commitment. Every single one without exception. You must understand – you already know this well, of course you do – that if one of us falters we are all, all of us, doomed. The man or woman who loses courage now, who believes that he or she can gain advantage by moving against the rest of us: that betrayer is the one Rizhin will kill first. You all know this as I do. Concerted collective decisive action, this is the only way. One swift and irresistible blow!'

3

Yeva Cornelius stares up at a tall cliff of concrete and windows. The concrete is grey but the building is somehow brown, and the windows reflect brown and yellow although the sky is blue. The paving of the street is brown and everything is strange.

Eligiya Kamilova has told them that this is Big Side, and this is the street where Aunt Lyudmila's apartment was, before the bomb; she's told them they can't go back to the raion where their proper house was, with the Count and Ilinca and the dog and all the other people who lived there too, because the raion isn't there any more. Yeva is beginning to doubt whether Eligiya is right about that or anything else. This doesn't look like Big Side at all. Maybe there was another city, the one they lived in, and this is a different place, another city with the same name but somewhere else, and everything is a bad mistake.

Eligiya doesn't say much any more, and Galina is thin and tall and her eyes are big and dark and she never says anything at all. They sleep in a dirty room with only one bed and come here very morning, but Yeva's more sure every day that it's the wrong place. The women who live here wear pale blue dresses and coats, and their hair is wavy and doesn't move in the breeze, and they wear small hats, though it's not cold or raining, and the hats are the same colour as the dresses and coats. Always the same colour. That's what you have to do here. The men wear hats too, and thin shoes.

Yeva Cornelius thinks she's eleven years old still, but she hasn't counted the days and the dates here are wrong. She knows what date it is here – the newspaper has that – but when the date of her birthday comes, it won't be her birthday. No one asks how old she is anyway. Birthdays are for children, and this is the wrong place; her mother is somewhere else.

'This is the wrong place,' she says again to Eligiya Kamilova, who's standing next to her with Galina. They come here every day at ten o'clock and wait for half an hour. That's their plan.

'You say that every day, Yeva,' said Eligiya, 'but it's not.'

A woman in black is watching them from the other side of the road. She looks like their mother but she's smaller and she has browner skin and shorter hair and the hair's grey and she's very thin. Even from so far away, Yeva can see her eyes are black and sad.

The woman in black is watching Yeva just like the dead soldiers used to watch her at Yamelei: patient and with nothing to say and watching for ever and never getting bored or wanting to look at something else instead. But the eyes are black and sad and that shows the woman is alive.

It is their mother.

Galina has seen her too but she doesn't move and she doesn't make a sound.

Yeva wants to run across the road but she doesn't because … because her mother is not the same and Yeva is not the same and nothing is the same. The awkwardness of strangers meeting. Yeva watches her mother back, from the opposite side of the road, and says nothing and doesn't move.

Eligiya doesn't know yet. She hasn't seen.

The woman in black makes a small movement, almost a stumble. Yeva thinks she's going to turn round and walk away. But she doesn't.

4

The Sixth Plenum of the New Vlast convened in Victory Hall in central Mirgorod under low ceiling mosaics of aviators and cherry blossom, harvesters and blazing naval guns, all depicted against the same brilliant lucid eggshell-blue cloudless sky. Victory Hall was not large: despite the brutal columns of mottled pink granite and the banners of gold and red, the atmosphere was surprisingly intimate.

The Central Committee took their seats on the platform in a pool of golden light. The floor of the hall before them – the sixty non-voting delegates from the oblasts, the observers from the armed forces in their uniforms, the leading workers in crisp new overalls of blue – murmured anticipation. Order papers were shuffled. An official in a dark suit tested the microphone at the lectern.

This was the day of accounting. Annual reports were to be delivered, production targets exceeded, measures of increasing wealth and prosperity noted, improvements celebrated without complacency. *Your committee can and must do better, colleagues, and in your name we will.* Revisions to the rolling Five Year Plan would be proposed, and adopted by acclamation.

Watching from the tiered side-galleries, the fifteen chosen representatives of the press, snappy in new dresses and suits, were relaxed and slightly bored, their copy already written and filed according to tables of information and officially approved quotations previously supplied. The seven ambassadors and their assistants from the independent border states measured their shifting relative importance and influence by the seating plan. In the rows behind them, squinting at the platform, trying to identify the members of the committee by name and thinking of what they would tell their families and friends later, sat several dozen selected members of the public – outstanding citizens all, decorated heroes of the Vlast. And among them, perched at the end of a row, inconspicuous in shadow, Vissarion Lom waited alongside Lukasz Kistler.

Every person in the Victory Hall was waiting for Rizhin to appear.

At two o'clock precisely he did. The small crowd gave a soft wordless visceral rising moan of delight.

Rizhin, simple white uniform blazing under the lights, paused a moment to acknowledge the reception – a modest deprecatory smile – and took his place with the rest of the committee. His chair was no grander, his place no higher than the rest.

I am the servant of our people. I do what I can.

As soon as Rizhin had settled, the Victory Hall was flooded with warm pink illumination. The chamber orchestra in their cramped pit below the platform began to play. At the sound of the first familiar bars every person except Rizhin rose to their feet, and they all began to sing, falling naturally into the fourfold harmonies of which everyone always knew their part.

Thank you! Thank you! Papa Rizhin!
All our peace is owed to you!
All new truth and all fresh plenty!
A million voices, a thousand years!

Kistler leaned across to whisper in Lom's ear. 'When the time comes they will not do it, Lom. All this, it's too strong. It's too much to go against. They'll lose their nerve.'

'It'll be fine. You've done what you can.'

The members of the Central Committee came to the lectern one by one to deliver their reports and were received with warm applause. The afternoon wore on. Rizhin was to speak last, and as the time approached he began to flick through his script. Shifting in his chair, preparing to stand.

Gribov was in the chair. He cleared his throat nervously and stood. 'Colleagues ...'

Rizhin was already coming to take his place. Gribov held up his hand to stop him. Rizhin paused and looked at him, puzzled.

Gribov motioned him back to his seat.

Rizhin hesitated, shrugged and sat down again.

'Colleagues,' said Gribov again, 'at this point the planned business of the Plenum is suspended. I require the public galleries to be cleared.'

There was a collective murmur of surprise. A burst of muttered protest.

Lom kept his eye fixed on Rizhin, who frowned and looked at Gribov, but Gribov was ignoring him. Then Rizhin glanced at Hunder Rond, but Rond was avoiding his gaze.

'Clear the room!' called Gribov. Plenum officials and officers of the VKBD began to usher the protesting ambassadors and the press corps towards the door. Lom and Kistler moved to one side, half-hidden from the platform. The officials ignored them as Gribov had arranged.

The non-voting delegates were permitted to remain. Gribov called the room to order.

'The Central Committee by collective agreement in accordance with Standing Order Seven has resolved to bring before you an urgent and extraordinary resolution.' Gribov's voice was gravelly. He struggled to make himself heard. Took a sip of water. 'The resolution, in the name of Secretary Yashina is, "To remove Osip Rizhin from all official positions, responsibilities and powers with immediate effect."'

Silence fell in Victory Hall. No delegate moved. None spoke. None made a sound.

Rizhin sat back in his chair. He looked relaxed. Almost amused. A wry scornful smile on his scarred face.

'So it comes to this,' he said, scanning the line of faces, fixing the committee one after another. 'Well done then. Bravo. Of course it's all shit, it's nothing, but let's see what you make of it.'

You mustn't let him react, Kistler had said to Gribov when they made the plan in secret conclave at Yashina's house. *Once you start, the momentum is yours, but you have to keep it. If he speaks, if he fights back, it'll be a battle between competing authorities and you could lose control. It'll turn into a shouting match. Don't get into a battle with him.*

Gribov turned to Rizhin.

'You may leave us now, Osip,' he said, 'or you may remain and hear what is said. But you may not speak. The resolution will be proposed and a vote will be taken. There is to be no right of reply. If you speak you will be ejected from the hall.'

There was a commotion on the floor of the hall.

'Shame!' someone shouted. 'Criminals! Betrayers!'

The cry wasn't taken up. It fell on silence. The shock and bemusement in the chamber was palpable. And fear, above all there was fear. The observer delegates collectively maintained a tense, terrified silence.

Lom guessed some of them were beginning to wonder if they would make it out of the room alive. If they would ever go home again.

He saw Rizhin look towards Hunder Rond again. The two men's eyes locked. Rond kept his face studiously, stonily impassive. Rizhin raised his eyebrows and gave an almost imperceptible nod: *And you, Rond? That's how it is then? Well it's your loss. It means nothing to me.*

Lom wondered what kind of deal Kistler and his cronies had made with Rond. He watched Rizhin's eyes slide from Rond to Yashina and from her to Gribov. Rizhin was obviously wondering the same thing.

Rizhin sat back in his chair and slipped his hands into his tunic pockets carelessly.

'Thank you, Gribov,' he said. 'I will not leave. This is my chamber and I am President-Commander of the New Vlast. I'll go when and where I choose. But this could be interesting. So come on, let's hear what you arseholes have to say.'

Gribov ignored him. He yielded the floor to Yulia Yashina.

'They're doing it,' hissed Kistler in Lom's ear. 'They're fucking *doing* it. I have to go now.' He squeezed Lom's arm as he left. 'Oh I could kiss you, you beautiful man. Look at that fucker wriggle.'

'It's not finished yet,' said Lom as Kistler disappeared.

5

Tall and slender, elegant, Yulia Yashina moved to the microphone and began to speak. Like Gribov, for the first few sentences her voice was dry and weak. She then drank some water and proceeded, more loudly and with growing purpose and confidence, speaking the words that Kistler had drafted for her.

'When we analyze the practice of Osip Rizhin in regard to the direction of the Vlast,' she said, 'when we pause to consider everything which this man has perpetrated, we see that his achievements in leading our country during war have transformed themselves during the years of peace into a grave abuse of power.'

A single gasp broke the silence in the hall. Yashina pressed on. She spoke slowly, with absolute clarity and determination, looking occasionally towards Rizhin as she went. By this moment she would live or she would die.

'As President-Commander, Osip Rizhin has originated a form of rule founded on the most cruel repression. Whoever opposes his viewpoint is doomed to removal from their position and subsequent moral and physical annihilation. He has violated all norms of legality and trampled on the principles of collective leadership.

'Friends, of the original ninety-four members and candidates of this plenum after the war, sixty-seven persons have been arrested and shot. Yet when we examine the accusations against these so-called spies and saboteurs we find that all their cases – all of them, every single one – were fabricated. Confessions of guilt were gained with the help of cruel and inhuman tortures—'

'No!' called a voice.

'Yes!' called another. 'Yes! It's all true!'

'Here we see it, friends,' said Yashina, looking out across pained faces. Shock and disbelief and fear. 'This is the fate that will come to us all if the man Rizhin remains in his position.

'He has elevated himself so high above the Vlast he purports to serve that he thinks he can decide all things alone, and all he needs to implement his decisions are engineers, statisticians, soldiers and police. All others must only listen to him and praise him and obey. He has created about himself a cult of personality of truly monstrous proportions, devoted solely to the glorification of his own person. This is supported by numerous facts.

'His official biography is nothing but an expression of the most dissolute flattery, an example of making a man into a god, an infallible sage, the sublimest strategist of all times and nations. It is a confection of lies from beginning to end, and all edited and approved by Rizhin himself, the most egregious examples added to the text in his own handwriting. I need not give other examples. We all know them.'

Lom noticed that Kistler had slipped onto the platform and taken a seat at the back. Rizhin had seen him too.

'Friends and colleagues,' said Yashina, 'we must draw the proper conclusions. The negative influence of the cult of the individual has to be completely corrected. I urge the Central Committee to declare itself resolutely against such exaltation of a single person. We must abolish it decisively, once and for all, and fight inexorably all attempts to bring back this practice. We must in future adhere in all matters to the principle of collective leadership, characterised by the observation of legal norms and the wide practice of criticism and self-criticism.'

She paused.

'I present the motion stated by Secretary Gribov to the Central Committee for the vote,' she said. 'Long live the victorious banner of our Vlast.'

Yashina returned to her seat, visibly shaken. The observer-delegates sat absolutely still. A woman was sobbing. A naval officer had his head between his knees, being quietly sick.

Rizhin sat looking at his fingernails with the same faint smile.

'I ask my colleagues,' said Gribov at the microphone, 'to indicate assent or dissent.'

For long moments nobody moved. Rizhin looked along the row of them, and none would meet his gaze. He began to smile. Then Kistler raised his hand.

'Yes,' he said. 'Assent. Assent.'

Another hand went up.

'Yes.'

And another, and another, and the dam broke, and all hands went up, every one, and the Victory Hall exploded into tumultuous shouting. In the body of the auditorium the observer-delegates – knowing now which way the wind blew – were on their feet, applauding, roaring, weeping their relief and joy.

Alone, Lom watched from the balcony corner. Rizhin was still sitting in the same attitude, still with the same supercilious smile. He seemed frozen in time. Gribov and Yashina embraced, and Kistler's face was alight with the clear happy grin of a child. The face of a man to whom the future belonged.

Lom listened to the ecstatic cheering and asked himself why he wasn't cheering too. He had won. He had done what he set out to do – Rizhin was fallen, the beast was down, the very idea of him in tatters – but his own first emotion was a flood of tired cynicism. Here he was, watching the rulers applaud themselves. All was decided now: Rizhin was a criminal; no one else was to blame, and the banners of the Vlast still flew. The roaring in the hall was the sound of survival, and of ranks closing.

He pushed that weariness aside: it wasn't right, it did no justice to the courage of Kistler, Yashina and the rest, and it did no justice to himself. The fall of Rizhin might not be an end, but it was a beginning. Things which only that morning could not have happened were once again possible now. Doors were opening. Possible futures multiplying second by second. He had done a good thing, and it had been hard, and he had a right to a moment's satisfaction. And more than that. *Maroussia*. He had a right now to go home.

He looked across at Rizhin once again, but his chair was empty. The man was not there.

Lom took the steps up to the exit from the gallery three at a time, crashed open the door into the deserted corridor and began to run.

Part IV

Chapter Eleven

Green shoots swell and burst
and your back is shattered, you broken
once-lithe hunting beast,
my lovely miserable century,
but still you go on, gazing backwards with a mindless smile
at the trail you leave.

Osip Mandelstam (1891–1938)

1

The man who was Osip Rizhin moves alone through the corridors of the Victory Hall. No praetorian troopers precede him, ten paces ahead, sub-machine guns in hand, sweeping the way. None follows ten paces behind. But he wears his white uniform still and he walks with the confidence of absolute power.

If you see him coming, press yourself against the wall, show the palms of your hands, lower your eyes. Do not meet his gaze. Papa Rizhin can break you open and smash your world. The modest gold braid on the white of his shoulder, the ribbons at the white of his breast: these are the crests of the truth of the power of death.

He looks at you with soft brown burning eyes as he passes.

The news of his fall has not yet escaped the plenum chamber.

*

Papa Rizhin, President-Commander and Generalissimus of the New Vlast, walks the passageways of the Victory Hall with measured pace and purposeful intent, but he does not exist. He is ghost. He is after-image. He is lingering, fading retinal burn.

The man who hurries towards the exit is Josef Kantor, wearing Papa Rizhin's clothes.

He pushes his way through heavy bronze doors and finds himself on a high terrace overlooking the River Mir. No one else is there. Above him the sky and before him the city of Mirgorod in the sun of the afternoon. He stands at the parapet and sees the city he saved, the city he rebuilt from the burned ground up: the great sky-rise buildings spearing the belly of cloudless blue, the tower that bears his face but Rizhin's name, the tower at the top of which Josef Kantor's immense and far-seeing statue stands.

Josef Kantor looks out across the city that is still his. Below him is the great slow silent river sliding west towards the sea. Barges call to barges, ploughing the green surface burnished in the afternoon sun, and a warm breeze palms his face. Summer air stirs his thick lustrous hair and gently traces the tight puckered scar on his cheek. Gulls wheel above the city lazily, flashing white in the sunlight. Their whiteness answers the whiteness of his tunic.

Josef Kantor does not move. He is calm. He is waiting. It is nearly time.

The revolutionary has no personal interests. No emotions. No attachments. The revolutionary owns nothing and has no name. All laws, moralities, customs and conventions – the revolutionary is their merciless and implacable enemy. There is only the revolution. All other bonds are broken.

He slips his hand into his pocket and folds his fat fingers round the tiny warm piece of angel flesh he always carries there. Always. He is never without it and never was.

He lets the last of Osip Rizhin drift away and dissolve on the air.

There is no past, there is only the future.

There is no defeat, there is only victory.

I am Josef Kantor, and what I will to happen, will happen.

There is a movement in the currents of the Mir, a disturbance at the near embankment. A roiling and rising stain of yellow sedimentary mud. An obstruction in the green flow.

The brutal faceless head and shoulders and torso of Archangel-in-mudjhik lifts itself out of the river, a blood- and rust-coloured thing of stone flesh spilling water as it punches holes in the embankment wall and hauls itself higher and higher, climbing towards the terrace of the Victory Hall.

Archangel tears open Josef Kantor's mind and pours himself in, flood after flood of vast glittering black consciousness, the voice of the shining emptiness between galaxies.

You remembered, my son, while I was gone. You remembered me and did well. You have built me ships for the stars.

Archangel! Archangel! Archangel!

I come for you now so that you can come for me! Carry me out from under the poisonous trees and bring me home!

It begins, oh it begins!

The voice of Archangel singing among the suns!

The foundations of the Victory Hall shook as Archangel-in-mudjhik, twelve-foot-high lump of mobile dull red angel flesh, climbed the embankment up towards the terrace, smashing through the skin of brick and gouging hand- and footholds in the concrete beneath. The waters of the Mir sluiced from him. The parapet crumbled and crunched under his weight as he heaved himself over.

Josef Kantor stood and faced him. He could not speak, his throat was stopped, but he did not fall.

The voice of Archangel filled his mind.

Join with me, faithful, beautiful son. Come inside me now and I will carry you.

Josef Kantor felt the mudjhik mind opening like a flower. It was a deep, scented well and he was on the brink. He was in a high and lonely place and desired only to fall.

Josef Kantor felt his body dying. His heart in his chest burst open, a dark gushing fountain of blood. His lungs collapsed. His ribs flexed and his throat gaped but no air entered. He was drowning in sunlight. His own name separated from him and drifted away.

Archangel-in-mudjhik pulled him in.

Vissarion Lom, running through the corridors of the Victory Hall, felt the irruption of Archangel into the world. A shattering rearrangement of the feel of things. A detonation of total and appalling fear.

He ran, and as he ran he felt the piledriver-pounding and -shaking of the floor. He was near and getting closer.

He ran.

There was no time and it was too far to go.

Lom shoved open the heavy bronze doors and burst onto the terrace. The paving stones were cracked and shattered, pieces of parapet broken and scattered across the ground. A corpse in a crumpled white uniform curled on the floor, leaking dark blood from mouth and nose. Lom looked over the wall down into the river. He could see nothing but he knew what was in there, moving eastwards, pushing strong and fast against the stream.

2

The River Mir is strong and green and brown. The last mudjhik in the world walks submerged, shoulder against the flow, up the river towards the forest. The archangel fragment, small and lonely and triumphant, is going home.

The river is a strong brown word, endlessly spoken, driving back towards the sea, but the mudjhik is stronger: every mighty footfall stirs puffs of silt. The dark voice of the river is loud: it is a hand against his chest, pressing. It ropes his feet and erodes the ground from under them. Eddies and water vortices stir and turn behind him, sucking him back, tugging him off balance. Thick mud in water whorls. The water ceiling just above his head glimmers and ripples.

Gravity operates differently here: he has no weight. All the forces shove and shear sideways and backwards, lifting and toppling, pushing back against archangel will.

Slip and fall. Tumble and roll. The strong brown river voice is running heavy. It turns everything over and over, slowly. Carries all away through city and marsh towards the ocean.

The river knows mudjhik is there. The river is a watchful, purposeful water ram. The river, the ever-speaking voice of the inland forest, opposes.

But mudjhik resists. Slow-motion walking like a brass-helmed diver in canvas and rubber, leaning forward into the slow conveyor of the water-wind, he hauls his clumsy mud-booted feet up and over lumps of half-buried concrete, brick and stone. Clambers clumsily over the weed-carpeted black and broken spars of a sunken barge, where worms and shell creatures rout and gouge the softening wood and frond gardens stream with the stream.

The engined hulls of riverboats lumber past his shoulder. He strokes their iron and timber with his palm and edges them gently aside. Eels and lampreys slide and flick, feeding in the silt clouds the mudjhik's feet kick up. Mudjhik pays attention to their slick dark mucus gleam. They flash like muscles of lightning in the paunch of storm clouds. They are bright marks of hungry life. Avid. Their needle teeth are sharp.

Larger fishes watch from shadow and darkness, curious, circumspect, holding themselves effortlessly in position against the force of the stream.

Mudjhik admires fish. Fish brain is cold, intent and unconcerned: the pressure of water currents is the book the fishes read. They trawl the turbid water with cold tongue. With cold and dark-adapted eye. They know what the river is: where it has come from, where it goes; the taste of earth and forest, lake and rain, and the fainter shadow-taste, the dangerous killing taint of oceanic salt. The river is their living god, and they are part of it, and there is nothing else and never was.

Josef Kantor knows that he is underwater in the river, and he knows that he is dead. The will of Archangel, heart and brain and total mudjhik commander, is a hot red fire that burns him. The overwhelming intent of Archangel drives all other thought away. Archangel is inexhaustible and unending dinning shout, all on a single note.

Archangel! Archangel! Archangel!

Archangel is bands of iron and wires of steel. Archangel is thunderous wheels on rails. Archangel is the blinding brilliance of internal suns. Archangel is the only force that drives. Archangel is ...

Joseph Kantor is dumb with it.

3

Mudjhik climbs from the river and stands in the evening sun to dry. The city is far behind him, a murmur in the wind, a skyline stain.

Archangel is well satisfied.

You remembered and did well, my son. You were my voice in the silence and prepared for me the way home. Walk with me now, back to the mountain under the trees. Be my voice a while and I will yet show you the light of the stars.

Josef Kantor is fist. All fist. He rises from the quiet floor (which smells of dead dog and stinks of dead Safran still) and fights.

I am nobody's son.

All the long day, all the river walk, Kantor has been watching from the shadows, crouching, growing tired of the taste of defeat and death. He has been gently, silently, testing the boundaries of Archangel, weighing strength against strength, will against will. He knows now that this Archangel is fragment only, stretched thin and small and far from home.

He knows the prize to be won, and that the risk of failure is death, but he is dead already, so what does it matter? And he is strong, stronger now than he was, and stronger than Archangel knows.

Josef Kantor hurls himself at the Archangel root shard. Pushes his fist into Archangel mouth.

I am Josef Kantor, and what I will to happen, will happen. I am nobody's prophet and nobody's labouring hand.

Archangel screams shock and indignation and turns on the sudden enemy within. Crushing. Squeezing. Smashing. He is speed beyond perceiving, strike and strike and strike again: he is the lancing burning blade and the crushing stamping heel. Burst upon burst of hammer-blow force. He is the turner-to-stone and the acid lick of a fire mouth. He is the bitter adversary against whom nothing stands.

Archangel! Archangel!

He is warrior nonpareil; his birthright is all the stars.

Josef Kantor goes down before him like a blade of dried grass under the wheel of a strong wind. Archangel burns him and he flares, weightless and brittle, crumbling to ash and dust. He vanishes into instant vapours of nothing like a scrap of paper in the belly of the white furnace.

The brevity of his destruction cannot be measured in the silence between tick and tick. Josef Kantor is simply instantaneously gone.

But Josef Kantor returns.

Every time Archangel destroys him he returns.

Archangel's force is fabulously, immeasurably, gloriously greater. He extinguishes Josef Kantor instantaneously every single time – blows him into nothing like a candle flame – but this is not a contest of force, it is a contest of will and nothing else. Archangel-fragment fights for pride and dignity and purpose, because he is Archangel and cannot fail; that cannot be conceived. But Josef Kantor fights because he will not die.

Study what you fear. Learn and destroy, then find a stronger thing to fear. Endlessly, endlessly, until the fear you cause is greater than the fear you feel. This is the dialectic of fear and killing.

Even before birth it began for Josef Kantor, the triumphant twinless twin spilling out onto the childbirth bed, accompanied by his shrivelled and half-absorbed dead little brother. Josef Kantor does not let rivals live. He doesn't share space in the womb.

All night long the mudjhik stands without moving on the bank of the river, and when morning comes the archangel-conscious fragment is dead.

Josef Kantor explores his new body, and oh but it is an excellent thing! Senses of angel substance show him the world in all its surge and gleam and detail, alive in a thousand ways he knew nothing of before. Mudjhik strength is power beyond dreaming: with a flick of his arm he splinters trees. This is the eternal body Khyrbysk dreamed of! Tireless, impervious, unfailing, free of death.

I have died once. I will not die again.

And yet this mudjhik body is imperfect. It has no face. No voice. No tongue with which to speak. It is a crude and clumsy roughed-out template of massive earthy red. So Josef Kantor does what no mudjhik dweller ever thought to do before, nor ever had the will: he begins to reshape the mudjhik clay from within. He gives it mouth. He gives it tongue (a fubsy lozenge of angel flesh, awkward now but he will learn). He gives it teeth and lips and palate for the enunciation of sibilants and plosives and fricatives, and all other equipment and accoutrements necessary for the purpose of making voice.

He gives its massive boulder head a face.

Josef Kantor's face.

Josef Kantor made of angel flesh the colour of brick and rust and drying blood and bruises.

Josef Kantor dead and immortal now and twelve feet high.

Josef Kantor in the warmth of the morning walking east towards the forest.

Find the thing you fear and strike it dead.

This is my world and I will not share it.

4

*T*housands of miles to the east, on the edge of the endless forest, Archangel feels himself in the mudjhik die. He knows that Josef Kantor has killed him, this one little piece of him sent out wandering across the world, and he knows what that means.

Archangel opens himself out like an unfolding fern and shouts at the oppressing sky of this poisonous world in absolute and ecstatic joy.

For Josef Kantor is strong!

Stronger than Archangel had ever guessed. The will of Kantor is harder than iron; his purpose is stronger than the heart rock of the world; his heat burns hotter than the sun. The strength of his arm grinds the wheels of time faster and faster.

Archangel knows and has always known that without Josef Kantor he is a dumb mouth shouting, a blowhard bully trundling about for ever in the forest, spilling futile anti-life: a liminal and ineffectual pantoufflard grumbling at the margins of history, claiming primacy but in clear-sighted truth merely scratching an itch.

And Josef Kantor without Archangel, one-time emperor of the Vlast though he may be, is brief-lived and tractionless. A powder flash in the pan.

But together!

My champion! My ever-burning sun!

It is Archangel who is the generator of power and endurance, Archangel the ever-spinning dynamo of cruel expansive energy, Archangel the permission and the totaliser. But it is Josef Kantor who is the conduit, the bond, the channel that lets Archangel reach out into the world and seize the bright birthright. Kantor is the face on the poster and the arm that wields the burning sword that turns the skies to ash.

Josef Kantor, freed now of his organic bodily chains, a will and a voice and a mind released into history and driving an angelic body, is coming to the forest with a mind to kill him, but there will be no need for that.

Faster and faster Archangel grinds towards the edge of the forest.

Kantor will come and break down the border.

Kantor will let him loose in the world.

Run my champion Josef Kantor faster and faster, run as I run towards you. Carry to me the banners of victory. The time is short and our enemies are upon us.

Archangel returns to his work with fresh vigour. There is much to do. His champion generalissimo needs a new army.

5

A week after the fall of Osip Rizhin, Vissarion Lom woke hollow and drenched with sweat from a dream of trees and Maroussia, and knew by the feeling in his belly and heart, by the anger and the anxiety and the desperate desolation, by the need to be up and moving, by the impossibility of rest, that it wasn't any kind of dream, no dream at all.

Maroussia was different – older, wiser, changed – she saw things he didn't see, she was distant, she was … august. She was something to be wary of. Something of power and something to fear.

Kantor is making for the forest. The angel is calling him there. Nothing is over yet, nothing is done. Come into the forest, darling, and I will find you there.

Helping. Answering the call. That was Lom. That was what he did.

In his dream that was no dream at all he'd seen the living angel in the woods. Seen the trail of poisoned destruction and cold smouldering crusted earth it left in its wake as it dragged itself, an immense hill the colour of blood and rust and bruises, towards the edge of the trees. A cloud of vapours burned off the top of the angel hill, cuprous and shining. Energy nets like pheromone clouds, dream-visible, dream-obvious. The soldiers of the Vlast were crawling about on its lower slopes like ants, digging and dying.

The living angel was recruiting an army of its own, infesting a growing crowd of dark things: bad dark things coming out from under the trees. Men and women like bears and wolves. Giants and trolls from the mountains and moving trees turned to ash and stone and dust. Lom's dream heart beat strangely when he saw the men like bears. The living angel found them in the forest and took their minds and filled them with its own. He gave them hunting and anger and desire and pleasure in death. He gave them bloodlust and greed and berserking. The smell of blood and musk. There were not many yet but more each day, and the nearer it got to the frontier of trees the more it found.

Lom heard faintly, insistently, the voice of the living angel in his own mind. It pulled at him like gravity, seeped through the skin, and polluted the way he tasted to himself.

I will not be silenced. I will not be imprisoned. I will not be harassed and consumed and annoyed and troubled and stung. I am Archangel, the voice of history and the voice of the dark heart of the world. My birthright is among the stars and I am coming yet.

Lom felt the living angel's attentive gaze pass over him and come to rest, returning his regard as if it knew it was watched. As if it knew its enemy and disdained him. It came to him then, dream knowledge, that he was Maroussia watching. He was seeing with Maroussia's eye. Alien Maroussia Pollandore, preparing to kill this thing if she could.

It was still dark when he woke but there was no more sleeping. In the first light of dawn Lom went to see Kistler, and then he went to find Eligiya Kamilova, who was back in her house on the harbour in the shadow of the Ship Bastion. That house was a survivor. Eligiya was there, and so were Elena Cornelius and her girls, Yeva and Galina. Rising for the day. Having breakfast.

I bring your children home to you Elena, Kamilova had said that day in the street. *I have looked after them as well as I could. You can stay in my house until you find your feet.*

What I owe you, Eligiya, said Elena, *it's too much. It can't ever be repaid.*

When he came for Kamilova in the early morning, Lom found Elena's girls just as he remembered them from when he and Maroussia stayed at Dom Palffy six years before. They had not grown. Not aged at all. That was uncanny. It disturbed him oddly. Kamilova was dark-eyed, thin and haunted. She had a faraway look, as if she felt uncomfortable and superfluous, marginal in her own home.

'I want you to come with me into the forest,' Lom said to her. 'Bring your boat and be my guide.'

Kamilova was on her feet immediately. Face burning.

'When?' she said.

'Now. Today. Will you come?'

'Of course. It is all I want.' She turned to Elena Cornelius. 'Keep the house,' she said. 'It is yours. I give it to Galina and Yeva. There is money in a box in the kitchen. I will not be coming back. Not ever.'

For all of the rest of her life Yeva Cornelius carried an agonising guilt that she hadn't loved Eligiya Kamilova and didn't weep and hug her when she left, but felt relieved when Kamilova left her with Galina and her mother. It was a needless burden she made for herself. Kamilova didn't do things out of love or to get love. She did what was needed.

Lom and Kamilova had the rest of the day to make arrangements. Kistler had arranged a truck to come for Kamilova's boat. The *Heron*. It was to be flown by military transport plane, along with Lom and Kamilova and their baggage and supplies, as far east as possible. As near to the edge of the forest as they could get.

Lom spent the time with Kamilova in her boathouse. She knew what she needed for an expedition into the forest and went about putting it all together while he poked about in her collection of things brought back from the woods. He felt excited, like a child, anxious to be on his way. He'd been born in the forest but had no coherent memories of life there. All his life he'd lived with the idea of it, but he'd never been there. And now he was going. And Maroussia was there.

When it was nearly time for the truck to come, Kamilova looked him up and down. His suit. His city shoes.

'You can't go like that,' she said.

She found him heavy trousers of some coarse material, a woollen pullover, a heavy battered leather jacket, but he had to go and buy himself boots, and by the time he got back the truck had come and the boat was in the back and Kamilova was waiting.

Elena and the girls were there to see them off.

'You're going to look for Maroussia, aren't you?' said Elena.

'Yes,' said Lom.

'You're a good man,' she said. 'You will find her.'

She looked across the River Purfas towards the western skyline where the sun was going down. The former Rizhin Tower, now renamed the Mirgorod Tower, rose dark against a bank of reddening pink cloud. It was still the tallest building by far, though the statue of Kantor was gone from the top of it. The new collective government with Kistler in the chair had had it removed and dismantled.

'They should call it Lom Tower for what you've done. People should know.'

'I wouldn't like that,' said Lom. 'I'd hate it. Nothing's done yet. It's just the beginning.'

Kistler had found jobs for Konnie and Maksim, working for the new government, and he'd sent out word to look for Vasilisk the bodyguard – Kistler was a man to repay his debts – but so far he could not be found. There was trouble brewing: many people had done well out of Rizhin's New Vlast, and not everyone was glad to see the statue gone. There were Rizhinists now. Hunder Rond had disappeared.

Kistler had offered to find a job for Elena Cornelius but she had refused.

'What will you do?' said Lom.

Elena smiled. 'I'm going to make cabinets again.' She hugged Lom and kissed him on the cheek. 'When you find Maroussia, bring her back here and see how we have done.'

'Maybe,' said Lom. 'That would be good.'

He swung himself up into the cab of the truck next to Kamilova and the driver.

'OK,' he said. 'Let's go.'

6

The plane carrying Lom and Kamilova and the *Heron* landed at a military airfield at the edge of the forest: three runways, heavy transport planes coming and going every few minutes. Soldiers and engineers and their equipment were everywhere: rows of olive and khaki tents in their thousands; roadways laid out; jetties and pontoons and river barges clogged with traffic; the smell of fuel and the noise of engines. Huge tracked machines churned up the mud and eased themselves onto broad floating platforms. It was an industrial entrepôt, the base camp of a massive engineering project and the beach-head for an invasion, all combined in one chaotic hub and thrown now into reorganisation and dismay. Orders had been changed: the collective government under Lukasz Kistler required the living angel not mined for its substance but destroyed. Eradicated. Killed. The order came as a signal, unambiguous and peremptory.

Destroy it? the commanders of the advance said to one another. *Destroy it? How?*

A few miles east of the airfield low wooded hills closed the horizon: rising slopes of dark grey tree-mass which stretched away north and south, unbroken into the distance, shrouded in scraps of drifting mist. Westward was clear summer blue, the continental Vlast in sunshine, but a leaden autumn cloud bank had slid across the sky above the forest like a lid closing, a permanent weather front coming to rest at the edge of hills.

In hospital tents men and women on low cots stared darkly at the ceiling. Others slumped in wheelchairs, legs tucked under blankets, or hobbled and swung on crutches, aimless and solitary, muttering quietly. Bandaged feet. Arms, hands and faces marked with chalky fungal growths and patches of smooth blackness.

'Have you seen this before?' Lom said to Kamilova.

'No. This is not the forest doing this.'

'The angel then,' said Lom. 'They've found it.'

*

Out of the trees through a gap in the low hills the broad slow river flowed, turbid and muddy green. An unceasing traffic of barges and motor launches and shallow-draught gunships cruised upstream, heavily laden and low in the water, and came back downstream riding higher, empty, bruised and rusting.

'There's another way,' said Kamilova. 'The old waterway joins the river downstream of here.'

The *Heron* and their gear was loaded on a flatbed truck. Early in the morning, before their liaison officer was up and about, Lom and Kamilova drove out of the camp alone. Nobody questioned them at the gate.

A day's sailing downriver and the sinking sun in their eyes was gilding the river a dull red gold when Kamilova swung the boat in towards the left bank under overhanging vegetation. Lom saw nothing but a scrubby spit of land until they were into the canal and nosing up slow shallow waters clogged with weed. Disgruntled waterfowl made way for them, edging in under muddy banks and exposed tree roots, or rose and flapped away slowly to quieter grounds.

'This way is navigable?' said Lom.

'It's a few years since I was here,' said Kamilova.

Ruined stonework lined the water's edge: low embankments, mossy and root-broken and partly collapsed, the stumps of rotted wooden jetties, rusted mooring rings. Back from the canal edge were low mounds and rooted stumps of standing stone. Broken suggestions of fallen ruins lost. Earth and grass and undergrowth spilled in a slow tide across ancient constructions and slumped into torpid water.

'It's an old trader canal,' said Kamilova. 'It connects with another river over there beyond the hill. In the time of the Reasonable Empire, when the Lezarye families were hedge wardens and castellans of the forest margin, you'd have seen a town here. Trading posts. Warehouses. Of course the trade was already ancient when the Lezarye came. There was always trade into the forest and out of it.'

'Timber?' said Lom. 'The canal seems too narrow.'

'Not here, that was always big-river trade. In places like this you'd find charcoal burners and wood turners. Fur traders selling sable, marten, grease beaver, miniver, fox, hart. There were markets for dried mushrooms and lichens and powdered barks. Syrups and liquors.

Scented woods. Wax and honey and dried berries. Antler and bone. Anything you could bring out of the forest and sell. And there'd have been shamans and völvas and priests. Giants of course, and the other forest peoples would come out this far too. Keres and wildings. This was debatable land then. Marginal. Liminal. A crossing place.'

They passed under the long evening shadow of a round-towered and gabled building of high sloping walls: red brick and timber, collapsing, overgrown, roofless and empty-windowed.

'A Lezarye garrison way fort,' said Kamilova. 'The trade leagues paid the Lezarye to keep the peace and the Reasonable Empire paid them to watch the border and make sure the darker things of the forest stayed there.'

The pace of the boat slackened as the evening breeze dropped away. There was thinness and a still, breathless silence in the air. Lom felt he was at the bottom of a deep well filled up with ages of time.

Kamilova shook herself and looked wary.

'Things are slowing here,' she said. 'I know the feel of this from when I was with Elena's girls. We shouldn't linger.'

She unshipped oars and began to row, nosing the *Heron* forward through thickening standing water. Lom watched her muscular arms working. The intricate interlaced patterns on her skin were like winding roots and knots of brambles and young tendrils reaching out across the earth. They seemed fresher and more vivid than he'd noticed before. There was much he wanted to ask her. But not yet. The wooded hills of the forest edge rose higher and denser before them, closer now, catching the last light of the setting sun. A rich and glowing green wall.

After an hour or so the waterway widened and the going was easier, but the last light of the day was failing. Kamilova tied up the *Heron*.

'We'll camp for the night,' she said. 'Tomorrow we'll go in under the trees.'

7

Yakoushiv the embalmer presented himself at the office of Colonel Hunder Rond, commander of the Parallel Sector. Yakoushiv was clammy with sweat. He felt sick. He could hardly speak for nerves. He thought his end had come.

'You did a nice job with the corpse of the old Novozhd,' said Rond. 'Very pretty. I have more work for you, if you're interested.'

Yakoushiv's legs trembled with relief. He almost fell. He felt as if his head had become detached from his neck and was floating a foot above his shoulders. He dabbed at his face with a sweet handkerchief.

'Of course,' he said. His voice came out wrong. Pitched too high. 'The subject? I mean … who is the … ?'

'Come through and I'll show you.'

Rond led him through to the other room. Yakoushiv's eyes widened in surprise. Another wave of sick nervousness and fear. The corpse of the disgraced Papa Rizhin was laid out in Rond's inner office on a makeshift catafalque.

'You will work here,' said Rond. 'You will write me a list of what you need and I will obtain it for you. There is need for great haste. He must be ready tonight. You understand? Is that possible?'

'Of course.'

'Make it your best work ever. And get rid of the scar on his face.'

Yakoushiv worked as rapidly and as neatly as he could. It was impossible to avoid making a mess in the room. There was … spillage. But when he had finished the corpse of Osip Rizhin was glossy and shining and fragranced with a cloying sickly sweetness.

When Rond returned he examined Yakoushiv's work from head to foot.

'You've done well,' he said. 'You should be pleased, Yakoushiv. Your last job was your best. I hope you can take some satisfaction from that. I'm only sorry you can't go home now.'

Yakoushiv turned white. 'No,' he said. 'Please. No.'

'There can be no blabbing, you see. No tales to be told.'

'I won't. Of course. I promise. Please—'

'I'm sorry, Yakoushiv,' said Rond.

8

Next morning Lom woke at the outermost, easternmost edge of the world he knew, he and Kamilova alone in an emptied ancient landscape.

The sun had not yet risen above the edge of the forest. Close now, the hills were dark shoulders and hogs' backs of dense tree canopy draped in mist and cloud. Home of ravens. On the lower slopes he could see the relics of long-abandoned field boundaries under bracken and scrub, and out of the scrub rose great twisted knobs and stumps of rock, shoulders and boulders of raw stone. Stone the colour of rain and slate.

The stone seemed to hum and prickle the air.

The Lezarye used to keep the debatable lands by patrol and force of arms, Kamilova had said, *but the forest maintains its own boundary. It's stronger now than I've ever felt it before.*

I feel it, said Lom. *Yes.*

Kamilova, bright-eyed and alive, raised the *Heron*'s brown sail, and the little wooden boat took them up the river and into the trees.

As they travelled, Kamilova kept up a stream of quiet talk, more talk than Lom had ever known from her before. She talked about the people who went to live among the trees.

'The forest changes you,' she said. 'It brings out who you are. The breath of the trees. Giants grow larger in the woods.' She talked about hollowers, hedge dwellers who dug shelters in the earth. 'They don't hibernate, not exactly, but their body temperature falls and they're dormant for days on end. They sleep out the worst of winter underground like bears do.'

She told him the names of clans. Lyutizhians meant people like wolves, and Kassubians were the shaggy coats.

'I saw things once that someone said were bear-made. They were rough things, strange and wild and inhuman, for paws and muzzles and teeth to use, not dextrous fingers. But it was just a rumour. Humanish forest peoples keep to the outwoods, but there's always further in and further back.

'The forest is a bright and perfumed place,' she said, 'with dark and tangled corners. It is not defined. It includes everything and it is not safe. The forest talks to you, but you have to do the work; you have to bring yourself to the task. Communication is indirect and you must pay attention. You have to dig. Dig!'

Lom hardly listened to her. The river was passing through a gap between steep slopes, almost cliffs, under a low grey sky, and there was the possibility of cold rain in the air. The troubling ache in his head that had been with him all morning, the agitated throbbing of the old wound in his forehead, was fading. His sense of time passing had lurched, dizzying and uncomfortable, but it was settled now. Time present touched the endless eternal forest like sunlight grazing the outer leaves of a huge tangled tree or the surface of a very deep and very dark lake. The forest was all Kamilova's stories and more, but it was also a breathing lung made of real trees and rock and earth and water. He felt the aliveness of it and the way it went on for ever.

Doors in the air were opening. The skin of the water glimmered and thrilled. Promising reflections, it almost delivered. The breath of the forest crackled. It bristled. There were black trees. There were grey and yellow trees. He was watching a single ash tree at the river margin and it was watching him back, being alive.

Lom was opening up and growing stronger. He was entering a place where new kinds of thing were possible, different stories with different outcomes. He was coming home. He reached up into the low roof of cloud and opened a gap to let a spill of warmth through that made the river glitter. A moment of distraction, lost in sunlight: there were many small things among the trees – animals and birds – and they were all alive and he could feel that.

Then he became aware that Kamilova had stopped talking and was watching him. Intently. Curiously. A little bit afraid.

From the slopes of the hills and among the trees they are watched. The small boat edging upriver against the stream; the woman whose arms are painted with fading magic; the man spilling bright beautiful scented trails from the hole in his skull, tainted with dark shades of angel: all this is seen and known by watchers with brown whiteless eyes, and by things with no eyes that also see. Word passes through roots and leaves and air. Word reaches Fraiethe and the Seer Witch of Bones. Word reaches Maroussia Shaumian Pollandore.

He is coming. He is here.

Chapter Twelve

Nothing that lives and dies ever has a beginning, nor does it ever end in death and annihilation. There is only a mixing, followed by the separating-out of what was mixed: and these mixings and unmixings are what people call beginnings and ends.

Empedocles (*c.* 490–430 BCE)

1

Kantor-in-mudjhik runs through the endless forest, tireless, exultant and strong. The continental Vlast is behind him. He has run it, ocean to trees, without a pause.

Under the trees he has heard the voice of Archangel talking and they have sealed the deal.

I will give you body after body, says Archangel, *a chain of human bodies without end, vessels for my champion son. Worthy and valid strength of my strength, bring me out of the forest and for you I will break down the doors and shatter the doorposts. For you I will raise up the dead to consume the living. I will give you armies without end, and you will carry me, speaking my voice, across the stars.*

Josef Kantor in his mudjhik body likes the sound of that.

I am nobody's son, he says, *but I will be a brother.*

It's not enough, but it will do for now.

2

Into the forest old beyond guessing, the first place, primordial, primeval, primal, the unremembered home, fair winds carried them day after day, deeper and deeper, up the river against the stream. Trees stood silently, lining the banks, fading away in every direction into twilight and indistinction.

'How will we find her?' said Kamilova. 'I mean Maroussia?'

'We keep going in,' said Lom, 'and she will come to us.'

Things that find their way into the forest grow and change. They grow taller, shorter, thinner, fatter; they change colour. Each thing grows out into its true shape and becomes more itself. A dog may become more wolf-like. It unfolds like a fern.

In the forest you can't see far or travel fast; detachment and analysis fail; you can't see the wood for the trees. Aurochsen and wisent, woolly rhinoceros, great elk and giant sloth browse among the leaves, and the corpses of those killed in great and terrible massacres are buried under shallow earth. The labyrinth of trees is filled with travelling shadows and all the monsters of the mind. In the forest, things long thought dead may be alive and the hunter become the prey. Green pools glimmer in the shade. More is possible here.

It is hard enough to get in, but leaving, that is the labour, that is the task. The forest is receding, back into its own world. Ancient silences are withdrawing like the tide.

Nights they slept out under blankets on the deck boards of the *Heron*. Kamilova cut thorns to make a brake on the bank against wolves and left a slow fire burning.

'If a big cat comes, set the thorns alight,' she said.

'Lynx is worse than wolf?' said Lom.

'Not lynx,' said Kamilova. 'Bigger than lynx, much bigger. Heavy as a horse, and teeth to snap your spine.'

Lom lay awake and heard the grumbling of predators in the dark, but nothing troubled them.

'I don't think wolves hunt in the night,' he said.

'You want to bet your skin on that?'

'No.'

Kamilova took the pan of stewed rosehips off the fire and set it in the grass. Pulled her knife from her belt and wiped it carefully clean. Unwrapped the axe and did the same, and sharpened the blades of both to a clean fineness with her stone. By the time she'd done, the stewed hips were cool enough. She picked a handful out of the pan and squeezed the juices back in. Lom watched the bright redness dribble between her fingers. She threw the seed-filled pulp away and scooped another handful, working it between her palms to release as much as possible of the blood-warm liquid. By the time she'd picked the last few softened fruits out of the liquid and pressed them between finger and thumb she had the pan half-full of rich rose liquor.

'Here,' she said and passed the pan to Lom.

He took a sip. Without honey it was bitter enough to roughen the roof of his mouth, but it was good.

'I know this place,' she said, 'but there were people here then, and fewer wolves. Everyone's gone, but there's somewhere nearby I'd like to see again. I'll take you there'

'OK,' said Lom. 'Tomorrow.'

Morning came quiet and cold, suppressed under low featureless skies. A drab unsettling breeze stirred brittle leaves. The forest felt shabby and grey. Snares and fish traps laid the evening before held nothing. Lom ate some berries and drank a little of the sour red rose-drink. It left him no less hungry.

The absence of Maroussia nagged at him. Her failure to come. Since they'd passed through the gap in the hills he'd felt nothing of her. Morning succeeded morning, timeless and inconsequential: a perpetual repetition of movement without progress against the narrowing river that always tried to push them back and out. The resinous taste of the air, the hungry excitement of opening up into the possibilities of the forest, was fading. Immensity and endlessness were always and everywhere the same, and he felt small and ordinary and lost. He was growing accustomed to the inexhaustible sameness of trees, and knew that he was somehow failing.

He crouched among fallen leaves, blotched and parchment-yellow and fragile, like dry pages scattered from an ageing and spine-cracked book, disordered out of all meaning. He picked up crumbling handfuls and sifted them, dealing them out like faceless cards in a game he couldn't play, returning leaves to the infinite mat of fallen leaves, every one different and all of them the same, abundant beyond all counting, further in and further on forever, abundant to the point of absurdity. Autumn was coming in the interminable forest and there would be no numbering of the trees.

He pushed his hands down, digging through the covering of dry leaves into darkening dampness and rot and the raw deep earth beneath. The cool fungal smell. Mycelium. Earthworm. Shining blackened twig fragment and softening pieces of bark. Truffle-scented leaf rot. Fine tangled clumps of hair-like root.

Lom closed his eyes and breathed.

Trunks of trees rise separately out of the earth and each stands apart from its neighbours. We overvalue sight. In the rich dark earth the roots of all the trees of the forest are intertwined. Knotted filaments and root fibres grow around and through each other, twist each other about, intertangled and nodal, meshed and joined with furtive fungal threads, digging down deeper than the trees grow tall. Slow exchange and interchange of mineral currency. Burrowing capacitors and conductors of gentle dark electric flux and spark. You can't say one tree ends and the next begins; it's all one sentient wakeful centreless tree and it lives underground.

Lom listened to the circuitry of the earth. He felt the living angel getting stronger. The first weakening of hope. A cruel thing coming closer and the rumourous growth of fear. There was a hurt in the forest and a wound in the world. He missed Maroussia and wished she would come.

3

Josef Kantor embodied in mudjhik reaches the lower slopes of the Archangel hill. The ground he stands on is burning with cool fire, thrilling to the touch, and the immense body of the living angel rises in front of him, higher, far higher, than he had imagined. Hundreds of feet into the sky. Even hurt and weakened, grounded as it is, it is a thing of glowering power. It crackles with life. The mudjhik body loosens and grows light. It feeds. Archangel feeds Kantor and Kantor feeds Archangel, strength mixes with strength, distinctions blur.

Archangel separates several hundred chunks of himself and sends them into the sky to circle his top on flaggy wings. The coming of his prince deserves such glorious celebration.

4

Kamilova took Lom to see the place she knew. She was happy in the forest. This was where she could be who she was.

They approached through old earthworks and turf-covered stone dykes. Redoubts. Salients. Massive boulders that had been tumbled into place and now settled deep into the earth. Rooks chattered and flocked among thorn trees.

The full extent of the stronghold was invisible, immersed in trees, and it felt smaller than it was because the chambers were small. Intimate human scale. Inside was gloomy, rich with earth and stone and leaf and wood, and the river ran through it, in under the hill. The place was burrow, sett and warren. Tunnels extended into darkness, every direction and down.

Kamilova took and lit a tar-soaked torch. The flame burned slow and smoked.

'Come on,' she said. 'This way.'

Distinctions between inside and outside, overground and underground, meant little. There were low halls with intricately carved ceilings and curving wooden walls, like the hulls of underground ships, polished and dark with age and hearth smoke, into which real living trees, their limbs and roots and branches, were interwoven and included. Chambers and passageways were floored with stone flags or compacted earth, leaf-carpeted. Older places were rotting and returning to the earth, moss and mushroom damp.

'I'd thought there might be someone still here,' said Kamilova. 'Stupid, but I hoped it.'

Lom's feeling of unease was growing.

'We shouldn't stay here,' he said. 'There's something not right.'

On the path back to where they had left the *Heron* they heard riders approaching. The footfall of horses. The clanking of bridles and gear. The scuffing of many feet through mud and forest litter. No voices. There was a quiet wind moving among the trees, but Lom could hear them coming.

'Get out of sight,' he said. 'Quickly.'

They crouched behind low thorn and briar. There was movement visible now through the trees.

Kamilova put her face next to his ear. 'Did they see us?'

'I don't know.'

He pulled off his pack and crawled forward on his belly, turning on his side to squeeze between thorn-bush stems. A root in the ground dug into him. He felt the spike of it gouging into his flesh, dragging at him. It hurt. He eased himself slowly forward across it, his face pressed close to the earth. Thorns snagged in his hair and grazed the skin of his scalp. A strand of briar hooked itself across his back. He reached back to pull it away and inched himself forward until he could see the track. He scooped a lump of earth and moss and rubbed himself with it, smearing it on his forehead and round his eyes, working it into the stubble on his face. The scent of it was strong and sour in his nose. He was sweating despite the cold.

Kamilova squeezed up next to him. The sound of her ragged breathing. He didn't look round.

There were three riders at the front, and men walking behind, strung out and silent. Lots of men, dirty and ill dressed. More riders followed, the horses dragging long heavy bundles wrapped in cloth. The bundles were heavy, deadweight, trailing furrow-paths through the leaves on the path. The horses pulled slowly against the weight.

The riders were bulky and hooded, soiled woollen cowls shrouding their faces, their heads heavy and too large. They rode alert, scanning the trees. Lom felt the pressure of their attention pass across him. It made him feel uneasy. Exposed. He inched his way cautiously backwards under the thorn.

'Don't move,' Kamilova hissed in his ear. 'There's one behind us.'

Lom lay on his back, face turned up, looking into the close tangle of the leafless bush. Outriders scouting the trail. Fear made his heart struggle. He wanted to breathe clear air. He forced himself to lie still and wait. Let them pass.

Long after the last sound of their passing had gone, the two of them lay without speaking under the thorns. The touch of the riders' eyeless gaze stayed with them, a taint breath, a foulness in the mind. They listened for any sign of more following or the scout returning, and when that purpose faded they still didn't move.

'What were they?' said Kamilova. She didn't look at him but stayed lying on her back, watching a spider moving slowly among the branches.

'I don't know.'

'Did you feel …?'

'Yes.'

'That wasn't … normal. That wasn't right.'

'No.'

Neither of them said anything for a long time.

'We should go,' she said at last. 'We should move on.'

'Yes.'

Stiff and cold, they picked up their packs and began to walk.

'Perhaps we should stay off the track,' she said. 'There might be more coming.'

'We have to get back to the boat,' said Lom. 'We have to keep going.'

It began to rain. Sheets of wind-driven icy water soaking their clothes. The noise of it was like an ocean in the trees. The track led them between shallow green pools, rain-churned and murky.

Lom didn't hear the splashing charge of the bear-man over the noise of the rain. Didn't smell it through the rain and the mud and the drench of the leaves. But he felt the appalling shock of the boulder-heavy collision that drove the air from his lungs, crunched the ribs in his chest and hurled him off the path into the water, crashing his spine against the trunk of a beech tree.

He could not raise his arms. He could not move his legs. The water came up to his waist. Propped against the slope of the tree root, he watched the grey-hooded figure turn and come back, wading towards him through the mud-swirled green pool. Its cowl was pulled back off its head.

Lom smelled the bear-man's hot sour breath on his face, on his wide staring eyes. He saw deep into the dark red mouth as its jaws widened to clamp on his face. The mouth reeked of angel. He observed with detached and distant surprise that half its head was made of stone.

Lom punched the side of the half-stone head with closed-up forest air, boulder heavy and boulder-hard. A swinging fist of rain and air. The bear-weighted bear-muzzled skull jerked sideways, crushed and broken and dead in a sudden mess of blood and bone.

5

*T*he bear-man, the angel rider of horse, opens his mouth to scream out the shock and outrageous surprise of his death, his death out of nowhere. He is instantaneously silenced. Cerebral cortex sprayed on the air like a smashed fruit.

But the screaming instant is heard.

Archangel, O Archangel all-surveying, connected by iron filaments of Archangel mind to all the doers of his will – all the absorbed living syllables through which he gives voice, all the soldiers in the army he is building for his brother in arms Josef Kantor – Archangel hears and feels the killing of the bear and knows it for what it is. It is familiar. Anomaly and threat.

And there is something else.

He has seen it now. Resolved out of endlessness and trees it has locality. The eye of his surveillance has pinned it, and this time it is close and he can reach it.

She shows herself and he has found her.

Everything comes together in the forest, and out in the forest hunting now is his racing engine, his destroyer, his fraternal champion and his pride.

Kill them all. Kill them quickly. Do it now.

Archangel calls and his champion runs them down.

6

'They were riding for the angel,' said Lom. 'I think we're coming closer to where it is.'

There was strain in Kamilova's eyes. She was watching him warily again. There was always a separateness about her: a wordless watchfulness, a lonely, withheld and self-postponing patience, doing what she must and waiting for the dark times to go.

'It was going to kill you,' she said. 'Then it was like its brain exploded.'

They were back at the *Heron*, and the rain had passed leaving watery afternoon sunshine. Lom had wiped the dark bear blood off his face and neck but still he felt unclean. The angel-residue in his own blood was strung out taut like wires in his veins again. He didn't like Kamilova's scrutiny and wanted to be alone.

'I'm going for a swim,' he said.

He followed a game trail up to the crest of a low slope and looked down on dark green water. The trail took him down to the edge of it, a stillness fringed on the far side with dense bramble. A fallen tree dipped a leafless crown and branches like arms into the mystery of the pool. Goosander gave muted echoless mews. Lom took off his rain-damp clothes and waded out. The water, cold against his shins, was moss-coloured, icy, opaque. He felt the thick cool of silt sliding between his toes and up over his feet. It felt like darkness.

After a few steps the lake bottom fell away steeply and he slipped, half-falling and half-choosing, into a sudden clumsy dive. The water closed over his head. How deep it might be he had no idea and didn't care. Bands of iron cold tightened round his skull and bruised ribs, squeezing out breath. He opened his eyes on nothing but pale thickened green light.

Floundering to the surface he swam with cramped clumsy strokes, arms and legs working through the cold. Broken twigs and fallen leaves littered the surface: he nosed his way through.

Once the first shock of the chill subsided, he immersed himself in the wild forgetful freedom of swimming in the forest, washing the sourness of killing and angel from his skin and hair. He took breath and dived for the bottom, reaching his arms down for it, but couldn't touch it, and surfaced, gasping. Floating on his back he watching the canopy of trees turning slowly overhead against the heavy sky.

He swam until the icy bitter cold of the water returned to the attack, then hauled himself up onto the bole of the fallen tree and lay there for a long time, face down, the bark's hard roughness against his skin, the air of the forest resting against his naked back. Lazy and reluctant to move he watched the pool opaque and green below him.

When he was dry he crawled back along the tree and swung himself down onto the bank, and she was there, her eyes brushing across him, bright and dark and happy.

Maroussia.

She put her hand against his chest, tracing the rise and hollow of his ribs. His hands and face were weather-brown, his body pale. The warmth of her fingers was on him. He smelled the sweetness of her breath.

'Is it you?' he said. 'Not a shadow but you?'

'You're cold,' she said. 'Your skin is rough and hard and cool like stone.'

She looked into his face and opened her mouth a little, and he kissed her, his arms around her shoulders awkwardly, uncertain. She tasted like hedge berries, and she leaned in and pressed herself against him. The scent of woodsmoke and forest in her hair. She took his hand and pressed it against her belly gently.

'Do you feel our child moving?'

For him it had been six years and more, but for her hardly any time at all.

7

It was late afternoon when Lom and Maroussia walked together back down the trail to the river where the *Heron* was moored.

Eligiya Kamilova received Maroussia with quiet reserve. She was generous and fine, but Lom could see her withdrawing. She was displaced again: having done her part she was finding herself edged to the margin of other people's reunions and plans. Lom found himself feeling slightly sorry for her. It was guilt that he felt, he knew that – he'd brought her here, he'd used her as his guide – but it was the path she'd chosen. The solitary traveller. She'd wanted to come. The forest was her travelling place, but she'd come back and found it an emptier, harsher place than before.

Kamilova had caught a fish in her trap. A pike. She shared it with them. The smoke of the cooking fire hung about in the still air of evening, clinging and acrid. It stuck to their skin. The flesh of the pike tasted muddy and was full of fine sharp bones. Not pleasant eating. Maroussia said little and ate less.

The sliver of an ominous new hill had appeared above the trees in the west. It glowed a dull rust-red in the last of the westering sun, and above it dark shapes circled like flocks of flying birds.

'I'm sorry, Eligiya,' said Maroussia.

Kamilova frowned.

'Sorry? Why?'

'A bad thing is coming and I am bringing it here. I show myself now to draw it out before it gets any stronger. It may already be too strong.'

Maroussia turned to Lom. She was almost a stranger, fierce and strong. Her hair was black, her eyes were dark and wide. She was carrying his child. He hadn't even begun to absorb the truth of that yet.

'Are you ready?' she said.

'Ready for what?' said Lom, but he knew.

He'd felt it coming for some time: the pulsing rhythm of blood in his head was the rhythm of a heavy, pounding footfall crashing through the trees, growing louder and coming closer. The hairs on the back of his neck prickled as he felt the touch of the avid hunter's tunnel-narrow gaze. He saw that even Kamilova was feeling it now: a faint drumbeat in the ground underfoot.

'Kantor is coming,' said Maroussia. 'I'm sorry. There is no time to prepare. It has to be now. Kantor is here.'

'Oh,' said Lom. 'Oh. Yes. I see.' A sudden sick lurch of fear. 'OK. Well there's no time like now.'

The mudjhik stepped out from the grey twilit birches, dull red and massive, balanced and avid and bulky and strangely beautiful and as tall as the trees it stood among. Its eyes – it had eyes – took them in with a gaze of confident relaxation and intelligence. Its expression was almost elegant and almost amused. It had grace as well as size and power. It was a perfectly realised angel-human giant of stone the colour of rust and blood and bruises, a new thing come into the world, and it had the face of a hundred million posters and portraits and photographs. The face on the statue at the top of the Rizhin Tower. The face of Papa Rizhin. The face of Josef Kantor.

And when it spoke it had the voice of Kantor too, warm and expressive, loud and clear among the trees. You heard it in your head and you heard it in your ear. Tall as the trees, it had a tongue to speak.

'So it is you, my Lom, my investigator, my troublesome provincial mouse, my annoyance still and always,' said the voice and face of Josef Kantor. He looked from Lom to Maroussia. 'And here is the trivial bitch-girl not my daughter too, my betrayer's bastard whelp, the spill of my cuckolding. You stink of the forest like your mother did. Both of you stink of it. Well the mother is dead and I will destroy the daughter also, and the man. You run and you wriggle and you hide, you sting me and skip away, but I have you cornered now.'

Kantor-in-mudjhik took a pace forward and spread its arms wide, arms with a suggestion of muscular flow. Fists opened flexing fingers. It had fingers. Thick stubby fingers. Josef Kantor's hands.

'I'm going to make quite a mess. Dog crows will clean it up.'

While the mudjhik Kantor spoke, Lom felt the dark electric pressure of angel senses passing across him, probing and examining. The touch of it, obscene and invasive, brought a surge of anger and hatred, a knot of iron and stone in his belly like a fist.

The mudjhik stopped mid-stride and gave a bark, a sudden laugh of surprised delight. Its blank pebble eyes glittered with warmth and pleasure.

'And there is a child!' the voice of Kantor said. 'How perfect is that? Good. Let me kill it too. Let it all end now, and then I will take the blustering bastard angel down and be on my way out of these trees and get my world back. This triviality has gone on long enough.'

Lom felt surge after surge of anger and desperation and the wired strength of his own angel taint welling up, overbrimming and bursting walls inside him. The taste of iron, a hot suffusion in the blood. He was the violence. The smasher. The fist. He was defender. He was bear.

That was the secret of his birthing. Fathered by a man-bear in the deeps of the forest, he was the blade-toothed muzzle, the gaping tearing snout, the heavy carnivore with heavy paws to break necks. He felt himself unfurling into bear and killing, and let it come. Let it come! Barriers and frontiers dissolving, he was coming into the myth of himself, he was the man-bear with angel in his blood.

Lom felt the power of the angel substance tugging at his mind, a hungry undertow pulling and hauling him out of his body, dizzying and disorientating. The forest sliding sideways. Peripheral vision darkening. Connection with reality slipping away.

It wasn't Kantor doing that, it was the thing his mudjhik body was made of.

Lom didn't resist. He threw himself into the pulling of the current and went with it into the mudjhik, leaving his soft body fallen behind, taking the war onto Kantor's own ground to kill him there.

All power is done at a price, but the price is not paid by those who wield it. It is paid by the victims. Kantor was human and he was not, and there was an end to it.

Lom in the mudjhik found Kantor there and fell on him, tearing and snarling, a blood-blind frontal killing assault of unwithstandable fierceness. To end it quickly before Kantor could react.

Lom hit a wall.

The wall of Kantor's will. Impregnable will. A hardened vision that could not be changed but only broken, and it would not break. Lom could not break it.

The force of his attack skittered sideways, ineffectual, like cat's claws against marble slab. It wasn't a defeat. The fight didn't even begin.

He felt the gross stubby fingers of Josef Kantor picking over his fallen, winded body. Ripping him open and rummaging among the intimate recesses of memory and desire. Kantor's voice was a continual whisper in his dissolving mind.

I am Josef Kantor, and what I will to happen will happen. I am Josef Kantor, and I am the strongest and the hardest thing. I am the incoming tide of history. I am the thing you hate and fear and I am stronger than you. You fear me. I am Josef Kantor and I am inevitable. I am the smooth and uninterruptible voice. I always return. I am total. I am the force of one single purpose, the voice of the one idea that drives out all others. The uncertain dissolve before and forgive me as they die. I am the taker and I have killed you now.

Vissarion Lom wasn't strong enough. He wasn't strong at all. He was dying. He could not breathe. He was dead.

And then Maroussia was in the mudjhik with him. Her quiet voice. A mist of evening rain.

The Pollandore was with her, inside her and outside her. Clean light and green air. Spilling all the possibilities of everything that could happen if Josef Kantor did not happen and there were no angels at all. The endless openness and extensibility of life without angels.

She followed him into death.

Come back with me. Come back.

8

Lom was in a beautiful simple place among northern trees. Pine and birch and spruce. The air was clear and fresh as ice and rain. Resinous dark green needles carpeting the earth. Time fell there in sudden windfall showers, pulses of night and day, evening and morning, always rising, always young, always new. There were broadleaf trees, and laughter was hidden in the leaves, out of sight, being the leaves.

Everything alive with wildness.

He could see trees growing: unfurling their leaves and spreading overhead, reaching towards each other with their branches until they met, a green ceiling of leaves, and all the light was a liquid fall, green as fire, that spilled through the leaves, enriching the widening silence.

Josef Kantor slammed together the walls of his will to crush Maroussia between them and extinguish her utterly, and it made no difference to her at all.

Lom saw Maroussia walking towards him, and a figure was walking beside her through the trees. It seemed at first to be walking on four legs like a deer, but it must have been a trick of the shadows, because the dappled figure appeared to rise on its hind legs as it came and he saw that it was like a woman. A perfume of musk and warmth was in the air. Her eyes were wide and brown and there were no whites in them. She was naked except that a nap of short smooth reddish-brown fur covered her head and neck and shoulders and the place between her breasts and spread down across her brown rounded belly.

'Who are you?' said Lom. *Engage in dialogue with your visions.*

She smiled, and a long warm pink tongue flickered between thin white pointed teeth.

'You mean, what am I?'

'Yes.'

'Do you want to know?'

'Yes.'

'You know what I am.'

'Tell me.'

She opened her mouth and spilled a flow of words, green foliage tumbling, heaped up, all at once. A chord of words.

I am the vixen in the rain and the hungry sow-badger suckling in the dark earth. I am salt on your tongue and the dark sweet taste of blood.

I am scent on the air at dusk, sweet as colostrum. I am the belly-warm womb of the she-otter in the river. I am the cub-warm sleep of the she-bear under the snow. I am the noctule, stooping upon moths with the weight of cubs in my belly.

I am the she-elk, ice-bearded, nudging my calf against the wind, and I am the mouse in the barn, suckling the blind pink buds of life. I am the sour breath of the stoat in the tunnel's darkness and I am the vixen's teeth in the neck of the hen.

I am the crunch of carrion and I am the thirsty suck and the flow of warm sweet milk. I am tired and cold and wet and full of cub. I am shit and blood and milk and salty tears. I am plastered fur and soaking hair.

I am the abdomen swollen taut as a drum and full as an egg. I am the ceaseless desperate hunger of the starveling shrew. I am the sow's lust for the boar, the hart's delight in the pride of the hind.

I am the fucker's laughing and the smell of droppings in the wet grass. I am the sweetness of milk on the baby's breath and the cold smell of a dead thing. I am the hot gates opening into light.

I am all of us and I am you. I am the mirror of your coming here to meet yourself.

'I don't understand.'

You understand, said Fraiethe. *Though understanding doesn't matter. You are green forest and dark angel and human world, compendious and strong. Forget what you cannot do and do what you can do.*

Fraiethe opened her mouth to kiss him, as she had kissed Maroussia once, though that he did not yet know.

She bit him, she swallowed him up and he was not killed.

9

Things can change. Borders are not fixed. Permeability. Mutability. Trees can speak. A man may become an animal. A woman may become time like a god. Everything is alive and humans are not separate from that.

There is power which is the exercise of will and there is power which is openness and letting go. It has to do with air and breath and consciousness. A freeing not a binding. A removal of bonds.

Josef Kantor – Papa Rizhin – fraternal angel champion – mudjhik – came lumbering at them out of the trees to silence and kill. Maroussia Shaumian and Vissarion Lom, side by side, the child inside a possibility between them, watched him come.

They saw right round him and through him and he wasn't there.

The mudjhik was an empty column of stuff like stone.

10

The prototype Universal Vessel *Vlast of Stars* stood on the concrete apron at Vitigorsk, a swollen citadel of steel, a snub and gross atomic bullet thirty storeys high. Hunder Rond had personally overseen the stowage on board of the embalmed corpse, the earthly remains of Papa Rizhin. A chosen crew had taken their places, eager and proud, the brightest and the best, prepared to live or die, but in their hearts they knew that they would live. They would reach their destination. There were other, better suns awaiting them.

Rond stood now on the asphalt, uniformed in crisp new black. The hot wind that disturbed his hair was heavy with the industrial chemical stench of Vitigorsk

'There have been no tests,' said Yakov Khyrbysk. 'It is the prototype. You know what that means.'

'You can come or you can stay,' said Rond. 'Your choice.'

Khyrbysk shook his head.

'I'm staying here,' he said.

Rond looked around.

'The backwash will destroy all this,' he said.

'We have evacuated. We will be far away. We will rebuild better somewhere else.'

'Perhaps,' said Rond. 'Perhaps. But we will get there first. You will not find us.'

Khyrbysk shrugged. 'I have to go now.'

Half an hour later and twenty miles away in Tula-Vitisk Launch Control, Yakov Khyrbysk gave the word. He was curious. It was a prototype. Whatever happened he would learn from it and move on.

The horizon disappeared in a flash of blinding light.

When the light cleared, a column of expanding mushroom clouds was climbing into the pale blue sky, puffs of distant smoke and wind illuminated by inward burn. Higher and higher they climbed, a rising stairway of evanescent stellar ignitions, a trajectory curving towards the west and the sinking of the sun.

*

At the sweet spot of the rising curve, several hundred miles high, the entire magazine of the *Vlast of Stars* exploded at once. The brightness of the detonation spread across the whole of the western sky. It overwhelmed the sun. The vaporised residue drifted for months through the upper atmosphere, borne on high fierce winds. Intermixed with the shattered molecular dust of the earthly remains of the corpse of Papa Rizhin it slowly slowly fell to earth, becoming rain.

The dust of Engineer-Technician 1st Class Mikkala Avril was in it too. Yakov Khyrbysk was as good as his word.

11

The great hill of the living angel, blinded, muted and unchampioned, abraded by wind and rain, crawled slowly on, lost among limitless trees. No fliers crowded the air above its sad peak. Already, scrubby vegetation was beginning to claim the crumbling lower slopes. The rain washed from it in slurries of tilth and rolling scree.

Directionless, inch by inch, withdrawing from the borderland, not knowing where it was, the ever-living angel turned inward from the forest margin into inexhaustible trees. There it would crawl on for ever and get nowhere at all. Of the heartwood, the inward forest, there is no end, and so there can be no ending of it.

12

Lom and Maroussia were together on the bank of the river. Fraiethe was there, and the Seer Witch of Bones, and the father also, though his presence was indistinct and Lom felt he had not really come there at all.

Eligiya Kamilova was standing apart. Alone again. A secondary role.

Fraiethe spoke to her.

'You can remain here, Eligiya Kamilova, in the forest with us. Go further in and deeper. If that's what you wish? You've done your part.'

'Yes,' said Kamilova. 'That would be good. I would like that.'

'In that case,' said Lom, 'perhaps we could borrow your boat?'

'You're not staying?' said Kamilova.

'No,' said Maroussia. 'No. We're going home.'

13

The Political Bureau of the interim collective government met in the former Central Committee cabinet room. Lukasz Kistler took the chair. Unrest was continuing. Rizhinites had barricaded themselves in the administrative block of the university and a large crowd had gathered in Victory Square. Already it had been there three days, penned in by a cordon of gendarmes. The crowd was smashing flagstones and levering up cobbles. Bonfires had been lit.

'It's a stand-off,' said Yulia Yashina.

'Negotiations?' said Kistler.

'No,' said Yashina. 'At least not yet. They have no leader; they have no clear demands to make. They want to turn back the clock, that's all.'

'Give them time,' said Kistler. 'We can do that. Are more people joining them?'

'Not for the moment,' said Yashina. She paused. 'We could end it now,' she said. 'The militia is standing by in the Armoury. There are tanks within two hundred yards.'

'The commanders are loyal to us?' said Kistler. 'They would fire on their own people?'

'Of course they would, if you give the word. Government rests on civil order. It's the prerequisite.'

Kistler looked around the table, each face one by one. They all avoided his eye. The decision was to be left to him, then, and they would follow where he led.

'We must not do it,' he said. 'And we will not. Give the order to withdraw the tanks and the militia to their barracks, and make sure the people of the city see them go.'